Threaded Destiny

Beth Brown

Belleyre Books

Published by Belleyre Books
Delray Beach, FL
www.belleyrebooks.com

First Edition

Previously published as *Threads*

ISBN: 978-0-9916657-6-1 (softcover)

Set in Adobe® Garamond™ Pro and Futura® Std Medium. Cover set in Preciosa.

Revision_1

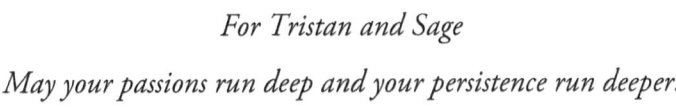

For Tristan and Sage

May your passions run deep and your persistence run deeper.

Two roads diverged in a yellow wood,
And sorry I could not travel both
And be one traveler, long I stood
And looked down one as far as I could
To where it bent in the undergrowth;

Then took the other, as just as fair,
And having perhaps the better claim,
Because it was grassy and wanted wear;
Though as for that the passing there
Had worn them really about the same,

And both that morning equally lay
In leaves no step had trodden black.
Oh, I kept the first for another day!
Yet knowing how way leads on to way,
I doubted if I should ever come back.

I shall be telling this with a sigh
Somewhere ages and ages hence:
Two roads diverged in a wood, and I—
I took the one less travelled by,
And that has made all the difference.

—Robert Frost, The Road Not Taken

CONTENTS

Chapter 1 ~ Left Behind

The family could have been any ordinary family just out for a walk in the park before stopping by the bookstore. It was a beautiful June day. The azure sky was spotless. The man and woman were casually dressed, wore comfortable walking shoes, and carried little with them aside from a small object in the grip of the man's hand. The girl between them looked to be a young teenager. She wore a serious, yet excited expression — the look of someone who was about to experience a rite of passage.

Together, man, woman, and girl walked to the back of the bookstore where they huddled closely, joining free hands. As the father extended his clutch in front of them, the mother turned her head for a fleeting look to the front of the store. A contented smile formed on her face just as the three of them faded from sight with less than a whisper.

Four-year-old Ellis sat with extended legs on the soft chenille braided rug amidst a half dozen books scattered about her feet. Her neck rounded, she gazed intently into the brightly colored book that lie open on her lap, her small chubby hands holding onto either side of it. Stretched out on the rug not far from her was a yellow Labrador retriever puppy, sleeping after a morning of play. The puppy's soft snoring was no distraction to the little girl and was all that she heard.

Nearby, another young teenager, resembling a miniature shopkeeper — her hair in a bun — was looking after Ellis. When less than a minute had passed, the young shopkeeper's expression changed from that of excitement to alarm and she ran from the girl and dog to find her parents.

Chapter 2 ~ Ellis

A bed and dresser were at one end of the room separated by a gable window. At the opposite end of the room stood a floor length mirror and a small desk, which would later be swapped with the dresser because the light was better on that side of the room. Next to the desk was a cardboard box with bumped corners and worn flaps hanging open. *Ellis* was scrawled on the side of the box. An upended bulletin board rested against the box. The pale yellow walls were bare.

The early morning light streamed through the gable window which was positioned above the front door of the two-story house and overlooked a small front yard that consisted of two square patches of soft grass bisected by a sidewalk connecting the small rectangular porch at the forest green front door to a sidewalk running parallel to Elm Street. When Ellis stands very close to the window and looks straight down, she can see the little slate roof that covers the front door and porch. On either side of the little porch, bunches of black-eyed Susans look up at her. Beside them, azaleas with a few lingering faded blooms border the front of the house. Sparkling dew droplets cling to the glass of the gable window, magnifying the rays that pass through them.

Ellis had awoken earlier than she needed too, but then again it was the first day of school. It was that very quiet time of morning when all the little noises can still be heard. A neighbor's car eased out of its driveway, songbirds welcomed the new day, the oven door in the kitchen below snapped closed.

Ellis was starting high school and was more nervous than she had ever felt about a first day of school. She walked over to the mirror and looked critically at her image before tentatively deciding the outfit was okay for a girl who had no idea what to wear on her first day to a school that she had never attended. Like every other first day of school for as far back as she could remember, Ellis was starting over again — new town, new house, new school. Ellis had barely had time to move in — let alone meet anyone — before the first day of school. So like every year before this one, she made a guess at what the other kids might be wearing, and hoped that she would not stand out like the newcomer she is.

Ellis continued to evaluate the fourteen-year-old who stared back at her from the mirror. The auburn-blonde-brown hair fell straight, ending just below the shoulders, with shades that some kids and many parents thought were a result of a lot of unsupervised hair-coloring experiments. On the rare occasion that a meddling mother or a thoughtless peer was bold enough to comment on the coloration, Ellis would smile embarrassingly and mutter to no one in particular, "That's just the way it grows."

She stared deeply into the blue eyes staring back at her and wondered when she would know her purpose in life. And then with a blink the inspection was over. Ellis turned away from the mirror and grabbed her backpack off the bed. The floorboard at the threshold creaked in protest as she stepped out of her room on the way to the kitchen.

The house she and her grandmother had moved into was old — "historic" she would later learn was the correct term — and the most interesting house Ellis could ever remember living in. The stone structure with its green slate roof looked like something that should be nestled in the woods. Inside, intricate crown molding and tall baseboards encircled each room. High ceilings and wooden floors of a deep honey hue were throughout.

Ellis's bedroom was upstairs along with a bathroom, her grandmother's room, and another bedroom that, for now, served as storage. The upstairs hallway was a room in itself. Irregular in shape, it was as wide as any bedroom and much longer. At one end was the front stairwell. That part of the hallway had an alcove with a built-in bookshelf and was large enough for a sitting chair and end table. At the opposite end of the hallway was a second stairwell that led to the kitchen. The bathroom, still steamy from Ellis's morning shower, was also at that end of the hallway. The room was barely large enough for the old-fashioned claw foot tub (with an added shower fixture) and pedestal sink, but it had a fun double casement window with lots of little panes that Ellis could unlatch and push open for fresh air.

Ellis tromped slowly down the stairs leading to the kitchen, mentally reviewing the contents of her backpack as she went. Last night she packed numerous pencils and pens and a notebook. Three creaky, wooden steps before the landing, Ellis detected the sweet, syrupy, wonderfully familiar smell of her favorite breakfast treat, which immediately distracted her from thoughts of her backpack contents.

With a thump, Ellis jumped the last two steps and landed in the dated, yet bright and inviting kitchen. The first time Ellis saw the room, she was reminded of the Julia Child's Kitchen display at the Smithsonian Museum in DC. She and Hen visited the DC museums often the year they lived in Virginia. Like the exhibit, Ellis's kitchen had butcher-block style countertops and simple wooden cupboards painted pale blue-green. The paint had a slightly shiny finish. But it was the retro chrome plated handles that dated the kitchen. Those and the white appliances with their rounded corners, chrome

accents, and chunky knobs. Most notable was the O'Keefe &
Merritt stove. The entire cooktop was covered in shiny
chrome and contained four burners and a griddle (Ellis loved
blueberry pancakes). On the stove backsplash was a small glass
window that Ellis later learned was a type of periscope with a
mirror for seeing down into the oven without having to open
the windowless oven door. To complete the picture, a bright
yellow, white, and chrome table was pushed against one wall,
leaving space for just three chairs on the exposed sides.
Landing in the kitchen was like stepping back in time.

A warmed pecan roll was the centerpiece of the table.
Hen, already seated on one of the matching yellow plastic and
chrome chairs, was sipping her tea.

"Good mornin' Hen," Ellis sang out, suddenly feeling
happier and lighter.

"Good morning, Ellis. Are you ready for school?" replied
Hen with a quiet excitement in her voice. Ellis was always
surprised by her grandmother's enthusiasm. At times she felt
little difference in age between herself and her grandmother,
who had always insisted that Ellis call her Hen, short for
Henrietta.

"I'm scared. . . ." squeaked Ellis, even though she knew
what Hen's response would be.

As expected, Hen gently rebuffed. "Scared? Or just
nervous about a new adventure?" It had become a sort of
game between them. Whenever Ellis said she felt scared, Hen
would redirect Ellis to think of the situation as a new adventure. At first this annoyed Ellis because she really did feel
scared and didn't want Hen making light of her feelings, but
after a few years, Ellis realized scared or not, she was going to
be starting a new school.

Ellis replied to Hen's query with a smirk and then said,
"Where did the pecan roll come from?"

At this point, Ellis was all eyes on the roll. It was as large as the dinner plate it was served on — one big roll, as if made in a Bundt pan — and then covered with pecan halves and a dark brown sugary glaze that glistened from being warmed in the oven.

"I went to the bakery early this morning. I wanted to surprise you."

Ellis cut a slice of the warm bread and moved into a chair. Poking at the roll with her fork, she lifted just a sweetened pecan to her mouth. "This looks so delicious. How did you find out about a bakery already?"

Hen took a drawn out sip of her tea. The silent pause prompted Ellis to look up inquiringly from her breakfast.

"It's the same bakery I visited when I was about your age," said Hen in a slow, deliberate way.

Ellis thought for a moment, her eyebrows knitted together, but all she could mutter was a confused "What?"

Hen waited. Ellis found her words. "What are you talking about? Did you visit this town before?"

"Actually Ellis, I lived here a long time ago. And Ellis, you were born in this town. You lived here until you were five."

Ellis sat speechless. Her mouth opened, nothing came out. She closed her mouth. Never before had she had any connections or knowledge of her life when her parents were alive. Her brain was racing, but before she could form any words, Hen said in a tone of finality, "You have a big day ahead of you. We can talk about this more after school."

Hen took another sip of tea and then added more gently, "Finish your breakfast. We have to get moving. I'll drive you." Ellis noticed a slight smile on Hen's lips before they were obscured by the tea cup once again.

With a smile that she couldn't keep off her own face, Ellis buttered her roll and took a big, gooey bite. She had never tasted a better pecan roll. But it wasn't the warmth of the roll that ignited a spark deep inside her. Ellis had never felt this way before. A glowing, hopeful feeling warmed her to the very core.

Chapter 3 ~ Ida May School

The yellow brick building stood four stories tall with a pillared front and three sets of wide, heavy wooden double doors that gave the school a grand look. *Ida May School* was engraved on the stone lintel that stretched the width of the pillars and rested on top of them. The very old school was once home to an all-girls school and dormitory. The building now served as the high school for boys and girls in the ninth through twelfth grades. Located in the oldest section of town, the school occupied an entire block, facing south on East North Street. Along its eastern perimeter was Locust Street and along the western perimeter was Franklin Street.

Even the news of being back in the town where she was born couldn't distract Ellis from her escalating apprehension as Hen slowed the car and pulled up to the front entrance of Ida May. At that moment the first-day-of-school feelings came rushing back to Ellis. Every year was the same. The horrible I'm-Going-To-Die-Feeling from thinking every eye is on the new girl. Ellis always wished that before they got to the entrance of a school her grandmother could press an Eject button that would invisibly pop Ellis out of the car and land her in the appropriate seat of her classroom, bypassing the whole "walk" into the new school.

Funny thing is, Ellis sensed that Hen was just as nervous when it came to getting Ellis enrolled in school. And rarely did Hen ever interact with the other parents. She and Ellis explored wherever they were currently living, but always just the two of them.

The car came to a complete stop. Ellis swung her head around and gave Hen the "stare." A look that she hoped revealed her distress and revulsion over the whole situation. Hen smiled and jerked her head toward the school.

Students approaching from every possible angle were making their way up wide stone steps to the double doors, which were wedged open to allow for easier traffic flow. There seemed to be no difference among the entrances, so Ellis focused on looking as inconspicuous as possible while being bumped and jostled up the steps. She poured into the school with several students at her side. The relative quiet of outside instantly changed to a loud drone punctuated by peals of laughter and the clanging metal of lockers opening and closing.

Ellis found a spot where she could stand still without getting trampled. She wanted a minute to look at her new school. She gazed up at high, ornate ceilings and then looked around to a large expanse of hardwood floors, walls lined with lockers, and a wide, winding staircase with more stone steps. Its winding wooden banisters were worn to a high luster and had finials that spiraled into infinity. Not like any school she had ever attended, Ellis was reminded of a museum with all its grandeur.

Before she had a chance to take in anymore, Ellis was pulled back to the present by an approaching voice. Surprisingly strong and commanding, the voice from a thin, bony teacher walking toward Ellis was directing the students to "Please proceed to the auditorium for your schedule . . ." and then her thin, but strong arm, with hand held flat open, motioned like a traffic cop, directing students to yet another set of open doors where traffic was flowing into queues according to alphabetical order by last name. Stepping back into the flow, Ellis headed for the auditorium and then settled at the back of a line where an older girl, a student from an upper grade Ellis decided, held a sign printed "A – G."

The line was moving steadily, but slowly, giving Ellis time to look around again. The auditorium had old-fashioned velvet covered chairs with wooden arms. The stage was a wooden floor with heavy maroon velvet curtains held back by gold rope tassel ties. A matching swag was draped across the front of the stage. Ellis wondered just how old the school was.

The line progressed as did the nervousness Ellis felt growing inside of her. Her stomach was lurching and she now wondered if eating had been such a good idea. She kept rubbing her sweaty palms against her jeans, looking around as she did, hoping that no one would notice. The students around her were chatting across lines, asking each other about their summer, discussing classes they might have together, and talking about where to go for lunch, which Ellis thought was odd when school lasted the entire day. The two girls behind her were apparently long-time friends. They talked and giggled without paying any mind to Ellis, for which she was grateful.

Ellis was just one student away from getting her schedule. She heard the girl in front of her recite her name — *Starling Archer* — and then she heard the rustling of a pile of papers.

The teacher held out a schedule printed on a mustard yellow sheet of paper. "Take this schedule and a guide will tell you about the school and show you to your first class," the woman recited in a deep, husky voice. The woman must have pointed toward the students at the doorway because she saw Starling look in that direction, where groups of older students, mostly girls, seemed to be waiting for something.

Ellis watched Starling walk toward the doorway. Before she saw exactly where Starling ended up however, Ellis heard "Name please."

For the first time, Ellis was able to see the teacher sitting behind the table. She was reminded of a bull dog with a curly wig. The teacher had slightly bulging eyes, a flattened face, and weighty jowls. She was rather stocky from what Ellis could see and extending from her rounded shoulders were heavy arms that connected to heavy hands and short, pulpy fingers. A front paw was resting on the pile of papers.

"Ellis Bell," Ellis squeaked out.

Disregarding all niceties, the curly head bowed as a stubby finger raised toward the lipstick-stained mouth. Ellis restrained a shiver when she saw a quick flick of the tongue wet the finger before it began pawing through the pile of papers. Nearly every sheet was white aside from one or two yellow sheets like Starling's. Ellis got a strange feeling in her stomach when a mustard sheet bearing her name was pulled from the pile. She wanted to ask why it wasn't white, but she had neither the courage nor the time, for as soon as the teacher spotted the required name at the top of the sheet she began reciting what she had just stated to the previous girl.

Holding the schedule out expectantly, the bull dog face stretched her short neck to see the next student behind Ellis, as if to say "move on." Ellis wanted to run. Her hands were ridiculously damp at this point. She mentally chastised herself for once again not being brave enough to face the situation. *How many times have I had to get through starting a new school?* she thought. *Why am I such a coward?*

"Thank you," mumbled Ellis as she took the paper and walked nervously toward the exit where the older students waited.

As she neared a group of chatting students standing by the door, one of the girls glanced over at Ellis. She seemed to be looking for something that Ellis might have. When her eyes rested on the schedule in her hand, the girl broke away from the group and moved toward Ellis. She had long curly blonde hair and wore thin wire-frame glasses. She was quite a bit taller than Ellis and had a refined look about her. Her face was friendly and her walk was bouncy.

"Hi, my name is Nia. So you're new to the school?"

"Uhm . . . Yeah," replied Ellis cautiously.

"New students have a yellow schedule." Nia smiled knowingly. "I volunteered to show new students around the school."

Oh, thought Ellis.

Nia put out her hand and asked, "Can I take a look at your schedule?"

Ellis handed her the yellow sheet. Nia took a quick look, handed it back, and said, "Follow me."

They headed out of the auditorium and back into the large hallway, which was now nearly empty. A clicking noise was coming from a locker where a boy who looked older than both Ellis and Nia was working to try to unstick the door.

"Hi, Anthony," said Nia in a way that seemed to make the words float over to the boy. He turned and smiled and gave a little nod to Nia. After a silent smile back to Anthony, Nia headed up the winding staircase and Ellis quickly followed.

"I like your hair by the way," commented Nia from over her shoulder.

Not sure if she was making fun, Ellis scrutinized Nia's expression and then half whispered "thanks," hoping she wasn't being foolish for deciding Nia was complementing her.

"No, seriously," Nia went on, picking up on Ellis's sentiment, "I love the color."

Nia and Ellis reached the top of the staircase and stepped onto the smooth wooden floor of the next level. The second floor had a bank of lockers and was lined with doors to classrooms. Tall windows illuminated the hallway; the crowns of large, old oak trees were level with the windows. There was another wide staircase like the one they had just climbed leading to a third floor.

"Most of the ninth grade classrooms are here on the second floor," explained Nia. "So you should get a locker up here."

They walked down the hallway. "There is a map of the school on the back of your schedule."

Ellis flipped the schedule over to see a layout of all four floors and a basement.

Ellis studied the map as Nia led her a short distance further down the hall. Ellis was surprised to see a swimming pool in the basement.

"Here is your first class, World History."

Ellis looked up. There were already a few kids gathering near the door.

After a brief pause in front of the World History classroom, they walked further down the hallway as Nia spoke.

"Ninth graders go to lunch at eleven forty-five. Most kids eat downtown. If you brought your lunch, you can eat it in the Club Room," Nia pointed out a large room on the first floor layout of the map. "There are tables and vending machines in there. Not very much fun though unless you actually have a club meeting."

"Where is downtown?" Ellis had never heard of kids eating anywhere but at the school.

Nia looked out a window and gave a wave toward the street below. "We have lots of eating places around the school. *Downtown* is Main Street, which is just a block away."

Ellis's confused look prompted Nia to keep explaining. "Go out the front doors and walk a block up and then over to Main Street. Hots has great fries; there's a lunch counter at Hubbel's; Madder Drinks is a coffee shop with smoothies and sandwiches — look for the red and white awning."

"Okay." Ellis wiped her hands on her jeans and hoped she sounded confident. She was grateful that Nia was so patient.

Nia pointed out other classrooms to Ellis who was now deep in thought. Ellis hadn't brought lunch with her, but the thought of walking several blocks in a town she had never been to, or at least didn't remember being to, seemed overwhelming. What if she got lost? What if her lunch took too long? Even if it was boring and she had to sit alone, Ellis decided she would go to the Club Room for today.

"Do you remember where your first class is?" Nia was staring curiously at Ellis who must have had a faraway look.

Ellis gave Nia what she hoped was a convincing smile and then said, "Yes, it's just over there." She pointed to the end of the hall where several more kids had now gathered.

"Good," said Nia genially, and then after a brief pause she added, "I'm going to go then. Class will be starting soon." With that she gave Ellis a light touch on the wrist, as if to say good luck, and then turned and walked away.

Chapter 4 ~ Starling

Ellis watched Nia walk away and then she turned and walked back to her World History classroom. The door was closed and evidently locked as several boys closest to the door kept trying the knob with no success. Ellis noticed the girl Starling from the auditorium standing among the students. She stood away from the wall and appeared to be casually observing her surroundings. For being new to the school, she didn't seem nearly as nervous as Ellis felt.

Ellis walked a few steps closer to the group. A boy sitting down with his back against the wall was sketching in a tablet. He was thin without being skinny and Ellis noticed he had long, slender fingers. His hair was somewhere between blonde and light brown and although it wasn't long, it sort of curled at the ends. He glanced up as if he could feel Ellis's stare, so she averted her eyes and looked straight ahead, pretending not to have been looking at him at all.

Ahead of Ellis, three rather husky boys with very short hair-cuts were jostling each other. They were snickering and talking in short grunts. The shortest boy seemed to be the leader. The other two were poking each other and pushing each other around while the third boy stood his ground.

The emptier the hallway got, the more it felt like the wrong place to be. The World History group, however, continued to wait outside the locked door. Looks were exchanged as students silently began to wonder where their teacher could be.

Four girls came rushing up the stairs. As they made their

way over to the waiting group, Ellis noticed their noisy, giggly approach drew a few annoyed looks. A tall, black girl with a strong, athletic build and hair so short her scalp was visible, and her friend, also athletic looking, moved away from the advancing foursome. The tall girl gave a sideways glance to the noisy girls as she whispered something to her friend, who then looked over at the group with narrowed eyes.

"I can't believe we made it," the short haired girl in the noisy group breathlessly stated to her three friends. A raucous laugh erupted from another in the group, a stocky girl with long, straight, dark hair and bangs. A door opened and a teacher stuck her head out to locate the source of the noise. A third girl in the group elbowed the laughing girl in the ribs who then put a hand up to her mouth in an effort to smother her loudness. The teacher looked down the hall and then back again at the group. For a moment Ellis thought the teacher might say something, but then she pulled her head back inside her room and closed the door.

Ellis had instinctively moved over when the noisy group of girls came toward the waiting students. She was now standing close to the new girl from the auditorium.

"Hi — I'm Starling."

Ellis looked up and saw the new girl was speaking to her. She had long dark hair that was somewhat frizzy. Her wide golden eyes sparkled and her light colored skin had a sprinkling of freckles that gave her a friendly look.

"I'm Ellis."

"Which middle school are you coming from?" asked Starling.

"I just moved here." Ellis hoped this answer was enough. She didn't want to explain that she'd been to six different elementary schools and three middle schools.

"Do you live in town?"

"Yes," answered Ellis, but didn't understand how there could be any other answer to this question as she thought about all the other schools she'd been to. As far as she knew, all the kids at her other schools lived in the same town as the school.

"I live in Muddy Creek so I take the train to school. Well, the train is called the Double Decker and there are only two cars, so it's not like a normal train," explained Starling.

Ellis had never heard of kids taking a train to school. It sounded interesting.

"Is Muddy Creek far from here?" asked Ellis, wondering how long the train ride was.

"My train ride takes about half an hour." Starling sounded a little bored with the situation. She looked around the hallway before looking at Ellis again.

"Do you walk to school?" asked Starling with renewed interest.

"No. My gra – I, I get a ride to school." stammered Ellis. She didn't want to bring up her grandmother. It usually brought up questions about her parents. Explaining her lack of parents wasn't usually a big friend attractor.

"I would love to live in town. There's so much more to do." Starling seemed to be explaining her interest in where Ellis lived.

"I thought maybe you were new too because you have a yellow schedule." Ellis hoped she wasn't sounding nosy.

Starling looked down at the paper in her hand. "Oh — no, I only missed the new student orientation because my family and I took my brother to college. He graduated from Ida May in June. I have two older sisters that go here too, so I kind of know my way around already."

Ellis thought having a brother and sisters sounded amazing. She always wished she had a sister.

"Can I see your schedule?" asked Starling.

Ellis held out the schedule. Starling took it and folded it and held it against her own schedule so that the class periods were lined up and then she held the two papers out so that she and Ellis could look at them together. Ellis leaned her head in and took a look. The girls looked at each other in surprise. "We have the same classes," they both said at once.

Starling's smile told Ellis she was just as happy about their schedules as she was.

"Lunch will be the best," said Starling. "Do you want to go downtown with me?"

Ellis was so excited she thought she might burst.

A clanging noise interrupted the waiting students, who looked up to see a teacher walking towards them, fumbling with a long lanyard that had many keys dangling from the end.

"Quiet down students," admonished the teacher, her head still bent as her thick fingers sorted through the keys.

The group of students parted as the teacher made her way to the door. With a key in her grasp, the teacher looked up just as she was passing Ellis. The flat face, slightly bulging eyes, and weighty jowls didn't look any friendlier than they had in the auditorium.

Ellis and Starling gave each other a knowing glance and then filed into the classroom with the rest of students. They quietly sat down beside each other at two desks near the back of the classroom. Ellis recognized the boy in front of her as the one who had been sitting in the hallway sketching. He tossed his backpack under the desk, but kept his sketch pad and pencil with him.

At the front of the classroom, a large modern white board rested on the ancient-looking wooden chalk tray of the original slate boards behind it. Without saying a word or even looking at them, for that matter, the teacher had their full attention as everyone watched in a state of suspense while she wrote on the white board. The classroom was so quiet that only the faint squeaking noise of the black marker on the white board was heard. Judging by the behavior of the class, Ellis sensed that silence was the correct protocol with this teacher.

Mrs. Dockleaf (that was the first bit of information written on the board) continued writing, making occasional brief snorting noises and breathing heavy enough to be heard, until nearly a third of the board was filled. Below her name, she listed the objectives of the class and her expectations. Ellis decided World History will be a lot of work.

A girl from the noisy group in the hallway began to whisper to another girl from her group. Before the second girl could respond, a deep husky voice reverberated off the white board and the slate boards behind it. "If I take the time to write something on the board, you need to take the time to copy it to your notebook."

Silence prevailed once again after a few moments of shuffling noises while notebooks and pencils were retrieved from backpacks. Ellis and Starling exchanged glances before busily writing in their notebooks.

Mrs. Dockleaf filled the board and then sat down at the wooden desk in the front corner of the classroom. She moved her keys and opened her grade book before speaking. "Please continue to take down the notes while I call roll. Say here and raise your hand when I call your name. If you have a preferred nickname, please say it when I call your name."

"Starling Archer."

"Here." Starling's hand went up long enough for Mrs. Dockleaf to see it.

"Thomas Baker."

"Here. Tom." Ellis looked at the boy raising his hand and saw that he was one of the short haired husky boys.

"Ellis Bell," continued Mrs. Dockleaf in a deep sounding drone.

"Here," Ellis said and then raised her hand. She felt the stares of several students on her. Many probably knew each other from living in the area and recognized her as a new girl.

"Joseph Butler."

"Here. Joey." He was a small boy with freckles all over his skin. He was working feverishly in an effort to copy the notes and forgot to raise his hand.

"Joseph Butler," repeated Mrs. Dockleaf sternly.

"Here!" Joey reached his hand high into the air and waved his arm to make sure he was seen. Several students giggled.

"Julian Connor."

The boy in front of Ellis raised his hand. A pencil was between his long fingers. "Here. Jules." His hand was up just long enough to respond and then his head was bent again and his pencil started moving.

Ellis went from watching Jules to looking at the three short haired husky boys who had begun snickering softly when Jules raised his hand. They made no gestures toward Jules, but Ellis knew, perhaps from experience, that the boys were laughing *at* someone, *at* Jules. She looked again at the back of Jules. He looked normal enough, his clothes weren't shabby or outdated, he didn't have an odd voice, he didn't seem awkward. He also didn't react to the snickering. Ellis felt a sense of respect for Jules. She admired his self-assuredness.

The roll call continued. Ellis learned the tall, black athletic girl is Keri; her friend is named Beatrix and likes to be called Bea. The four noisy girls are Violet (Vi) with the razor-cut short hair, Harley, the stocky girl with long, straight, dark hair and bangs, Gwen whose permanently pursed lips looked as if she's trying to suppress a smirk, and Peyton, a mousy looking girl that didn't really seem like she fit into the group at all.

Ellis now knew the names of everyone in her class with hearing them just once. Year after year of learning a whole new set of names and faces each fall taught Ellis how to remember a kid's name after hearing it just once.

Roll call finished and Mrs. Dockleaf began reciting what she had written on the board. Unfortunately, she managed to turn the early civilizations and their concepts and people — Babylonia, Mesopotamia, Sumer, Homer, Plato, Socrates, and class systems — into a dull, dry lecture. Ellis doodled around her notes and contemplated the class system of Ida May School.

The ringing bell jolted Ellis out of thought. When she looked up, Jules was standing by her desk. He said, "Interesting class. She's a work of art." And then he held out his sketch pad. Starling had walked over to stand beside Ellis. They looked at the drawing. It was a well-done sketch of a bulldog with Mrs. Dockleaf's head. They laughed the whole way out of class.

Chapter 5 ~ Downtown

There were two more classes before lunch. Math with Mr. Wilkins who looked like a throwback from the 1960s with his bearded face and longish hair, and English taught by Ms. Bennet who had a plain, long face and wore her hair in a simple bun at the base of her neck. Ellis thought of Jane Eyre, the central character from Hen's favorite book.

With just five minutes left to go in English class, Ellis was fidgety and paying more attention to the clock than the teacher. Her stomach was fluttery but not entirely from hunger. She kept trying to imagine what it will be like to walk downtown and eat lunch out. With less than a minute left to go in the class, Ellis felt a pang of guilt and had a moment of indecision when she suddenly remembered Hen's rule about always letting each other know where they are. What would Hen think about Ellis leaving the school?

The bell rang and Ellis completely forgot what she was thinking about. She and Starling gathered their backpacks and headed to their lockers. Ellis was feeling like the day was one adventure after another. Never in her life had she been so happy with a new school.

Together she and Starling headed down the wide winding staircase and through the double doors. It was a bright, sunny day without a cloud in the sky. The canopy of the tall oak trees surrounding the school sheltered the walkway. A light breeze whispered its way into the leaves, allowing dollops of dancing sunlight to filter through to the sidewalk below; the playful bits of light reflecting exactly how Ellis was feeling at this very moment.

Ellis and Starling walked past the school up to Franklin Street, made a left, and after hiking uphill a block Ellis saw a sign that read Main Street. Standing at the corner of Franklin and Main, Ellis was amazed. There were shops up and down and on both sides of the street. Pedestrians filled the sidewalks and the street corners were crowded with people waiting to cross the steady stream of traffic. A box truck was double-parked in front of a butcher shop while its driver made deliveries, making for a traffic bottleneck in the already narrow street. Ninth graders flowed from behind Ellis and up from the side streets on either side of her onto Main Street like a colony of hungry ants and then dispersed in every direction heading for their eatery of choice, mixing in with the pedestrians on the already busy sidewalk.

Ellis saw a red and white awning on the other side of Main, next to the butcher shop, and remembered the coffee shop Nia had mentioned. But after a tug on the sleeve from Starling they walked in the opposite direction.

They walked past a shoe store and then a small restaurant called the Courthouse Diner. Ellis saw a puffy haired waitress in a green dress and white apron carrying a coffee pot. The tables were mostly occupied by professionally dressed adults scribbling on yellow legal pads and clicking away on their electronics. Next, they walked past the courthouse. Ellis looked up to see a tall clock tower with clock faces on all four sides. Starling slowed as they approached a large department store that took up the rest of the block. The front was almost entirely plate glass windows. At the one end of the store, Ellis saw several U-shaped counters with bright red swivel stools mounted to the floor below. Servers wearing crisp sky-blue uniforms bustled up and down into the counter fingers delivering food and drinks.

As they walked up to the Hubbel's entrance, Ellis noticed an oddly shaped restaurant across the side street. The building faced Hubbel's, its entrance on the corner of Leo Street and Main Street. On the front of the building, in large old fashioned light up letters was the name "Hots." The building itself, however, was tall at one end and much shorter at the other, like something out of "Alice in Wonderland" or from a carnival fun house. Ellis then noticed that the roof line was level but the building was built on the slope of a steeply ascending street, making one end look much shorter than the other. Ellis hoped to see the inside of that restaurant very soon.

Starling pulled the distracted Ellis into Hubbel's. The linoleum floor was clean, bright, and shiny — with a lot of wear. The store was large inside and Ellis forgot about lunch altogether when she saw the many trinkets, gimcracks, and goodies.

"Let's go eat," pleaded Starling.

"Look at all this stuff . . ." Ellis's voice trailed off in wonderment.

"We'll look at things after lunch if we have time," said Starling with a laugh.

They walked through the store, passing a wide staircase leading to Hubbel's basement floor. A sign above the staircase read "Housewares in Basement." Just ahead was the lunch counter.

Ellis and Starling mounted two empty swivel stools and pulled menus from a holder on the counter. Ellis twisted left and right as she scanned the menu. There were burgers (with five choices of cheese), tuna melts, club sandwiches, wraps, and soups. There was also a nearly full page of desserts: twenty flavors of ice cream, ice cream sundaes, brownie sundaes, banana splits, pies, and cakes.

Ellis ordered the club sandwich and Starling a tuna wrap.

"Do you think we have enough time to eat lunch and get back to school before our next class starts?" asked Ellis.

"Yes," said Starling without hesitation. "Heron — my brother — told me that all the restaurants downtown are quick with Ida May students. See — look. . . ."

Ellis smiled in astonishment as the sky-blue server placed their lunches in front of them. The club sandwich was three slices of seeded toast layered with avocado, turkey, Canadian bacon, lettuce, and tomato. After extracting the tomato and setting it on the far edge of the plate, Ellis took a bite of the best club sandwich she had ever tasted.

"Heron — like the bird?" mumbled Ellis, her mouth a little full.

"Yes, and my sisters are Kestrel and Myna," Starling rolled her eyes and laughed. "My parents love birds. That's why we live in Muddy Creek. They go birding every chance they get — every day if they can."

"A heron is a big water bird, right?" asked Ellis.

Starling nodded. "Yes, and a kestrel is a small falcon, a myna is a bird known for its ability to mimic sounds, and a starling is a very social bird." Starling was struggling to keep her wrap together as lettuce and tuna started falling out. "Do you have any brothers or sisters?"

"No," replied Ellis without elaborating. She took a big bite of her sandwich and looked out the window in hopes of avoiding any other personal questions. It was then that she saw Vi, Harley, Gwen, and Peyton walk by.

"Tell me about those girls. . . ." Ellis jerked her head discretely in the direction of the window.

Starling shook her head slightly and said through a mouth full of tuna, "Trouble."

Ellis gave Starling a questioning look and waited for her to finish chewing.

"Violet, Harley, Gwen, and Peyton have been friends forever mostly because their parents are friends. They live here in town and they do everything together. Vi is obviously the leader. . ." Starling was talking with her hands and trying to eat at the same time. She spoke in a somewhat hushed monotone, like that of a well-seasoned narrator.

"Peyton's brother was dating Gwen's sister until they both left for college this year. There was some kind of falling out and now Peyton trails after her friends like a mouse allowed only the crumbs," continued Starling. "Harley is loud and obnoxious. Her mother works with my parents. In elementary school, Harley wanted to be friends. I tried a couple times. She came to my house . . . I went to her house. We just didn't click. I started to make excuses for why I didn't want to get together. She was loud and wanted to play football. I tried once — to play football — and she nearly broke my arm when she tackled me," Starling had a faraway look, like she was replaying the moment in her head. "Looking back, I was probably not a good friend to her. I really couldn't find a single fun thing about football and I remember her looking like she was about to tackle me when I called her a tomboy," added Starling with a shrug.

"Well, Harley took offense and she told the other three that I wasn't someone for their group. Since then they like to aggravate me whenever possible. But, I'm really good at ignoring that kind of stuff so they don't bother with it too often."

Starling got a more serious look before she said, "Those girls entertain themselves by feeding off the misery and embarrassment of others. They like to test new kids to see exactly how far they can push. They like to dominate." And with this last bit of information, Starling raised her eyebrows to emphasize the word *dominate*.

Ellis felt her face flush. She sighed to herself. She guessed it had been too much to hope that this school would be free of bullies and tyrants. She took her last bite of sandwich and weakly smiled.

With a few minutes to spare, the girls looked around Hubbel's. Ellis was fascinated by the aisle of hair care products. There were sprays that straightened hair for a day; gels that curled hair for a day. Shampoos that changed the color of hair until the next washing and shampoos that changed hair color gradually over several washings. She looked forward to having more time for this department another day.

They walked by the pet department in the far corner. It had a moist, earthy smell and sounded of chatter from parakeets bouncing around in a floor-standing cage. A soft gurgle was heard from the fish tanks where mollies, guppies, and goldfish darted back and forth. Other tanks housed slow moving frogs, lizards, and hermit crabs. The department sales person, wearing a sky-blue smock, was behind a short counter pricing bags of multicolored aquarium rocks. Ellis had been in lots of stores but never a department store like this one.

Feeling a little anxious about getting back to school on time, Ellis and Starling decided it was time to walk back to Ida May. As they meandered their way out of Hubbel's, Ellis noticed Jules in the Art Supplies aisle. He was holding several different pencils in his hand and staring down at them with a look of deep concentration. He appeared to be alone and Ellis wondered if he had many friends since she hadn't seen him talking to anyone else at school. It made no difference to Ellis who never judged a kid based on his number of friends because she knew what it felt like to rely on one's self most of the time.

Outside, the downtown was busier than when they had arrived. Upper class Ida May students were making their way to restaurants. Nia walked by with a group of friends and gave Ellis a wave and a friendly smile. Ellis never felt more at home.

Starling was easy to talk to. They chatted the whole way back to school. Ellis liked to listen. She felt at the top of her world right now just having someone to hang out with, but she wasn't ready to tell her deepest secrets to anyone yet. She had held them so close for so long that she wondered if they even mattered anymore.

Ellis and Starling walked up the winding staircase to their next class. Science was in an enormous room with rows of desks at one end and at the other end a lab with soapstone counter tops containing sinks and shiny silver-colored equipment. There were many tall windows on the far wall of the classroom; their ledges lined with potted plants and glass jars containing specimens floating in liquid. A woman who looked to be just out of college and wearing a white lab coat flitted about the classroom moving glassware and small pieces of equipment into storage cupboards as Ellis and the other students made their way into the classroom.

The students gravitated toward the desks, but couldn't take their attention off the busy woman. When the late bell rang, she immediately walked up to the front of the classroom where there was a teacher's desk, and turned to face the students. She instinctively smoothed her lab coat before looking directly at them. She was small boned and just a little taller than Ellis with long straight hair tied back into a low ponytail and dark vibrant eyes that drew attention.

She introduced herself as Ms. Lee and talked in a way that made you feel the Nobel Prize for Science was within your grasp — by the end of the school year. Her excitement was contagious and Ellis had no resistance to it. They learned they would be doing a lot of lab work throughout the school year and Ellis was thrilled. She loved science and loved the idea of being a scientist — something she'd never discussed out loud with anyone.

The last class of the day was PE. For the first time all day, class was not on the second floor, but in the gym, which was on the first floor. It was small for a gym, with wooden bleachers and wooden floors. Ellis was glad she was with Starling who knew her way around because getting to the gym took them down stairs and through several hallways.

Physical education had never been one of Ellis's favorite classes. Not because she lacked athletic ability — she was a pretty good runner — but because she never knew anyone well enough to hang out with. PE is the kind of class where most of the kids hang close to a friend, so they can go through all the embarrassing moments together, supporting each other.

Their PE teacher, Coach Cook, was a rather dowdy looking woman with a loud gravelly voice and a silver whistle that seemed to rest on her lips as often as it was hanging from her neck. In a long winded introduction, Ellis learned Coach Cook's favorite sports are soccer and field hockey, the latter of which Coach knew well because she was once a great field hockey player herself. Ellis took her at her word.

The end of the first day at Ida May felt like a triumph for Ellis, rather than a relief as she so often had felt at previous schools. She felt connected to the school, the kids, and the town in a way that she had never experienced before even after living somewhere for several months. She couldn't wait to tell Hen about her day.

Chapter 6 ~ Left Behind

Ellis didn't know why she woke up. It was Saturday morning and she didn't have to get up early for school. Maybe it was the wonderful smell of bacon drifting up to her room or maybe she was just too happy to sleep. Everything felt good: her comfortable bed, the soft sheet that was covering her, the warm sunshine that was streaming through her window, and her room. The room she had known as a child. She didn't need the memories of being in this room. It was enough to know that this was her first room. This was her room when she had parents.

Still too comfortable to make the effort to get out of bed, Ellis turned her head to see the bulletin board, which now hung on the wall by the desk. The school calendar was pinned in the center. A scrap of paper with Starling's phone number was wedged into a corner and one of Jules drawings was attached with a smiley face pushpin. Below, her desk was piled with school books and papers. The first week at Ida May had gone by in what felt like less than a minute.

Ellis heard Hen moving around in the kitchen below. She always made a big breakfast on Saturday mornings. The thought of over-easy eggs, toast, bacon, and hot tea was enough to finally push Ellis out of bed. She took a long look out her window to the quiet street below and then squinted as she tried to take in the town beyond. There were no sky scrapers or even really tall buildings in Harper. Ida May was close enough to walk to but was obstructed from view by the hilly streets. Ellis could make out a few church steeples and the tops of several Victorian style homes. She knew downtown was just a few blocks away even though her street was quiet as the country.

Ellis dressed in shorts and a t-shirt. The weather was beginning to cool, but Ellis loved the stress-free feeling of summer and wanted to prolong the season, even if just in spirit. The walls in her room were still bare aside from the bulletin board. The well-worn cardboard box remained beside the desk. Its contents were a collection of keepsakes, desk organizers, a few pictures, and school supplies. It was as much a piece of furniture as her desk. Year after year, Ellis pulled things from the box as needed, never fully unpacking it. She actually couldn't remember a time without the box in her room. Hen never discussed moving each summer with Ellis, but at some point Ellis began to expect it, so she just never completely unpacked.

After sliding into a pair of flip-flops, Ellis headed downstairs for breakfast, stepping on the creaky floorboard on the way out of her room. A bright sun was filtering through the kitchen's east-facing window. It was going to be another warm, end-of-summer day. Ellis was craving time to walk around outside to see the neighborhood, but she had promised to help Hen unpack today. Boxes were stacked waist high in the room Hen called the library. Ellis had no idea which books or knick-knacks the boxes might contain. Those boxes were among the many that remained packed from move to move.

Hen must have noticed Ellis looking outside with an expression of longing and then looking into the library with an expression of despair because out of nowhere she told Ellis that the boxes won't take long to unpack. Ellis looked at Hen and smiled.

"I might have an errand for you to do after we get through the boxes," said Hen, sipping on her second cup of tea.

"Really?" asked Ellis incredulously, spreading raspberry jam on her toast. She wondered what kind of errand she could do when she hardly knew the area.

"Yes, there's a bookstore — not far from here — that buys old books. We may find a few to sell when we unpack."

Finished with breakfast, Ellis and Hen carried their cups of tea into the library. Soft morning light poured into the room through two tall windows. A long, cushioned built-in bench stretched beneath the window ledges. The floor to ceiling built-in bookshelves on the adjoining wall were bare and painted an eggshell white like the bench. Another smaller bench made a cozy nook in the middle of the bookshelves. A large area rug in blue, gold, green, and tan covered nearly the entire floor. It was thin and antique, but had no heavy areas of wear. Two overstuffed chairs, each with their own small side table, were backed against the wall opposite the bookshelves. Ellis and Hen each placed their cups of tea on the two side tables, respectively.

The first box Ellis opened contained thin, oversized, hardback children's books. Most were brightly colored. Some had matching dust jackets; others had illustrated boards with no dust jacket.

"I remember this book," said Ellis as she pulled the first book from the box. She rubbed her hand lightly across the front cover as if the contact might awaken the memories.

"You liked having that book read to you and then when you learned to read on your own you read it over and over again," Hen was now standing near Ellis, looking over her shoulder.

Ellis opened to the middle of the book. Colorful illustrations involving a mouse caught her attention. She flipped through a couple pages. Ellis had the growing sense that this book represented something special. Her mind was reaching, reaching for the memory, but the harder she tried to remember the more slippery the memory became.

"Did my mom or dad read this book to me?" asked Ellis, her face still in the book.

"I think so . . . You better get moving or we'll never finish." said Hen as she moved back over to the stack of boxes. Ellis looked up from the book. Hen, looking pointedly at the shelf she was stocking, definitely seemed to be avoiding Ellis's eyes.

Several boxes held beautiful leather bound books with raised bands and gilt type. It felt nice just to hold one. Ellis pulled "The Three Musketeers," "Gulliver's Travels," and "Frankenstein" from the boxes. When she pulled Hen's favorite "Jane Eyre" she held it up excitedly for Hen to see. Hen smiled in a dreamy sort of way and then returned to her box. In a newer, but just as fine leather binding, Ellis found "To Kill a Mockingbird," "1984," "Fahrenheit 451," and a few others. Each book had intricate designs embossed on their cover and spine. Grouped together on the upper shelves, they gave the room an impressive air.

When the last box was emptied, Ellis sat down and studied the shelves, reading the titles to herself. She had absolutely no memory of any of the books. A few children's books seemed familiar and although they hit a nerve, they didn't actually seem to relate to a specific memory. Unpacking the boxes had turned out to be like opening a roomful of gifts — everything was new to Ellis. But yet she had never felt more at home.

"Hen . . ." said Ellis thoughtfully.

"Yes . . ." replied Hen in an equally subdued way from the overstuffed chair where she had settled to rest from all the standing and bending. She and Ellis were both eyeing the bookshelves.

"Why do we have all these books?" said Ellis, finishing her thought.

"Some are mine. Some were given to me by mom and dad . . ." replied Hen in a lazy, relaxed tone.

"Your mom and dad? Really? Which ones?" Ellis suddenly felt energized. Hen had never talked about her mom and dad. Whenever Ellis asked about them, Hen always replied that they lived a long time ago and then left it at that.

Ellis looked to Hen for an answer and saw that she was sitting up straight in the chair.

"Some of the older leather books. . . . The newer leather books were given to you by your mom and dad." The answer came out quick and short as if Hen wanted to close the subject. Ellis decided to go with it. She was even more interested in her own mom and dad, who Hen so rarely mentioned.

"Which ones?" asked Ellis.

"'To Kill a Mockingbird,' and the other newer leather ones."

"What's that book about?" Ellis wondered why her parents gave her something called "To Kill a Mockingbird." It sounded sad.

"It's about things not being as they appear. It's a great book. I've read it."

"What about those books? The ones about glass research, chemistry, and science." Ellis pointed to the lower shelves of hardcover textbooks as she squinted to read their titles.

"Those belonged to your parents." stated Hen simply.

Ellis recognized the finality in Hen's voice, and from past experience knew that it signaled a change in subject, but with so many of her parent's things in this room, Ellis had to know more.

"Why did they have those books? Please, Hen . . ." Ellis watched, hoping.

After a little sigh, Hen responded. "They were scientists. They specialized in glass research. Those were some of their reference books."

Ellis looked longingly at the books.

"They were considered to be among the best scientists in their field." Hen went on.

Glass? Ellis thought. She looked out at the bright sunny day through the glass window in the library. She had forgotten about wanting to be outside until now. *What does a glass scientist do?* Ellis knew there was still a lot to understand, but for the first time she was learning *something* about her parents.

Ellis looked back over at the bookshelves. Many of the bookends were made of glass. It didn't seem important while she was unpacking them. She slid off the chair and sat on the floor in front of one of the bookshelves. She reached out and touched a small — but heavy — glass bookend. It was a tall oval shape, flat on the bottom and the side next to the books, with brightly colored blobs of glass on the inside. As she ran her fingers down the smooth glass, Hen told her that her parents collected glass bookends.

"Why *are* we unpacking all of this now?" Ellis couldn't stop herself from asking. It was a question she had been thinking about since she saw the boxes in the library. She hadn't asked until now because she was afraid she might hear an answer she wouldn't like. She was afraid of the unknown.

The room was silent.

Ellis, again assuming there would be no answer, was about to rise from the floor when Hen began talking in a deliberate, calm way. "We have made our last move. We need to be here now. This is where your mom and dad last lived and this is where we need to be if we want to find out what really happened to them."

Ellis sat very still. An overwhelming feeling dropped down through the top of her head to land in her stomach where it rested as a heavy burden. She turned to look squarely at Hen and then she smiled. The odd feeling was still inside of her, but she had never felt closer to Hen.

"Tell me more, Hen," said Ellis as she climbed back into the chair where she began sipping on her now cold tea.

"Connor Glass is a research laboratory not far from here. Your mom and dad went to work there right out of college. After several years, they became the lead scientists in a project that revolutionized the way glass was made for solar panels. They discovered how to make glass so that it converted the sun's energy in such a way that one small panel provided hours of electricity for an entire home after just a few minutes of direct sunlight," Hen looked at Ellis, her eyes were sparkling.

"Do you think you understand so far Ellis?" asked Hen.

Ellis nodded.

Hen went on. "Before allowing the panels to go into wide-scale production, your parents conducted several tests. During one of these tests, they made a discovery that was beyond even their understanding. They immediately released a report indicating that the solar panels did not work as expected and could not be used. They said the test results reported earlier were erroneous and they took full responsibility," Hen stopped for a moment. She looked completely lost in thought.

"What was it?" asked Ellis.

"What?" replied Hen, bringing her attention back to Ellis.

"What was the discovery?"

"The glass in the panels not only converted energy from the sun, but it also bent light to *change perspective*," Hen stopped.

"Okay . . . now I don't understand," said Ellis.

"Your parents called what happened with the glass *changing perspective*. It was a term they decided on and one that I really cannot fully explain," said Hen.

In a serious, fearful tone, Hen added, "You mustn't discuss the last part of what I just told you with *anyone*. Many people in this town know that your parents worked for Connor Glass, and all they know is your mom and dad died in a car accident. They don't understand how you were left behind. They don't know about the glass your parents developed."

"What do you mean by *left behind*!" Ellis shook at the implications of these words. "I have a hard enough time being an orphan, but now you make it sound like I've been *abandoned*," Ellis continued, her voice shaky.

Hen was immediately at Ellis's side, "I'm sorry, Ellis. Please don't think that. I shouldn't have said that. Your mom and dad loved you. They would never abandon you."

Ellis got very quiet. She was too afraid for now to ask what Hen meant when she said *all they know is your mom and dad died in a car accident*. She felt like she needed to get away from Hen and the terrible things she was saying.

As if on cue, Hen said, "Enough for today. There is a place I think you'll like to visit."

Ellis stewed further over Hen's harsh comments while Hen wrote down the directions to a bookstore. "The person who runs the bookstore is a friend of mine," Hen said, while drawing a little map. "Her family was good friends with your mom and dad."

Chapter 7 ~ A Priori Books

The bookstore was as ancient as the building it was housed in. Passersby who took the time to peer into the large bay windows on either side of the store's arched doorway saw a display of old looking leather bound books and a few more newer looking hardcover books. Beyond the window display stood a long wooden counter, and beyond that, rows and rows of tall wooden bookshelves, which appeared to travel endlessly toward the rear of the bookstore.

The three-story stone building was on the oldest street in Harper. Bourner Street, as if forgotten by time, was still cobbled, with either end meeting present day blacktop paving. A walk from one end of the street to the other took less than a minute, for there were just three buildings in all to pass. Firmly abutted to the bookstore was a two-story apothecary and tightly adjoining that was a one-story flower shop. The three old buildings faced southeast, to view the brick backside of a row of tall townhouses that spanned the entire length of Bourner Street, leaving the street perpetually in shadows.

Protruding from the stone face of the bookstore was an elaborate wrought iron sign bracket. Among the flourishes were two small hooks from which hung a sign that read in large letters "A Priori Books" and beneath that, in much smaller letters, were the words "Buy and Sell." A heavy wooden arch door rested silently below the sign. Behind the heavy door, rippling through the otherwise silent room, was the muffled sound of soft snoring. Behind the counter, on her back with all four legs in the air, nose stretched out revealing the softest area on her neck, Daisy slept.

Ellis looked up at the sign and knew she had found the bookstore Hen described. She looked down the street again — it was still deserted — and dark shadows seem to silence any noises. Ellis readjusted the books in her arm, wiped her free palm against her shorts, and then opened the door. A soft jingle sounded as she pushed the heavy door inward. She had to push much harder than she expected for the door was heavy and it resisted with a stiffness that comes from not being opened for a long time. (At least that's what Ellis imagined.)

At the sound of the door, Daisy halted her snoring with a sneeze-like sound. She rolled her body to place her legs back on the ground, leaned down in a deep bow to stretch her back, and then unceremoniously walked around the counter and over to the entryway, a soft clip-clipping echoing through the store as her toenails made contact with the stone floor.

Daisy stopped a few feet away from Ellis, who by now was standing inside. And then Daisy sat. Her posture was erect and her snout was level. Ellis stood motionless, not feeling any fear, yet not sure what to do. Daisy looked Ellis in the eye before she turned her head back toward the counter. As though instructed to do so, Ellis followed Daisy's gaze. What Ellis saw gave her a start, and a whispered gasp escaped when she drew her breath. There behind the counter was a girl, or perhaps a small woman. It was uncertain. But Ellis was certain that she wasn't there a moment ago. A moment ago Ellis had the feeling that no one else was in the bookstore besides herself and the dog.

"Hello," said Ellis in a voice not quite her own as it escaped hoarsely from her suddenly dry mouth. She felt silly. She told herself that the quiet street and quiet bookstore have made her jumpy.

The girl-woman smiled. Her hair was piled into a curious

looking bun that had bits of hair sticking out at all angles. Somehow the effect was smart.

"May I help you?" asked the girl-woman. Her voice gave no hint to her age. She had angled her head slightly when asking the question. The bun bobbed along with the movement.

"I — I have books that my grandmother wants to sell," stammered Ellis. She held out the three books that had been wrapped in her arm. The books were old and rather worn looking.

"You don't look familiar. Are you an Ida May student?" The bun bobbed.

Perhaps the voice was more woman than girl Ellis thought. On second thought, maybe it was a girl looking for a friend. Ellis was feeling bewildered.

The girl-woman waited patiently. She looked kind. She was definitely older than a girl. Ellis remained silent. She had been told to never reveal personal information to strangers. Or even to most acquaintances for that matter.

Ellis cleared her throat. "I just want to sell these books," She answered with as much conviction as she could muster. She didn't want to disappoint Hen.

"Of course," replied the girl-woman without hesitation. "Please bring the books over to the counter so that I may take a look."

Daisy had been stretched out on the floor with her head resting on her crossed front legs, but the invitation for Ellis to approach the counter prompted Daisy to her feet again. She walked ahead of Ellis and when Ellis reached the front of the counter, Daisy walked around to the back and found her soft bed. A muffled snoring soon punctuated the quiet of the store.

Ellis placed the books on the wooden counter. It had a smooth, well-worn surface that could only come from years of use. Some areas were smoother and shinier than others. The rounded edges of the counter, where Ellis rested her hands, were particularly smooth and shiny. Separated by only counter space, Ellis looked up to meet the light gray eyes of the girl-woman. They sparkled against the dark lashes that framed them. Ellis pushed the books over to her.

As the girl-woman inspected the books, Ellis took in her surroundings. Mounted to the wall behind the girl-woman (who was now examining the first book) was a large pendulum clock. The time appeared to be correct even though the pendulum was motionless. Ellis turned her head to the right and saw several aisles of books. Tall rolling ladders rested against several of the shelves, which Ellis guessed to be at least twice her height. Ellis observed that no matter how hard she tried to focus her eyes, she could not distinguish the end of a row or even determine if there was a back wall. The aisles of books just continued on into darkness.

Hanging on to the rounded edge of the counter, Ellis twisted her body to look behind her. She observed the entry where she had stood, and for the first time noticed the short shelves of children's books. The shelves looked familiar — maybe she had subconsciously noticed them when she came into the store. Turning back to the counter, she looked up at the clock once more. The big hand had progressed two minutes but the pendulum remained at rest. There was no second hand to tick away the time.

"So, these books belong to Henrietta," the girl-woman suggested in an offhanded way. She hadn't raised her head from the book she was examining, but Ellis had the feeling that the girl-woman sensed the surprise that overtook Ellis.

"How . . . ?" questioned Ellis, her voice trailing off.

"You must be Ellis," the girl-woman said looking up from the books and into Ellis's eyes.

Ellis's cheeks instantly heated. She felt childish for not

introducing herself when she walked in. Hen said she knew the bookstore owner, Ellis remembered.

"Excuse me for not introducing myself earlier. My name is Tori." The girl-woman extended her hand across the counter.

"Nice to meet you," replied Ellis, politely shaking Tori's hand. The hand was small, even a little smaller than Ellis's hand. But Tori's handshake exuded confidence and experience. In that instant, Ellis felt as young as her fourteen years. Her surge of emotion was mixed with feelings of anger and inadequacy. She was, after all, old enough to handle selling the books, she argued with herself. So how come one minute she felt able to take on the world and the next she simply felt like she was going to be swallowed up by it?

Seeing Tori's confused look, Ellis put a feeble smile on her face and tried to remember where they were in the conversation.

"My grandmother said she knew you." Ellis tried to sound confident, knowing.

"Your grandmother?" questioned Tori.

"Yes, Hen."

"Hen?"

"Yes, my grandmother likes for me to call her Hen," Ellis was beginning to wonder if there was some sort of misunderstanding.

"Oh," answered Tori. She seemed distracted. "I have known Henrietta for a long time. I didn't realize — I, well, forgot she liked to be called Hen."

A heavy silence followed and Ellis sensed that Tori was deep in thought. Remaining silent, Tori paged through the books, but Ellis had the impression she wasn't really looking at the pages.

"I'm so glad that you and Hen have moved back here," Tori stated after a minute or so. She talked as if she and Ellis were old family friends.

Ellis glanced around the store. Still no other customers.

Tori shut the books and piled them at one end of the counter. "Does Hen want to sell the books on consignment? Or does she want me to purchase them outright?"

Ellis hadn't been sure what *consignment* meant when Hen told her to accept that offer, but she was glad she knew how to answer Tori. "Hen said to sell them on consignment."

"Very well," said Tori. "I will let her know when they sell." Tori picked up a tablet computer that was on the counter alongside a digital camera and started entering the book information.

"Okay," said Ellis. She knew their business had come to an end, and although she had a strange feeling about Tori and A Priori Books — like maybe she should leave and ask Hen what's going on with this big quiet place — she felt good being out on her own and didn't want to go home yet.

Tori seemed to pick up on Ellis's reluctance to leave. "Do you want to look around?" she asked.

"Uhm . . . okay," answered Ellis, feeling a little giddy about her freedom.

Hen must think this place is okay if she sent me here, thought Ellis, reassuring herself that she had made the correct choice in staying.

Ellis walked toward the children's book area she noticed when entering the store. A big rug with soft pillows made up a reading area in front of the short bookshelves filled with thin, colorful bindings. Behind them, she saw a few bean bag chairs and a couple upright chairs arranged to face a wooden table of teen books and classics. She recognized some of the titles from those that Ms. Bennet had on the reading list for English class this year.

"Do you go to Ida May School?"

Ellis jumped a little at the sound of Tori's voice so close by. Ellis hadn't heard her approach.

"Uh . . . yes," said Ellis, glancing at the front door, which still hadn't opened since Ellis came in.

"We get a lot of students from Ida May in here on school days," explained Tori. "We aren't so busy on the weekends. The books are listed online, which is how most customers buy their books now. . . ."

Tori looked thoughtful for a second before asking, "Have you been to The Apothecary?"

"What's that?"

"A candy store. It's right next door. Did you see the sign outside?"

Ellis remembered seeing another ornate sign above the door next to A Priori Books, but she wasn't sure if she had read the store name. "I remember seeing a store next door. . . ."

"Follow me," said Tori.

Chapter 8 ~ The Apothecary

Tori walked down the first aisle of books, which was backed against the store wall. Ellis followed. The bookshelves seemed even taller as she walked past them. She looked back and forth, right, then left, and back again, in an effort to take in the jagged terrain of the books on the shelves.

Tori continued further and further down the aisle of books. Ellis began looking less at the books and more at the bookends. They appeared on nearly every shelf. There were bookends of brass, glass, porcelain, wood, and shiny metals. A brass one was shaped like a high-backed chair with a cat curled up on the seat, a small wooden birdhouse held up a row of bird books, a snow globe rested against a long shelf of Christmas books. She thought of the glass bookends her parents had collected. When Tori abruptly stopped, Ellis was so distracted she walked squarely into her.

"Oh!" exclaimed Ellis, as she stumbled back a step. "Excuse me," she mumbled, her face reddening.

"We're here." Tori smiled while remaining firmly footed, looking unruffled by the incident. She was facing the wall of books.

Ellis looked at the shelf. The titles suggested plant and herb books. Among them "The Complete Book of Herbs," "Culinary Herbs," "Licorice and Mints for Candy Lovers," and "Sweet Herbs." The books were held in place by a large glass bookend in the shape of a giant purple and white starlight candy wrapped in a cellophane wrapper. Ellis was enchanted.

As if reading Ellis's mind, Tori placed her hand on the

giant starlight — her hand was only large enough to grip the top half — and began sliding the bookend toward her. Ellis decided the glass candy must be very heavy if Tori had to slide it off the shelf rather than lift it off. To her surprise, as soon as the candy reached the edge of the shelf, a section of the bookcase swung outward, revealing a large room.

A sweet, warm rush of air greeted Ellis. Tori motioned Ellis into the room and then followed behind her, closing the bookcase door with a soft swish behind them. Ellis took a few more steps into the room. At one end of the room were large vats of boiling, bubbling sweetness. Nearby were long tables topped with marble slabs. Leaning against each table was what looked like a long-handled spatula. The device had a wooden handle several feet long and a large — larger than two dinner plates — flat metal end (Ellis learned later they were for cooling and shaping taffy). Opposite the vats was a wall full of narrowly spaced shelves. Unlike the bookshelves with their books and bookends, these shelves were tightly filled with identical glass-stoppered jars. Ellis was not close enough to read the labels, but their contents appeared to be leaves, crystals, powders, and small dried berries.

"This is Mr. Neumann's store," said Tori.

Ellis remained still, in a silent awe.

"He owns The Apothecary," added Tori.

"The Apothecary?"

Tori began leading Ellis around the big room as she talked. "An apothecary is an old fashioned drugstore," she explained. "Mr. Neumann used to prepare prescriptions and sell other medicines along with some of his homemade candy. People told him that his candies made them feel better than the medicines. Joking or not, he saw that his customers were happier when they took along some candy with their medicine, so he created more candies. Eventually — " Tori waved her hand at the wall of glass-stoppered containers they had walked up to, "all the glass jars were needed for candy ingredients so he stopped selling traditional medicines. More people than ever now come to him for his homemade remedies."

Now that Ellis was standing closer to the glass containers, she read their labels. A row of pink, white, gray, and black crystals were actually salts. The handwritten paper labels were in decorative calligraphy. They read Ancient Sea Salt (crystals with flecks of pink, gray, brown), Himalayan Pink Salt (large pink crystals), Flaked Sea Salt, Kosher Salt, Pickling Salt, Fleur de Sel, Dead Sea Salts, and Black Lava Salt.

Ellis was mesmerized. It was like a science lab where everything was edible. Tori continued to speak, and Ellis listened while her eyes searched every inch of the space, analyzing the contents of the containers.

"Mr. Neumann has a candy for sore throats, one for ear aches, even one for acne."

The next shelf contained bottles of what looked like leaves, roots, and berries.

"Of course he has lots of candy for just enjoying too."

Ellis read their labels: Peppermint (small dark leaves), Spearmint (leaves), Applemint (leaves), Licorice Root (wood chip pieces), Ginger Root (a tawny gnarled tuber), Allspice (a small hard berry), Cinnamon Bark, Clove (whole), Tahitian Vanilla (a dark brown liquid), and Vanilla Beans (a long, dark brown, wrinkled bean pod).

There were more shelves with bottles, but Ellis had no time to read their labels as she hurried to stick close to Tori who was walking toward a door. They passed a long row of wooden barrels. The lids had engraved labels. Ellis gently tapped each barrel as she walked by and tried to decipher their contents. Caster Sugar (superfine), Powdered Sugar, Date Sugar, Fruit Sugar, Turbinado Sugar, Muscovado Sugar, Florida Cane

Sugar, Canada Maple Sugar, Vanilla Sugar, Spun Sugar, Piloncillo (partially refined Mexican Cane Sugar formed into little pylons), Jaggery (India), Melis (Scandinavia), Palm Sugar, Beet Sugar, Watermelon Sugar, Pumpkin Sugar, Birch Sugar, White Sugar, and Sugar Cubes.

As Ellis approached the door that Tori was directing her to, she caught a glimpse of the main store through a large pass-through window. On the other side of the pass-through was a counter with at least thirty jars of candies and a checkout register. Beyond that Ellis saw two aisles of stocked shelves displaying containers and packages of candy. The rest of the store was tables and chairs for hanging out and enjoying the treats. Cleaning one of the tables was an older man wearing an apron. As Ellis and Tori walked through the door to the main store, the man cleaning the tables looked up and smiled.

"Tori —" said the man warmly as he tucked his cleaning towel into an apron pocket. "You're back. And you brought a friend." He smiled at Ellis.

"This is Ellis — Ellis Bell," said Tori.

Ellis looked up to see Mr. Neumann's smiling expression turn to one of questioning. He looked at Tori and Tori nodded her head slightly. Mr. Neumann smiled again and looked at Ellis long and hard as if he were looking at an old friend he hadn't seen in a very long time. He was a tall, thin man with a few wispy strands of hair on top his head. His navy striped bib apron was crisp and clean.

Ellis instinctively looked down after a few seconds of his inquisitive stare. She found herself staring at his large brown leather shoes. They had brown laces and were well-worn, but like his apron, they were also neat and clean.

"It's so nice to meet you, Ellis," said Mr. Neumann.

Ellis looked up to see Mr. Neumann extending his hand. It was rather large, like his feet. Ellis shook his hand as he continued with the long-lost friend stare for a few seconds more before regaining his composure.

"So you ladies came through the secret passage?" Mr. Neumann smiled and let out a short chuckle.

Ellis couldn't help but smile. This was the most amazing thing she had ever experienced.

"Ellis, help yourself to anything you want to try. I have candies of just about every flavor you can imagine," said Mr. Neumann as he went back to cleaning tables.

Ellis looked longingly at the aisles of candy. "Go ahead," said Tori. "I need to speak to Mr. Neumann anyway. I'll come find you when I'm done."

Ellis left Tori and walked to the other side of the store. She went down one aisle and saw five shelves on either side. The middle two shelves were long rows of heavy round glass jars with glass tops. The other shelves contained packaged candies. Ellis became completely immersed in the offerings. She decided to start at the far end of the aisle and work her way back out.

The door to The Apothecary jingled as customers came in. Ellis didn't look up from the package of candied mint leaves she was examining. They were small dark green leaves that had a glittery, crystallized appearance, which Ellis guessed was created by a sugar coating. The package said they were great for dropping into hot tea or for chewing after a meal to freshen your breath. She placed the package back on the shelf and started looking at the large glass jars. The many shapes and colors they revealed made the jars as nice to look at as their candy contents probably tasted.

Below each of the jars was a label with the candy name and a short description of ingredients and even what to expect for the taste. A jar of shell-shaped candies called Scallops were described as tasting sweet and salty like the sea air. They were made with Florida cane sugar, sea salt, and sea grapes. Ellis thought that sounded interesting for at least one taste.

As she began to read the next jar, several other girls walked into the aisle. Ellis glanced over to see Violet, Harley, Peyton, and Gwen. She rubbed her palms against her jeans and hoped her face didn't look too pink. With Ellis still toward the rear of the aisle, the four girls blocked her passage out, so she pretended to keep reading the jar labels, hoping for the girls to move around and make room for her to slip out.

Even though Ellis wasn't looking at the girls she sensed them sizing her up. Only a moment passed before she heard Vi's intrepid voice.

"Aren't you the new girl?" she asked in Ellis's direction.

Ellis looked up.

"Where did you move here from?" asked Vi without waiting for Ellis to respond to the first question.

Ellis looked directly at Vi and waited. Maybe she would decide Ellis was deaf. Harley cast her eyes down and played with the string attached to her jacket zipper in a fidgety sort of way. Gwen and Peyton were staring at Ellis while intermittently glancing at Vi.

Violet got an exasperated look on her face and then said, "So . . . you are the new girl, right?"

"Yes," answered Ellis.

Vi looked over at her team and then back at Ellis.

"Excuse me," said Ellis, motioning that she wanted to squeeze past the girls, "but I need to find my friend."

Ellis's movement to get out of the aisle solicited no action from any of the girls. They all stood still and continued to block Ellis.

"Are you here with *Starling*?" asked Vi snidely.

"No," said Ellis.

"So you have more than one friend?" snapped Vi.

"Excuse me." Ellis tried again to push past the girls.

"Ellis?" A small, but confident voice came from behind the girls.

The surprised girls turned to find Tori standing behind them.

"Yes, coming," said Ellis. This time the girls grudgingly parted as Ellis made her way out.

Ellis and Tori left The Apothecary through the front door and after just a few steps were walking back into A Priori Books. "Is everything okay?" asked Tori. Ellis knew she was referring to Vi and her friends.

"Yes," Ellis sighed. "Thanks for taking me to The Apothecary . . . I better head home now."

Ellis was feeling too light hearted to let the encounter with Vi drag her down. She walked home thinking about her great first-afternoon-on-her-own in Harper.

Chapter 9 ~ Starling's House

By the beginning of the third week of school, Ellis was begging and pleading with Hen for permission to accept an invitation to Starling's house. Originally, Ellis had wanted Starling to come home with her so they could visit A Priori Books and The Apothecary together. But Hen said she wanted the unpacking to be completely done first. Apparently, what Hen didn't plan on was an invitation for Ellis to visit *Starling's* home to meet *her* family. Hen looked a little irked when Ellis excitedly told her how she and Starling planned it so that Hen wouldn't even have to go out of her way to drive Ellis to Starling's house. They would just ride the Double Decker together after school.

Hen finally gave in and after PE on Friday, Ellis and Starling excitedly grabbed their backpacks and headed to the Double Decker. The embankment behind the school to the tracks below was so steep that a zigzag path of alternating steps and ramped walkways was needed to allow for an easier descent. Ellis found she needed to grab the rail as they progressed, and she had the feeling that Starling was accustomed to moving faster. The trail was a bit dusty especially when quicker students stepped off the concrete path and scuffed their feet through worn grassy areas to keep from tumbling. By the time they reached the train tracks, Ellis felt a slight burn in her shins.

"Wow, that was work," proclaimed Ellis.

Starling laughed. "You get used to it."

Ellis saw that the train was old, like the school. Although clean and shiny, up close the car's bright red paint job couldn't hide the many ridges and valleys formed by the previous layers of paint beneath. The leather seats were a deep burgundy color. Hanging hand grips above each aisle seat allowed for standing passengers. Ellis was surprised to see the car get so full that there were students reaching for the hand grips. A narrow winding staircase at the front of the car led to the second floor, but before Ellis had a chance to start up the steps, Starling guided her to a seat on the lower level where they both sat down.

Through the window beside her, Ellis looked up at Ida May on its plateau. The number of students outside the school was thinning. Small groups were walking toward The Trivium, a park where Starling said students like to gather after school, especially on Fridays. Before Ellis could become further lost in thought, Starling interrupted, "So what do you want to do when we get to my house?"

Ellis smiled. It was so exciting to be able to go to a friend's house. "I'd love to see your room."

As soon as the words were out of her mouth, Ellis hoped she wasn't making a strange request.

Starling replied immediately, with no reluctance in her voice, putting Ellis at ease. "Sure. We'll drop off our stuff and then go for a walk before it gets dark."

The rest of the train ride was spent talking about what they saw out the window. The Double Decker track ran parallel to the four-lane highway that leads out of town. Ellis hadn't been outside Harper since she and Hen moved there, so she really didn't know anything about her surroundings. But as Starling explained the buildings and businesses along the route, Ellis had the nagging feeling that much of it was familiar.

The train brakes squeakily alerted Ellis to the Double Decker's first stop. She looked to Starling who said they get off at the next stop. As the doors opened to allow students off, Ellis looked out at the train station. It really wasn't much of a station, but rather a covered bench and a large parking lot. Parents were waiting in a car pickup line. In less than two minutes the doors were closed again and the Double Decker picked up speed.

Starling leaned over to gather her backpack, "Our stop is next and just a minute away."

As Ellis gathered her things, the brakes began to squeal again. She wondered if Starling's mother will be picking them up.

The remaining passengers stepped off the train. This station had a much smaller parking lot, but several covered benches.

"Is someone here to pick us up?" Ellis looked expectantly at the row of cars.

"Only on rainy days," replied Starling as she began walking through the parking lot. "I walk home from the station. It's not far."

Ellis followed Starling through the parking lot before they headed down an adjoining street. There were no sidewalks like in town. An occasional car made its way around them as they walked on the side of the street. The houses were more spread apart. Some had little white fences surrounding them. Mailboxes were placed on posts along the road, rather than attached to the front of the house. Ellis liked the way the houses were nestled among the trees, as if to not disturb the nature.

They turned down the next street, which had just a few houses and dead ended at a wooded area. As they approached the house at the end of the street, Starling said, "This is it."

The two story wooden house had shuttered windows and was surrounded by many trees. The walkway to the front door was lined with ivy, and rose bushes grew on either side of the door.

Facing the front door, Starling reached behind a window shutter and pulled out a small box with a key.

As Starling pulled out the key and unlocked the front door, Ellis realized neither of Starling's sisters was on the Double Decker. "Where are your sisters?" Ellis asked Starling.

"Kes and Myna went to The Trivium. They'll get a ride home later," answered Starling as she placed the box with the key back behind the shutter. "We'll put our stuff down and then walk to the lab to let my parents know we're home."

The front door opened directly into the living room. Beside the door was a high back bench with hooks. The bench had claw and ball feet to lift it from the floor, allowing room for shoes beneath. It was laden with jackets, sweaters, and umbrellas, and several pairs of shoes were stuffed below the bench leaving no room for more. Starling took her shoes off, but left them on the floor in front of the bench. Ellis did the same.

Stepping further into the living room, most of the remaining hardwood floor was covered by an area rug. Ellis could feel the warmth of the room. The sofa, covered in a flower patterned fabric, was long and inviting and had large overstuffed cushions. Comfortable chairs complemented the sofa and several side tables with small lamps were placed beside each sitting area. A coffee table was overflowing with magazines and books arranged haphazardly. The walls displayed beautifully framed bird prints. Ellis didn't move close enough to read them but the bird names were part of each print. A staircase at one end of the living room had a small, bright brass finial in the shape of a songbird. It appeared to be perched on the handrail with its legs and neck stretched up toward the sky and its beak open slightly as if time had stopped in the middle of a its song.

Starling grabbed Ellis by the arm and gave her a tug toward

the staircase, "My room is upstairs. Let's go quick because we still need to walk to my parent's lab."

As they ran up the stairs, Ellis gently brushed her fingers across the head of the songbird. At the top of the steps, a large landing with several doors greeted them. Starling chose the second door on the right and Ellis followed.

The room was bright and fun and very different from what Ellis had seen downstairs. The walls were a bright lilac. A large window overlooked part of an oak tree. A pile of clothing lay in the corner and the polka dot bedding was in a heap on the bed. The desk near the window was piled high with papers, books, and pencils. A few crumbled papers lie near the trash basket beside the desk.

Starling allowed her backpack to slide from her shoulder and hit the floor with a thud. Ellis placed her backpack next to it. "I love your room," said Ellis enthusiastically.

"Thanks," answered Starling. "It's kind of messy," she added as she half-heartedly straightened the comforter on the bed.

"No problem," said Ellis sincerely.

"Before we do anything, we have to check in with my parents at the lab," reminded Starling. Before Ellis could really take in the room any further, she and Starling were headed down the stairs.

Back outside, they walked at a quick pace to the end of the street and then Starling guided Ellis down a different street heading away from the train station. Ellis saw fewer houses ahead and beyond them was a densely wooded area. Starling continued toward the wooded area.

"Where are we going?" asked Ellis, confused.

"I'm taking the shortcut to the lab. There's a path up ahead."

Ellis squinted, looking for a path into the woods.

They stepped off the road and into the wooded area. Dry leaves and small sticks crackled beneath their feet as Starling led the way through the heavy brush and trees. Ellis noticed that they were clearly on a path, but it was so densely wooded around them that the path would be hard to distinguish from a distance.

They walked up a short incline and when Ellis glanced behind her — just minutes later — the road was no longer visible. Tall trees replaced the brush and began to filter more and more of the late afternoon sunlight. Starling walked with purpose. Ellis looked at the ground mostly, watching her step, occasionally pressing her damp hands against her jeans. They continued on for several minutes more without speaking, the near darkness and eerie quiet seemingly commanding a silent respect. All Ellis could hear was their crackly footsteps and her racing heartbeat until Starling said, "What do you think?"

"Wh — what?" stammered Ellis, jolting a little at the sound of Starling's voice in the quiet.

"I'm just wondering if you like taking this path. I know walking through the woods isn't for everyone," said Starling, and then hesitantly she added, "I hope you don't mind that I have to check in with my parents."

Ellis smiled. "I don't mind. I'm having a great time . . . honest. This is — this is exciting." Ellis didn't know how else to explain the sense of adventure she was feeling.

Starling stopped to rest against a tree, placing her back on the trunk of a narrow elm so that she faced Ellis. "I think it's fun too. The lab isn't that far now." Starling glanced in the direction of the path. Ellis craned her neck to look ahead but didn't see evidence of anything manmade.

"My parents used to work at Connor Glass. . . . When I was really young," said Ellis impulsively, surprising even herself by coming forward with information about her parents.

"Really?" said Starling, looking astonished.

"I lived in Harper when I was young . . . Until I moved away with my grandmother," said Ellis.

"Wow." Starling looked thoughtful, questioning.

"Yeah. My grandmother told me on the first day of school. I'm still getting used to the idea."

Starling's mouth hung open slightly as she looked at Ellis somewhat disbelievingly. After a moment she said, "Wait — so you used to live in Harper with your parents who worked at Connor Glass . . . and then you moved away . . . and now you're back with your grandmother?"

Ellis nodded. By the third day of school, Ellis and Starling were walking to every class together and eating lunch together every day. With that much conversation, Ellis found it awkward to avoid the topic of who she lived with so she opened up to Starling. She was nervous at first, but their bond deepened when Starling responded with "I'm sorry about your parents" and then continued on with the conversation like Ellis was just a normal girl. With that, even Ellis felt like living with a grandmother was not so strange after all.

"We better get moving," said Starling, still looking perplexed over the new information.

"Starling," said Ellis.

"Yeah?"

"I don't think I want to talk to anyone about my parents working at Connor Glass."

"Okay. I won't say anything," replied Starling sincerely, and then with concern she added, "They might recognize your name, you know."

"Okay, but I just don't want to bring it up or talk about it if I don't have to. I still don't know that much about it myself."

Starling nodded and then they walked on, their thoughts accompanied by the crackling, chirping, scurrying noises around them.

Only a few more minutes had passed when Ellis realized bright sunlight was warming her face. She looked up as if drawn to a beacon. Ahead of them the woods suddenly thinned and an iron fence crossed the path. Behind the tall fence several brick buildings protruded upward, where trees once stood. Ellis and Starling followed the fence line to a double gate that lead to a large parking lot. Ellis suppressed a shiver as a tingle went up her spine.

Chapter 10 ~ Connor Glass

Ellis and Starling walked through the gates and past a small guardhouse. Starling waved to the guard inside who did not bother to get up from his seat, but instead waved them on.

"I feel like we are in a secret place," said Ellis with a giggle.

"The owner likes birds and nature and wanted to put his research facility where he can go outside and see nature, not other buildings," responded Starling. "We really aren't that far away from other businesses. It just seems that way because it is so heavily wooded around the lab," Starling added, as she pulled open the door to the front entrance.

Ellis stepped inside the lobby. She heard a gentle trickle of water. Roughly cut glass blocks of many colors were piled in a sculpture-like way in the center of the lobby. The high glass ceiling let in natural light. Water slid down a sheet of glass behind a long receptionist desk.

"Hello, Starling," said an older woman sitting behind the desk. She was thin and wore horn rimmed glasses. "How was school today?"

"Great, thanks Miss Jayne."

"You have a new friend with you?" asked Jayne.

"This is Ellis." Starling gently rested a hand on Ellis's shoulder.

"Nice to meet you," said Jayne. "That's an unusual name."

Ellis politely nodded and smiled at Jayne who seemed to be distracted with her thoughts.

"Okay, we need to go," said Starling as she gestured toward an elevator.

Before stepping into the glass elevator, Ellis looked back to the front desk. Miss Jayne was intently organizing a stack of loose papers, but Ellis could swear that she hadn't heard the rustling noise of the papers before she turned around.

Two floors up, the elevator doors opened to a long hallway. Ellis peeked into every open door as she and Starling made their way to Starling's mother's office. She wanted to soak up as much of her own parent's past as she could. She wanted to *feel* their presence.

Unlike the lobby with all its colored glass, the walls and floors on this floor were a mix of white, or beige, or some other muted color. The rooms varied in size and looked sparse except for the occasional cluttered desk. A small room held just one large piece of equipment as tall as Ellis herself. The complicated looking machine displayed a digital screen and several electronic readouts.

The next room they passed had many shelves with lots of containers on them. The entire back wall was a series of glass doors, behind which were large vessels connected to tubes and controllers and housed in a framework of metal rods. A large room further down the hall had several sinks and counters, and reminded Ellis of the science lab at Ida May. This room however, also had large overhead vents which hung above the counter space in the center of the room.

Near the end of hallway, Starling directed Ellis into a room with long counters running along each wall. Three desks, facing three different directions, each laden with papers, a computer, and simple metal bookends that sandwiched books and folders, were situated around the room. Several high stools were placed beneath the counters. Ellis noticed each counter also had its own sink. Microscopes, flasks of liquid, and slides were strewn about the counter tops. Ellis was so distracted by the business of the room that she didn't notice the woman approaching Starling.

"Hi, mom," said Starling. "Ellis, this is my mom."

Starling's mother wore a white lab coat over her khaki pants and button down shirt. She looked like she was stopping by the office after a day of bird watching. Her short, straight hair contrasted Starling's long curly mane, but her golden colored eyes and straight nose looked almost identical to Starling's.

Dr. Archer warmly shook Ellis's hand and said hello.

"Nice to meet you," she said, as she continued to use both her hands to embrace Ellis's one hand.

"Hi" was all Ellis could manage to say, wishing she could extract her hand without seeming rude.

"Tom . . ." called Dr. Archer to a man walking into the room. Thankfully, the distraction caused her to release Ellis's hand.

The man turned and smiled.

"Hi, Dad," said Starling.

He too looked like a birder. He strolled over in his khaki's and button down and put one arm around Starling's shoulders. "How was your day, Star?"

"Great, thanks Dad."

"This is Ellis Bell," said Starling, smiling and putting her hand out, palm up, as if to say "ta da!"

"Ahh, nice to finally meet you Ellis," Dr. Archer shook Ellis's hand kindly. He wore thin wire frame glasses that rested partially down the bridge of his nose. His graying hair was short and thin on top, but there was enough for Ellis to see where Starling got her curls from.

"Thanks for having me over," replied Ellis.

Starling grabbed Ellis by the arm and said to her parents, "We're going to head back to the house now."

"Thanks for checking in," said Dr. Archer, and then she added, "Ellis, come again and we'll show you around the lab. Today is too busy for a tour, but we're glad you girls stopped by."

"Tom," said Starling's mom, turning her attention away from the girls, "I'm glad you walked in. I need to go over some data with you." And she and Starling's dad walked over to a computer on the lab counter.

Starling jerked her head slightly to indicate it was time she and Ellis head out. Ellis nodded in agreement but felt a pang of disappointment about leaving such an interesting place. A place that gave her a strange sense of connection to her parents.

They walked a longer route back along a roadway. It was late afternoon and Starling said the woods will be too dark to walk through. Ellis thought of Hen and was glad they took what Ellis was sure Hen would consider the safer way back.

The trip back to Starling's house seemed short as Ellis and Starling chatted the whole way. When they reached the walkway to the front door, Ellis noticed the house was well-lit and she heard noise coming from inside. Starling didn't seem to be surprised or concerned by the obvious occupation, so Ellis followed her lead.

Starling opened the door and the noise became blaring music from somewhere upstairs. Once inside, Starling shut the door behind her and Ellis and walked to the bottom of the stairs where she yelled, "KES! TURN DOWN THE MUSIC!"

The sound of the music diminished immediately. "Mom!?! Is that you?" yelled Kestrel from upstairs.

"No, it's me and I have Ellis with me. Keep the music down," called Starling up the stairs.

In response, the music went back up, but not quite to the deafening level it was at.

Starling walked through the living room into another part

of the house. Ellis followed. She smelled the aromas and felt the warmth of the kitchen before they entered the room. Myna was standing over a large pot of boiling water, stirring something. A large sauce pan contained what looked like red pasta sauce.

"Hi," said Myna, her hair looking a little wild and frizzy as a result of the humidity surrounding the boiling pot of what Ellis guessed to be pasta noodles. "Dinner is almost ready. Do you like spaghetti, Ellis?"

"Hi. Yeah, thanks," replied Ellis. Whenever Ellis saw Myna at school she seemed to be talking to someone or within a group of kids talking. On a couple of occasions when Ellis bumped into Myna walking alone, Myna immediately started up a conversation with Ellis, even if Ellis had no idea what she was talking about and therefore no idea of how to respond, which meant that most of Ellis's side of the conversations were nodding, and a lot of *humms* and *mmms* and *okays*. At first, Ellis thought Myna might be talking to her just to be nice, but over time she concluded that Myna liked to talk and Ellis did her part by lending an ear.

"Starling, you set the table," said Myna in a bossy tone.

Starling gave Ellis a look that showed she was annoyed by Myna's attitude.

"I'll help," volunteered Ellis, feeling so happy about dinner with a friend that she didn't want anything to spoil the occasion even if it was just sibling rivalry.

Ellis had just placed the last napkin and Starling the last water glass, when the Archers walked in. They seemed a little distracted, and Myna noticed. The house was suddenly very quiet. Ellis realized that Kes must have heard her parents come in and turned off the music.

"What's wrong?" asked Myna.

"Oh, nothing, My . . ." started her mom. "We've had a busy day at work is all," finished her dad. And they both seemed to make an effort to shake off the stress of the day.

"Dinner smells great," said Starling's mom, changing the subject.

Kestrel came strolling through the kitchen doorway. She and her dad were greeting each other when Myna proclaimed dinner was ready.

The oval wooden dining table seated them all perfectly. Everyone seemed to gravitate to a particular chair while Starling directed Ellis to a seat that she guessed must be Heron's usual place when he's home from college. Ellis loved the feeling of sitting around a dinner table with a big family. After a few minutes of utensils clattering and dishes being passed to serve dinner, talk shifted to general conversation.

"Ellis, how do you like Ida May?" asked Mr. Archer, while twirling pasta onto his fork.

"Oh, I like it a lot, thank you," answered Ellis, glancing over at Starling who was slurping up her own noodles.

Myna, looking discombobulated — her frizzy hair adding to the effect — broke in with the tale of what made her day a disaster.

"I'm never wearing this shirt again," said Myna as she plucked in disgust at the sleeve.

Ellis thought the shirt looked familiar, but didn't see anything wrong with it.

"Why?" her mother asked.

"I showed up to PE . . ." Myna said, and then seemed too emotional to go on.

"And . . ." Kes impatiently pushed her on.

Myna gazed at her plate and pushed her noodles around. "Well, Coach Cook comes out wearing this same shirt," she nearly wailed. "If I hadn't been wearing my PE clothes, I would have been standing there wearing the same top as Coach Cook!"

Ellis, not sure of how she should respond, at first bit her bottom lip in an effort to hold back her laughter, but when Starling and Kestrel chortled loudly, Ellis joined in.

After dinner, Ellis and Starling went back up to Starling's room. Hen was expected to pick up Ellis at any time.

"So, how long have your parents worked at the lab?" asked Ellis.

"I think about ten years," responded Starling. She was sitting on the floor of her room cleaning out her backpack.

Ellis was stretched out on her stomach on the hurriedly made bed. "How long have you lived here, if you don't mind telling me?" Ellis wanted to tread lightly on such questioning because she didn't like this kind of questioning aimed at her.

Starling smiled. The kind of smile she used whenever she's about to tell Ellis that she is being too polite.

"My parents moved us here for the job. This home is all I really remember."

"So your parents never met mine?" Ellis blurted out.

Starling didn't look directly at Ellis. After a moment of awkward silence, Starling said, "No, but they have heard of them. They asked me if you were related to the Bells that worked at the lab. I didn't know the answer until you told me in the woods."

Ellis wasn't sure how she felt about that information. She hoped Starling's parents had a good impression of her parents. She remained quiet, not sure what to say next. Ellis really liked being at Starling's house, but she wondered if Starling's family thought of her as an outcast.

Before she could change the subject, Ellis heard the front door open and the sound of Hen's talking as she was greeted by the Archers. Ellis thought she detected a slight waver of nervousness in Hen's voice.

Ellis jumped off the bed and headed downstairs. "Hi,

Hen," Ellis interrupted the Archers in her attempt to rescue Hen from any discomfort.

Hen smiled but continued talking to the Archers. They were asking what brought her back to the area. Ellis was just as interested in the answer as the Archers. She couldn't take her eyes off Hen who went on to say that she simply wanted Ellis to go to Ida May high school. Hen was good at not giving in to pressure to elaborate and the Archers seemed to know that they received all the answer they were going to get.

Ellis couldn't stop talking to Hen on the car ride home. She went on and on about how much fun she had with Starling and what a great room Starling had and how she and Starling set the table for dinner and how they had the best pasta ever. Even Ellis didn't understand why she left out the part about visiting the lab.

Chapter 11 ~ Threads

Throughout the weekend, Ellis would pass by Hen and see her lost in thought. She wondered if it had to do with her visit to Starling's house because she could think of nothing else out of the ordinary that had happened recently. By Sunday afternoon Ellis walked into the kitchen to find Hen just sitting at the table seemingly staring at the wall.

"Are you okay?" asked Ellis in a half laughing way not wanting to believe anything could actually be wrong. Hen was always the one to be cheerful. Each time Ellis started a new school, Hen was there with a smile, a hug, and for every negative incident Ellis had to report, Hen had a positive twist and a way to make Ellis laugh until she forgot why she was upset in the first place.

The way Hen looked over at Ellis made her half laugh disappear.

"Sit down Ellis, I want to talk to you," said Hen flatly. She reached for her cup of tea and then seemed to think better of it when her hand tremored.

Ellis pulled out a chair and sat with her legs over the side rather than over the front edge. She was in a position to flee if things got too weird.

"Ellis, your mom and dad disappeared when you were four years old," said Hen in a serious, monotone voice. "They created a device using the glass they developed at the lab — the glass that changes perspective. Do you remember what we talked about last week?" Ellis opened her mouth to respond, but Hen didn't wait for an answer.

"This device allowed them to visit threads," continued Hen.

Ellis squinted her eyes in an effort to concentrate. She really didn't understand what Hen was saying but something inside her told her to just sit and listen and hopefully the details would become clear.

Hen looked at Ellis as if trying to gauge her comprehension before she went on. "A *thread* is an alternate timeline, you might say . . . It's a life based on a different set of circumstances," Hen paused.

Ellis tilted her head and kept listening.

"A person has many threads, maybe even an infinite number of threads. If there is a way to move from one thread to another, then a person can see what their life is like on a different thread — what life is like under a different set of circumstances." Hen gave Ellis a look like *do you think you kind of get it?*

"What are you saying?" said Ellis, feeling mystified.

"The last time your parents visited a thread something happened to prevent them from returning. That is why your parents are gone . . . I don't know if they died," Hen took a deep breath and sighed. "They may still exist *somewhere.*"

Ellis thought she might faint. Still sideways on the chair, she leaned over and placed her elbows on her knees and held her head in her hands. She felt Hen's hand touch her shoulder, but she shrugged it away.

With her head still in her hands, Ellis said, "So my parents are *alive?*"

"I don't know. But there might be a way for you to find out."

Ellis lifted her head from her hands and looked into Hen's eyes.

"How?"

"Let's go to A Priori Books."

Summer was waning. There was a crispness in the air that suggested a change. Ellis and Hen wore light jackets and walked with purpose, oblivious to anyone else that might be out for a stroll in the cool, clear afternoon.

On the way to A Priori, Hen explained more about threads. She said that we live in a *main thread*, but because of the accidental discovery Ellis's parents made with the solar panel glass, they learned how to visit other *threads*. Ellis's parents theorized that everyone has many parallel lives in the universe, called threads, each progressing under a different set of circumstances. Our main life, or main thread, they said, is what we know in our consciousness.

Hen said that threads helped Ellis's parents understand that life is about our *perspective* — our interpretation of events. They learned that we can choose a different life by simply changing our perspective about events in our main thread.

Ellis's parents had told Hen that we can't go back in time and change our actions, but with threads we can see what happens under different circumstances and then use that information to guide our future decisions.

Ellis was overwhelmed by all the abstract information, but she remained focused on the idea that her parents might be alive *somewhere*. She and Hen turned the corner and were on the approach to Bourner Street. Ellis was still listening, too bewildered to ask questions.

Hen said that a visit to a thread can last for up to two days. At least the time on the thread feels like two days, but in our main thread only a few seconds have elapsed. Hen said that the device Ellis's parents made bends light in a way that places a person on a different thread in the universe. To end the visit, the device is used again to return a person to almost the same instant from where they left.

Ellis finally found some words. "You talk like time is just a location in the universe where we can visit."

"That's the way I've come to think of it."

"But we can't go to a place in the past?" Ellis was hopeful, thinking about the moment her parents disappeared. *What if they can be stopped from traveling that day?*

"I see what you're saying, Ellis," answered Hen sincerely. "If there is a way to go back in time, it can't be done with the device your parents made. I'm sorry."

They were a few steps away from A Priori Books. Before Hen entered the store, Ellis pulled her arm to stop her. "Why are we here? Why do we need to come to A Priori?"

"Tori was here when your parents disappeared. They left from the bookstore. You were reading books in the children's section . . . Your parents thought they would be gone for just a few seconds. . . ."

Before Ellis could ask any more questions, Hen pushed the door open. The familiar jingle sounded. Tori was working behind the counter and did not look up immediately. Daisy appeared and sat erectly, looking at Hen and Ellis with her big brown eyes. Her tail made a swishing sound against the floor as she wagged it vigorously from her sitting position. She clearly recognized both Hen and Ellis.

Hen had not moved from the entrance so Ellis didn't move either.

When Tori lifted her head in search of customers, she looked no further than Hen. Her expression immediately reflected overwhelming joy, and she looked as though she wanted nothing more than to run over and hug Hen, but she remained glued to her position behind the counter. Ellis thought she may have even seen tears in Tori's eyes.

The sudden outpour of emotion surprised Ellis who thought of Tori as a very calm, almost secretive person. Or maybe it was just the secret passage to The Apothecary that made Ellis decide Tori was secretive. When Ellis looked to Hen for an explanation, she was even more surprised to see Hen's face mirroring Tori's expression. And Hen too remained guarded, not moving. It was as if the two of them did not want to admit that they were longtime friends glad to see one another. Ellis knitted her eyebrows trying to make sense of such a strong friendship between two people with a big age difference. But then Ellis remembered that she had been left in the bookstore. Maybe Tori and her family took care of Ellis for a day or two until Hen could get to her after her parents disappearance. Ellis wondered if Hen and Tori kept in touch all the years she moved Ellis around. . . .

"Hen . . ." prompted Ellis.

Hen placed an arm on Ellis's shoulder, smiled, and together they walked toward the counter. Daisy seemed to take this as an invitation to run over and greet Hen.

Hen released Ellis and began vigorously petting Daisy, "Ahh, I remember you as a little pup. I can't believe you still remember me!"

Hen must have sensed Tori's presence because without looking up from petting Daisy, Hen said, "Tori, I told Ellis about her parents."

Tori walked closer to Hen who then raised herself up from Daisy. The two friends briefly hugged and smiled at one another. "I'm glad to see you," said Tori.

"Me too," smiled Hen with an expression that Ellis couldn't place.

Tori looked excited and nervous and flustered all at the same time. Without another word, she hurried over to the door, flipped the Open sign to read Closed, and turned the bolt. She hurried back to Ellis and Hen, her long skirt fluttering as she moved about so quickly.

Tori looked directly at Ellis and said a bit breathlessly, "Do you think you're ready to visit threads?"

Ellis looked at Hen, "Just me? Hen, you'll be with me too, right?"

Tori gave an exasperated looked to Hen as if to say, *I thought you told her everything.* . . .

"No, Ellis. You have to go alone," admitted Hen with a guilty look.

"I don' — don't know." stuttered Ellis.

Chapter 12 ~ Going on an Adventure

The three of them stood as silent as the stone floor beneath their feet. There wasn't even a snore from Daisy to break the tension. Ellis knew that Hen would never make her do anything she didn't feel comfortable doing, but she also felt that finding out what happened to her parents was as important to Hen as it was to Ellis. And then Ellis thought of her parents possibly existing somewhere. She had a nightmarish image of her mom and dad floating around in some unknown space. The image scared Ellis, but it also strengthened her resolve. "How do I do it?"

Tori disappeared behind the counter. Even her head wasn't visible, so she must have been leaning over. She popped back out within seconds and then revealed what was in her closed hand. In her palm lie a squarish piece of glass with rounded edges, about half the size and thickness of a deck of cards. It had a very dark center that lightened to a blue. It could have been a paperweight, but Ellis knew this must be the device for visiting threads.

Hen looked more nervous than Ellis about the prospect of what the device can do.

"What if I don't come back?" asked Ellis nervously. "Like my mom and dad. . . ."

Hen opened her mouth, but Tori spoke first, "We think the device your parents had may have dropped and cracked." Hen simply nodded. "They traveled many times with no problems. They felt it was safe," added Tori, turning to look at

Hen as she said the last sentence.

Tori led them to the sitting area with the high back chairs and sofa. The color had completely drained from Hen's face. Ellis wiped her hands on her jeans as soon as she sat down. She registered her concern for Hen but couldn't react because she was feeling so overwhelmed herself.

Ellis sat on the edge of the sofa next to Hen. She leaned forward and used her hands to emphasize every word, "How do I know where I'm going? How will I know what to do when I'm there?" Her tone reflected the panic rising in her. "This is crazy. I'm supposed to believe that I am going to go to some parallel life and hang out for two days and then come back to where I am right now? — I've never even gone on a sleepover."

"You won't know exactly where you are going when you leave, but you will recognize where you are once you get there." Tori calmly stated. "Each thread you visit will be *your* life. You cannot go where you do not exist."

Ellis took a moment to try and absorb this. Tori looked at Hen as she addressed Ellis, "We know this must feel overwhelming. It has been a lot of years since your parents disappeared and we really don't know what to expect."

Tori was silent for a few seconds and then said softly, "Ellis, we can't even be sure that you will ever see your parents." She sighed and went on, "Each time you use this device you may end up on a thread where your life includes your parents' decision to visit a thread the day they disappeared."

Ellis thought about this. "But what if I *do* see my parents?" She was suddenly feeling like the optimist in the wake of reality. "Will I be able to *bring them back*?" Ellis was still unsure of how visiting a thread worked.

Tori smiled at Ellis's optimism. Even Hen had a little more color in her previously pale face.

"Let's go over what we know. Your parents disappeared ten

years ago. They worked at Connor Glass and developed a more efficient glass for solar panels. We don't know how they discovered the special properties of the glass they developed, but once they knew about the properties they pulled the research data. They were afraid of what might happen once the glass was put into mass production and used for solar panels all over the world."

Ellis sat back in the couch. She rubbed her hands on her jeans. Her heart was pounding, but she remained completely focused on the unfolding story.

"Your parents removed the research data and their lab books from Connor Glass, but knowing your parents, they *never* destroyed the information. If we can find that information, it may help in finding them," Tori's voice became a little higher pitched and she was talking faster. "Your mother kept a notebook. After returning from a thread, she wrote down the coordinates of where they had traveled. She kept the notebook hidden and we haven't been able to find it."

At this point Tori held out the glass device. She flipped it over to show a small electronic readout with four two-digit numbers separated by spaces. "These numbers indicate the most recently visited thread," stated Tori.

"Since we don't have the device your parents used we don't know their last location — the location they never came back from," said Tori, gently rubbing her thumb across the device. It made Ellis think of a magic lamp and its genie. "This is an extra device they left behind. We think they made only two of these devices."

Tori stopped rubbing the glass and pulled herself out of the momentary distraction. "About the notebook your mother kept . . . We think she may have also hid the research lab books with it. *If* you end up on a thread with your mom, and *if* it's a thread where your mom is working for Connor Glass, *then* it's possible that you will go to the lab with her where you may learn of a secret place your mom stores research documents. Or maybe you'll see her hide lab books in your house here in Harper. Many times your parents were transported to a thread where they lived in your Harper house and worked at Connor Glass doing research unrelated to solar panels. Maybe you'll be transported to a similar thread."

"Do you think I will see where my mom might hide a notebook? — Do you think it will be the same hiding spot my mom used in her main thread?" Ellis asked, trying to figure out why her mom on a thread would do the same thing as her mom in her main thread.

"It's possible. In theory, a person is essentially the same on all threads because of innate characteristics — traits that are inborn or hardwired. It's the thread experiences and circumstances that influence how a personality develops, but a person will still use the same type of logic and thinking skills they were born with. So on another thread your mom may not know about the solar panel glass or the device, but she will still use the same logic when deciding where to hide something as important as research notes," Tori patiently explained. "But keep in mind, in your main thread — this life — even if we find the notebook, it won't contain the coordinates of where your parents disappeared because they weren't able to come back here to add the data to the notebook."

"And what if I end up on the thread with my actual parents — you know the thread that my parents never returned from?" asked Ellis.

Hen looked as if she might speak, but Tori jumped in first. "We think the chance of that is tiny. That's why we want you to focus on finding the notebook and lab books. . . ."

Tori looked thoughtful and then added, "We're not sure how you will be able to tell if the parents on a thread are your parents from your main thread." Tori then looked at Hen as she said, "And we're really concerned that you might risk your return from a thread if you try to find out."

Ellis, feeling frustrated with this new information, went back to the lab books. "So if I find a lab book on another thread, should I bring it back?" asked Ellis, thinking that any kind of research data might help.

Tori glanced at Hen before proceeding. Ellis was beginning to take these exchanges as a negative sign. "You can't bring anything back with you from a thread. However, you *can* take one picture by pressing this small button," Tori pointed to a small black button below the digital readout on the back of the glass.

"You must be extremely careful that no one sees you take the picture," said Tori, in a cautionary tone. "It can lead to suspicion . . . or worse."

"Okay, well, I'll just memorize the hiding spot . . ." suggested Ellis, afraid she might be careless when using the camera.

Tori and Hen exchanged another look.

In a remorseful tone, Tori said, "Ellis, you will not remember anything from a thread. When you return, you will remember that you intended to travel on a thread, but you will not actually remember anything about what you saw or did."

Ellis let this sink in. It all started to seem like an impossible task. She may never see her parents on a thread and if she does she won't remember anything about her encounter with them. She let out an audible "Hmmph!"

"Listen, Ellis," said Tori soothingly, "If you find hidden notebooks, take a picture of the hiding spot. Or, if you can, open the notebook and take a picture showing the last page of information. But, do not risk being seen. At no point can anyone realize you are on a thread. We are not sure what will happen, but your parent's research suggested dire consequences.

You might risk losing everything, including your ability to return to your main thread."

Tori was quiet. She seemed to be giving Ellis time to think about what she said. And then Tori added, "If you take a picture of where the notebook is hidden, we may be able to find it here in your main thread."

"What good will that be?" asked Ellis, sounding frustrated. "It won't contain the coordinates of where they last traveled."

"True," agreed Tori. "However, we think the notebook is stored with the research data. We can use your parent's research to help us find them."

For the first time since Tori began talking, Ellis looked directly at Hen. "What should I do?" she asked.

Hen looked tired — tired in a way that Ellis had never seen before. The soft wrinkles that accentuated her otherwise clear eyes looked more deeply creased than normal. Hen's already solemn face seemed even more so from the creases pulling on her mouth and forehead.

Hen forced a slight smile, "Ellis, you have to go with what your heart says. Your parents would never want you to risk your life in an effort to find them. They've been gone a long time. We don't know if they can be brought back. Or even if they exist to come back."

Then in a more upbeat tone, Hen added, "However, I don't think your parents disappearance had to do with the device malfunctioning. I think something else prevented their return. If you are careful not to drop the device. . . ."

"I'm scared," admitted Ellis.

For the first time all afternoon, Hen's eyes sparkled. "Scared? Or just nervous about a new adventure?" she said, trying to sound like her old self, and the attempt was contagious.

Ellis smiled. "I guess I'm going on an adventure."

Tori grabbed Ellis by the hand and the three of them walked to the back of the bookstore. As they headed down one of the endless aisles of bookshelves, Ellis asked, "Where are we going?"

"Your parents always left from the rear of the store so that the flash of light wouldn't be seen from outside," Tori explained.

Ellis felt her stomach flip flop. Her dry mouth prevented her from talking further.

Tori drew them all to a stop. She turned the device over and pressed a button to the right of the digital readout. The numbers disappeared and the screen was left blank.

Ellis looked at her questioningly.

"I blanked the destination. . . . When you travel you will be placed onto a random thread."

Ellis nodded, trying to appear outwardly confident in the hopes that she would feel more confident. "What is this other number for?" She pointed to what looked like a clock readout below the blanked destination readout.

"That indicates how much time you have left. You must return within two days — forty-eight hours. The clock counts down. We are not sure what happens when the clock reaches zero."

Ellis swallowed hard.

"To travel, hold this in the palm of your hand," said Tori while demonstrating by holding the device snugly in one hand, being careful to keep her finger tips off of the glass. "Press this button," Tori pointed to the button she had just used to clear the digital readout. "And then hold the device at arm's length, facing the device toward your body," She held out her arm in front of her. "Do the same when you are ready to return," she added.

After Tori's simulation, she handed the device to Ellis. It

felt heavier than Ellis expected. She was afraid to hold it and at the same time she was afraid of dropping it.

Tori continued her coaching, "Remember you can take only one picture. You can stay on the thread for up to two days, so don't waste your picture on something frivolous."

Ellis wasn't even sure if she knew what *frivolous* meant, but she intended to save her picture for something special — like her parents or the notebook hiding place.

Tori finished by saying, "You will not remember the thread once you return, so take a picture of something that lets us know where you were. Even if you don't find the notebook, having a picture to let us know you found your parents will allow us to set the device so that you can travel back to that thread."

With nothing left to be said, the three of them stood silently, waiting, waiting.

Ellis jolted at the realization that Hen and Tori were waiting on her. Waiting for her move.

Ellis looked at the palm of her hand with the device just resting there. She looked up at Hen and said, "So, I'll see you in a few seconds?"

Hen smiled, "Yes." And then she and Tori stepped further away from Ellis.

Ellis looked at the blank readout again and then with her other hand she reached over and pressed the button next to it. She immediately extended her arm to bring the device in front of her and then she looked into the bright light that swept over her.

Chapter 13 ~ The First Thread

Ellis must have been daydreaming. Her mind was feeling foggy and her world was just coming into focus: She was in a car with Hen and they were driving somewhere.

Where are we? thought Ellis.

Looking out the car window, Ellis saw familiar sites, but they seemed out of place. It was like seeing your math teacher at the mall — things didn't add up. Her heart began racing and her palms became damp.

And then Ellis felt the heaviness in her hand.

Adrenalin wiped out any remaining fogginess. Thoughts flooded her brain . . . she was on a thread . . . she was in a different version of her own life . . . she mustn't let Hen see the device.

Ellis looked over at Hen who was singing softly to a song on the radio and watching the road.

Hen gave Ellis a quick glance in return. "Why are you so quiet? Are you excited about going into Old Town?"

Old Town? thought Ellis, confused, but decided to answer Hen with "I can't wait."

"What flavor cupcake are you going to get?"

Cupcake? Oh wow, we're going to Old Town Alexandria, Ellis realized. She was impressed with her mind's ability to make such a connection. She also felt a little excited. She loved the cupcakes at Alexandria Cupcake! That question she had no problem answering. "I'm thinking the chocolate with vanilla frosting, or maybe Red Velvet. . . ."

As soon as the words were out of her mouth, Ellis inwardly

reprimanded herself, *How can I be excited about a cupcake when I should be focused on trying to find her parents?*

Ellis racked her brain to remember when she and Hen lived in Alexandria, Virginia. She remembered doing a field trip to Mount Vernon a few years ago . . . Ellis decided it was three schools ago — she was in 6th grade. When she and Hen lived in Alexandria, King Street was one of their favorite outings. They often took a Sunday stroll through the shops and stopped for a cupcake. On some visits, Ellis and Hen walked to the very end of King Street and looked out at the Potomac River before stopping by the Torpedo Factory Art Center. Hen especially liked the stained glass. Ellis found it fascinating that the place made torpedoes until 1945.

Hen turned the car onto King Street and started looking down the side streets for parking. She made a quick left onto Patrick Street and eased into a space less than a block away from Alexandria Cupcake.

"Ready?" asked Hen warmly. She always seemed happiest when she and Ellis were on an outing together.

"Sure," answered Ellis, hoping she sounded normal to Hen.

At this point Ellis knew she would have just a second or two of being out of Hen's view. As soon as Hen began raising herself out of the car, Ellis slipped the glass device into the crossover bag on her shoulder. It was a cute bag — sage green with pale turquoise trim and a tan leather strap — but it felt so odd to carry a bag that she had no recollection of buying or choosing.

They walked along the brick sidewalks — old bricks, many broken, with bits of moss and grass growing between — beneath the canopy of closely spaced trees. Ellis glanced at familiar storefronts and wondered why they were still living in the same place for three years.

"Ellis, I hope you're happy that we've moved back here for

high school," said Hen, seemingly reading Ellis's mind. "We had so much fun living in this area with DC being so close, and Georgetown, and of course Old Town. . . . Over the summer, I spent a lot of time thinking about where would be best for you to go to high school. I hope you're having a good year so far."

Ellis was speechless. The Ellis on this thread had no knowledge of what actually happened to her parents or where she was born. If this thread were her main thread she would not be visiting threads at all. She would still be going along thinking her parents had died, and there would be no Ida May or Starling or A Priori Books . . . yet this version of herself seemed happy and content to be going to have a cupcake treat with her grandmother. Or was she? How could Ellis know?

Ellis's head was swimming. She pressed her palm against the small bag hanging at her side. Feeling the glass device through the cloth was reassuring — she decided she wasn't crazy.

"Ellis?" Hen looked expectantly at Ellis as they were about to walk into the bakery. The converted historic townhouse was Victorian style with a steeply pointed slate roof complete with a small weather vane at the very point on top where a metal horse in a galloping stance rippled in the slight breeze but made no headway at all.

"Oh, I'm sorry, Hen. I was just thinking of something else. . . . Yes, I'm glad we moved back here for high school." Ellis flashed a smile that she hoped looked genuine.

Hen smiled back at Ellis and mumbled something about teenagers as she opened the carved red door and allowed Ellis to walk in first.

Alexandria Cupcake looked just as Ellis remembered it. The front room was as narrow as the house with four simple square white tables for patrons and a chilled glass case displaying the cupcakes of the day. Just seeing the condensation on the case brought to mind the cold, sweet taste of the buttercream frosting.

They walked up to the case. The familiar sight was welcoming, but it was the redolence in the small bakery that triggered an emotional response Ellis wasn't expecting. The rich scents of vanilla and cocoa, along with the lingering aromas of coconut and strawberries and peanut butter transported Ellis to yet another time — and the memories of coming here with Hen. Ellis realized at this moment how important it had been to her that Hen *wanted* to go out with Ellis. Hen always treated Ellis like she was a special friend. Ellis used to think that Hen dragged her on these outings because she felt guilty for moving her around and because she felt sorry for the girl with no parents and no close friends, but now Ellis saw that they were here because Hen wanted to connect with her — she wanted Ellis to be a part of the decisions Hen ultimately had to make.

"Mmmm, which cupcake . . ." Hen's voice faltered when she looked into Ellis's eyes.

"Ellis?" whispered Hen. "What's wrong?" The concern in her voice was more than Ellis could handle.

"I have something in my eye," stammered Ellis. "I'm going to the bathroom — I'll be right back."

Ellis shuffled off to the tiny bathroom and locked the door behind her. She braced herself on the pedestal sink for a moment before lifting her head to look in the ornately framed oval mirror. Ellis wiped her eyes and tried to find her strength. Her parents weren't going to be on this thread no matter how long she stayed. She pulled the device from her purse and looked at the button to push for her return. And then she remembered that she needed to take a picture.

Ellis looked around the tiny bathroom and saw an Alexandria Cupcake menu on the wall. She took a picture, and then rested her finger on the other button. She still had more than forty-six hours left on this thread. She felt sad about leaving Hen — like somehow this version of herself might be a nicer person to Hen. She pushed her finger down without giving herself the chance to change her mind.

"Ellis, you're back!" A tangle of arms wrapped around Ellis's neck. She was standing in the rear of the bookstore but couldn't remember exactly why she was there. She felt groggy. *And what are the hugs about?* she wondered.

Hen and Tori released her and then waited quietly, exchanging a few questioning looks.

Ellis became aware of the weight in her hand. She looked down to see the device clutched in her palm. She loosened her grip a little, taking care not to drop it. She wanted to get rid of it, but didn't know why.

The grogginess was fading as Ellis worked to focus her thoughts. She remembered planning to visit a thread, but it seemed so long ago. She tried to remember what happened after she held the device in front of her. There was a light, and then nothing at all or maybe something, or maybe the hugs from Hen and Tori was all that happened next. It was all in an instant but yet Ellis felt as if hours had passed.

Ellis became aware of the feeling inside her, or actually the lack of feeling. She felt empty inside, or maybe numb. She instinctively reached up to her eyes and felt some wetness. Hen was at her side. "Ellis, are you crying?"

"I feel so empty inside or maybe I feel sad, and my eyes are wet like I was crying, but I don't know why," said Ellis.

"Did you take a picture?" asked Tori, business-like, but her tone did not completely hide her concern.

Ellis handed the device over to Tori. She had no idea how to retrieve the picture, if she had taken one at all. She was glad she was no longer holding the glass device.

Tori walked to the bookstore counter while Hen guided Ellis to the sitting area. Ellis watched Tori move around behind the counter while she and Hen waited on the couch. Something behind the counter was working. *It sounds like a printer*, thought Ellis. She sat silently, not sure how to put her thoughts and feelings into words.

In less than a minute, Tori walked towards them holding a printed photo. Her expression was impossible to read. Ellis was now completely alert, her numbness gone. *Did I see my parents?* She wiped her hands on her jeans. Tori sat down between them and held out the picture. It took several seconds for Ellis to comprehend what she was looking at.

"What . . ." said Ellis in a deflated voice.

Hen rubbed her arm. "Ellis, it could take many tries to see your parents, if you see them at all." Hen tried to sound matter-of-fact, but Ellis detected disappointment in her voice as well.

"Do either of you understand what this picture might be about?" asked Tori.

"I can't remember anything about the thread," said Ellis sadly. "I remember Alexandria Cupcake though. Hen and I used to go there when we lived in Virginia."

Hen picked up the explanation from there. "It was a favorite place to visit on historic King Street. It's ironic that you would end up there, Ellis — I was thinking about moving us back there for high school instead of coming here to Harper."

Ellis looked at Hen in astonishment. "Why would you do that?" she admonished.

Hen smiled back. "So you like it better here?" she teased.

Chapter 14 ~ Déjà Vu

Ellis felt exhausted and energized at the same time. She was stretched out on her half made bed, still fully dressed, one pillow under her head, her arms tightly wrapped around another. Hen had ordered Ellis to rest while she made dinner, but after all that had happened this afternoon Ellis's mind was racing and even with lying down, her body didn't feel at rest. Hen said that Ellis's parents often felt tired after visiting a thread. They had guessed it was because their bodies were active for the time away, which added on to the activity level of their day on their main thread.

What was left of the setting sun was streaming through the gable window, illuminating everything in its path with a golden tinge. The soft light was relaxing but did nothing to help Ellis rest. She popped off the bed and clicked on her desk lamp before pulling out the chair and taking a seat at her desk.

Doodling on a blank sheet of paper, Ellis found herself sketching a cupcake. She thought about Jules and his look of contentment when he sketches. She wished she could feel the same effect. Instead, Ellis's thoughts continued to jump around in her head with no place to go. And then she remembered the scientific method.

Ellis had learned the steps for the scientific method in fourth grade and often used them when trying to organize her thoughts — like a game to help her make sense of the world. Below the cupcake, she wrote:

Step 1: Make an Observation
Step 2: Ask a Question
Step 3: Form a Hypothesis
Step 4: Conduct an Experiment
Step 5: Accept or Reject Hypothesis

The jumble of thoughts racing around in her head began to take focus and she picked out the details that matched each step.

As far as making an observation, Ellis didn't observe her parent's disappearance from what she remembered, so she used what she learned from Hen. Next to Step 1 she wrote My parents never returned from a thread. Step 2 was obvious. She wrote Where are my parents? Ellis thought for a moment about the hypothesis. After so many years of believing her parents to be dead, Ellis found it hard to write what she thought of only as a dream. For Step 3 she wrote My parents are living on a thread and cannot return. The experiment, Step 4, was her visit to a thread. For Step 5, Ellis could neither reject nor accept the hypothesis.

Ellis thought about the *experiment,* her thread visit. Most curious to her was the picture of the Alexandria Cupcake menu. The picture looked like the menu was hanging on a wall. Hen said she remembered seeing a small version of the menu on the restroom wall the last time they were there. *So why was I in the restroom of Alexandria Cupcake?* she thought. *And was I in there when I pressed the button to come back?* She shaded in her cupcake sketch while she thought about this. *And why were my eyes wet when I got back to A Priori Books?*

Ellis puzzled together her visit: I was in Alexandria Cupcake in Old Town Alexandria, Virginia. I was crying so I went to the restroom to pull myself together. I saw the menu, took a picture, and then pushed the button to come back.

"Why was I crying?" whispered Ellis to herself. "And were my parents there?" she said a little louder to herself.

Ellis started scribbling all along the edges of the page. Her pen leaving furrows in the paper as she pressed harder and harder, bordering the paper in inked spirals. Ellis felt that if her parents *were* there, her picture would have been of them.

"ELLIS!" called Hen from downstairs. "Dinner is ready!"

Ellis picked up the piece of paper and crumbled it before dropping it back down on the desk. The floorboard at her door creaked as Ellis left her room.

When Ellis saw the table already set, she knew Hen was worried. Ellis had to be either bleeding or throwing up to get out of that chore.

"Thanks for setting the table for me. . . ."

"How are you feeling?" Hen hovered. "Did you nap?"

"Hen, I'm fine. I couldn't sleep," muttered Ellis, ". . . too much to think about."

She gazed down at the table to see baked chicken, rice, and green beans. It looked delicious. Ellis hadn't realized until that moment just how hungry she was. The first few minutes of dinner were quiet while Ellis dug in. Hen broke the silence by asking, "Are you okay?"

Ellis nodded.

"You don't have to do this, Ellis," fretted Hen.

"I know," said Ellis, her fork held midair, spearing several beans.

The beans were crisp the way Ellis liked them. She crunched on them as she thought about school the next day. She wondered if the kids at Ida May will think she looks different somehow. *Did* she look different? Will Starling see something different in her?

And then Ellis came out with what she was really wondering. "Did I really go somewhere Hen?"

"I think so," sighed Hen. "How else could you get that picture? I trust your parents knew what they were talking about. *You* have a scientific brain like your mother — what do *you* think?"

Ellis felt her face get warm. "I do—" she stammered, feeling surprisingly flattered to be compared to her mother.

Hen smiled warmly. "Of course you do."

"I was thinking that I should try visiting a thread one day before school. You know — go at different times and days of the week. . . . I might have a better chance of finding my parents."

"I knew you had a scientific brain," said Hen, chuckling. "You're probably right to think that when you visit a thread, it's the same day and time as when you left."

"So, when I first get to a thread it's the same day and time, but the longer I stay the more I'm living in the future?"

"That's what your parents thought," said Hen, nodding.

Ellis ate without talking for a few minutes. The concept of actually visiting places in the universe, or wherever it was that she was going, was exciting, but strange.

"Why do I have to return before the end of two days?" asked Ellis.

Hen responded in a serious tone that shook Ellis. "Do *NOT* think about staying longer. You must return before the forty-eight hours are up. I am not certain of the consequences, but your parents felt very strongly that returning within forty-eight hours was imperative."

"Okay, okay," squeaked Ellis.

Ellis helped clear away the dishes and then she and Hen went with cups of peppermint tea to their library, which now felt so homey with its shelves full of books. Ellis had a new interest in the science books on the bottom shelves. She set her tea on the side table nearest her and then lowered herself into a crisscross sitting position in front of the bookshelves before pulling a textbook called *Glass Science* from the shelf. She paged through the heavy and complicated-looking text and wondered how anyone could understand such material.

"One thing I don't understand, Hen," Ellis said distractedly as she flipped the pages of *Glass Science*, "is how you are supposed to change your perspective about events in your main thread if you can't remember anything from a thread."

"Have you ever heard of déjà vu?"

Ellis twisted around to face Hen. She shook her head and sat up a little straighter.

"It's a French phrase and it means *already seen*."

Ellis slid the book off her lap and then curled up into the chair by her cup of tea. An uncontrollable shiver raced down her spine. She reached for her warm tea and cupped it with both hands.

"Déjà vu," explained Hen, "is when you are experiencing something for the first time and you get the strong feeling that you have experienced it before. Let's say you plan to visit a place you've never been but when you get there you feel like you've been there before. It can also refer to seeing something or someone for the first time. You go into a shop and you see something — a top or jeans — and you feel like you've seen it before even when you're sure you haven't. It's a very strong feeling. You feel it instantly."

"I think I know what you mean," said Ellis excitedly, realizing how déjà vu related to threads.

"You don't have to visit a thread to experience the feelings of déjà vu," warned Hen, "however, when you visit threads you are much more likely to experience strong déjà vu moments that are real. You need to be aware of this feeling so that you can take it into consideration."

Hen took a breath, while Ellis tried to absorb the information.

"So I will know it's déjà vu when I get a strong feeling that something is familiar — but how will knowing I've experienced something before help me know what to do in the situation now?" said Ellis anxiously.

"You'll have to trust yourself — you will have to go with what feels right."

Chapter 15 ~ Hots

Ellis had to drag herself out of bed in the morning. Even with feeling tired from visiting a thread, she couldn't get to sleep last night for thinking about déjà vu and wondering when she will have a déjà vu moment. What little sleep she got was filled with nonsensical dreams that she couldn't quite piece together. When her alarm clock sounded, Ellis was tired but relieved to finally have a reason to get up and away from dreaming.

Before heading downstairs for breakfast, Ellis studied herself in the floor length mirror. She wondered if Starling will see a difference in her. Ellis gazed at her reflection looking for the difference she felt. She looked at her clothes and hair wondering if the thread version had a whole different style. She wished she could remember, but her desire for this paled in comparison to the bubbly excitement inside of her. Ellis smiled. She may not look different, but she felt different. Her life had taken on a purpose.

Ellis lightly guided her hand over the well-worn banister as she made her way up the winding Ida May staircase. From the top of the stairs she could see Starling waiting by her locker. Ellis took a deep breath. She knew she would be able to keep her secret about threads from Starling, but she really didn't want to.

"Did the Double Decker get a bigger engine?" joked Ellis. Starling was never at school earlier than Ellis.

Starling half smiled, half grimaced. "Kes got her driver's

license yesterday so my parents let her drive Myna and me to school. We left at the crack of dawn because Kes was nervous about getting here on time — and after riding with her I think I prefer the Double Decker."

Ellis laughed. It felt good to be around Starling.

Ellis took off her jacket and stuffed it into the locker. Now that she felt comfortable with the school and the neighborhood, she usually walked to school. This morning she left the house early enough to make a stop at Madder's for a latte in hopes that the caffeine would counteract her tiredness.

Jules walked by and without stopping raised his hand and said hi.

"He is so shy," said Starling.

"And funny — I love his drawings," added Ellis, remembering her own cupcake doodle.

"He doesn't have any brothers or sisters." Starling went into chronicle mode. "My parents say they sometimes forget Dr. Connor has a son my age because he very rarely talks about his family. They think it's his way of maintaining a private life," explained Starling.

"Really? Are there other Glass kids here at school?" asked Ellis.

"Yes, many," answered Starling. "Heron said we even learn about glass in our science classes because it's so important to the people around here."

Ellis finished gathering her books and then she and Starling headed to Mrs. Dockleaf's class. The tall windows in the hallway reflected the dark and gloomy weather outside. It was only mid-September, and the days were getting shorter. The morning sun was still struggling to make an appearance and the overcast sky made it all the harder.

Starling nudged Ellis and jerked her head toward the four girls walking ahead of them. Ellis didn't need to see their faces

— she recognized the group by the short, razor-cut hair, the long dark hair swinging to the movements of self-absorbed animation, the nondescript brown head, and a petite-bodied girl spaced a little further apart than the other girls.

"They're all Glass kids," said Starling softly.

"All four?" whispered Ellis. "I thought just Harley."

"Harley's mother works closely with my mom, but the other three also have parents at Connor Glass," replied Starling.

Ellis inwardly smiled thinking about how she felt like she fit in. *I'm a Glass kid too*, she thought.

Just before English class ended, Ms. Bennet assigned their first novel, *The Odyssey*. When the bell rang, Ellis and Starling made a quick stop at their lockers for their jackets before heading out for lunch. It was still gloomy out and it had begun to drizzle. They were heading up East North Street when Starling asked Ellis if she planned to buy the book from A Priori Books. Ellis hadn't really thought about it, but shrugged her shoulders and nodded as if to say *sure, why not?*

Starling smiled — a smile that said she was up to something.

"How about if we go to A Priori Books after school today?" said Starling excitedly.

Before Ellis had a chance to answer, Starling filled in the details. "I bet I can talk Kes into waiting for me at The Trivium. . . .We'll go to the bookstore and make a quick stop in The Apothecary and be back in an hour. Kes can drop you at home before we leave Harper."

"I . . . don't . . . know," said Ellis warily.

On Main Street now, Starling changed the subject to where they should eat. "How about Hots? Warm food sounds good right now."

Ellis and Starling headed to Hots where hot dogs made to order were the specialty. Just across the street from Hubbel's, the Hots building was red brick with a large window at the kitchen where the short-order cooks could be seen grabbing tickets from the overhead order wheel, assembling hot dogs, or *hots*, and then pushing orders down the stainless steel order-up counter. Servers on the other side of the counter were grabbing orders and piling them onto their large round trays. From the side, the Hots building itself appeared weirdly proportioned in an Alice-in-Wonderland sort of way. The entrance was at the corner of Main and Leo Streets and from there the sidewalk angled so steeply up the side of the building that even small children were tall enough to look in, or actually down into, the restaurant's glass window.

Ellis and Starling pushed through the turnstile entrance and started looking for an empty booth. The brown vinyl high backed booths were impossible to see over so they began peeking around the sides. They had peered in on just a couple of patrons when a raspy voice called out, "Ladies! Over here."

They looked up to see a woman with a circular tray tucked under her arm jerking her thumb toward a presumably empty booth. She didn't seem to have the time to wait for Ellis and Starling to take their seats. As soon as she knew she had their attention, she started walking toward the cooks, yelling, "Two hots with everything! Fries with gravy! Fries!" The waitress brushed past Ellis without seeing her. She had on jeans and a white t-shirt covered with so much food that Ellis could only hope that it was clean this morning.

Ellis and Starling slid into the booth and slipped off their jackets. The mouthwatering aroma of chili, onions, hot dogs, and French fries was wafting through the warm restaurant. They looked briefly at their menus, which included a list of the many hot dog toppings, the available ice creams for shakes, and an entire column of homemade pies. Hots and fries seemed to be the main fare.

The waitress was back before Ellis had finished deciding on what to eat, but she knew she had to order quickly when on school lunch. She looked to Starling who suggested two chili hots and an order of fries with gravy. Ellis gave a nod of agreement. The waitress made a quick jot on the pad she held in her hand, and then without another word to Ellis and Starling, starting screaming the order as she walked away from the table.

"I didn't picture this place being so noisy," said Ellis.

"Used to be that they wouldn't even write the order down. The cooks would just have to remember everything," said Starling in a *can you believe it?* sort of way. "Now, they still yell the orders but the cooks have a backup order slip to look at."

Their waitress was back. She worked efficiently and silently as she set two large cups of water on the table and then placed a fork and napkin in front of each of them. She grabbed two straws from a pocket in her waist apron and laid them on the table and then she grabbed a towel hanging from the second pocket to wipe up the water that had spilled over when she set down the cups. She became distracted and looked toward the entrance when someone said "Hi, Rosa — how's it going?"

Ellis thought the voice sounded familiar but she couldn't quite place it and she couldn't see the person because of the tall booth back. Just as her memory clicked in, Tori stepped into her line of sight to move closer to Rosa.

"Ellis, are you okay?" asked a bewildered Starling, who was oblivious to Rosa and Tori's exchange, but noticed her friend was suddenly quiet and even looking a little flushed.

Ellis only nodded, hoping that her silence would somehow hide her presence. However, the next thing she heard was "Ellis! Hello — oh, you must be here for school lunch."

Starling's look of concern changed to that of questioning. Ellis avoided Starling's eyes and looked sheepishly over to the new customer. "Hi, Tori."

Tori smiled and said, "Rosa, this is Ellis, a friend of mine." Rosa gave a friendly smile, the first Ellis had seen.

An expectant pause in the conversation reminded Ellis to introduce her friend. "Oh, uhm, this is Starling," muttered Ellis, immediately feeling guilty for not being more enthusiastic.

"Tori, I have to get back to work, but it's been nice seein' ya," said Rosa with a quick smile before she was off to pick up orders.

Tori didn't seem to be in the same hurry because after Rosa's departure she turned back to Ellis and Starling with a rather curious look. "Starling, nice to meet you. I'm not sure if Ellis has told you, but I own A Priori Books."

Starling smiled broadly and said pointedly, "I've been wanting to go there with Ellis." She shot a knowing look to Ellis, who was wishing she could slide out from under the greasy Formica table and disappear.

Tori chimed right in, "You girls are welcome to come anytime."

"That would be great! Ellis and I were talking about coming after school today to get a book for English," Starling answered excitedly.

"Well . . ." Ellis began, looking uncomfortably toward Starling, "I really need to ask Hen before I go somewhere after school."

"Hummm," said Tori, nodding her head knowingly, "I'll be seeing Hen today. I'll let her know the plans."

Before Ellis could protest, Tori gave a quick wave and added as she walked away, "Have a nice lunch girls. I'm just here to grab takeout. See you after school!"

Rosa delivered the hots and fries as Tori was leaving. The hots were covered in a thin chili, which smothered the diced onions underneath. On top of it all lay a thin dill pickle spear. A bowl of thick cut, golden fries were covered in dark brown gravy. With two fingers, Ellis extracted a fry from the mound and distractedly bit into it, thinking about Hen and how she might react to the conversation she just had with Tori. And then she smiled to herself at the thought of going to A Priori Books with Starling. She wondered if Tori would let her and Starling go through the secret passageway to The Apothecary. . . .

"Tori seems really nice. She looks so young," commented Starling.

"Yeah," said Ellis, "but she really seems to know how to run a bookstore, so she must not be as young as she looks."

"And she's friends with your grandmother?" questioned Starling.

Ellis saw where that might seem odd. "Well, actually, her parents were friends with my parents . . . So I guess she's a family friend." Even Ellis thought her explanation sounded pretty good. Starling gave a little nod that seemed to say she was satisfied with that answer as well.

"I can't wait for school to end!" exclaimed Starling, who had taken a bite of her hot and was working at getting the chili overflow off her fingers.

Ellis smiled back and then tackled her own hot. It was worth every bit of messiness. The steamed bun and juicy hot dog were in perfect combination with the slightly spicy chili, diced onions, and the mild-flavored dill pickle.

Chapter 16 ~ Mr. Neumann

Hen leaned over the sink basin and splashed more cold water on her face. She grabbed a towel and blotted the dripping water before looking up into the mirror at her own reflection. She wanted to cry again. She was dusty and felt as worn as her reflection appeared. Another attempt at searching the attic, the basement, and every closet in the house was fruitless. She sighed and decided it was time to pull herself back together.

Hen had folded the hand towel and was hanging it on the rack beside the sink when she heard a knock at the front door. *Could it be that late?* she thought. She smoothed her hair as she hurriedly walked to the front of the house. When Hen opened the door, Tori's big smile faded as she registered Hen's puffy red eyes.

"What's wrong?" asked Tori, standing on the rectangular porch, her hands full of white cardboard carryout boxes.

Hen sighed in response, but was so happy to have Tori over for the first time since she and Ellis moved back that she broke out into a big smile.

"Come in," she said, feeling much better already.

Tori stepped into the house and without needing any direction headed for the kitchen table where she placed the delicious smelling boxes.

Hen was right behind her. The two friends briefly embraced and then stood back to look at one another.

"I am so glad you're back," said Tori.

"I'm glad to be able to see you," said Hen truthfully. "But I can't help feeling uncertain about coming back to Harper. . . . And I'm very anxious about Ellis visiting threads."

Tori's listened silently, her gray eyes sparkling.

"Sit, sit," said Hen. "What did you bring?" Her voice was slightly muffled as she talked into the cupboard where she was pulling out plates and glasses.

"Your favorite — a chili hot and fries with gravy."

Dishes clattered as Hen set the table. There was a soft swish from the cardboard box flaps as Tori opened the Hots takeout. The steamy aroma instantly had both their mouths watering. After quickly moving the food to their plates, they bit into their dogs before saying another word.

"Guess who else had Hots today?" said Tori, licking chili from her fingers.

"Ellis?" ventured Hen.

"Yep, I ran into her and Starling. They were in a booth together, looking like the best of friends."

Hen smiled.

"Starling seems like a nice girl." Tori was looking directly at Hen.

"Yes, yes. You know I'm just afraid," admitted Hen.

"Ellis needs to be able to make lasting friendships. Look how important is has been to us," argued Tori.

Hen silently nibbled at the fries.

"So why did you look like you were crying when I got here?"

"The usual. I spent the morning looking for clues, and I can't find any," said Hen dejectedly.

"We'll find something now that Ellis is visiting threads," promised Tori.

"Is it even safe for Ellis? — I would rather die than have anything happen to her," said Hen seriously, her wrinkled forehead furrowed even deeper.

Tori smiled warmly and then changed the subject, "Ellis and Starling want to come by the shop after school to buy a book for English class. I said I'd let you know their plans."

"What!" And then Hen added halfheartedly, "I like Ellis home after school."

"Let her go. She'll be fine," assured Tori.

"What about Starling — you know her parents work at Connor Glass — should we be concerned?"

"There are a lot of Glass kids at Ida May. Ellis might find out from anyone," warned Tori. "You should consider telling her, Hen."

Hen shook her head firmly. "No — and remember you promised not to let her find out."

"I'll try my best, but I can't control what happens at school."

Ellis and Starling grabbed what they needed out of their lockers and then headed out the Ida May double doors and down the exterior stairs. The sky was a dull gray, and a misty drizzle was turning the stone steps an even darker gray, but the weather went completely unnoticed by the two girls walking to the bookstore. Starling was practically skipping — Kes needed to go to the library after school anyhow and so agreed to pick up Ellis and Starling from A Priori Books when she finished.

The route to A Priori took Ellis and her friend to the north end of Main Street — an area that had few restaurants and therefore not yet visited by Ellis. Most interesting was the Main Street Cinema, an old fashioned movie theater that had just one screen. The carved wooden border of the marquee was painted a bright red and framed with big round light bulbs. Starling said that before each show a pipe organ with an organist comes up from the floor in front of the screen to play music while an old-fashioned silent cartoon played on the screen.

Bourner Street was noticeably busy. Ellis had never gone to A Priori on a school day and she was surprised by how many Ida May students they encountered. Starling considered it practically a rite of passage that she finally made it to A Priori Books. She said her brother and sisters would talk about going there during the school year, but her parents rarely went into town and preferred a smaller bookstore not far from Muddy Creek, in the opposite direction of Harper.

The big bay windows and the arch door seemed much more inviting than the first time Ellis came down Bourner Street. She and Starling stepped out of the misty dampness and into the warm, crowded bookstore. Every chair was occupied and several other customers were milling around. It seemed that this was a great place to meet up with friends.

"That table over there," pointed Ellis, "has school reading list books."

Starling nodded, and they started to work their way past several students. Even the children's section was being used by Ida May students, with teenage girls taking up the soft pillows and sitting comfortably on the big multicolored rug in front of the bookshelves sized for preschoolers.

"Ellis!"

Ellis and Starling turned to see Tori coming up behind them.

"Hi, Tori," said Ellis.

"Glad you girls made it," said Tori.

"Did you see Hen?" asked Ellis a little nervously.

"Yes, she said not a problem. Just don't be out late," said Tori. "So which book do you girls need?"

"*The Odyssey*," Ellis and Starling said together, giggling at each other.

"I see your teacher wants to ease you into English with some light reading," quipped Tori, while leading the way to the table of classics. Not understanding Tori's tone, Starling looked at Ellis who shrugged her shoulders in response.

Tori grabbed two copies of a thick softcover from the end of the table and then passed them out to Ellis and Starling.

Ellis and Starling felt the weight of the long tale in their hands and then gave each other a look as gloomy as the sky.

"Thanks," said Ellis.

"Yeah, thanks," replied Starling.

"It's an interesting book. . . ." assured Tori. "Since you're here, stop next door and get some candy. I know Hen loves the Hot Cinnamon Buttons."

Starling brightened at Tori's words.

Ellis looked at the wall with the secret passage to The Apothecary. Tori noticed — she smiled — and then gave an almost imperceptible head shake that said not today — before directing Ellis and Starling to the front door. Ellis hid her disappointment. Starling didn't know about the secret entrance, and Ellis didn't want to spoil the surprise for the day when she got to experience it. Ellis had the feeling that one day soon Starling will be coming with her through the wall — maybe it was déjà vu, she thought jokingly.

Ellis and Starling stepped back out into the chilly dampness for less than a minute before entering The Apothecary. It was sweet-smelling and just as busy as A Priori Books. Students filled every table and a small crowd formed around a young employee holding out a large tray of what Ellis guessed was candy samples. Starling looked around the former pharmacy in wonder. Ellis couldn't keep a smile off her face — the energy in the room was better than a sugar rush.

With no place to sit, and too curious to sit even if a table was open, Ellis and Starling walked over to the aisles of candy.

Walking down the first row, Starling looked for Sea Glass, a favorite candy Heron used to bring her after his visits to The Apothecary. Ellis wanted to find Hot Cinnamon Buttons to surprise Hen. They passed the jar of Scallops, the salty candy Ellis saw on her first visit. Lost in discussion over what the jar of Morning Glories might taste like (made with freshly ground coffee, pure Tahitian vanilla, ground cinnamon bark, and a hint of cocoa), Ellis and Starling both jumped and turned when a deep voice behind them asked, "Are you finding everything alright?"

"Oh, I'm sorry to have startled you," said Mr. Neumann kindly, and then with a look of pleasant surprise, added, "Ellis! Nice to see you again!"

"Hi — Hi, Mr. Neumann. This is my friend Starling," stammered Ellis, followed by a deep breath. "I'm loo — looking for — ahh — Hot Cinnamon Buttons for my grandmother."

"Oh, of course. Follow me." Mr. Neumann led Ellis and Starling to the next aisle over. There on the top shelf was a glass jar filled with bright red round candies about the size and shape of a small button. A plastic scoop was leashed to its lid. He pointed out the jar and then stood still, seemingly waiting for another request.

"Thanks," said Ellis, trying to fill the void in their conversation.

"Do you need help getting some?" asked Mr. Neumann brightly. Without waiting for a response he pulled a plastic bag from a roll below the jars. When he opened the candy jar, the distinctive, spicy smell of cinnamon got the attention of their eyes and noses. In one sweep he placed a scoop of candies into the bag and sealed it with a twist tie.

He held out the bag for Ellis to take and said with a delighted smile, "This is my treat. I hope Hen enjoys them."

"Thanks so much Mr. Neumann," said Ellis, taking the candies. "But how did you know these are for my grandmother, and how do know her name?"

"I've known Hen a long time." Mr. Neumann looked confused over the point.

"Really?"

Mr. Neumann seemed to understand something that Ellis didn't. He smiled and then asked, "You know Tori is my daughter don't you?"

Ellis felt her face flush. "No, I didn't."

The front door jingled as several more kids walked in. "Excuse me, Ellis, I have to get back to the tables. Nice to meet you Starling. Let me know if you two need anything else," said Mr. Neumann as he pulled a dish towel from his apron and set off to clear a table that had just vacated.

Starling looked at Ellis in her inquisitive, reporter way and said, "Wow, I bet my brother and sisters don't know that Mr. Neumann is Tori's father."

"Yeah," Ellis half-whispered without hearing what Starling said. She was still watching Mr. Neumann. He had been her parent's friend. She didn't know how she could be feeling joy and loss at the same time, but at this moment she was. Before now, her parent's existence seemed to hinge on only one fact — her existence. With nobody else to validate their lives — not even Hen because she avoided talking about them until recently — Ellis sometimes wondered if they lived at all. But now she had Mr. Neumann, friend of her parents. She wondered how much he knew about threads. . . .

"Ellis — "

Ellis felt someone shaking her shoulder.

"Ellis! Do you hear me?" Starling had her hand on Ellis's shoulder.

"Sorry. I was just thinking about something," said Ellis,

looking away from Mr. Neumann.

"What were you looking at?" pressed Starling.

"Nothing," Ellis shook her head to try and clear her thoughts.

"Let's find the Sea Glass — Kes will be here any minute," breathed Starling.

A few glass jars away from the Hot Cinnamon Buttons was a jar labeled Sea Glass. The candy chunks were triangular, rectangular, and many-sided in shape, in pastel colors of pale pink, shades of lavender, teal, aqua, and other shades of blue and green, and looked as though they had been sanded to soften the edges and further lighten the tints by scuffing the surfaces. Starling said each had a fresh, fruity flavor depending on the color.

As Kes drove her home, Ellis tried a piece of lavender Sea Glass. It tasted like a fresh plum.

Chapter 17 ~ Tori's Choice

Ellis was still thinking about the visit to The Apothecary when Kes pulled to a stop in front of her house. She slid out of the jeep and stepped onto the sidewalk, waving good-bye to Starling and Kes. The red jeep with black vinyl interior was Heron's. He didn't need a vehicle at college so Kes had the privilege of driving it. The SUV was a bouncy, fun ride and Ellis loved the feeling of furthering her independence. The short ride home though wasn't enough to distract her from the new information she learned about Mr. Neumann.

A few fallen elm leaves that had already changed from green to yellow and red were stuck to the damp sidewalk leading to the front porch. It was nearly dark and the porch light was on. On either side of the porch the Black-eyed Susans were staring upwards, their large brown centers even more prominent now that the petals hung shriveled and drooping. Inside, Ellis found Hen curled up in one of the overstuffed chairs in the library with a book closed on her fingers to hold the place where she left off reading. She must have heard the front door open by the way she was looking toward the library entry, apparently waiting for Ellis to appear.

As Ellis approached Hen, she noticed that she looked tired, or maybe even sad. Ellis stretched out her arm and dangled the bag of Hot Cinnamon Buttons in front of Hen. Ellis was glad they brought a smile to her face. She spilled a few into Hen's open hand and then took a couple out of the bag for herself.

"Thank you," said Hen. "Did you have fun at A Priori? —

and from the looks of it, The Apothecary?"

"Yes, it was a lot of fun . . . Starling had so much fun — it was her first visit," mused Ellis.

"How did you know I liked these?" said Hen, gesturing toward the Buttons in her palm.

"Tori told me," said Ellis, and then nervously added, "Hen, how is it that you and Tori are such good friends?" Ellis had been curious how someone she never knew existed until recently could know more about her family than she did.

"I was friends with her parents too." Hen fanned her mouth and then changed the subject. "I forgot how spicy these are." She continued to fan her mouth as she got up from the chair, leaving *Jane Eyre* face down on the seat, open at the place she left off, and headed to the kitchen seemingly in desperate need of a glass of water.

"Dinner's almost ready," Hen called from the kitchen.

Ellis poured what was left of the Hot Cinnamon Buttons into an empty glass candy dish on the side table by the chair Hen had vacated. The small crystal dish was yet another item new to Ellis because it was amongst the boxes that they usually left packed from move to move. She wondered if the dish had been special to her parents.

Breakfast the next morning started out quiet. Hen made scrambled eggs and toast. She and Ellis sipped on tea, clattered their forks against their plates of eggs, and crunched on toast. Ellis had thought Hen looked tired last night, so after a quick dinner, she headed upstairs to do homework until bed — there was plenty to do with *The Odyssey* weighing down her backpack. This morning, however, her questions were more burning than ever. Hen was reaching for a knife to add strawberry preserves to her toast when Ellis's voice came out sounding louder than she expected.

"Yesterday," Ellis cleared her throat and adjusted the volume of her voice, "Mr. Neumann told me that Tori is his daughter."

Hen appeared unfazed. "Yes, Tori took over the bookstore when her mother died a few years ago," she said, and then bit into her toast.

"I'm sorry . . ." Ellis nearly whispered before connecting that information to her next question.

"Does that have something to do with why Tori had the glass device? — I just don't understand why Tori had the device and not you. What if you wanted to visit threads to find my parents?" blurted Ellis, sitting up straight, her back away from the chair.

Hen's expression told Ellis that she was pushing too hard. Ellis resigned herself back into the chair and began picking at her scrambled eggs.

"Tori's father — Mr. Neumann — had the device for many years. I gave it to him before we left because I didn't want you to accidentally get hold of it. You were very young when we started moving around.

"When Mrs. Neumann died, Mr. Neumann felt lost. He was so distraught that he was willing to try anything for more time with her," Hen hesitated before going on. "He knew how to visit threads from your parents. . . . So he visited threads over and over again hoping to find a thread in which his wife was still alive."

Ellis thought this sounded very sad, but then she realized it wasn't much different from what she planned to do.

"Did he find her?" asked Ellis anxiously.

"No. Eventually he stopped looking. He decided that death on the main thread must mean death on all threads."

Ellis continued to listen quietly while she tried to process the information.

Hen sighed a little before saying, "Mr. Neumann gave the device to Tori and asked her to keep it safely out of his sight. He didn't want to be tempted to use it ever again."

"Did Tori try to find her mother?" asked Ellis.

"I don't think so. They had a wonderful relationship, and when she died, Tori was sad, but she wanted to find out what her main thread had in store for her."

Hen got up from the table and began clearing the breakfast dishes. "Hen," said Ellis, "I still plan to look for my mom and dad."

With no response from Hen, Ellis pushed her chair back and grabbed her backpack.

"Ellis," said Hen suddenly, "Mr. Neumann also stopped visiting threads because his main thread was suffering. His thoughts were so distracted by feelings of déjà vu that he was questioning his self-confidence. Most importantly he realized that his relationship with Tori on his main thread was beginning to suffer. He chose life with the living — a life that he could remember."

For some reason Ellis felt angry knowing this last bit of information. She grabbed her jacket and left for school. It wasn't until half way there she realized Hen never answered her last question: *Why hasn't Hen visited threads to find my parents?*

As Ellis walked to class with Starling she thought about how much she wanted to talk to Starling about threads. However, Hen and Tori told Ellis she mustn't tell anyone about threads. *Easy for them*, thought Ellis, *They have each other to talk to.* Ellis forced the notion out of her head, at least temporarily, but she didn't know how long she could keep this secret from her best friend.

"Are you okay?" asked Starling.

Ellis shook herself out of her thoughts. "Yeah, yeah. Just a little tired maybe."

"You are so quiet this morning," pressed Starling. She reached into her backpack and pulled out a plastic bag. It was the Sea Glass candy from yesterday. Starling held the bag out to Ellis and said, "Here, have one — it will wake you up."

Ellis smiled as she reached in for a light pink candy. When she popped it in her mouth, she tasted a ripe strawberry.

"I told my parents about Mr. Neumann being Tori's father," Starling started in a quiet, serious voice as if sharing a secret. They slowed their walking and drifted off to a place in the hallway that had little traffic before coming to a complete stop.

Ellis looked at Starling expectantly, waiting.

"They said that when Mrs. Neumann died, Mr. Neumann closed A Priori Books for almost two years — until Tori graduated from college."

"Really?" asked Ellis. She wondered what Tori studied in college . . . She wondered if Tori *wanted* to run the family bookstore.

"Yes, and apparently, The Apothecary was open very little for those same years A Priori was closed. A lot of people in Harper were concerned that Mr. Neumann had fallen ill," Starling looked at Ellis, making sure she had her attention. "When Tori returned from college, The Apothecary started to open for regular hours and eventually A Priori was also open regular hours again."

This all made sense to Ellis who knew that Mr. Neumann was distracted because he was visiting threads.

"My parents said Tori is only about twenty-four or twenty-five years old."

"Wow, *she* is really young," commented Ellis. *So why does Hen seem to have such a close friendship with someone so young?* thought Ellis.

With little time left to get to class, they started walking again, heads together, still talking.

"Do you think she likes running the bookstore?" asked Ellis.

Starling shrugged her shoulders.

They walked into Mrs. Dockleaf's classroom and took their seats just as the bell rang. Ellis didn't know why she had the feeling there was a mystery to solve.

The lunch destination was Madder Drinks. It was a cool, crisp autumn day. The oak trees surrounding the school were just beginning to show signs of changing from their summer green canopy to a fiery display of red and yellow and every blend in between.

"Did your parents say anything else about Tori?" Ellis couldn't stop wondering if there was more to her story.

"No," responded Starling, "my parents don't come into town much and what they know about the bookstore is because Heron was at Ida May at the time."

Ellis nodded.

"My mom asked me when you were coming over again. Do you think Hen will let you sleep over?"

"I'll ask," Ellis smiled.

The red and white awning of Madder Drinks was fluttering in the fall breeze. The two large front windows revealed the old fashioned soda fountain and mahogany booths. On her way to school, Ellis stopped by Madder Drinks once or twice a week for a latte and now that the weather was getting colder, she enjoyed their amazing homemade hot chocolate created from their own chocolate recipe and served with fresh whipped cream and chocolate shavings.

Ellis and Starling approached the soda counter to order

their lunch. It was a long wooden counter that reminded Ellis of the A Priori Books counter. Soda fountain heads stuck up at one end of the counter where an employee was busy with orders for custom flavored sodas and floats. Behind the counter, an industrial-sized modern machine for lattes and espressos was attended by a barista. A third employee was taking lunch orders and making smoothies. Madder's was busy in the morning, but nothing like this, Ellis noted. She and Starling ordered sandwiches and cream sodas before grabbing the last empty mahogany booth. The coffee house was full. Even the high tops reserved for drinking coffee or espresso were surrounded by standing Ida May students eating their sandwiches.

The coffee shop certainly had the feel of the oldest family-owned restaurant in Harper. Black and white photographs hanging on the walls showed the original store front, which had changed very little since 1875. The tan and brown checkered floor in shades of latte and chocolate complimented the mahogany soda counter, booths, and high tops.

Before Ellis could slip her coat off, she heard the waiter behind the counter call their order number. "I'll get it," said Starling, her jacket already hanging from a hook on the booth.

Less than a minute later, Starling returned empty handed. Beside her was Jules carrying a tray of food and drinks and smiling awkwardly.

"I invited Jules to eat with us since this place is so packed today," said Starling, and then seemed to remember that Jules was holding their orders. "Oh — thanks for carrying our lunches." She took the sandwiches and sodas off the tray and placed them on Ellis's side of the booth. While Jules returned the tray Ellis moved over to make room for Starling who slid into the booth and whispered, "He looked a little lonely."

Jules returned with his own sandwich and drink in hand.

As he slid into the booth opposite Ellis and Starling, Ellis thought he acted more at ease. He seemed to answer back by looking over at them and flashing an easy grin.

Ellis found her chicken salad sandwich to be a perfect fall lunch. It was packed with apple chunks, cranberries, and walnuts, and topped with arugula. "This is great," she mumbled.

Starling and Jules, with mouths full, nodded in consent.

"Jules, we went to The Apothecary yesterday. Have you ever been there?" asked Starling. Ellis looked over at Jules with interest.

Jules nodded and held up a finger to indicate he needed to finish chewing. After several seconds, he reached for his soda and said, "Yes, but not in a long time. My parents were friends with the owner and they used to take me there when I was younger — How is it?"

"Great," said Ellis, glancing at Starling, wondering what her agenda was.

"Ellis and I were just talking about how Mr. Neumann's daughter runs A Priori Books right next door," said Starling.

Jules arched his eyebrows while taking another sip of soda. "Wow, that's kind of cool. I remember he had a daughter older than me, but I really didn't know her. I don't think my parents have been to see Mr. Neumann in a long time. I can't wait to go to The Apothecary sometime after school."

"My sister drives now. Come with us one day," Starling pointed toward Ellis, "and then my sister can take us home after."

Jules grinned.

Ellis realized that Jules must live near Starling since his dad owns Connor Glass.

Jules lowered his eyes and looked at his tall soda glass as he reached for the last drink. Ellis nibbled on a cranberry that had fallen to her plate. Starling seemed to be contemplating the photographs on the wall.

"Uhm, you know, we were kind of friends when we were little," Jules said. Both Ellis and Starling looked at him to see who he was talking to.

Ellis felt her cheeks burn when she saw Jules looking back at her.

"Really?" croaked Ellis, and then clearing her throat.

"My mom said we had *play dates* when we were around four," chuckled Jules.

"Oh," said Ellis, her stomach churning. *Yet another person that knows things about my past that I don't*, she thought.

"Well, uhm, yeah, I guess we did story hour at the bookstore or something like that . . . until you, uhm, moved away," said Jules, now looking like he wished he never brought up the subject.

Ellis slurped up the last of her soda. She didn't want to be rude, but she had no idea how to respond to this new information. She was embarrassed that she had no one to tell her the little details of her life before her parents disappeared or even anyone to confirm the details presented to her now. She suddenly felt angry at Hen for not pasting together a picture of her past before bringing her back to it. Ellis spent many evenings in her bedroom trying to piece together her memories. She had a few vague ones of her first move when she was about six. But as hard as she tried, she couldn't remember anything about her parents.

"I need to get going. I want to get back to school early so I can sketch," said Jules, grabbing his jacket. "Thanks for the seat." He held up his hand to say good-bye and then walked out.

"Wow. I *never* had a play date with Jules," teased Starling.

Ellis smirked.

"I think it's kind of cool. You have friends here that you didn't even know about," comforted Starling.

"Yeah, that's what feels so weird about it," lamented Ellis. Although she was pretty sure that the cold shiver that went down her spine when Jules mentioned story hour wasn't from the last sip of her soda. Maybe she finally understood why the children's area of A Priori Books seemed familiar to her.

"Well, we're not any closer to learning Tori's story," said Ellis. "Maybe there isn't anything else to learn. . . ." Ellis realized that perhaps the part of Tori's story that she wanted to know about most had little to do with her work at A Priori Books.

"Maybe not," agreed Starling. "We better get back to school."

Chapter 18 ~ Harley

Ellis became more determined than ever to visit threads. Between learning that Jules was a friend many years ago and the gnawing feeling that there is more to Tori's story, Ellis felt passionate about finding her parents *and* her past.

It took Ellis more than a week of cajoling, coaxing, and ultimately begging to convince Hen to allow her to visit another thread. Ellis had wanted to visit a thread on a school morning so that she could spend at least a whole day at the thread school, but Hen flat out said no. She reasoned that going to a thread school for a full day to return and go to her main thread school all day would be too exhausting. Ellis, Hen said, would have to get used to visiting threads first. As a compromise, Hen said Ellis could visit a thread immediately after school one day. Ellis was disappointed but thought the option better than not visiting threads at all.

Ellis never heard Hen leave the house for the fresh pecan roll that was heated and sitting on the table when she walked into the kitchen that morning. She knew Hen must have gone out before dawn to get Ellis's favorite breakfast treat and so decided the effort was a peace offering.

"Thanks for the pecan roll, Hen," said Ellis quietly.

"You're welcome," said Hen, in an equally subdued voice.

They sat and drank their tea and ate the warm pecan roll, each thinking their own thoughts, together in the room, yet distant.

Ellis looked up at Hen who was taking a sip of her tea, a

faraway look in her eyes.

"Hen," prompted Ellis.

"Yes," said Hen, looking rather weary.

"I want to visit a thread after school *today* — please," said Ellis. "It's already Thursday and I don't think Friday will be a good day to go. Please . . . I don't want to wait until next week."

Hen looked aggravated but agreed to pick up Ellis in front of Ida May after her last class.

Ellis had the funny feeling that she had dozed off. The room was coming into focus: she was sitting at a table with Harley across from her.

What!?! thought Ellis, her head fuzzy. Why am I sitting here with Harley?

Ellis anxiously looked beyond Harley. She saw orderly shelves of books and a woman standing behind a circulation desk.

She gave a sideways look to Harley who was concentrating on the open book in front of her — a history book? Ellis couldn't tell exactly — she didn't recognize it. She gazed around the room again and saw the front entrance, which opened into a hallway that she recognized. She was in the Ida May library. She looked one by one at the students in the library, but didn't see Starling.

Ellis felt a heaviness in her hand. What is that? She looked into her lap and saw that she was holding the glass device. She was awake now.

Sitting very still, Ellis tried to remember why she was here. She remembered that she went straight to A Priori after school. She remembered standing in the back of the bookstore with Hen and Tori, but she couldn't remember anything after that moment. Ellis shivered as her spine involuntarily tingled. She wondered if she had this same eerie feeling the last time she visited a thread or perhaps she is feeling this eerie feeling now because it's her second time visiting a thread and she still has no sense of what's going on. Ellis wished she could at least remember going from one thread to another — the feeling of waking from a nap was bewildering.

So, she and Harley were in the school library after school . . . Ellis decided she must be assigned to do a project with Harley. What other reason could I have for being with her? she thought. Knowing how Harley treated Starling, Ellis was sure she could never be friends with such a person in any life, or on any thread of a life.

She looked over at Harley again. She didn't know what to say.

Harley looked up. She had sensed Ellis looking at her. "What?" whispered Harley loudly.

Ellis shook her head slightly and shrugged her shoulders. She felt embarrassed to be sitting alone at a table with Harley like they were friends. Ellis considered moving, and then Harley spoke again.

"I'm not finding anything for the history paper," Harley half whispered and half spoke, "You?" Harley's eyes fell onto the book in front of Ellis.

Ellis noticed for the first time that there was an open book in front of her. "Uhm . . . no . . . not a thing," said Ellis. She felt some relief over knowing that they were simply doing a history project together.

"Let's go," suggested Harley. "We'll ask Dockleaf tomorrow what she had in mind."

Ellis nodded. She found a backpack resting near her feet and guessed it must belong to the Ellis on this thread. She grabbed it, slipped the device inside, and together she and

Harley walked out of the library and then out of the school. It was a beautiful fall afternoon. The sun was getting low in the sky and the golden light emphasized the red and yellow and orange beginning to converge on the trees.

Ellis tried to act as nonchalant as possible considering she had no idea where they were headed. Maybe she was supposed to say good-bye and head for her own house? Did she even live in the same house on this thread? Her heart was racing and her hands were sweating.

Harley seemed distracted by the history project and spoke of how Dockleaf, as she called Mrs. Dockleaf, was so unreasonable for assigning a history project due next week. "Like we have no other homework . . ." ranted Harley.

Ellis nodded and mmm, uhed, and yeahed to everything Harley said. Ellis went with her instinct that as long as Harley kept talking, she should continue walking with her. Meanwhile Ellis was also trying to figure out where they were going since the route they were walking was not Ellis's usual way home.

"Why do you keep bumping into me?" asked Harley on the third time Ellis ran into her when she turned unexpectedly at a corner.

"Sorry," said Ellis. And then she decided she would have to risk sounding crazy, "Where are we headed again?" she asked as offhandedly as possible.

Harley looked at Ellis as if she had lost her mind. After a moment she said, "What? We're going to my house." Ellis apparently didn't look like she fully connected, so Harley went on, "You're staying overnight because your parents are at a conference. Remember?"

Ellis laughed. "Yeah, yeah . . . I guess I have that Dockleaf project on my mind." And then she rolled her eyes and smiled at Harley who gave Ellis a questioning look, but said no more.

My parents are on this thread . . . I found a thread with my parents! Ellis's thoughts screamed. She tried to suppress a smile, but knew she wasn't doing a good job of it. She started thinking about what kind of picture might let her later know that she found a thread with her parents. She had no idea, but decided she must make that her main focus.

As excited as she was though, she couldn't help feeling disappointed to learn her parents are out of town. It felt like a cruel joke. On the other hand, Ellis was confused as to why she was friends with Harley. But it was just a thread, not her main thread, and more importantly she was on a thread with her parents.

Ellis wondered how she could find out how long her parents will be gone without making Harley suspicious. If they come back tomorrow, Ellis decided, there will be time for her to stay on this thread until she gets to see her parents. Ellis felt like she was walking on air — she didn't realize how excited she was about seeing her parents until this moment, when the possibility seemed real.

Harley lived just two streets over from Ellis in one of the large Victorian houses that Ellis had admired when she and Hen first moved to Harper. The tall octagonal turret and large, wraparound front porch with gingerbread trim gave the house a magical feel. The steep roof was covered in black-green slate shingles and the house was painted pale yellow with white trim. The heavy wooden front door, twice as wide as an average door, had carved wooden panels and a leaded glass panel in the center. To open the door, Harley twisted and then pulled on a heavy metal ring as large as her hand.

Ellis followed Harley's lead and dropped her backpack on a bench in the enormously large front entry hall. A rectangular area rug with a complicated pattern of flowers, ivy, and borders in shades of burgundy, royal blue, gold, and forest green filled the space. To the left was a turret room with bay windows on each of the polygonal walls and a wooden octagonal table in the center. Ellis was feeling sorry she wouldn't remember this thread. The house was amazing — it even smelled welcoming — and Harley seemed to be a different person away from Vi and the others.

Ellis guessed that she must be a regular visitor to Harley's house because Harley started walking down a hallway toward another area of the house without so much as a "follow me" to Ellis. Ellis scurried after Harley and in a few seconds found herself in the kitchen. Harley's mother (Ellis guessed) was lifting cookies from a baking stone and placing them on a wire rack for cooling.

Mrs. Slade looked up and smiled. An apron was tied around her small waist. Harley was already as tall as her mother and had a much huskier build. Ellis decided Harley must look more like her father.

"Hi, girls. Just made oatmeal cookies with chocolate and peanut butter chips . . . who would like one?"

Ellis was famished, but wasn't sure how to respond. She wasn't even sure how the Ellis on this thread normally greets her friend's mother. Ellis settled on saying, "They smell great. I'd love one."

"Harley?"

"Yeah sure, I'll have one, thanks mom."

Harley's mom placed several cookies on a plate that she handed to Ellis. "Thanks," said Ellis, looking at Harley's mom for signs that she might suspect something. However, after handing the plate to Ellis, Harley's mom simply turned and wiped her hands on her apron and began cleaning up the kitchen.

"Ellis, honey, we're so glad you're spending a couple days. It will be fun having you here," said Harley's mom, her hands in soapy wash water.

Ellis's heart dropped. A couple of days! I can't stay for two days. Ellis did a quick mental calculation and guessed that she has been on the thread for close to two hours. She had less than two days left!

Harley grabbed the plate from Ellis and said, "Let's go finish our homework." As she headed out of the kitchen, Ellis scampered after her, feeling a little lost.

They worked at the turret room table. Ellis found it hard to concentrate. She located her planner and from that deciphered her homework assignments, which were remarkably close to what she was doing at Ida May on her main thread. Harley wasn't talking much. She seemed intent on getting her homework done, but Ellis had a different focus — she needed to find out more about her parents without making Harley suspicious. And how would she ever find the notebook if her parents aren't even in town?

Ellis distractedly worked through her homework. She almost laughed out loud at herself for feeling like she had to get homework done when she planned to stay in this life for only a day or two. But then again, she thought, I want the Ellis on this thread to do well. With that thought, Ellis decided she could easily make herself crazy trying to figure out threads. She also decided that she was thankful after all not to remember the threads she visits — it would feel like too much responsibility.

Harley seemed to be winding down with the homework. Ellis took this as a signal to start closing her own books and acting like she had her homework done as well. Ellis felt awkward sitting in Harley's house like she was a friend, but Harley didn't seem to notice anything out of the ordinary.

"I can't wait to go to the movie tomorrow night," said Harley.

"Me too," replied Ellis, trying to sound enthusiastic.

"I think we'll see a lot of Ida May kids there," continued Harley.

Ellis nodded in agreement.

"Why are you so quiet?" said Harley in the shorter tone Ellis was accustomed to hearing from her.

"I kind of miss my mom," said Ellis, feeling like it was a childish thing to say, but she wanted to turn the topic around to her parents.

"You do?" questioned Harley. "Why?"

Ellis shrugged her shoulders and tried to think fast. "It's silly, isn't it?"

Harley's tone softened and she looked thoughtfully at Ellis and said, "I guess I would miss my mom if she had to go to a lot of conferences and work a lot like your parents do . . ." said Harley before rushing to add, "but my mom likes working with your mom."

Ellis was touched by Harley's seemingly genuine concern. Ellis remembered Starling saying that Harley's mom works closely with her mom. They must all be in the same research division as Ellis's parents.

"Do you think we can walk over to my house so I can get my clothes and stuff?" asked Ellis.

"You brought your clothes over this morning — are you having memory problems?"

"No, no, I remember that," replied Ellis casually, "I just decided I want to wear something different to the movies tomorrow night."

Harley eyed her suspiciously for a moment before replying. "Sure . . . We'll go after dinner."

Chapter 19 ~ A Different House

Ellis and Harley's family ate dinner in a small dining room off the kitchen where Mrs. Slade served meatloaf, mashed potatoes, gravy, and yellow beans. Just minutes before dinner, Mr. Slade arrived home carrying a briefcase and wearing a suit and tie, but his formal attire didn't hide his bright smile and jovial disposition. At about the same time, Harley's eleven-year-old brother, Rod, came in — his knees covered in mud and hair sticking in every direction. He had been playing football with neighborhood boys and his stocky, solid build led Ellis to believe him to be one of the better players. He flashed a boyish smile at Ellis and said hi. Ellis said hi back and tried to act like this wasn't their first meeting.

Over dinner, Ellis heard that Harley's older brother, Brock, is in his last year of college. Mr. Slade talked excitedly about having him home next weekend to go to the big game together, which Ellis interpreted to mean a football game. He spoke with his hands and made enthusiastic gestures. Ellis noticed Mr. Slade's thick neck and heavy, muscular build and guessed that he played football himself at some point.

Harley knew as much about football as anyone. She spoke of downs, sacks, and snaps, and asked her dad about strategy, plays, and tactics. Ellis smiled a lot and listened quietly because she couldn't decide if she should act like she knew what they were talking about or not. She and Hen never made time to watch football, so Ellis couldn't bluff her way through a football conversation even if she wanted to.

"Harley, he *didn't* have *time* to make the pass — the linebacker was right on him. . . ."

"Dad," gestured Harley wildly, "the quarterback was too slow . . . he needed to throw as soon as he stepped back. . . ."

Watching Harley interact with her dad had Ellis wondering if she and her dad watched football together on this thread, or on any thread for that matter. She pictured herself sitting with her dad and mom, eating, laughing, talking — if only she had a brother or sister — if only she had her parents.

"Boom!" Mr. Slade clapped his hands together loudly. Ellis jumped, but only Mrs. Slade seemed to notice, and she just smiled politely.

" . . . and down he went," finished Mr. Slade.

"Dad, dad, that's like the play I made today!"

And all attention was on Rod, everyone laughing over the retelling of his afternoon game.

After helping with the dinner cleanup, Ellis and Harley grabbed their jackets and headed over to Elm Street. The shorter fall days meant that it was already dark out. However, there was no bumping into Harley on the walk over now that Ellis knew where she was going.

"You have such a great house," Ellis said as they walked. She hoped the comment wouldn't sound too odd.

Harley glanced at her with another look of concern before saying, "Ahh . . . okay. Yeah, it's a great house — You know it's where my father grew up. . . . We've been friends since we were two. . . . Why are you acting like this is the first time we've met each other?"

Ellis hoped the dark was hiding the heat that crept into her cheeks and the fact that she was sweating when it was cool out. She wiped her palms against her jeans before answering. "I don't know what you mean," said Ellis innocently.

"Never mind," grunted Harley, shaking her head in exasperation.

They arrived at Ellis's front door within minutes. Ellis thought her house looked a little better attended on this thread. There seemed to be more azalea bushes and yellow mums growing on either side of the walkway. As Ellis approached the front door, she anxiously realized she didn't have a key. She swung her backpack off her shoulder and opened a small zipper compartment and pretended to rummage for a key.

"What are doing?" asked Harley rather impatiently.

"Uhm . . . looking for the key," said Ellis, hoping an idea would come to her.

Harley sighed. "I'll get the spare." She jumped off the porch and lifted a rock nestled among the black eyed Susans and extracted a key.

"Thanks," mumbled Ellis, working the key into the door. Ellis didn't know what she would find inside, nor did she understand why she wanted to go to her house, but she liked the idea of being closer to her parent's presence even if they weren't physically there.

There was enough moonlight shining through the windows to allow Ellis and Harley to make their way to the kitchen without turning on the entry lights. Harley flipped on the kitchen switch and sat down at the table. "I'll wait here," she said. "Hurry though . . . my mom wants us back early on a school night."

Ellis noticed that the table was pulled away from the wall and centered in the kitchen, but aside from that she didn't notice much else different in the room in her quick survey before going upstairs.

Ellis reached the top of the stairs and breathed a little easier without the pressure of Harley at her side. She wanted to look around in every room and every drawer and closet, but she knew Harley wouldn't have the patience for the time that would take. The only open door was the bathroom and Ellis didn't feel she had much to gain by searching it. She turned and opened her bedroom door and went in. A chill went down her spine as she walked around her room. It looked so lived in — the walls were covered with pictures and posters; the desk was filled with papers, knickknacks, and a framed picture of her and Harley looking about eight years old; there was more furniture in this room than the room on her main thread . . . the girl that lived here had lived in the same place all her life and it showed. Ellis felt like an intruder in her own room.

Harley yelled another reminder for Ellis to hurry up.

"Coming," Ellis called back, as she ran to the closet and grabbed a top and jeans.

With clothes in hand, Ellis took one last look at her unfamiliar room. Of little consequence was the familiar creak from the threshold floorboard as she left the room.

"I'm ready," Ellis said to Harley who by now was standing up waiting impatiently.

The walk back to Harley's was quiet. Ellis found it hard to make conversation when all she could think about was the visit to her own house, except that it wasn't her house.

On the premise of getting ready for bed, Ellis went into the bathroom with both her school backpack and the tote bag she apparently left at Harley's earlier that day. As with the rest of the house, this room had high ceilings and Victorian accents. The octagonal window high on one wall had thick leaded stained glass to let in light, and currently, moonlight from the nearly full moon outside. Ellis walked across the wooden floor to the white rug in front of the white porcelain footed tub and dropped her bags. In the wall nearest the bathtub was a small fireplace with a wooden mantel painted white, above which hung a large gilded mirror. Ellis gazed at her reflection momentarily before she lowered herself into a crisscross position on the rug and systematically began to go through her bags for any clues to her current thread existence.

Ellis rummaged through the tote but found only a change of clothes and her toiletries. Setting it aside, she opened the backpack. One by one she took out each book and held them by the spine and shook them over the rug, hoping for something of personal value to fall out. A page of science notes was all that landed on the rug. With the books piled beside her, Ellis looked through every pocket of the backpack. The small front pocket held a planner, pencils, pens, and what looked to be a candy wrapper from The Apothecary. She flipped through the planner and noticed her class schedule written on the first page. A quick look told her that the schedule was different from her main thread class schedule. The classes were the same, but in a different order. She was disappointed to think that maybe Starling won't be in all of her classes tomorrow.

Ellis memorized her schedule before packing away the planner and the other books. She shoved the page of science notes into her backpack and checked the floor for anything she may have missed. Ellis knew by now Harley must be wondering why she was taking so long, so she quickly changed and got ready for bed, gingerly moving the device from her jeans pocket to the small outer pocket of her backpack.

When Ellis came out of the bathroom, only a small night light was on in the bedroom, and Harley was in one of the twin beds. "You were in there a long time," she mumbled, sounding half asleep.

"Yeah . . . stomach issues."

This seemed to rouse Harley because in a more alert voice she said, "Are you feeling okay? Do you need something?"

"No, no. I'm just going to get to bed. I'm tired." *This isn't what I expected from my first sleepover*, thought Ellis. *But then again I won't remember it anyway*, she sighed.

"Okay," said Harley hesitantly, and after a moment, she muttered sleepily, "Good-night."

Ellis slipped into bed and turned out the small night light on the dresser between them. She tried to lie very still, which was difficult when her mind was moving so fast. She couldn't see what she had to gain by going to Ida May tomorrow on this thread, but Ellis felt she hadn't learned enough about her parents yet to leave. She was also really curious as to why Harley's mother worked with her parents and why Harley seemed friendly on this thread when she was regarded as a bully on Ellis's main thread. She wanted to stay angry at Harley for the way she had treated Starling in the past, but Ellis realized this was ridiculous. It's possible that Harley is friends with Starling on this thread. Ellis still had a hard time believing that she and Harley were such good friends though. She wished she could figure that one out. . . .

Chapter 20 ~ They Never Travelled That Day

When Ellis opened her eyes it took her a few seconds to remember where she was. Harley was not in the twin bed beside her, but Ellis could hear water running from the bathroom.

Ellis jumped out of bed and began searching the room. As quietly as she could manage, Ellis opened drawers and looked in the closet. No clues there. Ellis almost laughed out loud. *What did I think I would find?* she asked herself.

The water had stopped running in the bathroom, so Ellis gathered her tote bag of clothes, slipping the device from her backpack into the tote. Ellis decided she should keep the device with her at all times. She turned it over and checked the readout: 32:12. She still had more than a day left. Less than twenty-four hours had passed, yet Ellis felt like she had been away much longer.

Mrs. Slade was hurriedly rushing around the kitchen with a mug of coffee in one hand. "Good morning, girls. Help yourself to some scrambled eggs and toast. It's all ready, but I need to get to work early today, so I'm about to scoot out of here."

Ellis saw a plate of scrambled eggs and a pile of toast with a jar of jam next to it on the small table in the kitchen where some magazines were stacked at one end. A built-in wooden bench on the far wall of the kitchen was the seating for one side of the table; on the opposite side of the table were two high-backed wooden chairs.

"Thanks, Mrs. Slade," said Ellis.

"Oh, Ellis — over on the table," Mrs. Slade turned her head in the direction of the kitchen table. "The journal on top has a picture of your mom and dad. It's a report about the new glass technology we developed at Connor. Okay, gotta go!" Mrs. Slade rushed over and gave Harley a kiss on the forehead and then headed out with cup still in hand.

Ellis was at the table picking up the journal as soon as Mrs. Slade walked out of the room.

Harley sat down at the table and started fixing her plate. "You want some eggs?"

"Okay," said Ellis distractedly, as she lowered herself onto the bench while continuing to read the journal. The article pictured her mom and dad smiling at the camera. Her mother wore a pencil skirt and jacket and stood close to her father. His hair looked a little gray, but in general they both looked — well, they looked happy. *So this is what they look like when I'm fourteen*, Ellis thought.

"Ellis, we have to get moving," reminded Harley, as she smeared jam on her toast.

Ellis set the journal down long enough to put eggs and toast on her plate, but she didn't want to stop reading to eat. She held the journal in one hand and ate with the other.

"What's so interesting?" asked Harley.

"Have you heard about this? — Connor Glass has recently developed a unique porous glass that shows promise for use in sea water desalinization . . ." read Ellis. "It says here that my parents are the head researchers for the project."

Harley shrugged her shoulders. "Yeah, our parents talk about the day when we are able to drink ocean water."

Ellis read on silently while munching on toast with blackberry jam. The article went on to say that her parents are scheduled to present at a conference in Washington, DC and it listed today's date.

Harley stood up and gathered her backpack. "We have to go," she emphasized the last word like a football coach rallying her team, making Ellis jump in response.

"Can I bring this?" squeaked Ellis, still trying to get used to Harley's brusque tactics.

"I guess. Just give it back to my mom when you're done."

Ellis smiled at Harley's bossiness.

Ellis looked at the journal in her hand. Unless something major came along, this will be her picture, she decided. Now Ellis had to find the right moment to return to her main thread.

Ellis was anxious to finish reading the article, but for now she added it to her backpack and she and Harley walked out the door to school. Ellis took what she assumed would be one last look at Harley's house. As they walked, Harley talked about how excited she was for the movie tonight. Harley revealed enough detail in her conversation for Ellis to determine that the plan was to come back to Harley's after school to change clothes and then head back downtown to eat and then meet up with several friends at the Main Street Cinema for a movie. Ellis caught herself thinking that it sounded like a lot of fun.

In an awkward moment for Ellis, Harley let on that she was very self-conscious about her tomboy appearance. She said it in such a way that Ellis got the feeling it was something she had talked to her about before. Even so, Ellis had a pang of guilt, like she wasn't entitled to be hearing such personal information intended for someone else, even if that someone else was another version of herself.

"You look great in those jeans," assured Ellis.

Harley sighed.

"Why don't we braid your hair — you know, just for

something different," Ellis bit her lip, waiting for Harley's response.

"I don't know . . . Do you think it'll look nice on me?" Ellis could see the gleam of hope in Harley's eyes.

"Of course! You have awesome hair!"

What am I doing? thought Ellis.

They were climbing the Ida May steps when Ellis realized that although she had memorized her schedule, she had no idea where she sat in each of her classes. Her heart was pounding and her stomach clinched harder with each step they climbed. When they walked through the double doors of Ida May, Ellis heard the clanging rattle of lockers being opened and closed. Now she really wanted to disappear on the spot — she had no idea where her locker was! With no better plan in mind, Ellis continued to walk alongside Harley, who hadn't yet reacted as if Ellis's actions were out of the ordinary.

Ellis and Harley walked up the wide staircase to the second floor. Ellis recognized several students in passing and noticed a few others that she had never seen before. Harley seemed to be veering toward the first bank of lockers, and Ellis stuck with her, keeping a lookout for Starling and her sisters, neither of whom she had seen yet.

Ellis leaned against another locker trying to act nonchalant as Harley opened her locker and started exchanging its contents with items in her backpack. After a minute, she looked at Ellis and said, "What's up?"

As if to reply *What do you mean?* Ellis raised her eyebrows and said nothing.

"Why aren't you getting stuff out of your locker?" pursued Harley, raising her hand and tapping a knuckle on the locker beside her.

Oh, so I have a locker beside Harley . . . But what's the combination? thought Ellis, and then said matter of factly, "I'm having trouble with the lock, and besides I have everything I need in my backpack." *I hope,* she added silently.

Harley shrugged and then reached over and started spinning the dial on the locker she had rapped on a moment ago. Two more quick turns and the locker sprung open. It was Harley that then raised her eyebrows to Ellis.

"Thanks," Ellis wiped her hands on her jeans and diverted her eyes from Harley's in hopes of hiding the pink flush warming her face as she mumbled, "You've helped me with two locks now."

Ellis rummaged through the locker, "Oh, yeah, I do need this English book . . ." she said offhandedly. After reorganizing her backpack, Ellis, feeling as ready as she would ever be, was getting antsy to go to class. Her first class in this thread was science and she was hoping that Starling would be waiting for her.

"I'll see you later Harley. I'm off to science." Ellis was also anxious for a little separation from Harley so that she could work out the plan for returning to her main thread, a place that seemed oddly distant.

"What?" barked Harley. "Why aren't you walking with me?"

"Uh — Oh, I just wanted to re — read the rest of the article your mom showed me," said Ellis, stammering an impromptu excuse to cover up the fact that she didn't know Harley was in her class.

"Okay, well, we usually walk to class *together*," said Harley apologetically, apparently realizing her abruptness. "Look, I'm ready. Can we walk together?"

"Sure."

Ellis and Harley walked into the Science classroom, which looked the same as the classroom in Ellis's main thread, but there were still several empty seats — too many for Ellis to guess which was her seat. As they walked further into the classroom, Ellis began to cough. And cough and cough.

Harley stopped and looked at Ellis as she continued to cough.

With one hand over her mouth, Ellis muttered between coughs, "Please — *cah cah* — take my backpack to my seat — *cah cah* — I need — *cah cah cah* — a drink from the fountain."

Harley gave Ellis a mixed look of concern and questioning, but grabbed the pack and headed toward the desks near the front of the classroom.

Ellis dashed out of the classroom, coughing every few seconds. Once in the hallway, she found a vantage point to observe Harley without being obvious. Ellis watched her walk to the second row of desks and sit down. Harley then turned and placed Ellis's backpack under the desk behind hers. Ellis took a moment longer to look at each of the students seated in the classroom. *Where was Starling?* she wondered.

"Hey! What are you doing out here?"

Ellis jumped at the sound of an unexpected voice so close by and then turned to see a laughing Jules standing behind her.

"Sorry . . . I didn't mean to surprise you," said Jules, smiling brightly, his apology one of mock sincerity.

"Oh — hi," said Ellis, trying to regain her composure. Ellis thought about how she and Jules were friends when they were very young in her main thread. Apparently they were friends on this thread as well. Perhaps since they were very young.

"Are you going in?" asked Jules, stretching out his arm in a chivalrous way to indicate that she should go first.

Ellis walked into the classroom and took her seat behind Harley just as the bell rang. Harley was twisted around, ready to say something to Ellis, but lost her chance because the science teacher — a woman that Ellis didn't recognize — started speaking to the class as soon as Ellis sat down. Harley sighed and reluctantly turned around in her seat to face forward. Jules walked down the row of desks to the right of Ellis. As he took his seat next to her, Ellis got the feeling that Jules was different on this thread.

The teacher — Ellis still hadn't learned her name — was talking about chemical reactions. One reaction could set off a chain of reactions, one after another. Ellis thought it sounded like her life. Her parent's one discovery has led to a chain of reactions. Reactions that Ellis just couldn't piece together yet. Nagging at her was the journal article in her backpack. Why were her parents speaking about a porous glass instead of solar panel glass? This thread seemed more like what her life should have been. She had two seemingly longtime friends, Harley and Jules, and she lived at home with her parents who worked at Connor Glass. Why wasn't this her main thread?

Ellis glanced over at Jules periodically. There was something different about him. He was listening to the lesson and taking notes like everyone else in the class — his long, thin fingers twiddling the pencil back and forth when not writing. And then it hit her, Jules wasn't sketching. There were no doodles in his notebook; nor could Ellis see a sketch pad in his open backpack on the floor by his desk. She thought about how different a life could be depending on the path taken while still trying to focus on taking the notes that the Ellis on this thread might need.

Ellis bluffed her way through the rest of her morning classes, finding her seats by feigning another coughing fit, a need to go to the lavatory, and a leg cramp which made her fall behind and require help with her backpack. Harley wasn't in all her morning classes but the one she wasn't in, Jules was. Vi was in Ellis's English class along with Jules (but not Harley) — she chatted with another girl Ellis had never seen before while completely ignoring Ellis and Jules altogether. Gwen and

Peyton appeared to be good friends as they walked into Ellis's Spanish class together, but Harley made no notice of them. Math again included Harley. When Keri and Bea walked into the classroom together — apparently friends on this thread as well — they both said hi to Ellis and Harley. By lunch, Ellis was feeling like she had been playing musical chairs the entire morning. On top of it all, she was dismayed and confused by not having seen Starling or either of her sisters.

Chapter 21 ~ Return from Harley's

As Harley, Jules, and Ellis walked to Hots for lunch, Ellis contemplated her return to her main thread. In her mind's eye, she visualized walking to the Hots ladies room with her backpack, taking a picture of the journal article, and then pressing the appropriate button to return. But her plan evoked an odd feeling of sadness that Ellis couldn't seem to push away. She felt obligated to go to the movies with Harley, to help her with her hair, to be a good friend to her. Ellis had never felt so torn in her life.

"ELLIS!"

Ellis had been so deep in thought that she forgot entirely about Harley and Jules being right beside her. "What?" she said distractedly.

"We've said your name three times," grunted Harley. "You're off in another world."

She has that right, thought Ellis. "Sorry," Ellis smiled and tried to make light of the situation.

Harley, still looking a little put off, explained what she and Jules had discussed, "We're talking about the movies tonight. Jules is planning to stay here in Harper after school — it's easier than taking the train all the way home and then getting a ride back into town.

"We were asking you about going to A Priori Books and The Apothecary after school. It's too chilly to hang around The Trivium."

"Sure," Ellis found herself gladly agreeing. Seeing Tori and

141

Mr. Neumann was reason enough to stay on the thread — she might learn more about her parents. Although at this point it seemed like a weak justification when Ellis now believed that her parents on this thread don't know about threads, nor did she believe they even had a device for visiting threads since it appeared they invented a porous glass, not a solar panel glass, for Connor Glass.

After lunch, Ellis had just two classes left in which to find her seat. Her last class was the same in her main thread — PE, and thankfully they didn't have seats to worry about. Harley was in that class as well. Ellis had just one class without Harley or Jules, Keyboarding, and because there were the same number of computers as students, Ellis simply waited until the entire class was sitting before rushing to the remaining open seat just as the bell rang. Her first afternoon class was with Mrs. Dockleaf. Ellis had the impression that on any thread Mrs. Dockleaf would be about the same — grumpy and stern. Ellis had created yet another excuse for Harley to take her backpack to her seat, which ended up being just one seat away from her main thread seat. Aside from missing Starling, Ellis felt pretty much at home in World History.

Ellis and Harley hurried from PE to meet up with Jules who was waiting for them in front of Ida May. He was sitting in an out-of-way spot on a bottom step. Although he had clearly been waiting for several minutes, Ellis still saw no sign of a sketch pad. She again thought about how the same person could be so different under different circumstances. *What drove him to pursue drawing on one thread, but not on another?* wondered Ellis.

Ellis, Harley, and Jules headed up East North Street, left onto Franklin, and then west again on Main on their way to Bourner Street. It was a crisp, clear afternoon, less than a week into fall. The three friends walked comfortably, laughing and talking.

They turned the corner and started down Bourner Street. Ellis saw the familiar A Priori Books sign and just a few steps further, the sign for The Apothecary. She felt herself visibly shiver and her spine tingled.

"Are you cold?" asked Jules.

"No . . . I'm fine," said Ellis. Just a little more than twenty-four hours ago she had left from inside this bookstore and now she was outside looking at the very place she started. In her mind's eye Ellis saw Hen and Tori standing at the back of the bookstore, waiting for her return.

They walked inside to find A Priori crowded with Ida May students. Students were lounging on big pillows by the children's books and every high-back chair was occupied. Ellis couldn't stop herself looking to the back of the bookstore. She craned her neck to look at the spot she left from, knowing she would see nothing, but feeling better about checking none the less.

"What are looking at?" asked Harley, straining to see what Ellis was seeing.

Ellis pulled her head back and said, "Nothing, just thought I saw someone down that aisle."

Jules had wondered off and was talking with a group of guys near the Reading List table.

"Jules is very social, isn't he?" commented Ellis, more to herself than anyone else.

"When hasn't he been?" Harley shot back.

Harley started walking in the direction of Keri and Bea who were leaning against the far wall, talking amongst themselves. Ellis was about to follow, but stopped in her tracks when she heard someone say her name. She swung around in the direction of a familiar voice. Tori was standing behind her, holding a stack of books in her arms.

"Tori — hi," said Ellis. She suddenly felt very homesick and it must have shown because Tori asked if she was feeling okay. Ellis flashed a smile and acted as if she had no idea why Tori would ask such a thing. Although what she really wanted to do was take Tori aside and ask her a hundred questions about life on this thread and tell her that this life wasn't real for her. She wanted Tori to help her. In that single moment, Ellis realized that she wanted someone to help her. How was she supposed to know which picture will mean the most? How was Ellis supposed to find a notebook, when in this thread, her parents hadn't even developed the glass for transporting someone to a thread?

"This place is a madhouse," said Tori, shaking her head and rolling her eyes, oblivious to Ellis's anxiety. "Sorry I can't talk right now — I just wanted to say hi." She blew at a strand of hair that fallen into her eyes, readjusted the heavy stack in her arms, and started to move away. Before going very far, however, Tori turned and yelled back at Ellis, "Hey, is Henrietta around this weekend?"

"Henrietta?" Ellis whispered to herself and then replied more loudly, "Ah, yeah, I think so." Tori nodded her head and then moved on.

What was that about? wondered Ellis. *Even on this thread, Tori is friends with my grandmother?*

Ellis saw Harley talking with Keri and Bea. She walked in that direction simply because she didn't know what else to do. She didn't feel much like talking with anyone at this point. She suddenly felt like nothing more than a stand-in for someone they knew.

Ellis had nearly reached Harley when Jules intercepted her. "When are we going to The Apothecary?" he asked.

Ellis shrugged her shoulders and said, "I'm ready. . . ."

"I'll let Harley know." As Jules zig zagged his way through

groups of students to where Harley was standing, Ellis decided to stay where she was and wait. No one seemed to notice her just standing there, not reading and not talking to anyone.

Jules returned straightaway and reported that Harley will meet them over there. They turned and made their way out of the packed store and onto the sidewalk, where a blast of cool air greeted them if for but just a minute before they opened the door to The Apothecary, which was equally packed.

"Wow!" Ellis lamented.

"Yeah," Jules agreed somberly, noticing there were no vacant chairs, let alone open tables. "I still want to grab some candy to take to the movie though," he said, nodding his head toward the aisles of candy to indicate they should walk in that direction.

Jules seemed to know exactly what he wanted because they headed directly for the packaged candies and he grabbed a bag of taffy strips. "Anything?" he asked Ellis, indicating he was ready to follow her now.

"No, thanks," she mused.

Harley appeared as Ellis and Jules approached the cash register. "You want anything?" Jules asked Harley. She looked around, as if to decide whether getting through the crowd would be worth it, and then she said no.

Ellis was thankful to be heading back to Harley's house. It wasn't until they were well beyond Bourner Street that she realized she hadn't seen Mr. Neumann at all. She really didn't even care anymore — she wouldn't remember the encounter anyway.

"I love it!" Harley exclaimed as she looked in the mirror at Ellis's handy work. Ellis had plaited Harley's hair so that a single long braid wrapped around the back of her head to hang down in front of her left shoulder. Ellis smiled at the effect on both the way Harley looked and the way she seemed to feel. In that instant Ellis realized that she thought differently of Harley now — her perspective had changed. By making the choice to help Harley, Ellis now knew that Harley wasn't the enemy. Maybe this is what her parents meant when they said perspective can be changed by making different choices. But Ellis wondered how seeing Harley as a friend will change her perspective on her main thread and guide her future decisions.

Harley was still seated at the vanity in her expansive bathroom admiring her hair. "I think I want to change the hair tie to match my top," she said with the excitement of someone who had just received an exciting new gift.

Ellis watched with curiosity as Harley walked over to the fireplace and then rubbed her hand along the frame of the gilded mirror above it until she heard a soft *click*. Trying to keep the surprise off her face, Ellis watched a section of the fireplace mantel pop out from the wall. Harley then pulled on the mantel piece to expose a drawer.

Harley looked inside, studying the drawer's contents. Ellis peeked over her shoulder and saw an array of barrettes, hair ties, combs, and other hair accessories. Harley turned toward Ellis, "Which one?"

Ellis, still shocked at the presence of the secret compartment, was speechless.

"How about this one?" asked Harley, picking up a red and silver hair tie.

"Yes," muttered Ellis.

Harley closed the drawer, a click confirming that the mantel piece was back in place. She sat back down at the vanity and then asked Ellis to help her with the new hair tie.

"We should get going," she said, referring to the movie they planned to see. Jules was waiting downstairs, watching a sports show with Rod.

"I'll be down in a minute," said Ellis, as Harley walked out of the bathroom's second door that opened to the hallway at the top of the stairs.

Harley, still clearly happy, nodded and then headed downstairs. Ellis closed the door and listened from the inside until she couldn't hear Harley anymore. She double-checked that both bathroom doors were locked before grabbing her backpack, which she had purposely deposited inside the bathroom before braiding Harley's hair.

Ellis fumbled in the main compartment of the backpack until she located the journal, which was still folded back to the article that pictured her parents. She laid it on the floor next to her and pressed on the crease to flatten it more. She reached into the outer pocket of her pack and immediately felt the smooth glass she was seeking. She held the device a few inches from the journal page, took a deep breath to steady herself, and clicked the button to take a picture. All that was left now was to go to the movie theater where Ellis planned to excuse herself in the middle of the movie and return to her main thread. . . .

Chapter 22 ~ Maeve and Aiden Bell

Ellis felt groggy. Through hazy vision she saw Hen and Tori standing just inches from her, looking like they might try to catch her if she falls. They had rather strange smiles on their faces. And then Ellis remembered. She had been on a thread. She brought her hand up to verify she had the device. It was there. The fogginess was clearing.

"Ellis," said Hen tentatively.

Ellis continued to stare at the device. She tried to remember what happened. She tried to remember the thread. She went through her day in her head. What was the last thing she remembered? Breakfast, school, the back of A Priori, ready to visit a thread — it all seemed so long ago. But she could remember nothing beyond the bright flash of light.

"Ellis," repeated Hen.

Ellis looked up into Hen's aged face, her gray hair pulled back into a low bun. "I wish I could remember. The last thing I remember is leaving the store, but it seems so long ago."

Tori put her hand out. "Let's see how long you've been gone."

Ellis didn't know immediately what she meant and then realized Tori wanted to see the device.

Ellis handed it to her and then let her arm drop, feeling tired. Hen put an arm around her shoulders, but didn't say anything.

Tori flipped the device over and studied the readout. "You've been gone more than twenty-four hours. And you took a picture — go have a seat. I'll bring it to you."

Ellis and Hen slowly made their way over to the couch and sat down. Ellis really didn't like the washed out feeling she was left with after visiting a thread.

"You were gone a long time," commented Hen. "Do you feel okay?"

Ellis shrugged her shoulders in a noncommittal way. "Yeah. It's just weird to know you've been somewhere for a whole day and not remember any of it." Ellis chuckled sarcastically to no one in particular.

Ellis and Hen both looked up when they heard Tori rushing toward them. Excitement showed on her face. "Look, look," she held out a paper, waving it in the air.

Ellis and Hen leaned in to look at the printed picture Tori held between them.

Ellis's eyes lit up when she saw a picture of her parents. She smiled brightly at Hen who was holding her hand over her mouth and wore an expression of mixed disbelief and joy.

"This looks like a page from a journal article," said Hen, her eyes scanning the text in the picture. "It says your parents are attending a conference to present their work on porous glass . . ." mumbled Hen. "Whoa, the conference dates are today and tomorrow?" Hen looked up from the picture, but her eyes were focused on her own thoughts, a look of deep concentration on her face.

Ellis and Tori stared at Hen, waiting for her to continue.

"I don't think your parents would take you to a conference," said Hen, processing her thoughts, not looking at either Ellis or Tori. "The device glass isn't made of porous glass. It's made from a solar panel glass. . . . Maybe you were on a thread where your parents existed, but they were working on a different project.

It looks like they were away. You must have stayed with

someone. . . ."

Hen looked directly at Ellis and Tori, her eyes now focused on them. "It may have been a thread where your parents worked for Connor Glass but never discovered the solar panel glass properties, or perhaps they never developed the solar panel glass at all."

Ellis was frustrated and her tone of voice reflected her sarcasm over the situation, "So it was a thread where they knew nothing about threads. I probably just lived at home — in one home — while my parents went to work every day and I went to school in the same town with the same friends I had known all my life. Sounds like a nice normal life. Sounds like a nice main thread to me."

Hen gave a weary grimace and then awkwardly looked away.

Ellis watched Tori make notes below the picture. She wrote down today's date, the coordinates, and the amount of time Ellis spent on the thread.

"I'm no closer to finding the notebook, am I?"

Tori avoided answering the question and hypothesized instead, "You must have had a reason to stay so long on the thread. Maybe you were with some Ida May friends?"

Ellis felt a tingle in her spine. *Maybe my subconscious remembers the thread? — Tori's suggestion sounded possible.* Ellis thought about what it might be like living in the same house in Harper her whole life. She would have lots of friends, probably some of the same friends she has now at Ida May — kids that have been in Harper their whole life, or at least since they were very young.

Ellis decided she must have felt comfortable on the thread to stay for more than twenty-four hours, especially if she stayed overnight with a friend while her parents were away at a conference. Ellis remembered Jules saying they were friends when very young. And Starling had been a Glass kid since she was four. Ellis imagined herself, Starling, and Jules hanging out together in a different thread. She pictured herself sleeping over at Starling's house, having a great time, staying up late and talking. . . .

Her fantasy came to an abrupt end when Hen stood up and declared, "Ellis, you have homework to do. We better get going."

Ellis pushed herself up off the couch, and then pointing to the printout in Tori's hand, asked, "Can I keep that?"

Tori looked at Hen briefly, as if to obtain permission, and then handed the paper to Ellis. Ellis glanced down at her parents smiling at a camera in some other life.

Ellis and Hen rode home in silence. Ellis thought Hen might be upset about something, maybe even upset with her. However, Ellis remained stubbornly quiet because she herself was feeling resentful towards Hen for taking her away from her life in Harper. Ellis knew her feelings were unreasonable, which was the only thing that kept her from voicing her thoughts. Instead, she daydreamed about what she may have been doing on the thread.

They pulled into the driveway at the same time Ellis came to the conclusion that she must talk to Starling and find out all she can about who lived in Harper at the time her parents disappeared. But then how would Starling remember such things when she would have been so young herself?

Hen left the car parked in the driveway and she and Ellis walked up to the front porch. Even with all the unpacking they had done, the detached garage was still too full of boxes to park the car inside.

The black-eyed Susans, tiny sentinels at the door, peered up at Ellis as she waited for Hen to unlock the door. Once inside, they stopped at the closet to stow their jackets.

"Hen," said Ellis, still contemplating her life as a long-time Harper resident, "who was I friends with before I left Harper?" Ellis was sure to phrase the question so as not to imply that Hen took her away from her friends in Harper, although Ellis was feeling a little like that right now.

Hen continued facing the closet where she was hanging up her jacket. She turned half way around and held out her hand for Ellis's jacket. She didn't start to answer until she was facing the closet again. "I'm not sure I know," said Hen elusively, her voice somewhat muffled by the jackets.

"What do you know about my life here before Mom and Dad left?" Ellis almost begged. "Didn't you come to visit me before I lived with you?" challenged Ellis.

Hen had finished hanging the jackets in the closet and was walking to the kitchen. "It was so long ago," she answered vaguely.

Ellis caught up with Hen and gave her a pleading look.

"You had several playmates — mostly kids from the lab because you hadn't started school yet," Hen's voice was trailing. It seemed difficult for her to recall old memories and reveal them at the same time.

"Why do you want to know about the friends you had when you were little, anyway?"

Ellis lowered her eyes and said, "I'm wondering who I might have been if I had never left here."

"Ellis . . ." said Hen in a disappointed tone. She put a hand on each of Ellis's shoulders and then looked searchingly into her eyes for several seconds before pulling out a chair at the kitchen table and directing Ellis to take a seat.

Hen stood wringing her wrinkled hands for a brief moment and then she fretfully took a seat at the table with Ellis. "Ellis, you are who you are meant to be. It's okay to wonder what might have been, but don't get so caught up in asking yourself *what if* that you forget to live your life in the present."

Ellis silently nodded in agreement. She knew Hen was right, even though it will be very hard to stop wondering about the what ifs.

"Why did they visit threads, Hen?" asked Ellis sadly, rhetorically, her eyes looking down at the chrome edge of the table she was picking at with her fingernail.

Hen's response was unexpected and her voice carried such deep conviction that Ellis completely forgot about the chrome and looked into Hen's lined face now hardened with determination.

"They traveled for the sake of science. They were scientists at heart. And your mom and dad always visited threads together so that they would end up on a thread where they both existed — like a team."

"Did they *love* science more than they *loved* me?" Ellis knew she sounded selfish, but at the moment she was feeling very selfish — cheated from a life that she thought sounded better than what she had right now. Hen looked sternly at Ellis, but she was understanding enough to ignore the childish outburst.

"Often they learned of new discoveries they made on a different thread. It was like cloning yourself and having each one do research so that you could make as many discoveries as there were clones.

"Science was their calling. They felt they had a greater purpose — and they wanted *you* to be proud of them."

"Me? Why would it matter if I was proud of them?" Ellis tried to look and sound as offended as possible.

"They loved science because it was their calling," repeated Hen, "but they loved *you* to the very depths of their souls. That's why it mattered."

Hen paused for a moment, looking as though she was considering whether to go on.

"Your mother was thorough, detailed, committed to doing what she thought was right. She made careful notes about the discoveries on other threads. But as you know, you can't bring anything back from a thread, so she hid her notes on the thread. If they went back to that same thread again, she would continue her notes.

"Your mom said that they often ended up on a thread where they were scientists at Connor Glass, but each thread was under a different set of circumstances and their work at the lab was for different projects. They visited those threads over and over again to add to their hidden notes as the version of themselves on that thread continued their research. They were spies on themselves," laughed Hen. "When they gathered enough information, they proposed a new project at Connor Glass. But your mother always said there was so much more. She added her device research to the hidden notes. . . . All that information is somewhere. Finding those notes might give us the information we need to bring them back."

"Why didn't mom ever tell anyone where she kept the notes?" Ellis felt charged by the mystery behind it all.

"I don't know," said Hen, shaking her head.

"What about the pictures mom brought back? . . . Do we have those? Maybe they will give a clue about the notebook location," said Ellis, her voice rising in excitement.

"Your mom focused on the research so she took only a close up photo of a few notes related to a project, or a photo of a diagram that would help further research. That's all, and besides, the photos are with the lab books."

"But how did she know where to find the notebooks when she couldn't remember anything from a thread?"

"Your mom placed notebooks in a secret place in her main thread and then retrieved them on the other threads. They were lab books, like the ones on the bookshelves." Hen pointed with her thumb toward their library in the next room.

The excitement was building inside of Ellis — Can she find the notes? Ellis's mind was a jumble of thoughts as she tried to process the information. She and Hen sat at the table, quiet, seeing not each other, but only what their mind's eye saw. Ellis envisioned her mother (using the image from the photograph she brought back) reaching for a lab book. She saw her mother's hand clearly, but the lab book was surrounded by a foggy cloud because that was a far as Ellis's imagination could go. She couldn't see the location of the book.

And then a question came to Ellis.

"When on a thread, the traveler is living in the future. . . . How can a lab book containing my mother's notes exist in her main thread if the notes aren't added until a day or two in the future?"

Hen smiled. "Weird, huh? Good thinking, Ellis. Your mother would not touch the lab books until two days after she returned to her main thread. She left them in their hiding place to allow her threaded self the time to add the notes."

"Wow."

Hen looked into Ellis's eyes, making sure she had her attention. "Your mother was confident that it was her fate to visit threads — your mom and dad decided their discovery was what was meant to be," Hen pushed the words in a way that sounded a little defensive. "They were transported to Connor Glass threads over and over again even when they allowed the device to transport them to a random destination. Each thread showed them a different Connor Glass project. With this, they felt it was their *responsibility* to bring these discoveries to the world by developing them at the Connor Glass in their main thread." Hen now looked reflective, like she was considering every word carefully.

"Your mom and dad were happy with their lives because

they had you and because they had a special purpose in life. I think they felt their destiny — their *threaded destiny* — was to use threads to further their scientific contributions." From the look of Hen's expression, the last statement seemed to be a new realization for her as well.

Ellis had never thought of her parents as more than the mother and father she no longer had. She hadn't ever wondered what else they did besides parent her. Ellis suddenly felt a little ashamed for not thinking of how they might be missed by the other people that were involved in their lives. She realized that her daydreams about what life would be like if her parents came back were all about what life would be like only for *her*. The journal picture came to mind. The caption discussed Maeve Bell and Aiden Bell, scientists recognized for their achievements. Even though she still felt the loneliness of being orphaned, Ellis now had a source of pride that occupied a part of her. It felt tangible, like something that Ellis could latch on to.

A thought came to Ellis. "On the threads where they were scientists at Connor Glass . . . did they live in the same house?"

"I think so," answered Hen, in a tone that said she knew where Ellis was headed.

"So . . . maybe the lab books are in our house?"

Hen smiled. "I've been searching." And then she put an arm around Ellis's shoulders. "It's so nice to have a partner in this quest." Hen's eyes sparkled, as she chuckled.

"Why do you think they lived in the same house on so many different threads?" asked Ellis.

"It takes a long time to realize — I'm still figuring it out — that if you listen to your heart and trust yourself, you'll end up where you need to be. Maybe this is where they needed to be."

Ellis nodded her head and felt finished with her questions, at least for now.

Hen looked up at the kitchen clock. "Egads, it's getting late," she said, pressing a hand to her grumbling stomach. "I'll make dinner. You get started on your homework."

Ellis grabbed her backpack and started for the stairs but then turned around and went back to the table to grab the printout picturing her parents. Her actions didn't go unnoticed by Hen who glanced over at Ellis but continued to pull items from the refrigerator without commenting.

"Hen," said Ellis, waiting for Hen's full attention.

"Yes."

"Is it okay if I take one of the empty lab books from the library?"

Hen silently nodded her head.

Ellis popped into the library and pulled one of the unused lab books from the bottom shelf and then went up to her room where she dropped her bag before taking a seat at her desk. Ellis opened the top desk drawer and found a wrinkled sheet of paper. She laid it on the desk and ironed it with her hands, trying to smooth it. As she did, she reread the five steps for the scientific method and her conclusions. She chuckled at how little she knew after visiting that first thread.

She reached in another drawer and pulled out clear tape. She opened the lab book and pressed on the gutter of its stiff binding. At the top of the first page, Ellis wrote the date of her first thread visit and then taped the still wrinkled paper in the space below.

On the next page, she wrote today's date and then taped the printout in the space below. Ellis rested her hand on the facing page, pen in hand, as she reread the text below the picture of her parents. It was a brief article that said Dr. Maeve Bell and Dr. Aiden Bell have been working at Connor Glass for twenty years, spending most of that time developing a glass filtration system for purifying ocean water to make it safe for human consumption.

Ellis looked at the blank page where her hand rested. This being an actual lab book, Ellis wanted to do a good job with writing down her "experiments." She included Hen's idea that Ellis did not go with her parents to a conference and Tori's idea that Ellis spent the night with an Ida May friend. With this last experiment Ellis decided she was closer to accepting the hypothesis *My parents are living on a thread and cannot return* but she did not write a conclusion.

Ellis was looking over her new lab book when Hen called up the stairs that dinner was ready. She shut the book and pushed it to the back of the top desk drawer and closed the drawer.

Chapter 23 ~ Sleepover

Hen quietly sipped her tea and sighed for a second time since Ellis sat down to eat some scrambled eggs and toast. Ellis was spreading the Amish-made butter on her toast when she heard Hen sigh yet again. Ellis impatiently looked over at Hen but said nothing.

More than a week had gone by since Ellis's last thread visit. As much as Ellis wanted to visit another thread, or actually go back to the last thread where she knew her parents existed, Hen seemed to come up with one excuse after another to keep her from going. By midweek though, Hen had little need to make excuses because Ellis became distracted with her weekend plans.

After finishing her eggs, Ellis placed her breakfast plate in the sink and took one quick last swig of tea. She grabbed her backpack and swung it around to place her arms in the straps before picking up the straps of another bag and crossing it over her body.

Ready to walk out the door, Ellis looked at Hen and said, "Don't worry. I'm just going for a sleepover. I'll call you when I get there."

Hen smiled for the first time that morning. "Have fun." With true Hen style, she didn't want Ellis to walk away with any hard feelings between them. Ellis felt her defenses melt away at the sentiment and for the first time since she started badgering Hen for a sleepover at Starling's house, she felt sorry about leaving her grandmother all alone for the night.

"Hen . . ."

Hen held up her hand, as if to say stop. "Go. Have fun. Tori is coming over for a visit tonight, so don't worry about me."

Ellis smiled and nearly skipped out of the house. "Call you later," she yelled back as she went out the front door. Ellis even surprised herself at how at ease she was about doing a sleepover — it didn't even feel like a first sleepover.

Ellis had left the house a few minutes earlier than usual. She wanted extra time to make room in her locker for the messenger bag she had packed to take with her to Starling's. As Ellis turned the corner, she noticed another girl walking almost a block ahead. Her long straight hair swayed from side to side as she walked. Ellis was too happy to feel intimidated. She kept her pace and was soon less than half a block from the other girl. Ellis could hear the swishing sound of Harley's jacket and wondered if Harley was aware of Ellis, who was now closing in.

Harley glanced back to see who was behind her. She hesitated for a moment when she made eye contact with Ellis, but then turned back around without changing pace or acknowledging Ellis in any way.

Rather than try to pass Harley, Ellis decided to cross the street — she could see Ida May just up ahead. But when Ellis stepped off the curb, Harley made the same move. Ellis sighed inwardly and wiped her palms on her jeans. She was gaining ground on Harley and she would either have to slow down or speed up and pass.

Ellis stopped and adjusted her messenger bag strap — which didn't need adjusting. Even with that deliberate delay, she and Harley approached the Ida May steps at the same time, where fortunately the wide berth gave them the opportunity to spread apart and go their separate ways. As soon as Ellis hit the first step she picked up her pace again. As she did, she noticed from the corner of her eye Harley glancing over at Ellis, and then as Ellis passed she heard a low, "Hi."

Ellis was ahead of Harley before she was able to take in the gesture. In a split second she decided to say nothing and to keep moving as if she hadn't heard Harley at all. Ellis felt a slight clinching in her stomach, but she reasoned that at this point it would be awkward to turn back just to say hi.

Her momentary guilt disappeared when she saw Starling, who looked as excited as Ellis felt. Ellis made room for her messenger bag in her locker — pushing books to the back and pulling out loose papers and candy wrappers — while Starling reviewed their sleepover plans.

"So, right after school, we have to come back to your locker for your bag and then race to the Double Decker," said Starling warningly.

"Right — If we don't get to the train in time, the Double Decker will leave without us and Kes can't drive us home today," recited Ellis, nearly giggling.

Ellis was still stuffing her bag into the locker when the bell rang. "Quick," said Starling, and she reached over and pushed the bag inside while Ellis slammed the locker door shut. They grabbed their backpacks, dumped the trash in a bin by their lockers, and hurried off to reach their seats in Mrs. Dockleaf's class before the late bell rang.

As Ellis settled into her desk, Jules nodded a hello. When Ellis smiled back at him, she caught a glimpse of Harley several seats ahead. She was turned around in her seat looking in Ellis's direction, but rotated back around when Ellis caught her eye. Had Harley been looking at her?

They wrapped up *The Odyssey* in English — both Ellis and Starling looked forward to moving on to a different book. In Science, Ms. Lee discussed next week's lab — a chromatography experiment for separating the pigments that make up the fall leaf colors. She explained that by soaking ground up leaves in rubbing alcohol, the alcohol will absorb the pigments, or coloring, and then a paper filter strip partially immersed in the liquid absorbs the pigments, separating the colors into bands along the strip — Ellis couldn't wait. The day came to an end as quickly as it started with Ellis and Starling finishing PE and then racing to their lockers.

Ellis took a seat on the lower level of the Double Decker and Starling slid in beside her. Jules grabbed a hand grip alongside where they were sitting and swayed his arm slightly while standing beside them. Ellis couldn't keep the smile off her face. Her stomach fluttered in excited anticipation, not for another ride on the Double Decker, but for the time with friends.

The Double Decker jerked to a start and then gradually gained speed. Jules wore his backpack on his shoulders, but as usual he had his sketch pad tucked under his arm. A pencil had been pushed into the spirals along the top of the notebook. It was an art pencil like one Ellis had seen at Hubbel's. It had a metal cap where the eraser should be, which Ellis thought was a ridiculous design for a pencil. Even so, Ellis noticed that Jules always used the art pencil when sketching. When he needed to erase something, Ellis watched him use what looked like a blob of gray putty. He would systematically pull on the gray putty, stretching and reforming it several times before rubbing it against the paper to remove his pencil marks.

Ellis's excitement filled her with confidence. "Can I take a look at your drawings?" said Ellis, immediately regretting her zealous request because she felt it was probably a personal one.

Jules hesitated for a moment, making Ellis feel a bit awkward, before he held out the tablet for her to take.

Ellis slowly paged through the sketch pad, becoming more and more surprised as she went. She glanced up at Jules with a questioning look. He was telling Starling about a new movie and caught Ellis's eye midsentence. He continued talking to Starling, but Ellis thought she heard a nervous hitch in his voice.

At the end of the sketch pad, Ellis paged backward to the beginning, where Mrs. Dockleaf's likeness was featured on the body of a bulldog. As she smiled at this, Ellis suddenly became aware of the silence around her — Starling and Jules were no longer talking, and Ellis had the feeling someone was watching over her shoulder. She looked up to see Jules staring into his sketch pad and Starling craning her neck over Ellis's shoulder. Ellis looked back down at the pad and unzipped her jacket because she suddenly felt too warm.

Jules still hadn't said anything.

"These drawings are amazing," said Ellis, with deserving admiration in her voice.

"Thanks," replied Jules, sounding comfortable with the compliment and wearing a relaxed smile.

Ellis flipped the pages of the sketch pad until she came back to some of the more recent drawings. Starling voiced what Ellis was thinking a few minutes ago. "Wow . . . what are these?"

Jules chuckled. "I like to do scientific drawings. That's a plant cell."

Ellis observed the complexity of the drawing while Jules continued with an explanation.

"My father took me with him to a conference in Boston several years ago. While we were there we visited the Glass Flowers exhibit at Harvard University. It was incredible. Each flower was an exact replica of its living counterpart. What was amazing was the coloration and scientific accuracy, allowing the models to be used as substitutes to study in place of the real thing. The glass flowers looked real. I couldn't believe my eyes. Along with the flowers were a few sea creatures — a jelly fish and a squid, I think. It inspired me to make realistic models from glass.

"I asked my father if we could buy one of the glass flowers or animals to bring home with us so that I could study it. He laughed and said that they were one-of-a-kind, not for sale, unable to be duplicated. He told me that when the German father and son team who made the glass models passed away, so did their secrets because they never wrote down their techniques or formulas for the colors and textures they obtained in the glass. It became all the more fascinating to me when I learned that the development of such unique glass is a mystery."

Jules paused for a moment, looking as if he was recalling the glass flowers exhibit. Ellis thought about her parents and the mystery they left behind.

"I told my father I would like to do something like that. I don't think he took me seriously. He'd rather see me as a traditional scientist like him. But my mother convinced him to let me try."

"So these drawings," asked Ellis, "are used to make glass models?"

"Exactly," nodded Jules confidently.

"Do you go to the lab to make these?" asked Starling.

"Yeah."

"Really?" asked Starling, her voice sounding more mischievous than questioning.

Jules smiled knowingly. "Yes," he said. "Actually I'm going in to the lab tomorrow to work on something." It seemed like an invitation to Ellis. Starling obviously came to the same decision because she jumped at the opportunity.

"Can we come?" asked Starling excitedly.

"Sure," said Jules. "Meet me there at nine."

The Double Decker squealed to a stop and Jules grabbed

his bag. He raised his hand to signal good-bye and said he would see them tomorrow.

Ellis didn't even notice the short time to the next stop — she was preoccupied by her own thoughts of going to the lab where her parents used to work. Ellis knew the next visit to the lab will have a very different meaning to her than the first visit. Now that she felt like she knew better who her parents were, Ellis planned to find out as much as possible about the lab that meant so much to them.

Off the Double Decker, Ellis zipped her coat against the brisk air. It was getting dusk and Ellis could faintly see her breath.

"You wanted to go too, right?" questioned Starling, sounding a little unsure of herself.

"Go where? — To the lab? To see Jules?" replied Ellis.

Starling nodded her head.

"Yes! I can't wait."

Starling smiled.

They walked on for another minute or so breathing in the chilly fall air, shuffling among the leaves that had fallen into the street. "Do your parents ever talk about the projects they work on at Connor Glass?" asked Ellis, wondering if her parents started any projects from other threads.

"Not so much. I don't think they're allowed to talk about their work until the information is published — even to their own kids," said Starling thoughtfully. "They try to invent new uses for glass so that they can patent their ideas."

"What's a patent?" asked Ellis.

"A patent means that only Connor Glass is allowed to produce the product. It allows Connor Glass to make money off a product. The more patents a company holds, the more money they make. If a scientist invents a new use for glass, then Connor Glass can patent the idea and receive money from other companies that want to use one of their patented products or ideas in a product they sell."

Ellis nodded.

"One thing my parents *have* mentioned lately is how Connor Glass needs more patents to remain in business. They have great researchers, but they can't do research without the backing, as my parents say. . . ." said Starling. "Some nights they look pretty stressed about the work they love."

Ellis remembered the night she had dinner with Starling and how Myna asked her parents if something was wrong.

Starling unlocked the front door using the key from behind the shutter. Ellis made a mental note to ask Hen if they had a hidden house key. For some reason, she thought they might.

Myna and Kes were off with friends for the night, and it was getting dark too early to walk to Connor Glass after school, so Ellis and Starling headed upstairs to Starling's room. On the way up, Ellis gently glided her fingers over the song bird finial that silently sings forever.

After dropping their backpacks inside the bedroom door, they both plopped down on the bed. Ellis sat crisscross on one side while Starling propped up some pillows and rested her back against the headboard. Starling grabbed the magazines on her bedside table and put them between her and Ellis. As they absentmindedly leafed through the pages, they chatted easily about whatever came to mind. When Ellis saw a picture of a girl with long, dark straight hair, she said the first thing that came to her.

"How did Harley get to be such good friends with Vi and that group?" asked Ellis.

Starling laughed. "Where did that come from?"

Ellis laughed. "Harley just popped into my head. She was in front of me on my walk to school this morning. When I passed her on the Ida May steps, I think she said hi to me."

"Really?"

"I think so. . . . And you know what's really strange? When I got to Ms. Dockleaf's class, I swear Harley was turned around in her seat staring at me."

"Why do you think that?"

Ellis shrugged her shoulders. "I feel kind of bad for her. Maybe she's nicer when she's not around Vi."

"I don't know," said Starling, sounding unconvinced.

"I'm not saying I want to be friends with her or anything. It just sort of seems like maybe we shouldn't think of her in the same way as Vi," rambled Ellis.

The front door opened and voices traveled up the staircase. Starling closed the magazine in her lap and jumped off the bed. "Let's go. Sounds like mom and dad are home."

Ellis and Starling hurried down the stairs. The aroma of pizza filled the living room.

"Hi girls," said Mrs. Archer.

In unison, Ellis and Starling said hi and then giggled.

"Help me out. Take the pizza to the kitchen and let's have dinner."

Starling took the pie from her mother's outstretched arm and she and Ellis headed into the kitchen.

"That smells sooo good," said Ellis.

Starling agreed as she filled glasses of water and Ellis set the table.

Mr. and Mrs. Archer walked into the kitchen and the four of them sat down to dinner. Ellis suddenly missed the presence of Kestrel and Myna. The last time she visited, the kitchen had a steaming pot of pasta going and it was bustling with the activity of a large family. Ellis had enjoyed the noise and energy, which was so unlike the way things were with just Hen and Ellis in their house.

The one-to-one ratio of parent to kid had Ellis wiping her

hands on her jeans before she had her first bite of pizza. Ellis was grateful the conversation started out as an update on Heron. The Archers had spoken to Heron the night before and this was their first chance to fill Starling in on the classes he was taking and how college life is.

Starling served Ellis a second piece of pizza, which she hungrily lifted to her mouth just as Mrs. Archer said, "Ellis, it's nice that you're staying over."

"Thank you for having me," responded Ellis, cheese sliding from the vertex of the triangular slice she was about to put in her mouth.

Mr. Archer picked up the conversation, directing his question to Starling. Ellis took the opportunity to bite into her pizza. "What do you girls have planned for tomorrow?"

"Jules invited us over to the Factory to watch him work," said Starling.

Mrs. Archer nodded her head, "Mmm, Dr. Connor said that Jules was trying to create realistic models from glass."

"Yes, he showed us some sketches," said Starling. "They look amazing."

Ellis nodded in agreement.

"I hear he's very talented," said Mr. Archer.

"We are leaving early to go hiking with our birding group," informed Mrs. Archer. "You girls will have to get off on your own."

"No problem," said Starling.

Chapter 24 ~ The Factory

Starling's alarm felt like a rude awakening. Ellis was barely able to open her eyes when Starling grumbled that it was time to get up and that they had to hurry if they wanted to meet up with Jules by nine.

Ellis continued to lie in bed for a few minutes more as she listened, with her eyes closed, to Starling tromp off to the bathroom. When Ellis heard the water running, she knew she couldn't put off rising any longer. She dragged her body from the bed and then squinted at herself in the dresser mirror. Her hair was messy and her face had bed wrinkles. She remembered last looking at the clock when it read 2:20 am. She and Starling had stayed up until well past midnight talking in Starling's room and then when Starling's mother said it was time for lights out, Ellis and Starling whispered in bed in the dark until well past two, using their hands to press tightly against their own mouths in an attempt to smother the uncontrollable bursts of giggles and laughter.

"We have to hurry," said Starling, bursting back into the room, her hair now pulled back into a low ponytail. She grabbed a pair of sweatpants out of the dresser Ellis was standing by and began hurriedly dressing. Ellis grabbed her bag and headed for the bathroom.

Within ten minutes Ellis and Starling were in the kitchen looking for something to eat on the go. The house was quiet. There was evidence that Starling's parents had made coffee and breakfast, but they clearly left early for birding. Starling said

Kes and Myna would sleep for hours.

After rummaging around, Starling turned from the pantry with what looked like two protein bars in her hand and a couple of reusable water bottles dangling by their hooks from Starling's other hand. After filling the bottles, Starling packed them into a small backpack and handed Ellis a protein bar and signaled it was time to leave.

Ellis bit into an oatmeal raisin nut bar combination. It was a brisk morning. "Where's the Factory?" asked Ellis, remembering Starling referring to it last night. She thought Jules would be at Connor Glass.

"Oh," said Starling, realizing Ellis's confusion. "The Factory is the building beside Connor Glass. It's where they keep the large furnaces and annealing ovens."

"Do we still go into the other building? The one where we visited your parents?" asked Ellis, trying to sound nonchalant while hiding her disappointment at not going to the lab where her parents once worked.

Starling looked searchingly at Ellis, her eyes slightly narrowed. Ellis looked down at her feet, afraid of what her expression might reveal. They had turned onto the wooded path to Connor Glass, which was now cushioned with fallen leaves. With the early morning light and the bright tree canopies, the wooded trail was much less intimidating than the first time Ellis walked the path.

"No, the main building isn't open on the weekends except to the scientists with permission to go there," said Starling.

Ellis felt Starling continuing to look at her. She glanced up to see if Starling's expression had softened.

"Why do you want to go to the lab?" asked Starling in a challenging tone.

Ellis felt her face flush. She couldn't speak. She didn't want to lie, but she wasn't sure if she should tell the truth either. Ellis wasn't even sure if she *could* tell the truth. At times when she thought about her parent's disappearance, she had a hard time believing it was the truth.

Starling silently, politely looked away.

The sound of the rustling leaves below their feet as they walked on was suddenly deafening. It was all Ellis could hear. It was the sound of a wall going up between her and her only-ever best friend. Ellis pulled her incredibly damp hands from her jacket pockets and wiped her palms against her jeans.

"Starling —"

There was no response.

Ellis continued with her head hanging, watching her feet shuffle through the dew-dampened leaves. "Starling, I *need* to know more about my parents. I think they may have left behind some research. Hen said their research was really important to them — everything they did for Connor Glass meant a lot to them. I feel like I can connect with my parents by knowing more about what they did there."

Ellis wiped her hands against her jeans again. But this time, she felt relieved instead of nervous. She looked up to see Starling walking backwards, facing her. Starling's eyes sparkled and she had a mischievous smirk on her face.

Ellis arched her eyebrows.

"I love a good mystery," replied Starling with a broad smile.

"What?" laughed Ellis.

"After we visit Jules, we can check out all the old journals we have at home. My mother has kept every journal that mentions Connor Glass since she started working for them. Maybe they mention your parents' research," said Starling, as she turned back around.

Ellis excitedly thought about the photo of the journal article that she brought back from the last thread. Did she take the photo from a journal at Starling's house? Ellis didn't know which was more exciting; thinking that she may know where she was on the last thread, or the prospect of discovering more about her parents by going through journals while on her main thread — a thread where she remembers her actions.

They were at the boundary fence of Connor Glass. Starling led Ellis past the main entrance, which was gated and locked, and down a short path to another building.

The Factory was a tall, brick building that looked like it had been around for more than a century. Ellis saw a bright light dancing in the windows at one end of the building. When they walked inside, Ellis immediately noticed a figure dressed in heavy, white clothing and a face guard, carrying a long pole near an open furnace where a brilliant fire was burning.

Starling directed Ellis to walk to the other side so that they could get a closer look. When they settled on a position, Starling got close to Ellis and spoke loudly into her ear. The atmosphere was exciting. Music was blaring and the fire in the furnace roared. There were clanging and tapping noises and Jules appeared to be matching the beat of the music, working the molten glass blob into what Ellis guessed was one of his sketches.

"Jules is acting as the gaffer — the glass worker in charge of the project," said Starling, loudly enough for Ellis to hear. Starling used her thumb to point to something. For the first time, Ellis noticed another man standing near the furnace, apparently watching over the process. "That's Mr. Nigel. He's in charge of the Factory, so he must be here to help out Jules and to make sure everything goes okay."

Ellis smiled in wonderment. Jules was dipping a pole into what looked like a crucible of glowing yellow-orange liquid and then raising it up with a molten mass on the end.

"That rod is called a punty and Jules is *gathering* with it," informed Starling. "I'm not sure what he might be doing with the glass on the punty. . . . If gaffers want to make a vessel, they use a blowpipe, which looks kind of like a punty, except that it's hollow so the gaffer can blow air into the gathered glass."

Ellis nodded, not completely understanding what Starling was talking about but enjoying the information none the less. It was hot inside. Ellis pulled off her jacket and held it in her arms. They moved a few steps closer and Ellis now clearly recognized Jules behind the face shield.

Jules tossed his head in greeting and Ellis and Starling both waved back.

Starling moved closer to a tall table and Ellis followed. Starling pointed out powders, little pieces of colored glass, and what looked like metal shavings. "These are called frit — they are chips of colored glass used to add color to the object. The powder and metal shavings are used for color too. Hot glass can be rolled in the powder or shavings and then reheated to release the color."

Ellis gave a slight nod while looking closer at all the colored pieces, like little candy bits.

"Hey," a voice from behind called.

Ellis and Starling turned to see Jules walking toward them. He had pulled off the face mask and unbuckled the white jacket he was wearing.

"I got here really early because my dad said that Mr. Nigel can't stay past nine thirty."

Starling called a hello to Mr. Nigel and he raised a hand in response.

"I have something in the annealing oven. Do you want to take a look?"

"Sure," Starling nodded excitedly.

Jules lead the way to what looked similar to the pizza oven at the Pizza Den where Hen liked to order takeout on Fridays. The large metal box had a thick door with a long metal handle.

"The annealing oven is a type of kiln that gradually cools the glass so that it doesn't crack," said Starling.

"How hot are the ovens that melt the glass?" asked Ellis.

"About 2,200 degrees," answered Jules.

Jules picked up a large pair of insulated gloves, Kevlar gloves, Ellis later learned. He opened the door of the annealing oven and pulled out a delicate piece of ivory colored glass. Ellis recognized the shape immediately.

"It's honeycomb!"

Jules smiled.

The texture looked smooth and waxy just like real honeycomb. "It looks so real, Jules."

"Thanks. That's what I'm aiming for."

"What were you working on over at the furnace just now?" asked Starling.

"Actually, I'm trying to make a lifelike bee to place in one of the honeycomb cells," said Jules, as he guided them to the table where he had been working earlier. There rested the striped abdomen of a bee. The small gold and brown appendage was life sized and looked so realistic that Ellis shuddered.

"The challenging parts will be the wings, thorax, and head," said Jules absentmindedly, as he examined his work on the bee abdomen. "I'll make each of those separately and then attach them later." He seemed to be thinking out loud more than talking to his visitors.

Ellis jumped slightly when she heard a deep voice behind them. "Jules, I have to get going soon," said Mr. Nigel, approaching the table.

"Nice work, Jules." commented Mr. Nigel, looking down at the developing bee Jules was holding.

"Thanks, Mr. Nigel." Jules gently lay the bee abdomen back on the bench. "I'll take care of closing things up."

Mr. Nigel nodded his head and worked his way over to the furnace area where he seemed to be putting things away.

"What were you doing with the punty though?" asked Starling. Ellis was impressed with Starling's knowledge about glass making.

"Oh, that," said Jules, "I was combining some frit and other materials to try to get the color I'm looking for. If it's the color I want, I can melt it again later and use it in a project I'm planning."

Starling nodded knowingly. "Wow, you know a lot about glass to be able to make your own."

"I really like chemistry, and let's face it, my dad has taught me a lot," said Jules humbly.

The three of them lingered in silence for a few seconds. Jules absently looked around the room. Ellis followed his eyes. Mr. Nigel was grabbing his jacket. Starling also picked up on the signal that it was time to leave. Ellis pulled her jacket back on and after thanking Jules, she and Starling headed back outside.

Chapter 25 ~ Another Journal Article

"That was really amazing," said Ellis, as they walked away from the Factory.

Starling agreed. "I had no idea Jules knew how to work with glass like that."

Starling turned in a different direction from the path they took to the Factory. Before Ellis could ask why, Starling said, "Let's take a different way home. It's so nice out . . . we can explore a little." Ellis detected a hint of excitement in Starling's voice.

The unfamiliar path was well travelled, wider than the other trails Ellis had been on. Starling seemed confident about where she was going so Ellis relaxed and trusted her friend to lead the way. The sun was bright and the day crisp, still chilly even though the dew had dried from the leaves. Ellis followed along thinking about how her life might be different had she continued to live in Harper. She wondered how much she would know about glass. Would her parents have taken her to the lab and the Factory to teach her about glass? Jules was really interested in glass and art. But, Ellis thought consolingly, perhaps she wouldn't have been so interested even if she had grown up here.

"This way," said Starling, making a quick turn onto a less obvious path.

"How do you know your way around here so well?" asked Ellis, pulling a twig out of her hair.

"My parents are birders. They used to drag me and my

brother and sisters through these woods every weekend when we were younger. In the summer, we came out almost every evening. Most of the time I really hated having to tag along, but now I'm glad I know the trails so well. I don't think I could ever get lost in these woods." Starling was sounding breathless between the talking and the incline they were climbing. She grabbed the branch of a tree for support and then stopped walking. "Let's catch our breath," she panted. Starling swung the backpack around where she could get to the contents and handed Ellis a water bottle before grabbing the second bottle.

As Ellis sipped, she wondered if Starling had this detour in mind all along.

"Do you think about your parents a lot?" asked Starling, her voice softer than usual.

Ellis swallowed. "Yes."

"Do you miss them?"

"Hen is really great. She feels like a mom," said Ellis, and then paused, not really sure what else to say or how much to say. The conversation felt awkward. She had never before talked aloud to anyone besides Hen about her parents.

Ellis had been avoiding Starling's eyes, but when there was no immediate response to what she just said she looked up. Starling was listening intently. She was quiet, respectful. There was nothing in her expression to suggest that she thought Ellis was saying something odd. Feeling more confident, Ellis went on. "I miss not knowing what my life would have been like with my parents."

"Do you remember your parents at all?"

"No, I don't think so. I was only four when they left."

"Left?" said Starling in a high-pitched voice.

"Uhm — when they died," stammered Ellis.

Starling seemed distracted. "We moved here when I was four," she said thoughtfully.

They began walking again, slower. Ellis saw how the pieces might fit together, but she wasn't sure she wanted to believe in the possibility.

Ellis stole a glance at Starling to get a sense of what she was thinking.

Starling caught her eye. "Do you know what part of the lab your parents worked in?" she asked.

"No," answered Ellis. So they were both on the same track. "Do you know why your parents moved here?"

"No," said Starling.

They walked a few steps more. The quiet seemed to amplify their noisy footsteps on the leafy path and the sounds of the chirping birds. A chipmunk scurried across the path so close to Ellis's feet that it brushed against her shoe. She laughed nervously.

"Does it make you feel weird that my parents probably took over for your parents at the lab?" asked Starling candidly.

It had been said, and now it was real, thought Ellis. She lightly touched the palm of her hand to her suddenly lurching stomach. A light sheen of perspiration had cooled Ellis's forehead and she felt chilled. *Starling is in my life because my parents left my life. . . . I know Starling only because my parents disappeared.* The thoughts weighed heavily. Ellis needed more time to think about this.

Starling was waiting for an answer. Ellis shrugged her shoulders. "I don't know."

"Do you still want to go through the old journals?" asked Starling.

Ellis nodded. "I would love to." For now, Ellis decided, she would put off thinking about what ifs.

"Here we are," said Starling.

Ellis looked up to see Starling's back yard, and she laughed at her own lack of sense of direction. "We walked in a circle!"

Ellis and Starling entered a still quiet house. They pulled off their jackets and pushed them onto already loaded hooks on the tall bench by the front door. The house felt empty.

"Are your parents still out birding?" asked Ellis.

"They'll be gone until after lunch," said Starling. "And Kes is working and Myna is downtown with her friends."

They went into the kitchen and Starling put on the tea kettle. "Have a seat," said Starling, indicating a chair at the kitchen table as she disappeared through a door off the kitchen.

Ellis sat down at the table and looked around. She still felt unsettled about the circumstances of Starling's move to Muddy Creek. It really seemed that the Archers moved here to fill the positions of her parents.

A loud whistle pulled Ellis from her thoughts. She went over to the stove where steam was erupting from the kettle, condensation dripping down the back wall. Ellis found the control knob and turned the kettle off. Its scream was replaced by a loud thud. Ellis turned to see Starling standing beside a tall pile of journals that she had dropped onto the table.

"Here you go," she proclaimed.

Ellis walked back to the table and began leafing through the top periodical. "How many are there?

"Dozens. . . . I pulled the oldest ones first," Starling panted, as she pushed a curly wisp of hair out of her eyes.

Ellis grabbed the top journal and slid into a chair. She heard Starling rummaging around behind her making mugs of hot tea. When she sat down next to Ellis, Starling had paper and pencil in hand.

"Thanks," said Ellis, not lifting her head from the journal's table of contents, trying to determine which article was about Connor Glass.

"What are you looking for?" asked Starling, slurping her tea.

"I want to make a list of the Connor Glass projects mentioned and the date," said Ellis, her face in the journal. "How long before your parents come back?" she added, unable to keep the nervousness out of her voice.

"We have a couple hours," said Starling. "We're not really doing anything wrong, though. . . ."

Ellis looked up at Starling. At that very moment she wanted to tell Starling everything. Threads, the device, everything. But right now she had to focus on getting information from the journals. Ellis didn't know what this data mining might provide, but it felt useful, like she was doing *something* that might help her understand, and possibly find, her parents. "Thanks, Starling," was all that Ellis muttered.

Starling grabbed a couple journals from the pile and started flipping through them. "I'll let you know what I find. There is probably something in each of these journals — my mom seems to bring home only —"

"I found one!" shouted Ellis, cutting off Starling.

They leaned in together, heads touching, to read the article. It was entitled "Glass: Liquid or Solid?" by Connor Glass Laboratories:

We've all seen or heard about old panes of glass that are thicker at the bottom than at the top and likewise been told that it is due to the gravitational flow of the glass over hundreds of years. The glass flows, we are told, because it remains a liquid even at room temperature. There is much evidence to dispel this myth. (Actually, the process involved in making those old panes is the likely culprit for heaviness along the edge.) Glass is said to "melt" at approximately 2,200 degrees Fahrenheit at which point it can be blown, molded, or floated (to create float glass, i.e. sheet glass). The purpose of this article is to explore the molecular structure of glass as it transitions from liquid to solid in order to determine the . . .

"Wow, this isn't exactly light reading," said Starling.

Ellis nodded in agreement, but refused to feel discouraged. She knew there wasn't time to read all the articles today, or even some of the articles from the looks of it. Working through the scientific jargon alone appeared to be an insurmountable task. And Ellis couldn't imagine how understanding each article would help her find her parents. But at least she could try to track the research coming out of Connor Glass.

Ellis began writing the article title and the journal data and number on the sheet of paper Starling provided. The idea of collecting more information for her lab book felt good.

Starling picked up the next journal and began going through it.

Ellis flipped through the pages of the journal she was holding to see how long the *Liquid or Solid?* article was. It ended two pages later. Just as she was closing the journal, the last sentence of the article caught her eye. She opened to the page again and read:

Therefore, the state of glass must be viewed from the perspective of both time and space.

Ellis was transfixed. She stared at the words. *Perspective — time* — these were the words of her parents.

"Starling," whispered Ellis.

"Are you okay?"

Ellis cleared her throat and tried to speak in a normal tone. "Uhm, yes," her voice crackled. "Uh, can I take this journal and return it in a couple days?" Ellis felt her spine tingle. Was it déjà vu? Ellis looked at the pile of journals. Did Ellis take the journal picture in the last thread while staying at Starling's house? It seemed unlikely now that she knew Starling and her parents only moved to the area after Ellis's parents disappeared. So where was she when she took the journal picture?

"Yeah, sure. Just give it back to me at school and I'll slip it back in the pile later. My parents will never notice."

Ellis pushed the journal aside to separate it from the others. She shook her head to try and clear her mind and then picked up the next journal. . . .

Golden rays filtered through the drapes and illuminated the living room where Ellis and Starling sat curled up, talking and having another cup of tea. Ellis's backpack and overnight bag were with her jacket at the front door — the journal and the sheet of paper she and Starling filled out tucked between books in the backpack. Hen was due any minute.

Chapter 26 ~ Time and Space

Jules was already in his seat when Ellis and Starling walked into Mrs. Dockleaf's class. He acknowledged their arrival with just a head nod. Ellis and Starling each whispered back a "hi". Mrs. Dockleaf's back was to the class as she furiously wrote her notes on the white board. The bell rang. The only remaining sounds came from a few students rummaging through backpacks for their books and notebooks. It took only a class or two to learn that it was best to get quiet fast and stay quiet upon entering Mrs. Dockleaf's World History classroom.

With notebook open and pencil in hand, Ellis looked up at the board to begin taking notes. Upon reading the underlined topic at the top of the board, Ellis gave Starling a questioning look. Starling shrugged her shoulders in response and went back to her note taking.

Ellis wrote "The Trivium" and then continued copying the notes from the board. Unless she was seriously mistaken, the notes were about the park in downtown Harper, not Mesopotamia as they had been studying the class before. She learned that the park had been built in 1856 as a tribute to the town's founders and significant figures, and that trivium is Latin for the juncture of three roads. Other notes included the building of the war memorial, names of prominent war heroes, and the names of those responsible for getting The Trivium monument built. Ellis knew lots of kids gathered at the park after school, and she had seen The Trivium from a distance when she rode the Double Decker home with Starling, but Ellis had yet to walk over to the park.

Ellis continued scribbling down the notes from the board even as Mrs. Dockleaf faced the class to begin her lecture. She seemed a bit happier than usual and was sort of bouncy as she walked back and forth across the front of the room talking about The Trivium.

"The reason for the diversion from Mesopotamia, class," said Mrs. Dockleaf in a rather slow, serious tone, "is that we are having our annual Harper Fall Festival this weekend." She waited a moment before going on as if the seriousness of the subject matter needed time to be fully comprehended. "This year, I am pleased to announce that I have been invited to unveil the new plaque that honors our more recent military heroes." Mrs. Dockleaf paused, her eyes darted back and forth scanning the students, and then she cleared her throat with a loud "Umm hmm."

The class sat silently, unsure as to what their response should be. Ellis looked around. Should they *clap*, she wondered. The silence continued.

Mrs. Dockleaf looked at the class for a moment, and then said, "Well — so — I decided we will discuss the history and relevance of this important Harper festival." With that, Mrs. Dockleaf went back to her usual monotone and Ellis heard everything she thought she could ever want to know about the Harper Fall Festival and its origins (which are based on celebrating the peak of the fall foliage).

The bell finally rang and Ellis and Starling grabbed their bags and headed out of the room. Just outside the door, Ellis looked at Starling and rolled her eyes.

Starling laughed, and then said, "The Fall Festival is actually a lot of fun. There will be all kinds of food and music."

"And it's this weekend?" asked Ellis. "Are you going?"

"Maybe . . . depends on if Kes will bring me in. . . ."

Ellis thought about her weekend plans — she wanted to try

a new thread. But what came out of her mouth next was, "I'll talk to Hen. I'll convince her to let you stay over Friday and then we can go to the Festival together on Saturday!" Ellis looked hopefully at Starling who was nodding her head and smiling back before Ellis had even finished her sentence.

Ellis neared her house. She was less than a block away. She wiped her palms on her jeans for the third time since she left Ida May. She slowed her walking to give herself more time to organize her thoughts. She planned to ask Hen to allow Starling to stay over on Friday night. And then she would ask Hen about visiting another thread after school on Thursday. Ellis was more excited than nervous, but the feeling seemed to render the same heart-racing effect.

Before Ellis got to the walkway leading up to her front door, she stepped off the sidewalk and cut through her yard to walk around to the side door which opened directly into the kitchen. As she kicked up the leaves in her path, Ellis remembered her promise to Hen to rake the yard this weekend. "Ugh!" she grimaced.

She stepped onto the leaf-covered stepping stones — a path made from the same type of stones that were used to build her house — and then onto a small side porch before opening the kitchen door. The room was warm compared to the brisk air outside and fully lit to offset the overcast skies and dusky fall afternoon pushing its way in through the many windows of their house. Hen was at the table, her computer and several papers in front of her.

"Hi Hen," said Ellis warily. Hen looked up from her computer. Ellis was always impressed by how computer savvy her grandmother was.

"How was your day?"

"Good," said Ellis, as she pulled out a chair and took a seat at the table. "What are you working on?"

"Well . . ." said Hen in a mysterious way, "There is a downtown festival this weekend. It's called the Harper Fall Festival."

Ellis couldn't believe her ears. She continued to listen excitedly, wondering what Hen's connection was to the festival.

"Tori has decided to have a booth there with A Priori books and merchandise, and I've agreed to help her. I'm making an order form and a flyer." Hen lifted a printout from the table. Ellis recognized the A Priori logo.

"Are you going to *go* to the festival?" asked Ellis teasingly. Ellis knew Hen typically stayed away from events where there were lots of people, especially lots of people that knew her or Ellis. The few times Ellis attended an elementary classmate's birthday party, Hen dropped her at the door without staying, saying she had an errand to run. Since Ellis was usually only invited to parties that included the whole class, she was left feeling even more awkward about attending because her invitation was simply a matter of etiquette and had little to do with friendship.

Hen looked at Ellis suspiciously. "Do you know something?"

Ellis laughed, "Mrs. Dockleaf was talking about the festival in class today. Starling said it's a lot of fun."

Hen nodded her head. "Yes, lots of music and food and from what I can remember all the big oaks, maples, elms, and sassafras in The Trivium are usually at peak fall colors — they look amazing." Hen seemed to be looking through her mind's eye at the fall trees before she looked back at Ellis and said, "I hear the weather will be perfect this weekend — an Indian summer."

As excited as Ellis was about the festival, she sat silently, working out how to ask Hen for a sleepover.

Hen must have thought that Ellis's silence was in anticipation of the answer to her earlier question because she suddenly said, "Yes, I will be working the booth at the festival."

Ellis smiled. "Hen . . ."

"Yes?"

"Do you think maybe Starling can sleep over Friday after school so that we can go to the festival together on Saturday?" Ellis sat on her hands to keep them still.

Hen looked up with an *I didn't expect this* look, but didn't immediately say no. Ellis took the opportunity to plead her case.

"Please. Starling might not be able to get a ride to the festival on Saturday. We really want to go together." Ellis gave her most anguished look. With head tilted and eyebrows tightly knitted, she pulled her hands out from under her legs and pressed them together in front of her as if in prayer. "Pleeease."

Hen was obviously in a good mood. She laughed at Ellis's intensity and said, "Okay."

Ellis, shocked, jumped up from her chair. "Are you serious?"

"Yes," Hen nodded.

Ellis gave Hen a quick squeeze and then grabbed her backpack and took the stairs two at a time. She was too happy to risk disappointment — Ellis would wait until tomorrow to ask about visiting another thread.

A creak so familiar that Ellis no longer heard it sounded as she stepped onto the threshold of her bedroom. An underhand swing landed her backpack on the unmade bed on her way to the desk. Ellis sat down and, as if seeing her room for the first time, noticed that the wastebasket was overflowing and some clothes were piled in a corner. She reminded herself to clean up her room before Friday for her first-time ever sleepover at her house.

Ellis pulled the lab book out of her desk drawer and paged through it. She had taped the list of journal articles to the next empty page and on the facing page she wrote her notes. One note related to an article published last year entitled "Glass Filtration Systems for the Purification of Salt Water." The writing on the list was in Starling's hand. Ellis hadn't looked over the list until the day after the sleepover at Starling's. When she first saw the title, Ellis felt a gush of pride. Her parents must have brought back data from another thread to get the filtration project started in their main thread. Ellis even felt a sense of camaraderie with her parents knowing that perhaps the last thread she visited may have been the same one her parents visited to get the filtration data. But now, as she stared at her notes, a sense of loss surfaced, turning to anger that this is all she had of her parents.

Pushing aside the urge to slam the lab book closed, Ellis again looked over the words she quoted from the "Glass: Liquid or Solid?" article: "the state of glass must be viewed from the perspective of both time and space." Her parents had said the glass device changed perspective. And the glass device somehow transported a person to a different time and space.

Ellis had read the article in full after she got home from Starling's. She really didn't understand a lot of the technical information, but illustrations showed that the molecules in solid glass have the same chaotic structure as the molecules in liquid glass. There was no way to distinguish the two without bringing in the factor of time.

Most solids, Ellis remembered from science class, had an organized structure of atoms and as the material melted or liquefied, the atoms scattered in an unorganized way just as an ice cube goes from being a structure with a defined shape to a puddle of water that takes on the shape of whatever holds it. The article shows that the only difference between liquid glass and solid glass is time and space. Perspective, time, and space. The words resonated with Ellis and she was sure they were related to the discovery made by Maeve and Aiden Bell.

Chapter 27 ~ Harley's House

Friday morning arrived. Ellis was resentful at first when Hen had said no to a thread visit on Thursday, but the hard feelings passed as quickly as the days. By Thursday afternoon Ellis still hadn't redd up her room, so she felt relieved to have the time to prepare for Starling's visit. She hoped for as much fun at her sleepover as she had with Starling two weeks ago.

"Good mornin' Hen," Ellis sang out cheerfully.

"Good morning," mumbled Hen distractedly, holding a tea cup in one hand and some papers in another. She was reading the papers intently while standing by the O'Keefe & Merritt where a cup of already dark black tea was still steeping.

"Is this for me?" asked Ellis, picking up the cup of overly steeped tea.

Hen simply nodded.

"What are you looking at?"

"Double-checking the flyers for the festival."

Ellis sat down at the table and began spreading jam on a piece of toast. She took a bite before getting back up to serve herself some scrambled eggs from the stove.

"Hen . . ." said Ellis, scooping eggs onto her plate.

"Yes," said Hen, this time looking up from the papers, her eyes a bit bleary.

"Starling and I want to walk around town for a while after school." Ellis sat down again, this time her plate full of eggs. She pushed her eggs around with her fork, keeping her eyes down. Hen had mentioned that A Priori would be closing early to get ready for the festival tomorrow. Ellis secretly thought this would be the perfect opportunity to take Starling there to show her the mysterious entrance to The Apothecary.

"Promise me you'll stay together. And be home before dark."

"I promise," said Ellis, looking up now and smiling at her grandmother before she began shoveling down her eggs.

Ellis stepped outside wearing a pullover cotton cable knit sweater and a light denim jacket with jeans. The sky was spotlessly blue. Red, orange, yellow, and a few green leaves clung precariously to the oaks, elms, and maples that lined the streets of Harper. The vibrancy of the palette energized Ellis as she walked to school. The Indian summer Hen forecast was here.

Ida May was buzzing with excitement. Mrs. Dockleaf suspended her regular lesson and talked again about the history of Harper. Judging by the way she kept glancing at some notes spread out on her desk, Ellis had the suspicion that Mrs. Dockleaf was practicing at least part of her speech for tomorrow on them. But her unusually light mood was contagious and everyone listened attentively without grimacing. Mrs. Dockleaf didn't even take notice of the occasional whisper between excited students talking about their weekend plans. Ellis wanted to ask Jules if he planned to be at the festival, but every time she looked over at him he was staring into his notebook, doodling absentmindedly. Ellis shot a questioning glance to Starling who just shrugged her shoulders as if to say *I don't know what's bothering him.*

The rest of the morning seemed to follow suit. Teachers were allowing group work (which in reality meant that kids gathered in groups and talked about the upcoming weekend), off topic discussions (which festival group will have the best music), and shorter lectures with time to do homework in class (kids whispered amongst themselves about the weekend).

Ellis and Starling were stowing books in their lockers when Jules walked by. "Hey Jules . . . do you want to come to lunch with us?" Starling called out.

Jules paused and looked over at them. He had a distracted look on his face and clearly he hadn't heard Starling's question.

"Do you want to come to lunch with us?" repeated Starling.

"Uh, no thanks. I have to do something," He half smiled and looked apologetic before walking away.

"What does that mean?" asked Ellis, pressing her locker shut with a click.

Starling shrugged her shoulders. "He definitely has something on his mind."

They walked down the staircase, Ellis lightly dragging her hand along the smooth wooden banister, discussing how much fun it will be to walk around town tomorrow for the festival.

Ellis and Starling pushed through the center double doors and walked down the stone steps, catching glimpses of a transformation over at The Trivium. Even with little time to spare, they couldn't resist first walking to the edge of the park for a preview of the festival.

The canopy of the tall oak trees surrounding the school was now completely bright red-orange. Ellis and Starling made their way under the fiery cover, an occasional leaf drifting onto the path as they walked to the corner of East North and Locust.

"Wow," exclaimed Ellis. The Trivium was obviously the center of the festival. Dozens of canopy tents filled the grassy areas, and a parking lot at one end was being transformed into a pumpkin patch. Workers in a bucket brigade unloaded the truck, passing pumpkins person to person, from the truck to a bed of straw covering the asphalt. A few other workers continued to lay down straw, expanding the bed for more pumpkins.

"Come on . . . we still have to eat lunch," said Starling, as she teasingly tugged at Ellis's sleeve.

"Wait. Look." Ellis pointed to the canopy tents along the far edge of the Trivium. "That looks like Jules!"

Starling squinted. "Yeah, that looks like him. . . ."

"What is he doing over there?"

Starling was quiet with a thoughtful expression.

"What?"

"I'm not sure," said Starling. "Let's go to lunch."

They turned around and headed their usual route to Main Street where even the day before the festival, the street was busier than usual. A huge banner had been hung high at Leo Street, spanning the light posts from one side of Main Street to the other, announcing the Annual Harper Fall Festival. Smaller banners attached to the other lamp posts up and down Main flapped in the easy breeze.

Ellis and Starling stepped into Hots for lunch — they were both hungry for fries. The table in the booth closest to the door was piled high with Hots boxes — a one-piece plain white cardboard box with flaps on the lid that tuck into the sides, the perfect size for a row of hots or a pie. Since these boxes were free of the telltale signs of grease, Ellis guessed they were for the Hots pies that everyone in Harper seemed to love. When they got closer, Ellis saw each had a sticker on the side with a pie name — apple, pumpkin, shoo fly, lemon meringue, chocolate meringue, and chocolate pecan.

"Look at all the pies," laughed Ellis.

"They sell a ton of pies at the festival," said Starling. "Actually, all the stores on Main will have sidewalk sales. And most of the restaurants will sell food from sidewalk stands." She rubbed her hands together and smiled in anticipation.

Ellis laughed. She and Starling loved to eat. They both agreed lunch was their favorite subject.

Their hots and fries were delivered within minutes as usual, but Ellis and Starling were running late. They wolfed down their food without speaking again until they were ready to leave the restaurant.

"What are we doing after school?" asked Starling, as they started back for school.

They walked at a quick pace. "Do you want to go to A Priori and The Apothecary?" asked Ellis, tying her jacket around her waist because it was too warm outside to wear it.

"Yeah!" Starling replied enthusiastically — just as Ellis had expected.

"We'll go to A Priori first — I want to show you something," said Ellis, trying to feign indifference and not fooling Starling at all.

"What?" Starling smiled brightly, knowing full well that her question would go unanswered.

"You'll see . . ." chuckled Ellis.

Ellis and Starling ran up the stairs and into Ida May just as the bell rang. The classes after lunch had the same Fall Festival excitement going as the morning classes. However, Ellis found herself wondering what was going on with Jules. He was quiet for the rest of the day and every chance Ellis thought she might be able to talk to him he suddenly became busy with a book or notes.

The cloudless sky made for a bright afternoon even with the shorter days. Ellis and Starling decided to drop their bags and books at Ellis's house before walking to A Priori.

"Hi, Hen," Ellis called out, the kitchen empty. She dropped her bag at the foot of the stairs and then helped Starling with her bags.

"Hen!" Ellis called again.

"Are you home?" asked Hen, her voice coming from the top of the stairs.

Ellis walked over to the bottom step and looked up at her grandmother. "We're just dropping our stuff off. We'll be home before dark." Ellis noticed dark circles under Hen eyes as she gave a quick wave and smile.

"Let's go down a different street," suggested Starling. "They all lead toward A Priori. We can do some exploring. Have you been down any side streets?"

Ellis shrugged her shoulders. All she could think about was showing Starling the secret entrance to The Apothecary. At the moment she felt a little annoyed that Starling wanted to take a different route.

"Let's take this street to A Priori," persisted Starling.

Ellis followed, at first feeling a bit resentful, but soon decided she was being silly. After all they were heading in the right direction.

"Look at the tower on that house," Starling pointed out. The street they had turned onto boasted one Victorian house after another.

Ellis nodded in agreement. The round tower looked like something from a castle. It was really cool. Ellis was enjoying the new route. *These houses are beautiful*, she thought.

Ellis and Starling began picking out their favorite features on each house. Ellis really liked the wrap-around porches. Starling was oohing and aahing over the stained glass windows.

"This is a great house," said Starling when they got to one of the bigger houses they had seen so far. It had an octagonal turret and a large, wrap-around front porch with gingerbread trim.

Ellis stopped to look longer. She was drawn to the house. She found herself staring at the front door, which was unusually wide with carved wooden panels. She saw the metal ring door knob and in that moment she knew her subconscious was aware of something she was not. Ellis felt her spine tingle and the sensation proceeded all the way up to her scalp. Her hair raised on the goose bumps that formed. She shivered.

"I know this house," Ellis heard herself say, but didn't know why she was saying it.

"Yeah," laughed Starling, as if to say *of course you do*. "This is where Harley lives."

Ellis looked at Starling.

"You didn't know that?" asked Starling, seeing Ellis's surprised expression. "Are you okay? You look pale."

Ellis nodded almost imperceptibly.

"Harley lives here?" said Ellis just above a whisper.

"Maybe you were friends before you moved away — you know, when you were really little," suggested Starling.

"Yeah, maybe," Ellis said. "It just feels really familiar. Like I was here recently."

"I think you would remember hanging out with Harley," laughed Starling. "Come on, let's get moving. We won't have much time at A Priori Books and The Apothecary if we have to be home by dark."

They started walking again. Ellis knew now what déjà vu truly feels like.

Chapter 28 ~ Starling's Timeline

A Priori had a Closed sign hanging in its window, but as Ellis had hoped, Tori was moving around inside.

Ellis tapped on the glass window. Tori looked up, at first with a blank expression. When she recognized Ellis and Starling, she waved and walked toward the door.

"Hi, ladies," Tori smiled warmly. Her hair was in its usual bun, but it looked especially disheveled. Many strands were sticking out from the bun and a few wisps of hair were hanging down onto her shoulders. "I closed early today to get ready for the festival."

At first Ellis thought that Tori wasn't going to invite them in because she stood in front of the open door, blocking their way.

"We wanted to stop by anyway. I hope you don't mind," said Ellis. "Starling is sleeping over tonight." Ellis added this last bit of information as she silently willed Tori to understand how much she wanted to show Starling around.

"Come in, come in," said Tori apologetically. "Of course, you're welcome to stop by." Tori pushed the door open wider and welcomed the girls in. She tucked a few tendrils of hair behind her ear just to have them fall again as soon as she moved her hand away.

"I've never set up at the Harper Festival before, so I'm trying to figure out what will work best at the booth," Tori looked around the store, like she was searching for items to put in the booth.

"Can I show Starling around?" blurted Ellis.

"Uh, sure . . ." said Tori, sounding confused.

Starling had wandered a short distance away to look at a display of new novels. Ellis leaned in close to Tori and whispered nervously, "Can I show her the secret entrance to The Apothecary?"

Tori chuckled. "Okay. Dad is putting together bags of candy for his booth." Tori glanced toward the secret entrance. "Close the shelf behind you after you go through," she added.

As Tori moved back to the boxes she was filling for tomorrow, Ellis walked over to Starling.

"What's going on?" Starling had obviously seen Ellis whispering to Tori.

"I want to show you something," said Ellis, grabbing Starling by the hand. "Follow me."

They walked down the long aisle of books. It wasn't nearly as dark and secretive looking as Ellis remembered. Starling was quiet but when Ellis looked at her she had a smile on her face and her eyes sparkled.

"Okay, we're here," said Ellis.

"Here?" Starling examined the bookshelf. She bent over to look on the lower shelves and then stood on her tippy toes to see the higher shelves. "Am I missing something?"

Ellis reached out and rested her hand on the purple and white starlight candy bookend. She had Starling's attention. Unsure of what to expect, Ellis placed her free hand in front of the bookend for fear of having it drop off the shelf. But as she pulled on the bookend, Ellis could tell by the resistance that it was somehow attached to the shelf and wouldn't come off.

Ellis continued to pull the bookend toward herself and Starling, who was excitedly staring at the moving bookend. Ellis felt a latch give and the shelf swung outward with a soft click.

"What's in there?" asked Starling in wonderment.

Ellis stepped into the sweet smelling room and then waved Starling in before shutting the shelf door. "We're in The Apothecary!"

"This is amazing," said Starling, shaking her head in disbelief.

"Hello?"

Both Ellis and Starling were startled by the sound of Mr. Neumann's deep voice.

"Hi — It's Ellis," Ellis called out.

Mr. Neumann appeared from around the corner and entered the room where Ellis and Starling were standing.

Ellis felt her face heat up. "Uh . . . Tori said it was okay to come through the secret passage."

"Of course, of course," said Mr. Neumann kindly. "I'm working to get ready for the festival tomorrow. You girls help yourself. I'm going to get back to filling bags."

Mr. Neumann grabbed a handful of plastic bags from the counter of the pass-through window and then left the room.

"Wow, it's like a science lab in here with all those jars of stuff," said Starling, as she walked toward the glass-stoppered jars. "What is all this?" She lifted the jar of vanilla beans and examined the long brown wrinkled specimens through the glass.

Ellis looked closely at the labeled jars. The salts were beautiful. Pink, tan, black, and white. All lined up. Some salts were chunky pieces, others looked like fine sand. Seeing it brought to mind playing in the sand at one of the children's areas in New York's Central Park. New York City was one of the first places she moved to with Hen. Every Saturday Hen took Ellis to the park and while Hen sat nearby poring over books from the university libraries, Ellis played in the sand, sifting it through her fingers.

"Mr. Neumann was friends with my parents," said Ellis, more to herself than anyone else.

"What?" said Starling.

"I was just thinking that Mr. Neumann might know who I was friends with when I lived here before," pondered Ellis. "Let's go talk to him."

"Yeah, and maybe we'll learn more about Tori and the bookstore," said Starling.

They walked through the deserted candy shop until they found Mr. Neumann sitting at a booth stuffing bags with hard candies from a large bowl. As they approached the table, Ellis saw candies shaped like leaves in colors of red, orange, yellow, and green.

"Hi, Mr. Neumann," said Ellis cheerfully. Even though she hadn't spent much time developing a friendship with him, Mr. Neumann's easy-going personality and kind disposition made Ellis feel happy when she was around him. Ellis had calculated that he was a little older than her father would be, so she considered him a grandfather type.

Mr. Neumann smiled and waved a hand toward the chairs at the next table. "Pull up some chairs girls. Please. And help yourself to my fall treats — the red leaves have a hint of cinnamon, the yellow are a warm vanilla, the orange is a pumpkin spice, and the green tastes like pure maple syrup. They all have a hint of maple flavor because I used maple sugar to sweeten them."

Ellis and Starling pulled two chairs closer to the booth and used the large serving spoon to retrieve two candies. The yellow elm leaf shaped candy melted in Ellis's mouth with a wonderful flavor of sweet vanilla.

"Mr. Neumann," said Ellis, suddenly feeling very awkward and a little embarrassed.

"Yes," he looked up from his work.

"Well, I just wondered if you knew much about me before I left Harper. You know — before I moved away with Hen." Ellis was so nervous she almost choked on the candy.

"Like what, Ellis?"

"Well, like, who I might have been friends with," Ellis hesitated, not sure herself of what exactly she wanted to know, and suddenly feeling desperate about defending her question. "Jules Connor said he used to go to A Priori for story hour with me. Do you know who else I was friends with?"

Mr. Neumann had a thoughtful expression before he looked down at the bag in his hand and continued to fill it. "You were very young when you first lived here. If my wife were still alive she could tell you more because she ran the bookstore and was close to all the parents who came in with their children." Mr. Neumann placed a tie on the bag and picked up another.

After a brief pause, he added, "I remember that you were always with Harley Slade." Mr. Neumann stopped filling the bag before he went on. "She was very sad when you left. Your parents worked closely with her mother, so I have the impression you two spent a lot of time together."

Ellis couldn't believe what she was hearing. "Harley? Are you sure?" She asked.

Mr. Neumann nodded his head. "Yes, I do remember that."

That might explain the déjà vu feeling Ellis had when they saw Harley's house. It might also explain Harley's odd attempts to connect with Ellis, like the quick hi as she passed Ellis on the stairs that morning, and the time that Ellis thought she caught Harley staring at her in the classroom. But this information from Mr. Neumann didn't feel like enough. It wasn't satisfying Ellis. Besides, how could she have such a strong impression from seeing Harley's house when other places in Harper didn't leave her with a feeling of déjà vu? Ellis was even more convinced that Harley's house had something to do with her last thread.

Ellis blurted out her next thought. "What about Tori?" Ellis obviously had Mr. Neumann's attention. "Did she babysit me? Maybe she knows more about my past."

Mr. Neumann had a guarded look. "No, no," he answered, dismissing the notion too casually, Ellis thought. "Tori never babysat you. She was too young at the time. Just a young teenager." He seemed to be pushing Ellis away from the idea that Tori might remember something.

Before Ellis could decide which question to ask next, Starling asked, "Mr. Neumann, why is the bookstore named A Priori?"

Ellis felt a little put off that Starling had jumped in and completely changed the subject — and with such a random question, but then she saw Mr. Neumann relax. He smiled.

"A priori is knowledge based on reason. A priori knowledge is independent of physical experiences like touching, listening, or seeing," Mr. Neumann paused and stopped filling the candy bag. He had a faraway look in his eyes. "In other words, the bookstore is full of opportunities to read about new ideas which ignite our thinking, from which we generate new knowledge."

Mr. Neumann went back to filling the bag. Ellis wasn't quite sure she understood his explanation of a priori, but Starling pursued the subject. "Did Mrs. Neumann pick the name for the bookstore?"

"Yes, she did." He looked squarely at Ellis and Starling. "Catherine, Mrs. Neumann, understood that we must go beyond physical experiences to believe in the possibility of new ideas. . . . Time, for example."

It was Ellis's turn to jump in and continue the conversation. "Time? I don't understand."

"Time is an a priori concept. We use it to order the events in our life. We don't need to feel it or see it or hear it to know that it is there. However, there may be aspects of time that we don't understand or perhaps don't even know about. For example, is there only one timeline? Or are there many instances of time going on simultaneously? If we think and study enough, can we figure out a way to move back and forth in time? On the other hand, if we sit idly by and not think about concepts such as time, we may miss out on the opportunity to experience all that there is," said Mr. Neumann, before he abruptly stopped, perhaps feeling like he divulged too much.

Starling looked at Ellis and raised her eyebrows slightly. Ellis gave a barely perceptible shoulder shrug and avoided full eye contact altogether. Ellis had a better idea of what Mr. Neumann was getting at than she wanted to let on.

Ellis glanced out the window at the dusky sky. "We better go. I promised to be home before dark." Ellis had hoped to find out so much more and the disappointment came out in her voice.

Mr. Neumann handed them each a bag of candies. "Ellis, who you were when you first lived here doesn't matter as much as who you are now."

Although Ellis knew she should appreciate the sage advice, all she could manage was a muffled thanks before she and Starling went out Mr. Neumann's front door, bypassing A Priori Books altogether.

They were barely off Bourner Street when Starling brought up the conversation with Mr. Neumann.

"What do you think he meant by all the timeline stuff?" asked Starling, a candy clicking against her teeth.

Ellis didn't want to reveal too much, but she decided there was no harm in discussing what Starling had heard. "I'm not sure. Maybe he thinks there are different timelines. The timelines have all the same people, but living different lives. If we could hop onto a different timeline, then we could see all the same people, but they might have different personalities because they are living under a different set of choices and circumstances."

Judging by Starling's face, Ellis thought she had revealed too much, and then Starling broke out into a laugh, "How did you come up with that!" she said. "Wow, that's really using your imagination."

Relieved, Ellis laughed back.

"Actually," said Starling, "that's an interesting way to think of things. . . ." her voice trailed off and she looked down at the ground as she walked. She appeared to be concentrating hard on the possibility of different timelines.

They had decided to walk back the way they came. Harley's house was up ahead and this time Ellis felt for sure that she had been in the house recently. She made a mental note to record everything she learned today in her lab book.

At home, Hen was still busy with festival preparations, so she asked Ellis to order Chinese for dinner. As Ellis expected, Hen kept herself busy in the library while she and Starling ate lo mein together in the kitchen. It was only after she and Starling headed up the stairs that Ellis heard Hen walk into the kitchen.

Starling plopped down onto Ellis's bed. "You know, I was thinking . . ." she said.

Ellis felt happy seeing her friend so comfortable in her room. "Yessss . . ." Ellis, sitting in her desk chair, giggled light heartedly.

"The timeline theory," said Starling in a more serious tone. "You know it's possible that you and I would never have met if you hadn't moved away and then come back," and then more sheepishly, she added, "— if *my* parents hadn't filled the positions *your* parents had." Starling seemed to be holding her breath, waiting for a response.

Ellis had been avoiding this subject. She didn't even allow herself to think about it much when she was alone. It made her feel uncomfortable.

"Yeah" was all Ellis could manage.

"Well, back to the timeline theory . . . isn't it weird to think that maybe on a different timeline you're living in this house and your parents are working at Connor Glass and you're friends with Jules and *Harley* (Starling emphasized Harley's name in a joking way) and I'm living some other life?"

As startling as Starling's revelation was, Ellis had to restrain the giddiness she felt well up inside of her. It was like Starling knew all about the device and timelines without Ellis even telling her. She wanted to share everything with her right then and there. Instead, Ellis closed her eyes, for only a second, but it was enough time to strengthen her resolve to keep the secret that Hen and Tori entrusted in her. "It's really weird to think about," said Ellis.

"But here we are on the same timeline, so it seems like this is the way it was meant to be. . . ." Starling trailed off.

It was still all too much for Ellis to understand. And now that they were talking about it, Ellis wished she had visited a thread yesterday.

Chapter 29 ~ Harper Fall Festival

"Ellis . . . Ellis," someone whispered. Ellis opened her eyes just enough to see a white head of hair poking through the cracked open door.

"I'm leaving," whispered Hen.

Ellis lifted her head enough to nod an acknowledgment and then she let her heavy head drop back to her pillow as she heard the door softly close. Ellis was too tired for her eyes to bring the digital clock into focus, but she knew it must be about 6:00 am because that's the time Hen had told her she needed to meet Tori to set up the A Priori booth. Ellis drifted back to sleep feeling happy that she and Hen had great friends and fun things to do.

The shower was still running so Ellis kept writing. She updated her lab book with the clues from yesterday, including the déjà vu feeling when she saw Harley's house and the timelines discussion with Mr. Neumann. Ellis was pushing the notebook to the back of the desk drawer when she heard the bathroom door open. Within seconds, Starling came walking into the bedroom, her hair in a wrapped tightly towel.

Ellis dressed quickly and then she and Starling headed out to Madder Drinks for breakfast. The air was cool with a promise of warming up under the bright sunshine and clear sky, like a spring morning, rather than a fall day.

"You've lived in a lot of different places," Starling began, "do you miss your other friends?"

At first Ellis didn't understand Starling's question. And

then she laughed out loud. "I really didn't have any other friends," replied Ellis truthfully, feeling only a little intimidated by what Starling might think about a girl who never had friends until now. "When I think about all the other places I've lived, I feel like I was simply visiting."

"Really?" said Starling disbelievingly.

"Yeah," said Ellis, nodding because the realization was new to her as well.

"But you lived in some great places — New York, DC, Boston," Starling looked at Ellis with admiration in her eyes.

"It really doesn't seem that special to me. But, we did see some amazing sites," said Ellis, reflecting on the past few years. "Hen and I went on outings nearly every weekend. She can be like a kid herself."

"I think it sounds like fun," pressed Starling.

Trying to keep the frustration out of her voice, Ellis said, "And I think living in the same house and town all my life sounds like fun."

"So you really didn't have many friends?"

"No — I never really connected with anyone. But then again I never went to a school where I ate out for lunch every day, and I never lived near a downtown that Hen would allow me to walk around in, and I never felt so *at home*. Now that I'm living in Harper, I feel like I'm where I should be. I don't feel like a *visitor*."

Madder Drinks was packed. Ellis and Starling jostled their way through the line and ordered lattes and kiffles (which Ellis mistakenly called a croissant the first time she ordered one). They didn't even bother to try and find a place to sit — every inch was claimed. Instead, they squeezed their way through the unending stream of incoming and popped back out into the cool, fresh air.

Ellis had never seen Main Street so busy. It was still early, but Ellis had promised to check in with Hen when they got downtown, so they walked at a start and stop pace toward The Trivium, eating and glancing at the sidewalk sales.

The festival was set up throughout the park, with booths grouped in grassy areas between the large trees. Many of the booths were still partly covered, their respective owners inside working to ready each tiny shop for the ten o'clock opening. As they neared the booths closest to the back of the courthouse, Ellis heard Hen's familiar voice in the distance — a bit crackly while still sounding energetic. A few steps more and they were at the A Priori Books booth. It was twice as large as most of the other booths, located at the end of a double-sided row of booths, facing the tall clock tower of the courthouse. Like the other vendors, Hen and Tori still had the white vinyl booth sides down to maintain privacy while they set up.

"Hi, Hen," said Ellis.

Hen looked up from the box she was unpacking. White wisps of hair had come loose from the small bun at the base of her neck. "Hi, girls!"

Tori said a quick hi without stopping working.

"Did you eat?"

"We had kiffles from Madder Drinks," said Ellis.

Hen nodded distractedly, looking around the booth. There were two long tables and a few small bookshelves. Electronic readers and baskets of colorful pens, erasers, and bookmarks filled one end of a table. Tori was pulling books from boxes and placing them spine up at the other end of the table. The bookshelves were full but the second table was still empty.

"Do you need help?" asked Ellis.

"Actually, that would be great," said Hen, looking relieved.

Ellis and Starling went to work unloading boxes of books onto the tables. Tori rolled up the tent side flaps as the last of the boxes were emptied. The once nearly empty park was now crowded with people.

"Thank you so much," said Hen. "We couldn't have done it without you."

Tori looked up at the clock tower and noted, "Just five minutes until the festival officially begins."

Ellis suddenly remembered The Apothecary had a booth as well. "Where's Mr. Neumann?" Ellis asked Tori.

Tori pointed to a group of tents. "He has a smaller booth over there."

Ellis and Starling started scanning the tents, looking for signs of Mr. Neumann and his candy. Ellis stopped short and tugged on Starling's sleeve. "Look —" gasped Ellis, "It's Jules." She pulled on Starling's hand, not waiting for her to answer. "Hen, we'll see you later," called Ellis, without looking back at her grandmother.

The festival had come alive. People were milling about everywhere. Music was heard coming from near the parking-lot pumpkin patch and the tents were all open. Ellis already smelled the aroma of grilled onions and funnel cakes coming from the food carts parked along the perimeter.

"Jules!" yelled Starling.

When Jules turned around, his hands were jammed into his front pockets, and his cheeks were flushed pink.

Ellis had the uncomfortable feeling that she and Starling had interrupted something.

"Hi," Jules croaked and then cleared his throat. His color faded slightly.

"We didn't know you were coming today . . ." Ellis started, and then she noticed the booth was filled with glass objects. "Is this a booth for Connor Glass?" asked Ellis, trying to piece together Jules presence in the booth.

"Not exactly," said Jules with a nervous chuckle, his voice still a little raspy.

Ellis realized Starling was looking at a display on the table in the back of the booth, so she walked over to see what she saw. The ivory colored glass looked familiar. When she got close enough to see the detail, Ellis became enchanted. The tiny bee was a perfect replica. The wings were somewhat transparent and the black and yellow body appeared to be hovering over a cell of the waxy honeycomb. Ellis had to remind herself that the whole piece was made of glass.

Ellis sensed Jules behind her and Starling, looking over their shoulders.

"This is really incredible, Jules," said Starling.

Ellis nodded her head in agreement.

"So this is *your* booth?" asked Ellis after a few more seconds of silence.

"Yeah. It's the first time I've ever had a booth at the festival," said Jules. "It feels really strange," he added just above a whisper.

Several people were crowded into the small booth looking at the realistic models Jules had so artfully made. In addition to the bee on honeycomb, Ellis saw realistic models of a small branch with an oak leaf and acorn attached and another plant structure that looked like berries on a stem with leaves. Jules kept glancing at the visitors, putting his hands in and out of his pockets, as if he didn't know what to do with them.

Starling gave Ellis a look that said *let's go*.

"It's amazing that you're doing this Jules," said Ellis in a rush.

"Yeah," agreed Starling as she and Ellis left the booth. "We'll come back to visit you later," she added.

After they walked a short distance away, Ellis said, "So that's why Jules has been acting strange."

Starling nodded, "I had a feeling that it was something like this. When you saw him yesterday over here during lunch, I put two and two together, remembering how many models he had made when we visited the Factory."

"Hey, look!" Ellis pointed just ahead. Mr. Neumann, wearing his familiar apron, was standing by his booth holding a tray of samples.

"Hi ladies," said Mr. Neumann cheerfully when Ellis and Starling approached. "Have a candy." He extended the tray so that they could reach for a treat.

"Thank you," they said in unison, each taking a small sample cup and then moving off to the side, their space immediately filled by others behind them reaching for The Apothecary's famous treats.

Ellis peered into the tiny white paper cup expecting to see one of the maple leaf candies that Mr. Neumann was packaging the night before. Instead she saw a crescent shaped moon candy. It was creamy white with a finely sparkling surface. Its taste was as smooth and creamy as its appearance. The longer it sat on Ellis's tongue the more flavorful it became, gradually melting into a sweet, slightly almond flavor, reminding her of the Italian wedding cookies Hen made during the holidays with their delicate texture and generous powdered sugar coating.

"Mmmm," said Starling. "This star candy is so delicious."

Celestial bodies were the appropriate shape for a candy that tasted otherworld. With the last of the heavenly treats melting on their tongues, Ellis and Starling began walking among the booths, surveying their contents, which ranged from jewelry to original art to crafts to potted herbs and fresh cut flowers. Ellis slowed as they walked by a booth attended by an older woman wearing a straw hat with flowers tucked hodgepodge in its cloth band. A sign hanging from the entrance of the booth read Flowers by Florita. Ellis had never been in the flower shop next to The Apothecary but she recognized the name.

A small crowd was gathering near the memorial at the

center of The Trivium. A temporary stage had been erected and Mrs. Dockleaf and a few others were arranging the podium and preparing for a presentation.

"Looks like Mrs. Dockleaf is getting ready to make her speech," said Starling.

"Do you want to go listen?" asked Ellis, her nose scrunched up as if she was experiencing something unpleasant.

"I think we heard most of it in class."

"Yes," agreed Ellis. "How about a funnel cake?"

"Good idea," Starling nodded. And they followed the scent of onions, grilled meats, oils, and fried dough. On the way, they passed the Hots booth, which was piled high in boxed pies and crowded with customers. Rosa had on a fresh white apron and was selling pies as fast as she could manage. A few steps further, Nia and her friends, including the boy Anthony that Ellis had seen on the first day of school, were standing together sharing fries. Anthony appeared to be dousing them with vinegar. Nia brightly smiled and waved hello. Her straightened hair was a bright copper color. Her lip color was a perfect match and she wore a golden yellow cotton sweater. Ellis half expected to see a "Miss Harper Fall Festival" sash draped across her shoulder.

"Wow, did you see Nia's hair?" asked Ellis.

Starling nodded knowingly. "She changes her whole style like we change our clothes. . . . One day a blonde, another a red head and one day glasses, the next none." Starling chuckled.

"And her clothes! Always the perfect outfit . . ." said Ellis as they stepped into a long funnel cake line.

Starling and Ellis continued glancing back at Nia. "Look at the tree Nia is standing under . . . her hair matches the red fall oak leaves," said Starling.

"Amazing . . ." said Ellis.

In front of them, a group of three excused themselves and

left the line, mumbling something about ". . . this is taking forever."

Moving up to fill the gap, Starling's eyes got large and she silently motioned Ellis to notice the person they were now standing behind. Ellis raised her eyebrows but didn't move from the line. She recognized her chance to make a choice based on déjà vu.

The palpable silence behind Harley was probably what prompted her to glance around. She obviously recognized Ellis and Starling, but acted as if she were looking beyond them rather than at them. She faced forward again, and then craned her neck, seeking someone, perhaps looking for Vi and the others. Harley shuffled her feet slightly. Ellis could almost hear her thinking.

"Hi, Harley," said Ellis. Starling looked surprised, but followed along. "Hi," she muttered toward Harley.

Harley twisted her neck once again and said hi. And that was it. She turned back around, her long straight hair a wall between them.

Starling shrugged her shoulders. Ellis felt frustrated. She didn't know what she was expecting, but it was certainly more than this. How did her parents know what to do with déjà vu? Ellis's heart sank. She realized just how little she knew about threads and how far she was from finding her parents.

A nudge pulled Ellis out of her thoughts. Starling gently elbowed her again, "Let's move." The line had progressed, but Ellis, lost in thought, hadn't stepped forward.

They eventually made their way to the front of the line, not talking again with Harley, who took her funnel cake and left, never looking back.

Once Harley was out of hearing range, Starling asked, "What was that about? Why the sudden urge to be friends with Harley?"

"I don't know," replied Ellis honestly. "I just have this feeling that Harley isn't so bad." And in a distracted tone, she added, "And somehow I think Harley can help me learn more about my parents." The two of them grew quiet, Ellis mesmerized by the way the funnel cake attendant danced the funnel over the hot tub of oil to release the batter in a pattern of swirls that immediately began to rise and turn golden brown.

Chapter 30 ~ The Cinema

Ellis went straight from sound asleep to wide awake. Her eyes snapped open the moment her body sensed the morning sun crest the hilly horizon. She felt rested and energized, even though her mind was whirring — as busy now as in the moments before she fell asleep. Her sleep had been deep and dreamless — just a lull between thoughts. Ellis smiled, squeezed her eyes shut and then opened them again. Joy welled up in her heart.

The house had been quiet when Ellis arrived home last night. She found Hen asleep in a chair in the library, obviously trying to wait up for Ellis.

"Hen," said Ellis softly.

Hen jolted awake, a book slipping from her lap, her hand reaching to rub the crick out of her neck. "I drifted off," she said apologetically. "How was the movie? Did you have fun at the festival?"

Even half asleep Hen's first thought was about Ellis.

"Yes, we had a great time. The movie was funny."

By late afternoon the festival was showing signs of winding down, but Ellis and Starling weren't ready to end their day. They went back to see Jules. He had several pieces, including Honeybee on Honeycomb, and was now packing the remaining pieces. The booth was empty, so Ellis and Starling finally had the chance to talk with him.

"How did you do?" asked Ellis.

"Great. It was pretty amazing to hear compliments about my models. And then to have people actually *pay* to buy them. Wow," said Jules with a smile.

"Jules," a voice sounded from the booth entrance. The three of them turned around.

"Hi, Dad," said Jules.

Dr. Connor was a few inches taller than Jules. His dark hair was close cut and he had dark eyes. Jules, long and lanky with longer, lighter, wavy hair, looked very different from his father. Their similar mannerisms and way of speaking, however, were immediately recognizable.

The man took in the presence of the others. His face brightened. "Hello, Starling."

"Hi, Dr. Connor," said Starling. Dr. Connor glanced in Ellis's direction. "This is my friend Ellis Bell," added Starling.

The change in Dr. Connor's expression was noticeable, but he recovered quickly. "Hello, Ellis." Dr. Connor extended his hand, which Ellis politely shook. "I heard you had moved back to Harper. I hope you're enjoying high school."

"Yes, thank you," replied Ellis without elaborating. She was surprised by her own feeling of confidence.

"Well . . . so," said Dr. Connor, sounding a bit flustered, before returning his attention back to Jules. "Son, I am parked right behind your booth. We need to load so I can move the car out of the way."

The unsold models filled just two crates, which Jules and Dr. Connor managed without help. After a few minutes, Jules returned alone. "My dad is taking my stuff back to the house for me." Neither he nor Starling seemed to want to recognize that Dr. Connor was yet another person from Ellis's past that Ellis had no recollection of.

"Hey . . ." interjected Starling, "How about a movie at the Cinema? Kes and Myna said they'd be there with friends. They can take us home after."

Ellis shook off the feelings from the meeting. She'd wanted to go to the historical theater since she first saw it. "That sounds like fun!" she replied enthusiastically.

While Jules finished clearing out the tent, Ellis and Starling walked over to check in with Hen. The Trivium had gone from festive and busy to something that seemed a little like a ghost town. Dusk was falling and only a few remaining stragglers drifted past booths. Clicking and clanking noises echoed through the park as tents were dismantled. A light thumping echoed from the pumpkin patch where a pickup truck was being loaded with leftovers.

Hen's eyes were drooping and she was resting on a stool, drinking from a bottle of water. When Ellis asked to go to the movies, Hen paused for just half a breath before she smiled and said to have fun. Within fifteen minutes Ellis, Starling, and Jules were at the Pizza Den — and from the looks of things, so were half of Ida May.

Den seemed to be the appropriate name for the restaurant located down a cobbled alleyway just half a block from the theater. The entrance was a glass door set flush with the brick wall. No awning covered it, probably because any type of extension in the narrow alley would make it impossible for a passing delivery truck to get through. A flat metal sign, faded with age, bolted to the brick wall near the door, labeled the hidey-hole. Two small windows, condensation at the edges, exposed the interior and all its many customers.

The three friends formed a single line to walk through the dimly lit and crowded restaurant. The noise level was so high that Jules had to yell their order to the server at the counter, gesturing and pointing toward the menu posted on the wall above to make himself clear. Serving the best pizza Ellis ever tasted, the Pizza Den was where a lot of movie nights started or finished, she later learned.

"Where are we going to sit?" shouted Starling.

Jules simultaneously shrugged his shoulders and looked around. High tops for two were surrounded by five or six people. The booths were packed and had chairs pulled up to the ends for extra seating. The Harper Fall Festival had moved indoors. Ellis looked around, but was more focused on the atmosphere than looking for a vacant table.

Suddenly, Jules brushed past; Starling hooked arms with Ellis and pulled her along — diners were leaving a high top in the back.

Ellis and Starling hiked themselves into the chairs while Jules stood between them. It was much quieter now that they were away from the front counter. "Did you see who we passed?" asked Starling, her eyebrows raised.

Before she could stop herself, Ellis instinctively looked back the way they had come and then wished she hadn't. Harley made eye contact. It seemed as if she had been watching them. Ellis nonchalantly turned her head back toward Starling and waited a moment before talking. She knew she had been caught looking, but wanted to appear unaffected none the less.

"What's going on?" asked Jules, obviously confused about the interest in Vi and her group sitting a few tables away.

"We bumped into Harley earlier and she was none too friendly," said Starling casually.

Jules nodded, but didn't seem completely convinced. "Did you expect anything else?"

Ellis had never heard Jules speak so bluntly.

Noticing Ellis's surprised look, Jules added, "I've known Harley a long time. And Vi, Peyton, and Gwen have been around for a long time too. When they grouped together, they brought out the worst in each other. Harley became part of that group because their parents all work together and she didn't have many other friends. They aren't nice to anyone outside their group."

"What about you?" asked Ellis. "Your dad owns Connor Glass. . . . Are they nasty to you?"

"I think they are careful around me because of my dad," said Jules. "Besides, I'm not bothered by what other people think, so they have nothing to gain by targeting me."

A Den waiter, arm held high to balance the order and avoid bumping into the crowd, lowered a piping hot pizza onto a metal stand in the center of the table. The combination of fresh crispy crust, homemade sauce, and a bubbly blend of cheeses (the Pizza Den professed to a five-cheese blend) was instantly mouthwatering. Lost in thought as the server lifted cheesy slices onto their plates, Ellis couldn't help but wonder if Harley's current path in life was influenced by Ellis moving away. . . .

The smell of baked oatmeal drifted up to Ellis's room. The aroma of raisins and cranberries and extra cinnamon — the way Hen liked to make it — was drawing Ellis out of her bed. The pudding-textured breakfast served in a bowl with milk was a favorite because it tasted like a warm oatmeal cookie dipped in milk.

Ellis washed her face and dressed. But even with the O'Keefe & Merritt baking up a distraction, Ellis sat down at her desk and pulled out the lab book. After Hen went to bed last night, Ellis was too wired to sleep. She had decided to write down her findings to help her unwind. . . .

After finishing every bit of the pizza, the three of them headed over to the Cinema. Ellis had an odd feeling of familiarity when she walked into the lobby of the 1920's theater. A huge crystal chandelier hung in the center, and concession attendants wore flapper dresses or buttoned vests with baggy, pleated pants.

Still feeling stuffed from the pizza, Ellis, Starling, and Jules bypassed the popcorn and proceeded to the theater, where nearly every seat was occupied. Ellis noticed Harley, Vi, Peyton, and Gwen were already seated and apparently so did Starling and Jules because without a word of discussion the three of them headed for seats well away from the four girls. Waiting for the movie to start, Ellis found herself staring over at the back of Harley's head, wondering why she was drawn to Harley and why she was concerned about her happiness.

Ellis's heart jumped. A deep chord had sounded from the direction of the screen, but with no visible source for the sound. And then music — bold, strong notes — flowed. The sound vibrated Ellis's rib cage and her heart changed its beat to match the rhythm. Ellis was scanning the theater when she noticed movement from a small stage in front of the screen. She focused her eyes and watched in wonder as a man's head began to appear, rising up through the floor, and then little by little, the rest of his body, sitting erect on a bench, playing a pipe organ, appeared as well. Once the organ was level with the stage, the man began to play even more vibrantly — his back, shoulders, and arms moving wildly as if needing to first capture the keys to create the sound he desired.

After just a few minutes, the playing came to an end. The organist, in a tux with long tails, slid off the bench and turned toward the audience and bowed. The whole theater exploded in applause. Ellis clapped too, excitedly, but not with the enchantment of someone seeing the organist for the first time because Ellis was experiencing déjà vu. . . .

Ellis opened the lab book to review her updates. She had started a new page with a list of people from her "former life" and included Jules, Harley, and Dr. Connor in the list. And then she made notes about her interaction with Harley at the festival. A second list included déjà vu moments. So far, she listed seeing Harley's house and going to the Cinema.

Ellis now felt confident in recognizing déjà vu moments. The feelings of familiarity when she walked into the theater could be explained away, but the overwhelming feelings of knowing that she had recently seen the organist play could not be explained by anything other than déjà vu. She flipped back to the page with the thread picture of the journal article featuring Maeve and Aiden. At the bottom of the page she noted that she probably stayed with Harley and they went to the movies.

Ellis closed the book and tucked it back into her desk drawer. She headed out the door, the threshold creaking on her departure. As she hurried down the stairs, Ellis heard Hen open the O'Keefe & Merritt oven door.

"Mornin', Hen," said Ellis from the landing.

Hen served Ellis a bowl of baked oatmeal. Ellis poured milk onto the warm mound and then prepared her tea, putting first one tablespoon of sugar and then another into the steeping brew before staring distractedly into the cup and moving her spoon in slow circles.

"Ellis, you seem quiet . . ." said Hen, sipping on her tea.

"Hen," said Ellis. "I am sure I experienced déjà vu last night at the theater. When I saw the organist, I had a feeling like no other that I recently saw him. . . . And I've never been to the Main Street Cinema before," reasoned Ellis.

Ellis nervously glanced over at Hen before continuing. "I think I stayed with Harley on the last thread and we went to the movies."

Hen didn't answer. Ellis ate.

"Hen, I really want to go back to that thread . . . today,"

said Ellis, moving her spoon around in the little bit of milk left in her otherwise empty bowl. She noticed flecks of cinnamon floating on top.

"Ellis, this might be too much. The déjà vu will start interrupting your life. I feel I've made a mistake to let you visit threads," said Hen, and then she placed her head in her hands. "I'm sorry . . . this isn't the right thing for you to do," she said, her face still covered by her hands.

"What are you talking about, Hen?" asked Ellis angrily. "This is what I want to do. I want to find my parents."

After a few moments more of silence, Hen pulled her face out of her hands so that only her chin rested on her fingertips. She looked thoughtful. "If you go again, you should go to a different thread. Your parents didn't develop the solar panel glass on the last thread."

"I want to go to the thread where I know my parents exist," insisted Ellis.

"Why? You may never learn about the notebook on that thread," said Hen, sounding frustrated.

"I want to visit my mom and dad," admitted Ellis weakly.

Hen looked squarely at Ellis, her eyes squinted a bit. "You can't remember what you see and do on a thread. . . ."

Ellis looked defiant. "I just want to know that I have seen them."

"Ellis . . ."

"Please, Hen," begged Ellis.

After a tense silence, Hen said, "Promise me you'll come back." She looked at Ellis with a serious expression, "I know what you're thinking, Ellis. But, you don't understand everything about threads. You must come back. You might destroy any chance we have of bringing your parents back . . . the parents who are lost on a thread somewhere."

Ellis was silent. She was angry at Hen for denying her a

chance to live what Ellis decided was a normal life.

"What about your main thread?" asked Hen. "You're such good friends with Starling. Sounds like she may not exist on a thread with your parents."

Ellis was angered even further. She hated that Hen pointed out the details she didn't want to think about.

Sullen and feeling rejected, Ellis began to rise from her seat when Hen said, "Okay, let me get dressed and we'll go to A Priori."

Chapter 31 ~ Mother

As if awaking from a daydream, Ellis felt the fogginess clear from her mind and saw her surroundings come into focus. She was sitting at her kitchen table. It felt familiar, but small differences confirmed that Ellis was visiting a thread. The table was pulled away from the wall, and had four chairs, one on each side. The kitchen was more cluttered; books and papers were on the countertop, a sweater was tossed on the back of a chair. The tea kettle on the stove top was not the one that she and Hen use.

Ellis heard noises from another part of the house.

"Ellis, you had better hurry up or we'll be late," a voice sounded from the library.

Ellis noticed a half-eaten egg sandwich on a plate in front of her. This threaded self, however, was not hungry. She leaned in from where she was sitting to get a look into the library. There stood a woman by the bookshelves, her head bent over, intently reading the book that lie open in her hand. On the shelf in front of her was an empty space where the book had previously rested. Ellis couldn't immediately tell which book it was because the shelves were arranged differently from the way she and Hen had organized them.

After she finished scanning the room, Ellis turned her focus back to the woman. Could it be her mother standing there? Ellis was holding her breath. She felt like a spy. She studied the woman from top to bottom. She was more petite than Ellis had expected. She had a professional yet somehow casual appearance. Ellis would love to be able to put together a skirt, top, and heels that way. Maybe, thought Ellis, the style gene will kick in later. The woman was slim and younger looking than Ellis had imagined her mother. She looked so *alive*. With her head bent over the book, she had an academic air. And then Ellis noticed it. The woman — her mother — had the same hair as Ellis. It was a little longer, but the coloration was there. The morning sun streaming into the library illuminated the highlights. The blonde, the auburn, the rich brown were all there. Ellis had never been able to distinguish her mother's hair from the few pictures she had seen. But seeing her mother now — it was an answer to one of the many questions Ellis had.

Ellis felt a burn at the edges of her eyes. She silently chastised herself and then concentrated on not giving herself away as the impostor she felt like. She began by reminding herself to breathe. And then Ellis's thoughts raced. What was it her mother said? They were going to be late for something? What would the Ellis from this thread reply? "I'm done eating breakfast," said Ellis loudly, directing her voice toward the woman, hoping it didn't sound shaky.

She waited, hoping her mother — that was a weird thought — would respond with a clue as to what Ellis was going to be late for.

Ellis sat glued to the chair. She didn't trust herself. The excitement bubbling up inside of her might just cause an explosion. She wanted to scream into a pillow or jump up and down, but of course neither of these could happen.

Heels tapped against the linoleum tiles of the kitchen floor. Ellis looked up expecting to see her mother's face, but instead was greeted by the top of a head because Maeve still had her nose in the book she was holding. "Ellis, I need to stop at the lab before I drop you at Jules house." Maeve spoke into the book.

And then she lifted her head, and looked Ellis squarely into the face.

Ellis thought she might faint. She smiled instead. A loopy, I-can't-believe-I'm-seeing-my-mother-for-the-first-time smile.

"Are you being silly? Please put your dishes in the sink. . . . *Let's go,*" Maeve said the last command with enough force to make Ellis jump in her seat, momentarily losing her grip on the device. Ellis gasped as she adjusted her clutch around the device to prevent it from falling.

Maeve snapped the book shut and looked with concern at Ellis. "Is something the matter?" She looked curiously at Ellis, apparently wondering why she had gasped.

"No — no," stuttered Ellis, clenching her hand around the device even tighter.

Maeve laid the book on the table and then gathered her bag and jacket from hooks near the kitchen door. Ellis slipped the device into her front jeans pocket at the same time she stood up to take her dishes to the sink. She noticed a messenger bag at the foot of the stairs with a jacket tossed on top, and headed over to retrieve them, all the while watching her mother's smooth, confident actions move her from the kitchen to the car parked outside.

Inside the car, Ellis wanted to stare at her mother the whole way to the lab, but she forced herself to look out the front windshield instead, allowing only occasional glances in her mother's direction that she hoped wouldn't raise any suspicions.

Maeve was going on and on about something. Ellis just loved hearing her voice. It was like a song that she had only ever heard in her dreams. And through her dream-like state she picked up on only snippets of the conversation — ". . . project . . . Dr. Connor's office . . . pick up before dinner. . . ."

Ellis looked out the passenger window. The route was

much the same as the one she had seen on her main thread. She recognized several of the buildings and businesses from her travels on the Double Decker to Starling's house. When she saw an unfamiliar building, Ellis didn't know if it was because it existed only on this thread or if she just wasn't familiar enough with the route to recognize the building from her main thread.

Maeve wasn't talking anymore. Ellis stole a glance. She was lightly humming to a song on the radio. The moment was relaxed — average — as if she and her mother were just on a drive together, running an errand, with no sense of urgency. Ellis wanted to shout *Look at me mom! I'm here for only two days! Help me know you! Help me remember you!*

Maeve looked over at Ellis. Had she heard the screaming in Ellis's head?

"You okay?" asked Maeve.

"Yeah," Ellis nodded her head rapidly, shakily.

Although not looking quite satisfied with the response, Maeve was forced to look back at the road.

"Like I was saying," Maeve continued looking out the windshield, seemingly picking up the conversation from where she left off a few minutes ago, "I'll pick you and Harley up from Jules house before dinner. I hope the three of you get the project done today."

Maeve pulled into the Connor Glass parking lot and came to a stop. She hurriedly opened the door and began exiting the car. Ellis moved to keep up with her mother.

Mauve stopped, giving Ellis a quick glance. "What are you doing? I just need to run in for a lab book."

Ellis froze, unsure of what to do. "Uhm, can I come along? I, uh, don't want to sit in the car."

"Please hurry," said Maeve, sounding a little exasperated, the tick-tock of her heels moving toward the Connor Glass entrance.

Ellis was half walking, half jogging to keep up. She pressed her hand against her front jean pocket. She felt relieved knowing the device was there.

Maeve swiped a card at the door and entered a code. A heavy click prompted Maeve to pull on the door allowing her and Ellis to scoot in.

As Hen and Tori faded into view, Ellis immediately knew this thread visit was different. "I miss my mom . . . I bet I saw her, didn't I?" It was more of a statement than a question. Like the previous threads, Ellis couldn't remember anything, but this time she came back *feeling* something. The exact feeling was indescribable, like a word lost on the tip of the tongue.

Hen looked shocked. Tori's eyes began to shine. "If you did, you know she is very proud of you for coming back."

"That's crazy!" shouted Ellis. "We're talking about my mother as if she exists in my life right *now*. As if she could even care that I came back."

Ellis felt her face get very hot. She looked down in an attempt to avoid Tori's eyes and saw in the palm of her hand the device — its weight burdening. With her free hand Ellis wiped her eyes dry and then with a sigh of resignation held the device out for Tori to retrieve.

Hen seemed especially agitated as she and Ellis waited on the bookstore sofa for Tori to print the photo recorded on the device. When Tori came hurrying over, Ellis noticed Hen become still and straight-backed, as if to brace herself. "What is it?" asked Ellis excitedly, feeling more like her old self wanting to solve a mystery.

The three of them huddled around the picture. "I want to go back!" demanded Ellis.

Tori was shaking her head while Hen was saying, "No . . . no . . . no."

Ellis looked toward the A Priori counter, squinting, willing herself to see through the solid wood. For the first time, she was ready to find the device and go with or without permission.

Hen sensed Ellis's reckless desire. She reached out for Ellis who wanted nothing to do with reason or discipline.

Tori planted herself firmly in front of Ellis and said calmly, "You can't go back *now*."

Ellis was baited by the way Tori said *now*. She eyed her with reserved curiosity. It was enough to hold her back.

"What do you mean?" asked Ellis.

"You can go back, but not right now," said Tori calmly. "You must wait at least two days to travel back to the same thread. You understand?"

Ellis understood. It made sense. Her main thread self is still on the thread. She took a deep breath and then shuddered to think what might happen if her main thread self tried to replace itself on a thread.

Chapter 32 ~ Alone

"You know I want to go back tomorrow," said Ellis defiantly over breakfast. "As soon as I can," she added for emphasis.

Yesterday was like a dream come true. Ellis had spent the day with her mother. The picture proved it, sort of — it showed the back of her mother reaching for the door handle of a car. Tori and Hen said it looked like Maeve may have been in the Connor Glass parking lot, which raised the possibility of Ellis being at the lab with her mother. Unfortunately, Ellis must have been in a rush because the picture was a little blurry. Maeve had something tucked under her arm, but neither she nor Hen or Tori felt confident in saying it was a lab book.

Just knowing that she was with her mother in the last thread was enough. Remembering the experience would have been nice, but for now Ellis was happy knowing that she had a mother somewhere that she could spend time with.

Hen gave her an exasperated look. Without responding, she sipped her tea and crunched on a piece of toast. It was covered in a homemade blackberry jam that Hen brought home from the festival on Saturday.

Ellis ate another spoonful of the leftover baked oatmeal. She stared at Hen and then resigned herself to a different tactic. "Please, Hen," she said in a quieter voice.

Hen didn't look won over. But she put her mug of tea down and gave Ellis her attention.

Ellis looked at her pleadingly.

"Will you try a different thread?" asked Hen.

Ellis hesitated before responding, but knew that compromise might be the only way. "Why can't I go back to the thread with my parents?"

"We've talked about this," said Hen, a forced patience in her voice. "Your parents haven't developed the solar panel glass on the thread you were on yesterday. They don't know anything about the device. They were a threaded version of your parents, not the parents that disappeared from your main thread."

Ellis was aching to go back to where she knew her parents existed, but she agreed to try a different thread. There was a chance that she'd see her parents anyway, she reasoned. And if not, she always had her lab book with the coordinates for the thread where she knew she'd find her parents (or at least a set of parents).

The walk to school was cloudy and chilly. The Indian summer was over it seemed. Ellis made a quick stop at Madder Drinks for a latte. As much as she hated to admit it, a visit to a thread was tiring. Ellis didn't sleep well at night after a thread visit either. She had the feeling those nights were dream-filled, but as hard as she tried, she could never remember the actual dreams.

Starling was spinning the dial on her combination lock when Ellis walked up and started opening her own locker. "Hi!" said Ellis.

Starling sighed and said good morning.

"Ellis pulled her combination lock open, and then turned to Starling. "You okay?" she asked.

Starling looked at Ellis. She didn't look herself and apparently neither did Ellis. "You look tired," said Starling.

"Oh, I didn't sleep well, but I'm okay."

Starling turned away and started switching books out between her locker and backpack. After a moment of awkwardly expecting Starling to start chatting like she usually did in the mornings, Ellis turned toward her own locker and started gathering what she needed.

Their walk together to history seemed to be more out of habit than out of friendship. Nearing the door to Ms. Dockleaf's class, Ellis drew to a stop and said, "Starling? Did I do something wrong?" Ellis felt her stomach flop.

Starling stopped walking. She looked confused. "Oh. No, no. I'm just distracted by something else. I had a great time this weekend. It was so much fun." said Starling in a monotone, her face wearing the blank expression she'd had since Ellis arrived at school.

"Oh. Kay. . ." said Ellis expectantly before they started walking again.

"I'll talk about it at lunch," assured Starling, as they took their seats in the classroom. Jules nodded a hello. He was looking a little tired himself.

It definitely felt like a Monday. A gloomy one at that, thought Ellis.

The morning dragged on until finally Ellis and Starling were walking out the big double doors and down the stone steps for lunch. It was still overcast and hadn't warmed up much. Even the vibrant leaves looked a little less so without a bright sun illuminating them.

"How about Hubbel's for soup and sandwiches?" Starling asked Ellis.

"Sounds good," answered Ellis, wondering more about her friend than what she might eat for lunch.

Within seconds Starling began talking. Ellis immediately felted relieved. It wasn't what Starling had to say that relieved Ellis, it was that Starling was chatting like the friend she had come to know.

"My parents didn't go birding yesterday," said Starling, her tone serious.

Ellis couldn't decide how she was expected to respond, so she just kept listening.

"I can't remember my parents ever not birding on a Sunday," continued Starling in a worried tone.

Ellis nodded to let Starling know she was listening.

"And they just sat at the table and talked about Connor Glass. . . . I heard them say they still needed several years to develop a project. . . . And then they were saying that Dr. Connor may not be able to keep the funding going long enough," Starling sighed and looked at Ellis for a response.

"Are your parents worried about their jobs?" asked Ellis.

"I think so," said Starling. "They've mentioned before about a need for patents, and all that, but it never sounded serious. Until last night."

"I'm sorry," mumbled Ellis, wishing she could be more helpful.

"Ellis, I don't want to move away," lamented Starling.

Ellis felt her eyes pop. "What? You might have to move?"

"I'm not sure. My parents sounded like they were looking for another lab to work in."

Main Street was busy, so Starling stopped talking about her parents in case other Connor Glass kids were walking nearby.

The sky blue Hubbel's server was quick to bring out chicken noodle soup and grilled cheese sandwiches, but Ellis wasn't very hungry and just picked at her lunch. Starling didn't do much better and neither had much to say throughout lunch. As upset as Ellis was about Starling's news, she couldn't stop thinking about visiting a thread. Somehow, she thought, finding the lab books would make everything better.

With time to spare, Ellis and Starling walked around Hubbel's and mindlessly contemplated the hair products that temporarily turns hair purple, green, or orange. Halloween was just a little more than a week away and even the older kids of Ida May planned to trick-or-treat.

The walk home from school was chillier and grayer than in the morning. It would be dark in a couple hours. Ellis walked through the kitchen door harboring a mood that reflected the weather.

In the kitchen, however, a simmering pot of turkey chili filled the room with a sweet, spicy aroma. Ellis dropped her backpack and gave the pot a stir, her mouth watering.

"How was your day?" asked Hen as she appeared from around the corner.

"Okay," sighed Ellis.

"Something wrong?"

"Besides wanting to visit more threads and find the notebook?" said Ellis sarcastically.

Hen sighed, apparently hoping the topic would have disappeared for a while.

Ellis argued with Hen that since she agreed to go to a random thread, then she should be able travel this afternoon instead of waiting until tomorrow.

Hen firmly stood her ground. She said that she was certain Ellis's parents always waited at least two days between visiting threads. "Even with a random thread, there is the slight chance you could end up on the thread you are still visiting."

"Can I visit a thread before school then?" asked Ellis.

No, too tiring," retorted Hen, "besides tomorrow morning is still too soon."

"When then?"

"After school tomorrow. Tori said she'd close the store for us," answered Hen.

"Ellis, please run upstairs and get the store tablet," said Tori.

What? Ellis thought. *I've never been upstairs where Tori lives. Why is she asking me to do that?* Ellis then noticed she was standing by the reading list books instead of in the back of the bookstore. She looked around for Hen. *Where did Hen go?* she thought.

And then Ellis felt the weight in her hand.

"Ellis?" Did you hear me?" Tori's voice was getting closer.

"I'm going!" Ellis called back. She slipped the device into her front pocket and then jogged toward the doorway that she knew led upstairs. She reached out for the knob. Ellis's heart raced as she opened the door to an area she had never been invited before. She slipped inside the door and started up the wooden stairs.

Halfway up, she saw a hardwood floor. At the top of the stairs, Ellis took a quick look around. Living room to the left; dining room to the right. Further in, she spotted part of a small kitchen. Straight ahead were more stairs leading to a third floor. The bedrooms, she guessed.

A few steps away on the dining table was the tablet. Ellis grabbed it and turned around to go back down the stairs, but what she saw brought her to a dead stop.

There on the wall behind her was a family portrait. She thought she must be seeing wrong. Ellis squinted as she got closer to the portrait.

"Ellis?" Did you find it?" Tori's voice sounded from the bottom of the stairs.

Ellis grabbed the device from her pocket and took a picture. She heard Tori ascending the stairs. Ellis had finger was on the button to return, but before she could press it, the top of Tori's head was visible in the stairwell.

Ellis slipped the device back into her front pocket just as Tori surfaced.

Tori looked from Ellis to the family portrait and then back again. "What's going on?" asked Tori, her voice not sounding quite right.

"Noth — nothing," stammered Ellis. "I have the tablet." She raised her hand holding the tablet in an exaggerated show.

Tori looked at Ellis searchingly. She seemed to be looking for something in particular. "What were you looking at?" she finally asked.

"Nothing," said Ellis, as she shrugged her shoulders and then started for the stairs, which Tori was still blocking.

Ellis was now next to Tori. "Are we going back down," said Ellis, glancing down the stairs to avoid Tori's eyes.

"Ellis?" asked Tori, her voice questioning, her eyes trying to make contact with Ellis's.

Ellis felt her face flush. She pressed her damp free hand against her jeans. Her other hand held the tablet to block the view of the device in her front pocket. "Are we going?" asked Ellis again.

Tori nodded and then slowly stepped aside, still looking intently at Ellis.

Ellis ran down the steps jumping the last two, not waiting for Tori. She went directly to the long wooden counter and put the tablet down. Ellis heard Tori coming up behind her.

Without looking back, Ellis headed to the restrooms.

"Where are you going?" Tori demanded.

"I have to wash my hands," said Ellis without looking back.

Ellis walked as fast as she could without running. She pushed the ladies room door closed behind her at the same time she held the device in front of her.

"I think something went wrong," panted Ellis. She dragged her fingers across her damp forehead.

Hen stood beside Ellis, wringing her hands. She and Tori glanced at each other.

Ellis placed a hand on her chest. "My heart is beating so hard," said Ellis. She looked at Hen for an answer.

Tori held out her hand. "Let's see if you took a picture."

Ellis released the device to Tori and then wiped her palms on her jeans.

"Do you want to sit?" asked Hen anxiously.

Ellis shook her head. She was too shaken to move just yet.

"Why is Tori taking so long?" asked Ellis. Not waiting for an answer, Ellis started walking toward the counter with Hen close behind.

Tori stood at the counter, holding a printout.

"What is it?' asked Ellis.

Instead of answering Ellis, Tori looked into Hen's eyes.

"Let me see," demanded Ellis.

Tori held onto the printout. She looked at Hen again.

"I went to the thread. I want to see the picture," persisted Ellis.

Tori continued to look at Hen.

"Ellis, maybe I should see it first," said Hen cautiously.

"No, I want to see where I was."

Hen and Ellis stood on the opposite side of the counter, across from Tori.

Tori turned the printout so that it would be upright for Ellis and Hen and then placed it on the counter.

Ellis picked it up and looked at it disbelievingly, and then she handed the printout to Hen.

"I don't understand," Ellis said.

Hen stared at the printout. It showed a family portrait. A mother, a father, a teen about sixteen, and a small child about six. The Neumanns, it seemed, had adopted Ellis.

Chapter 33 ~ Madder Drinks

The two friends sipped on tea, the kettle on the O'Keefe & Merritt still warm. They sat across from each other, quietly contemplative. "It looks like your family adopted Ellis."

"Yes, it does seem that way," said Tori.

"Do you think I died?" asked Hen.

Tori shook her head. "We know from my father's thread visits to look for my mother that if you die on one thread, then it appears you are dead on all threads. You're alive now — you must be alive on other threads."

"It's scary to be talking about my existence like this." Hen shivered.

Tori nodded. "Ellis was on the thread for just nine minutes."

"She came back looking as if she were running away from something," added Hen.

"The picture leads me to believe that you weren't part of her life."

"Yes, well, now that we've decided I was alive, we know what that picture probably means."

Tori nodded. "Maybe. . . but there are other possibilities."

"Unlikely. You know I would be with Ellis if I could be."

Tori agreed.

"Do you think the reason Ellis returned after such a short time is because the Tori on the thread figured out that Ellis was from another thread?"

"I think so. The Neumanns — my family — on the thread

238

must of known about the device and visiting threads. Why else would Ellis be without her parents?" said Tori.

"You and your parents were probably waiting and watching for someone to visit from another thread," said Hen.

"It's mind boggling. To think that I would be aware of threads on a thread. . . . What does that mean?" questioned Tori. "Is that thread version of myself thinking that she is the main thread?"

Hen sighed. "I can't let myself think about it too much. After all my research over the past ten years, I still haven't come any closer to figuring out how it all works."

"How can we even be sure that *we* are living on the main thread?" said Tori.

Hen shrugged her shoulders and nodded her head slightly. "I feel so old."

"Don't lose hope. Ellis may find something on the very next thread," said Tori in an upbeat tone.

Hen at first looked at Tori without saying a word, her creased face sagging and her wrinkled hands embracing the mug of tea while her finger pads tapped the surface, and then she said sadly, "I don't know how much longer I can live this way."

Ellis slurped down the last foamy bit of the Madder's latte before depositing the empty cup into a recycle compactor at the base of the Ida May steps. Ellis walked up the stone steps, her legs feeling a bit heavy, and into the school where she dragged herself up the next flight of stairs with the help of the banister.

Last night had been more restless than usual after a thread visit. Ellis could not clear her head of the image of her six-year-old self in a family portrait with the Neumanns. There she stood near Tori, who didn't look much older than Ellis does now, resting her arm around Ellis's small shoulders, with Mr. and Mrs. Neumann standing behind them. As kind as Mr. Neumann is and as much as she likes Tori, it disturbed Ellis to her very core to think that she may have been raised by anyone other than Hen (besides, of course, her parents). On top of this, she found her heart ached knowing that with the Neumanns she would have been left motherless at a young age for a second time.

Ellis lie awake in bed for hours last night after updating her lab book with the new photo and her thoughts. Why did she have the feeling that she was escaping from something when she returned from the thread? And where was Hen? If Ellis were part of the Neumann family, does that mean the Neumanns on that thread knew about threads? More than anything, Ellis had a heavy heart for ever feeling resentful toward Hen for her current life. It could be much worse she now knew.

"Hi," said Starling. Ellis had been so lost in thought that she hadn't noticed Starling standing at her locker.

"Hi."

"You seem distracted."

"Just some things on my mind . . ." said Ellis, clicking open her locker. Starling was in much better spirits since she got back to the routine of school. She had been completely shaken after an unsettling day at home over the weekend when she overheard her parents discussing the possibility of leaving Connor Glass.

"Did Kes drive you to school again?" asked Ellis, realizing that Starling was at school unusually early.

"Yes — that old jeep does not heat up in the cold," said Starling, rubbing her hands together.

Ellis smiled briefly, but even Starling couldn't hold her attention for long. As they walked to class together, her mind kept wandering back to what she knew about the threads she's visited. In one life she had neither parents nor a grandparent. And in another, probably in many others, she didn't have Starling as her friend. And then there was the life where she probably didn't know about threads at all — a most likely friendless life in Virginia, going to a school where the kids ate school lunch instead of eating in restaurants downtown. And finally there were the countless lives that Ellis would never know about. And after all this Ellis wasn't any closer to finding the notebook or her lost parents.

"Ellis? Ellis!"

"Yeah?"

"You haven't heard a word I've said," chastised Starling.

"I'm sorry," said Ellis. She had been so deep in thought she also didn't realize that they had arrived at Mrs. Dockleaf's class.

Starling sighed and walked into class and sat down. Ellis followed and took her seat, never learning what Starling had been saying to her.

After her fifteen minutes of fame at the Harper Fall Festival, Mrs. Dockleaf was back to her usual self. She mumbled something about being behind schedule after spending so much time on The Trivium subject and began the class by writing the requirements for a history project on the board. They were allowed to work in teams of two or three, and the project was due in a week.

As Ellis wrote the details into her notebook, she had the funny feeling that she knew this assignment was coming.

"Wonder where Jules is today?" Ellis asked Starling on their way to math.

"As I was saying on our way to history . . ." said Starling in an exaggerated, sarcastic manner to make sure Ellis remembered that she hadn't been listening to her on the way to class, "Jules has a meeting with the art teacher this morning because he is up for an award."

"Okay, okay, I'm sorry I wasn't listening," said Ellis, feeling a little embarrassed for ignoring Starling earlier. "But, wow, that's awesome!"

"Yeah, he said he'd tell us more at lunch today," said Starling.

"What do you think about the history project?" asked Ellis.

Starling shrugged her shoulders. "I think we should get started right away. I can't believe she's giving us just a week."

"So, you'll work with me on the project?" asked Ellis.

Starling looked at Ellis with raised eyebrows, as if to say "I'm not even responding to that," and then she said, "Let's talk to Jules at lunch to see if he wants to work with us too."

Ellis nodded.

"I'm already thinking that we should go to the library tomorrow after school," said Starling, "and then we may need to meet over the weekend to finish it up."

Ellis inwardly sighed. She was planning to visit a thread on Thursday and again on Sunday. "Maybe we'll get a lot done tomorrow," said Ellis, mostly to herself.

The morning dragged on until Ellis, Starling, and Jules walked down the Ida May stone steps and onto the nearly oak leaf covered sidewalk. Jules had requested lunch at Madder's and so they headed for the red and white awning on Main Street.

Jules was visibly excited about his art award nomination and Ellis enjoyed seeing him so animated. When they neared Madder's Jules took the lead. Ellis giggled as Jules guided her and Starling — not to the counter to order lunch — but to the glass cases on the other side of the store, which displayed the chocolates Madder's was known for.

Ellis and Starling looked at each other, unable to guess what Jules had in mind.

"What do you think of the chocolate covered espresso

beans?" he asked, directing their attention to the top shelf in the case where a long shallow bowl presented the energy treats.

Ellis stared at the chocolate beans trying to understand what was so special, and then she noticed the plant stem next to the bowl. It looked familiar. She bent over to look closer. And then she pulled on Starling's coat sleeve to draw her attention to what she was looking at.

"What is it?" asked Starling.

"Look at that plant stem," said Ellis. "Is it made of glass?" she asked, tilting her face up toward Jules. He smiled.

Starling looked closer. "Wow, it looks so real. What is it though?"

Jules was beaming. "It's a stem from a coffee bush. The berries are fresh, unroasted coffee beans. The plant belongs to the Madder family of plants."

Ellis stared at the plant. It had slender glossy green leaves and many clusters of small, round green and reddish berries growing from the stem. "Why do the beans look like berries?"

"They have to be picked from the plant and the outer part removed to get to the coffee bean."

"Well, now I know where the name Madder comes from," mused Starling.

"Did they buy this model from you?" asked Ellis.

Jules nodded. "I made it hoping the Madder Drinks owner would want it for the coffee shop. He bought it from me at the festival and told me to look for it here."

"Smart," said Ellis, nodding her head.

"We better get some food while we still have time . . ." said Jules, looking at his watch.

The lunch special was a tuna wrap served with veggie chips. They ordered three and ate without talking.

"Your models are so real looking. Does this mean you figured out the secrets of the German glass makers?" asked Ellis, mumbling through a bite of tuna wrap packed with shredded carrots and lettuce.

Jules chuckled. "I don't think so . . . their models are very complex with lots of little pieces." Jules looked thoughtful for a moment, and then said, "But I may be developing some of my own secrets instead."

"Are you writing everything down?" asked Starling. "You know . . . so your secrets aren't lost with you?" she added in a teasing way, referring to the way the German glass flower makers died without leaving any record of how they created their models.

Jules smiled.

Ellis finished off her wrap in silence, her mood darkening. Like the Germans, when her parents left they took their secrets with them. Ellis wondered if she would have time to explore her own life and develop her own secrets if she kept visiting threads, living lives that leave no memories yet rob her of sleep and drive her to distraction.

Between afternoon classes, Starling told Ellis again that she seemed distracted, which only darkened Ellis's mood further. As Ellis walked home from school, she continued to brood over Starling's comment, her jacket unzipped, the chilly air chafing her cheeks to numbness, and not feeling any pain except that from a frustration growing deep inside her.

Ellis walked off the sidewalk and into her yard, kicking up the leaves that had fallen since she raked just a few days ago. The stepping stones to the kitchen door were once again nearly covered in yellow elm leaves.

Hen was standing at the O'Keefe & Merritt stirring a large pot of something. "Hi, Hen," greeted Ellis.

"Ellis, how was your day?" asked Hen. Steam from the pot gave off the aroma of vegetable soup.

"Okay," Ellis tried not to sound mopey. "We were assigned

a history project. I'm doing it with Starling and Jules, so I need to go to the library after school tomorrow to work on it with them."

"Okay," said Hen, as she turned around to face Ellis. "So why do you sound so down about it?"

"I wanted to visit a thread tomorrow."

"Ellis, I know you want to find your parents, but it's important not to get so obsessed that you forget to live in the here and now," said Hen, wringing her hands and then pushing at invisible strands of hair on her already bare forehead.

"So can I visit a thread after school on Friday then?" Ellis's tone was challenging.

Hen shot back, "You don't have any plans with Starling after school? You seem to like to be with her on the weekends."

Ellis stubbornly responded, "I haven't made any plans. I want to visit a thread on Friday."

"I'll talk to Tori," resigned Hen.

Chapter 34 ~ Squeaky

Ellis awoke feeling more like her normal self. She had slept well and was not feeling distracted. Of course, Ellis discussed none of this with Hen for fear of being made to stop visiting threads. She was ready to visit another thread Friday. Today she would work on the history report. . . .

Ellis and Starling walked into the Ida May library. Jules said he would meet them there. A large circulation desk was in the center of the room. Ellis saw Harley sitting at a table with Gwen with several open books between them.

Ellis looked from Starling to Harley and back again.

"Have I been here before?" Ellis asked Starling.

"What?" asked Starling. "Are you okay? You look a little sick."

Ellis looked around the library. She had been here before. She concentrated on remembering. "When was I here?"

"What?" asked Starling again. "I don't think you've ever been here before. At least not with me." Starling grabbed Ellis by the arm and began leading her. "Jules is waving at us from the table over there," she pointed toward the back of the room.

Ellis let Starling guide her. She felt like she was walking in a bubble — everything around her not quite in clear focus.

Jules usual smile turned to a look of concern. "Are you feeling all right, Ellis?"

Ellis tried to nod, but wasn't sure if her head moved.

"Do you need to go home?" asked Starling, "I can call your

grandmother. . . ."

"No," said Ellis too loudly and heard a *Shhh* from the librarian in return. Ellis and Starling took a seat in the chairs across from Jules.

"No, no," whispered Ellis, pulling her chair in closer to the table. "I'm okay. Let's work on the report."

As they muddled through several heavy reference books, Jules and Starling continued to give her occasional sideways looks of concern. Ellis pretended she was fine and avoided looking at the table where Harley and Gwen were sitting. Eventually, Ellis was able to shake off the feeling of déjà vu.

With most of the report done, they packed their backpacks and walked out of the library. Ellis still felt a bit shaken by the déjà vu and avoided looking around the room as they left. In the nearly vacant Ida May hallway, the whole school took on the hushed tones of the library.

"So how about we finish the project at my house on Sunday?" asked Jules, his normally soft-spoken voice sounding loud as it penetrated the quiet.

Starling agreed and Ellis in turned nodded as well.

"Why did we have to use library books anyway? We could have found the information on the Internet a lot faster," commented Ellis.

Starling laughed — the empty hallway echoing in response — and then reminded them that Mrs. Dockleaf said she wanted to give the class the experience of using library reference books.

"Did you talk to your grandmother about Friday night?" Starling asked Ellis.

Ellis was suddenly interested in looking at her trimmed, but unpolished finger nails. "Ummm, no, I haven't had a chance to ask if I can sleep over tomorrow."

"Do you still want to sleep over?" asked Starling, her voice trailing a bit.

"Well, yeah, but Hen has some chores she wants me to do with her after school," said Ellis, forcing herself to look up at Starling.

"Is everything okay? I thought you really wanted to come home with me after school on Friday."

"I do. I just forgot that Hen wanted me to help with some stuff after school," said Ellis. She started to bite her thumbnail.

"So you can't come over at all? Will Hen bring you out to my house after the chores?" asked Starling. "I mean only if you want. . . ."

"I'll talk to Hen tonight," said Ellis, guilt and confusion wracking her. She had been so focused on arguing over a thread visit with Hen last night that she completely forgot about the sleepover Starling had planned.

Kes was waiting outside the school with the jeep running. Ellis and Jules slid into the back seat. The heat was blasting, but Ellis didn't notice any difference from the outside temperature. Starling jumped into the front seat and sat on her hands.

"Where's Myna?" Starling asked Kestrel.

"She took the Double Decker. She said it was warmer," grunted Kes.

"Thanks for the ride home," Ellis called from the back seat.

"Sure."

As the jeep picked up speed, Ellis heard a faint whistling noise coming from the door seal where cold air pushed its way in and began circulating around the inside of the jeep. Ellis shivered and stuck her hands into her coat pockets.

Ellis was home in less than five minutes. She entered the house through the front door. The entry area was small, the floor tiled in the same green slate used on the roof, and contained just one piece of furniture, a long bench. Ellis unzipped her jacket and kicked off her shoes, pushing them under the bench with her sock feet. For the first time, Ellis noticed a picture hook on the wall above the bench. It made her think of the family portrait with the Neumanns. She wondered what used to hang there.

With a new found awareness, Ellis began looking around. She slipped out of her jacket and hung it in the closet, all the while looking at the walls around her. There were two hooks on the wall across from the closet.

She walked over to the foot of the front stairs, which she rarely used in place of the back stairs that lead to the kitchen. She peered up the staircase and saw several bare hooks hanging in a staggered path trending upward.

"Ellis?" Ellis jumped at the sound of Hen's voice so close by. "What are you doing?"

"Why do we have all these empty picture hooks hanging on the walls?" asked Ellis. "Where are the pictures?"

Hen looked at the wall as if noticing the hooks for the first time herself. "We still have unpacked boxes. I think there are pictures in them."

"Family pictures?" asked Ellis.

"Um, I'm not sure. . . . We'll come across them eventually," said Hen, and then without waiting for a response from Ellis, she changed the subject. "How was the library? Did you get the report done?"

"Most of it," said Ellis. "We need to meet again on Sunday."

Hen nodded and started walking toward the kitchen. "I'm making dinner. Come join me in the kitchen."

Ellis felt frustrated, but decided it was no use making a big deal about the hooks when Hen was clearly not willing to discuss them. She followed Hen into the kitchen to the smell of sautéed onions and green peppers and knew immediately dinner was Hungarian goulash. The pasta dish was a favorite for both of them.

As she set the table, Ellis thought about whether or not to tell Hen about the déjà vu in the Ida May library. Even though she knew Hen might worry, Ellis needed someone to talk to.

"Hen," said Ellis.

"Yes." Hen was scooping goulash into a serving bowl.

"I experienced déjà vu again today, at the library."

At first Ellis thought Hen hadn't heard her until she looked over and saw Hen staring at her without moving.

"Please don't be worried," pleaded Ellis.

"What happened?"

"I walked into the Ida May library and I knew I had been there before, but really I hadn't. Well, at least not in my main thread," said Ellis. "I've been thinking. . . . Maybe I went to the library with Harley on the thread where my parents were at the conference."

Hen took a deep breath. "Maybe," she said, as she finished scooping dinner into a serving bowl.

"Hen, I still want to visit a thread tomorrow. Remember you said I could visit a thread on Friday?"

"I didn't exactly say that," said Hen. "It might be better if you take a break. Why don't you have Starling over instead?"

"Well, now that you mention it," said Ellis in her sweetest voice, "Starling invited me to stay over at her house tomorrow, and I was hoping you would take me there after I visit a thread."

Ellis reached over and placed two heaping spoonfuls of goulash on her plate. The wide noodles, ground beef, tomatoes, onions, and peppers with ample Hungarian paprika made for the perfect meal on a chilly, damp night.

Rather than answer Ellis, Hen served herself some goulash and began eating.

"Please, Hen," begged Ellis.

"Skip the thread and go to Starling's."

Ellis looked at her plate and ate in silence. She knew Hen had her, but there had to be a way to do both.

Stretched out on her bed, Ellis read through her lab book hoping to identify a pattern or find a clue. She paged through a second time, and then began to feel frustrated. Looking around her room Ellis thought about how much has changed for her in the short time she's been in Harper. The evidence was everywhere she looked. The cork board was covered — mementos, flyers, drawings, a Pizza Den menu. Clothes scattered about revealed a top borrowed from Starling. An empty Madder Drinks cup sat on her desk. On her dresser lay a new bag — sage green with turquoise trim and a tan leather strap — which Ellis just had to have when she saw it in a store window downtown. A Harper Fall Festival poster — a surprise from Hen — hung on the wall. Ellis found the brightly colored abstract collage a fun distraction — like a hidden picture puzzle. She would scrutinize the colors, shapes, and lines to pick out maple, oak, and sassafras fall leaves, gourds of many shapes and sizes, musical instruments, and artist's tools including a paint brush and palette.

Ellis began paging through the lab book again, determined to find a reason for Hen to let her visit a thread tomorrow. She paused on her entry for the last thread she visited and studied the Neumann family picture. She was about six. Ellis thought about her life at six. Six. She couldn't remember much about being six. It was the year she started moving around with Hen.

Ellis stared at the picture some more, trying to pick out every detail. She noticed for the first time that Tori's pose was relaxed, with her arm around Ellis, but her expression looked somewhat sad. They were all casually dressed for the impromptu photo, which was taken inside the bookstore. At the six-year-old Ellis's feet lie a children's book. Ellis rotated the picture to have a better look at the cover. It looked familiar. She had seen the book before, and she knew she wasn't experiencing déjà vu.

Maybe she had seen the book at A Priori, thought Ellis. She turned the photo back to upright.

The memory came to Ellis in a flash. . . . Hen had said Ellis liked having that book read to her and then when Ellis could read on her own, she read it over and over again.

Ellis ran downstairs and into the library. She scanned the shelves looking for the brightly colored book she placed there just a couple months earlier. She pulled an oversized, hardback children's book from the shelf and headed back upstairs.

She compared the image in the thread picture to the book she was holding. She couldn't be absolutely positive, but they looked very similar.

Ellis looked at the book in her hands, "Squeaky." The front cover featured an animated brown mouse standing on its hind legs. He was holding a marble in his two front feet and his expression seemed to say it was a special treasure. He was apparently a house mouse because beneath his hind legs was a wooden floor and behind him was a baseboard in place of the usual field of grass with woods in the background.

When Ellis opened the front cover, she saw an inscription from her parents. *To Ellis, There are hidden treasures for you to find, Love Mom and Dad.* It was dated the year Ellis turned two.

Ellis read the story, which contained just a few lines of text on each left hand page. The right hand pages were bright, full-page illustrations depicting the text on the facing page.

Ellis enjoyed the detail and artistry in the illustrations. At first she didn't remember the story, but as she read along, it all came back to her. A little house mouse, Squeaky, lived beneath the floorboards of a big house. At night, when he was out seeking crumbs, he would often come across a treasure for his living area. After taking a tiny key, Squeaky was afraid when he heard that the house people were frantic about the missing key. Squeaky agonized over what to do. If he returned the key he may be thrown out of the house forever, but if he kept the key the house people might have to move out and leave Squeaky with no food or family. He was afraid, but the next night he bravely brought the key back out. As he tried to place it where he found it, a house person caught him. Squeaky squeaked with fear, but the house person gently rubbed his head before releasing him to go back to his home beneath the floorboards.

"Good mornin' Hen," chimed Ellis.

"Good morning," Hen said, unable to hide a tone of curiosity at Ellis's cheerful greeting.

Ellis placed two pancakes on her plate before sitting down at the table where Hen was sipping her tea. She pulled the children's book out from under her arm and laid it on the table in front of Hen.

Hen raised her eyebrows and set her mug of tea on to the table. "What's this about?" she asked.

"I was looking at the picture from the last thread — you know — the one where I'm with Tori's family. . ." Ellis paused.

"Okay," replied Hen.

"In the picture there was a book at my feet," said Ellis excitedly. "I think it was this book." Ellis gestured toward the copy of "Squeaky."

Hen contemplated what Ellis was saying. "Yes, but it was a different thread. It probably just looked similar to this book."

"Remember what Tori said?" asked Ellis. "She said that on all threads a person has the same characteristics. Maybe I liked this book on another thread."

"That's possible," agreed Hen.

"Look," said Ellis, opening the book and pointing to the inscription in what she guessed was her mother's handwriting.

Hen leaned in and looked surprised to the see the writing. "I didn't know there was an inscription," she said in a thoughtful tone.

"What do you think it means?" asked Ellis.

Hen had a wary look. "Ellis, it's probably just a sweet play on words from your mom. . . ."

"It says 'There are hidden treasures for you to find'," recited Ellis, looking at Hen expectantly.

Ellis got out of her chair and stood beside Hen, hovering over her, as if her proximity would somehow make the meaning of the inscription clearer.

"What do you think it means, Ellis?" said Hen.

Ellis sat down again. She looked Hen in the eyes. "I think my parents want me to keep visiting threads to find treasures — to find them."

Hen sighed. "Ellis, look how old the inscription is . . ."

"When did they start visiting threads?" countered Ellis.

Hen was thoughtful, and then admitted that she didn't know exactly when they started visiting threads, but that they had been visiting threads for at least a couple years before they disappeared.

"Hen, I think they want me to visit threads. My parents just didn't realize at the time that the treasure I would be looking for is them."

Chapter 35 ~ Through The Apothecary

Tori was clearly not happy about closing the store on a Friday night. Not only was she losing business, but she was worried about all the activity on the sidewalk with kids going to and from The Apothecary. After displaying the Closed sign, she also pulled down the window shade.

"Thank you," Ellis said to Tori.

Tori raised an eyebrow, "Sure."

There was much argument over whether Ellis should try a new thread or go back to the thread where she knew her parents existed. Between the three of them the discussion seemed to go in circles. Ellis got to the point where she didn't care one way or another. She just wanted to go to Starling's tonight before it got too late.

It was finally decided that Ellis will try a new thread. Hen was nervous after what happened on the last thread, but Tori felt it was statistically unlikely that Ellis would end up on the same thread again.

Tori insisted that Ellis leave from the furthest back corner of the bookstore this time. The three of them headed down an aisle of books that ranged in subject from biographies to historical fiction. Ellis was further back in the bookstore than she had ever been. When they reached the end of the shelves running perpendicular to the entrance, they were faced with the back wall of the bookstore, which was completely covered from floor to ceiling with bookshelves filled with books. A tall ladder with wheels along the bottom was hooked onto the top of the shelves to access the many books that were beyond reach.

Ellis hurriedly positioned herself and without another word placed her finger on the button to visit a thread.

"Wait!" shouted Hen.

"What?" said Ellis and Tori together.

"You are rushing, Ellis," lamented Hen. "This is serious. You can't rush when using the device. Anything could happen."

"Hen's right," added Tori. "We're going too fast. This is not something to take lightly."

Ellis took a deep breath. As frustrated as she was with Hen at the moment, she knew Hen was right. Ellis cleared her mind of wanting to get to Starling's and thought about what was happening here and now. After several seconds, she said, "Okay, I'm ready."

"Please grip the device firmly," warned Hen.

Ellis squeezed her hand a little tighter and nodded. Without further delay, there was a bright flash of light.

Ellis wondered what she was thinking about. She was thinking of something just a moment ago . . . what was it? Why was she standing in her room? She felt the device in her hand at the same time her thinking cleared. *Wow, I'm in my own room. Maybe threads are not so random after all. I seem to keep finding my way back to Harper.*

"Ellis! What's taking so long?"

Ellis thought fast. Who is calling? The stranger's voice sounded too young to be an adult's. "Coming!" she yelled back, unsure of what else to say.

Ellis looked around wishing she had time to search her own room. She slipped the device into her front pocket, and stepped out into the hallway, the threshold at her door creaking when she stepped on it. Ellis smiled at the familiar response.

Ellis liked the look of the large hallway on this thread. There was a chair or a small bench by every bedroom door. A long bench was situated at the top of the front stairs. On the opposite side of the front staircase, a comfortable looking chair and end table were placed in front of the bookshelves, which were filled with books and knickknacks, along with several bookends. She recognized "Squeaky" at the end of a row of books, propped up by a built-in bookend.

Across from her room, the door to the master bedroom was open. She stepped closer and then stood very still, listening for any signs of a presence. Ellis heard only her own breathing, which seemed very loud. She tiptoed to the open door. Ignoring the goose bumps that formed on her arms, she peeked inside. The telltale signs of her parents were there — clothing, ties, women's shoes, and journals, like the ones she and Starling looked at. Ellis wanted to scream with joy to be on another thread with her parents.

What if they are downstairs? Ellis took a deep breath through her nose, trying to take in the scent of her parents, before stepping back out into the hallway and then down the front stairs, where she heard the voice come from.

"What took you so long?" grunted Harley.

Ellis tried to keep the surprise off her face. Even though they were friends when young, seeing Harley standing in front of her as a friend now was hard to believe.

"Sorry," mumbled Ellis, since she wasn't sure why she was upstairs to begin with.

"Are you ready to go?" Harley nearly barked. "Jules is probably already at The Apothecary waiting for us."

Ellis noticed Harley had her jacket on.

"By the way, your parents left while you were changing your clothes," said Harley. "They said they were going to be late for their dinner reservation."

Ellis's stomach dropped. "My parents left?" She practically whined.

"Yeah," confirmed Harley, and then noticing Ellis's tone of voice, added, "Hey, is there something wrong?"

Ellis made her best effort to hide her feelings. "No . . . Uhm, I just need my jacket." She turned to walk to the closet behind her. Where empty hooks hung in her main thread, pictures hung on the walls of this thread. And Ellis was frozen by what she saw hanging in the entry.

"Ellis?" Harley questioned from behind her, "Are you going to get your jacket?"

Ellis rubbed her palms against her jeans. "Yeah . . . I was trying to decide if I need the scarf on the bench," she said in the calmest voice she could muster before stiffly walking to the closet and grabbing a jacket that looked to be her size, leaving the scarf where it lie.

Harley seemed to have a lot she wanted to talk about on their walk to The Apothecary, for which Ellis was glad because she really didn't think she could manage to say anything for a while. For the first time, Ellis realized there was more going on than just her parent's disappearance. She didn't understand what she saw in the picture back at her house, making the whole thread experience feel surreal. Ellis was beginning to wonder what was real and what wasn't. Maybe this thread was real and her main thread wasn't, she mused. Aside from small differences in the way the houses looked and the fact that Ellis was with Harley, the walk to The Apothecary was like any other trip to Mr. Neumann's store.

"Isn't it great about the patent our parents got for Connor Glass?" asked Harley, getting Ellis's attention.

"What?"

"You know — the new wearable glass. I think it's amazing

they made a glass so thin and flexible that it can be stuck to your shirt or jacket and display pictures and colors," said Harley excitedly.

"It is interesting," said Ellis, wondering if such an invention existed on her main thread. "Do you remember how long they've been working on the project?"

Harley gave Ellis an odd look. "A *really* long time," she replied.

"Yeah," mumbled Ellis. *On this thread*, she thought.

They turned down Bourner Street where Ellis got a shock. Kids were walking in and out of The Apothecary, but A Priori was quiet. When Ellis was in front of the bookstore, she couldn't help but stop and look into the windows of the closed up building. Overcome with a sense of panic, Ellis blurted out, "What's going on here?"

"What's wrong with you?" asked Harley. "You know as much as anybody. Tori and Henrietta are supposed to reopen the store in the Spring."

Henrietta? thought Ellis. *Why was Harley calling my grandmother Henrietta?*

Harley had no patience to look in the A Priori windows. She reminded Ellis that Jules was meeting them at The Apothecary. Ellis wished she could go back to her main thread at this very moment.

The Apothecary was packed. Jules was standing at a table talking to several Ida May students, a couple of which Ellis recognized. Ellis hung slightly behind Harley as they approached the table to hopefully avoid interaction with the kids she didn't know.

"Hi," said Jules in his usual happy voice and lifted his open hand in greeting.

Ellis smiled. Harley said hi to the kids at the table.

Harley and Jules got into a conversation about what to do

tonight. There was talk of a movie or just pizza. Ellis felt like an outsider looking in. She looked around the busy store and thought about going to the restroom so that she could return from the thread. Instead, her gaze fell on the doorway leading to the rooms behind the cash register, where Mr. Neumann made the candy. Ellis wondered if she could go through the secret passage from this direction and get into A Priori.

Ellis pointed toward the restroom and told Jules and Harley she'd be back in a minute. She wasn't sure why she wanted to go into the bookstore, but since that was where her parents last left from, perhaps she would find a clue. She'd also never had free reign of A Priori and the idea of looking around with no one to answer to intrigued her.

Walking toward the restroom, Ellis scanned the area for Mr. Neumann — she spotted the top of his head in the furthest candy aisle — and then she double-checked that Harley and Jules were still deep in conversation, before turning sharply and slipping through the door to the back of the store.

The air, saturated with sugar, was soft and syrupy. The sweet peppery smell of cloves wafted in from another room. Ellis did a slow jog through the candy laboratory, past the tables where taffy was pulled, past the sugar barrels, past the many glass jars lined up in rows, making her way to the secret entrance. Soothing vanilla, invigorating mint, sharp ginger, and other herbal and spice scents barraged her already acute senses.

With shaky hands, she felt the edges of the wall where Tori had first brought her through to The Apothecary. There was no handle from this side, but she detected a panel. Desperately, she pulled and pried on the panel edges — her fingertips whitening. Frustrated, Ellis stopped prying and leaned her back against the wall to think. When her weight pressured the panel, she heard a click. She stepped away and the door popped open.

Chapter 36 ~ The Pendulum Clock

Ellis walked into A Priori and pulled the door closed behind her, a click confirmed that is was latched. She nearly giggled aloud. Leaning her head back slightly, she sang out, "Hello." Ellis wiped her hands on her jeans and then placed a palm over her heart in an effort to calm it.

There was no response to Ellis's greeting, as she expected. A Priori felt empty and she knew it would be.

Ellis walked around the empty bookstore, being careful to keep a lookout for passersby that may see her through the front windows. She walked over to the Children's department and sat on the rug. She realized that Daisy wasn't around and wondered if the Neumanns had Daisy on this thread.

Ellis saw the door to the upstairs and had a strange curiosity about the living area, but she also felt a little too frightened to go up there.

Standing up, Ellis looked over at the counter. She knew then what she wanted to see. She walked over to the long wooden counter and went behind it. She searched the area, knowing that the device wouldn't be there, but wanted to see where it could be kept. The back of the counter was more complicated than she imagined. Several built in shelves offered storage space. She rifled through several of the cubbies and then stopped searching, realizing it was pointless — she wouldn't remember any of it when she returned from the thread.

Being behind the counter felt fun. The perspective was different and she felt in charge. Ellis turned around and found herself facing the pendulum clock. Just like on her main thread, the pendulum was at rest, but the clock continued to keep time. A small wooden step stool, tucked away behind the counter, seemed to be inviting Ellis to take a closer look at the clock.

Ellis pushed the stool to below the clock and then took the two steps to stand on top. At first, Ellis just looked at the clock. She cocked her head slightly to better hear the sound of a soft ticking, which was not audible when standing on the other side of the counter.

Meaning only to touch the clock lightly, Ellis gasped when the whole thing slipped off its hook. With quick reflexes, she brought her other hand up to catch the clock as it fell from the wall. Ellis anxiously tried to place it back on the hook, but she wasn't tall enough to see where to hang it. After what felt like several minutes of repeatedly trying to hang the clock, Ellis stepped off the stool and carried the clock to the counter. Her arms felt exhausted from the effort and she was beginning to feel panicked about being gone for so long. Harley and Jules must be looking for her by now.

Ellis decided she must either go back to The Apothecary or return from the thread. She really wanted to go back to her house and take a picture of the photo hanging in the entrance. She glanced down at the clock, its soft ticking reminding her that she was wasting time. *It was now or never*, she thought, resting her hand on the clock.

Something about the width of the clock caught her eye. The panel behind the pendulum was not the back panel of the clock. It seemed the clock was taking up just the front half of its wooden frame.

Ellis carefully flipped the clock over. There was a small recess in the wood. She stuck her fingertip in and then pulled. The back came off to reveal a compartment. The space was empty, but Ellis noted that it was large enough for a lab book. Her heart racing, she placed the clock on its side, revealing the compartment, but also showing that it was the A Priori pendulum clock. She pulled the device from her front pocket and took a picture.

After closing the compartment door, Ellis flipped the clock over and left it on the counter. She jogged to the back of the bookstore, away from the front windows. Before pressing the button to return, Ellis willed herself to be calm. She didn't want Hen to have any reason to keep her from going to Starling's and then she told herself that she must return to this thread. "I must come back here, I must come back here," she whispered to herself before pressing the button.

Ellis was dazed. Hen and Tori were staring at her. The back of the bookstore seemed oddly familiar. Ellis remembered she was visiting a thread. She looked down at the device in her hand and then handed it to Tori.

Unable to remember anything from the thread, Ellis felt a strange calmness. "I want to see the picture," she said.

Hen eyed her suspiciously. "Are you okay?"

Ellis nodded her head, the fogginess was clearing. Tori had already left to print the photo. After another minute, Ellis felt focused enough to walk with Hen to the counter where the printer could be heard. Ellis wanted to go behind the counter for once, but felt too drained at the moment to press the issue.

Tori's head disappeared momentarily before she came up with a printout in her hand. Rather than pass the paper over immediately, she stared at the photo, obviously intrigued by something she saw.

"What is it?" said Hen.

Tori silently handed the printout over.

Ellis leaned in and looked at the photo, which Hen now held. Their heads moved in unison from the printout to the wall where the pendulum clock hung. Tori was already moving. She carried a small step stool from behind the counter, and placed it below the clock. She gingerly ascended the steps and lifted the clock from its hook. It looked rather large in Tori's arms, as Hen and Ellis waited breathlessly for her place it on the counter.

The three of them nervously looked at the clock. "Do you think there's a hiding place?" asked Ellis.

"This clock has been passed down through my mother's family. They were German, and the clock arrived with her descendants from Germany," cited Tori, as she looked over the front and sides of the clock. "My mother always said this clock was special, but she never even hinted to a secret compartment that I can remember."

"Should we ask your father?" suggested Hen.

Tori shook her head. "He's too busy with the store right now. Let's just see what we find and ask him later. Come around," Tori motioned.

Ellis and Hen moved along the length of the counter and then around to the other side where Tori stood. Daisy was on her bed, lifting only her head when Hen and Ellis approached. She looked from Tori to the unexpected visitors in her space before resting her head on her front paws and letting out an audible groan.

As curious as Ellis was about the clock, she was also excited about being behind the counter. When she glanced around, she saw several shelves and storage cubbies built into the back of the counter. A printer was off to one side on a bigger shelf. A small drawer was slightly ajar and appeared to be empty.

Tori began inspecting the clock. She turned it over and lay it face down on the counter. An indentation in the rear of the clock looked like a way to open the panel.

Without discussion, Tori put her fingertip into the recession and pulled. The back of the clock opened and exposed an inner compartment.

Hen, Tori, and Ellis placed their hands over their mouths and screamed. They embraced and jumped up and down and chanted words and expressions of joy, all the while Tori saying, "Shhh, shhh, someone at The Apothecary might hear us."

The compartment was stuffed full of papers, a lab book, and what appeared to be some jewelry. Tori gently pulled each item out, nervously looking around periodically as if someone might come in and steal the treasure from them.

Ellis was most interested in the lab book. Could it be the one her mother kept? she hoped. When she smiled at Hen to share her excitement, she saw tears in Hen's eyes.

Tori lingered on each piece of paper.

"Tori, what about the lab book?" asked Hen. She seemed to be as anxious as Ellis about knowing the contents of the lab book.

"These papers all seem to be in my mother's writing," said Tori, holding a sheet of paper in her hand. "And the lab book has her name on the front," she said, picking it up to have a closer look.

Tori began flipping through the familiar looking book with its burgundy binding and olive green spine. "I'm not sure what this is, but I don't think it's what we're looking for," said Tori, looking perplexed and sounding sad.

Ellis looked at Hen disbelievingly. Hen grabbed the lab book from Tori. "It has to be it." Hen began examining the contents.

Tori spoke in her usual calm voice, the excitement completely worn off, "It seems like a really inconvenient place for your parents to hide a lab book. My mother was very good friends with your mother, Ellis, but even so, why would your mom want to hide something where she could only access it during nonbusiness hours?"

After a few more minutes of leafing through papers and separating out jewelry, it became clear that this treasure was intended for the Neumanns.

"Can I still sleep over at Starling's?" Ellis asked Hen. She wanted to escape, and Hen seemed to sense that.

"Sure. Let's go." Hen looked exhausted. "Thanks for closing the store and everything, Tori."

Tori nodded solemnly.

Chapter 37 ~ Starling's Plan

The car ride to Muddy Creek was a quiet one. Ellis thought about Mr. Neumann's decision to stop visiting threads. She understood now why he came to that decision. Even though Ellis couldn't remember the threads, she felt she was losing her sense of self. Ironically, Ellis reflected, before I knew about threads I felt I didn't have a life. Now that I've been visiting my many different lives on threads, I feel I'm losing myself to all the other selves living their lives.

However, the difference between her and Mr. Neumann, Ellis reminded herself, is that her parents may be waiting for her to find them and bring them back.

When Ellis arrived at her friend's house in Muddy Creek, Starling was there to greet her at the door. Ellis walked in while Starling politely waved to Hen before she pulled away. The house was quiet.

Ellis had asked if anyone else was home, while slipping out of her shoes and hanging her jacket on top another jacket on the crowded high back bench.

When Starling responded that her parents were meeting some friends and her sisters were out with their friends Ellis felt an immediate sense of relief. The facade she had been holding on to tight since she returned from the thread loosened and dropped away.

"Starling," said Ellis. "I need your help."

Starling smiled.

Ellis looked into her friend's eyes and wondered how much

she should divulge. How much would anyone really believe?

"Ellis?" queried Starling, her tone echoing concern.

Ellis sighed. "I don't know where to start," she said honestly.

"Let's make some tea," suggested Starling. "And then we'll go up to my room."

They carried large mugs of black tea, sweetened with many tablespoons of sugar and lightened with just a splash of milk to neutralize the tannins. Ellis used the tip of her finger to tap the head of the silent songbird when she stepped onto the stairs.

Starling's room was a comfortable mess, clothes on the floor and bed unmade. They put their tea mugs on the two bedside tables on either side of the bed, and then sat crisscross on the bed facing each other.

"So . . ." nudged Starling.

Ellis decided to go from the angle of what was really bothering her. "I don't think Hen ever wanted me to live in Harper because there seem to be secrets here related to when I was young."

Starling gave Ellis a look that said go on.

"There is something odd about Hen and Tori being friends. I can't explain it, but I sense that there is a secret between them that affects me," said Ellis.

"What makes you think that?" asked Starling, her detective cap firmly in place.

"Just the way they seem to avoid talking too much in front of me. It's as if they are afraid of spilling a secret."

"If Hen never wanted you to live in Harper, then why did she move you back?" asked Starling.

"I overheard Hen and Tori talking several weeks ago, and Tori told Hen she did the right thing moving back to Harper and she said something about me being fourteen and how that was the age I needed to be to help Hen," said Ellis, using her mind's eye to see herself standing on the stairs, overhearing the loud whispers between Hen and Tori when they thought Ellis was upstairs.

"It is very strange," mused Starling, taking a sip of tea. "Help Hen with what?"

"I don't know," said Ellis. "It's strange, I've lived with Hen for as long as I can remember, but I don't really know much about her. It's as if she left her life and started a new one with me when I no longer had my parents."

Ellis leaned over to the end table and took several sips from her tea mug before sitting up again.

"And there are strange things about my house. We have empty picture hooks on the walls. When I asked Hen what used to hang there, she said she didn't know and changed the subject. I think she knows but doesn't want to tell me."

"You said you needed my help," Starling reminded Ellis.

"Yes . . ." said Ellis, and then paused. She realized at that very moment that she no longer wanted to live her life visiting threads. She wanted her life to be here, on her main thread, spending time with friends and figuring out what she wanted to do when she grows up. She missed her parents and wanted them to return, but the key to their return was in the missing lab book, which existed somewhere on this thread. Visiting other threads — other timelines — was making Ellis feel lost, confused, and distant from her real life, the one on her main thread. Deep down something was telling her she had to go back to the last thread, but that would be her last thread visit. She now knew what she needed help with.

Starling was waiting, still staring at Ellis.

"There is something hidden at A Priori and it has to do with my parents. I need your help distracting Tori, so that I can have a few minutes to find it."

"What is it?"

"You're my best friend and I know you'll understand if I say I can't tell you about it right now, but it's important for me to find it."

"I'll help you," said Starling without a second thought.

Starling's plan was beyond anything Ellis ever imagined. It helped that Starling knew so much about Harper and Ida May.

Ellis slept little that night and the cups of tea weren't the culprit.

Hen met up with Tori on Main Street, just a little south of Bourner Street. They wore heavy windbreakers and light scarves. Madder Drinks was just a few blocks away. When they stepped inside, they immediately felt overheated and worked to untwist their scarfs and hang their jackets on the hooks of an empty booth before ordering breakfast.

Madder's wasn't nearly as busy on Saturday morning as during the work week. Hen and Tori each ordered the same breakfast — an egg, Swiss, and arugula on kiffles. They strayed from their usual tea and had Madder's lattes.

Seated at the booth and sipping on their coffees, they finally settled into talking, both staying alert to anyone close by that might overhear them.

"Hen, I really think it's time you talked to Ellis," said Tori. "She needs to know exactly what's going on."

Hen nodded. "I am feeling the same way, but how will she react?"

"Ellis is getting too close. If she figures it out on her own, she may be even more upset than if you tell her," warned Tori.

"After all these years, I just don't know how to tell her," lamented Hen. "Time has gone by so quickly. I thought I would find a way by now to bring back her parents."

At the sound of someone calling out their order number,

Tori slid from the booth to pick up the breakfast tray. Hen clasped her wrinkled hands around the latte mug and realized it had been a very long time since she sat in a restaurant with a friend.

Hen and Tori were quiet for several minutes as they started on their sandwiches. Hen got back into the conversation by mentioning the book Ellis had matched up to the Neumann family thread picture.

"I remember that book," said Tori, her face brightening at first. "Ellis read it all the time. . . ." Tori trailed off, her expression clouding as if her memory suddenly became sad.

Hen seemed to understand, but pressed on. "Well, Ellis discovered an inscription in the front of the book. An inscription from her parents. I never knew it was there."

Tori gave Hen a curious look, and put her sandwich down. "Really? What did it say?"

Hen recited what Maeve had written and was careful to emphasize the date. "Ellis was only two. I don't think it means anything related to our *quest*," said Hen, raising her eyebrows as she spoke in code.

"It's exciting," said Tori as she squeezed her friend's hand. "It's the first communication you've come across in a long time."

"I want to be excited, but I also don't want to be let down again," stated Hen.

Ellis and Starling dragged themselves up. They had decided last night to take a hike before breakfast so they could discuss their plans without being overheard.

They filled a thermos with hot cocoa and packed it along with two bottles of water into a drawstring bag that Starling wore like a backpack. The morning was crisp and cool with a cloudless sky. Starling led the way, walking in neither the direction of the Double Decker station or Connor Glass. Ellis was still trying to wake up as she stumbled along behind.

The street narrowed and became less defined the further they went. There was just one other house on the road that Ellis could see. The pavement gave way to a gravelly mix of broken asphalt pieces, soil, and small stones. Before the road completely disintegrated, Starling veered off into a wooded area and stepped onto a narrow path covered with leaves.

"We'll walk this way for a while. Up ahead there's some bigger rocks where we'll break to have our cocoa," said Starling, her cheeks pink beneath her freckles from exercise and cool air.

Ellis smiled. The fresh air felt good and walking felt good.

They padded along, sun streaming through the thinning tree canopies; the walk punctuated by the crispiness of the thick ground cover. The soft, supple leaves of early fall were less frequent now, turning into dry, glossy leaves in shades of brown, deep maroon, and tan that cracked when stepped upon.

Ellis and Starling rested on the large rocks that were big enough for them to sit on with their legs up off the ground. The hot cocoa was sweet and rich, and the curling moist steam warmed Ellis's face when she took a drink.

"I think the plan will work," said Starling confidently.

Ellis nodded slightly. "I'm a little nervous."

"It will work. You will have the time you need, as long as we stick to our plan."

"Okay," said Ellis, feeling guilty that Starling didn't know the full extent of what Ellis had planned to do.

"We have to work with Jules tomorrow until we get the history project done. If our plan is to work, we will need Monday and Tuesday free to get ready for Halloween on Wednesday."

The hot cocoa suddenly seemed sickeningly sweet. Ellis

dumped the rest of her cup onto the dirt next to the rocks. A muddy puddle formed and then the liquid seeped into the dry ground. Ellis's stomach was flip flopping and she felt light headed.

They slid off the rocks and took a different route back to Starling's as she went over their plan again. Ellis thought about Connor Glass and nearly asked Starling if they could walk by the lab, but Ellis knew they wouldn't be able to go in, and besides, Maeve and Aiden wouldn't be there, at least not on this thread.

Hen laughed when Ellis climbed into the car carrying a shopping bag overflowing with feather boas, hats, and sequined materials. "Let me guess," she said, "Halloween."

Ellis laughed as well. "Has Tori mentioned a big Halloween open house at A Priori?"

"It's been that way for a long time," Hen seemed to reminisce. "Mrs. Neumann started the tradition when she opened the store. Mr. Neumann gives away treat bags of his candy."

"Starling wants to come over after school on Wednesday," said Ellis. "We'll get ready at our house and then go to A Priori."

Hen nodded her approval with a smile.

They drove on for a while in comfortable silence. Ellis noticed that she could no longer tell if she was experiencing déjà vu when they drove along the route. At this point she had been along the road enough times that it felt familiar in the normal sense.

"Do you think I can visit a thread today?" Ellis almost whispered.

"No," said Hen definitively, looking straight out the windshield.

273

Ellis was silent.

Hen glanced over and said, "Tori is too busy to close the store for us."

Ellis sighed. It was the confirmation she needed to know that she and Starling had to follow through with their plan.

Chapter 38 ~ Halloween

On Halloween morning Ellis treaded down the back stairs wearing jeans and a hoodie. The weather had warmed since the weekend, which along with predicted clear skies and a nearly full moon would make for a perfect Halloween night.

"Good morning," said Hen.

Ellis smiled. She saw a plate with eggs and toast waiting for her on the table.

"You're running late," remarked Hen.

Ellis bent over the table without sitting down and scooped scrambled eggs into her mouth and gulped down some lukewarm tea. She grabbed the toast from the plate and straightened up. "I have to go. I'll eat the toast on the way."

"Is Starling still coming here after school?" asked Hen hurriedly, trying to address Ellis before she was completely out the door.

"Yes!" yelled Ellis, closing the kitchen door behind her.

Ellis walked briskly down Elm Street, munching on the toast. After a second bite, she threw the remnants into a neighboring yard where a dozen or so finches and chickadees had gathered. The elm in the yard came to life, its branches quivering and leaves dropping, when its occupants went into a frenzy, swooping down to join their friends on the ground for a share of the treat.

Ellis ran up the stone steps of Ida May along with the few other student stragglers. Inside, she propelled herself up the next set of stairs with the help of the sturdy wooden banister.

She breathlessly arrived at her locker just seconds before the first bell rang. Starling was leaning against the lockers watching the clock on the opposite wall.

"I thought you might not be coming to school," said Starling, sounding concerned.

"I — I was just feeling nervous and the time got away from me," stammered Ellis. In truth, she had awoken early but spent entirely too long looking through her lab book for more clues, desperately trying to find a way to avoid even one more thread visit. After going to Jules house on Sunday to finish the history report, Ellis had a whole new understanding of *anxiety attack*, a term which she had only ever heard used in relation to tests, boys, or hair. As soon as she and Hen pulled into Jules driveway, Ellis knew she had been there before, and the déjà vu feeling overwhelmed her. Her heart raced, she couldn't think clearly, and a general fogginess paralyzed her. But with no other clues, Ellis came to the conclusion that she needed to trust her strong instinct that there was something else on the previous thread that needed to be seen.

"Let's go," said Starling, her hands moving in a quick circular motion in an effort to move Ellis along.

Ellis slammed her locker closed and she and Starling ran to Mrs. Dockleaf's class, sliding into their seats as the late bell rang. The dampness on her back reminded Ellis of just how rushed the morning has been. She really didn't like the way the day was getting started.

After an already hectic morning, lunch was more about shopping at Hubbel's than eating. Ellis had always found their hair products fascinating, but until now never had a reason to buy any of them.

"Which one?" asked Starling, holding two bottles of temporary hair color up to her head.

Ellis laughed and realized how much fun this could be.

"The purple," she said.

"So that means you're green," concluded Starling.

Ellis looked at the bottles of colors. She was feeling guilty about betraying Hen and Tori.

They picked up a few more products that Starling deemed necessary and then hurried out of the store to get back to school on time. Ida May was abuzz with excitement over Halloween, and as anxious as Ellis felt, she couldn't help but also feel excited along with everyone else.

Ellis gasped out loud when she stepped in front of her full length mirror. She was unrecognizable. Her normally distinct hair with all its highlights was now completely, solidly green. And it flared out in a frizzy wildness. Her face, neck, and arms were green as well. Most amazing was the transformation of her face. Starling had chastised her about holding still while she applied heavy black eyeliner and bejeweled false eyelashes, but now Ellis appreciated her friend's persistence. The effect was impressive. She literally couldn't recognize herself. To complete the costume, Ellis wore a green sequined top and miniskirt that had been part of a recital outfit belonging to Kestrel, along with green tights and spray painted ballet slippers.

In a similar style, and just as transforming as Ellis's look, if not even more, Starling was all in purple. With one rinse from a Hubbel's hair product, Starling's hair was now completely straight, making it hang several inches longer. Another bottle changed her hair to solid lavender. She also applied body paint, making her upper body match her hair. Myna had a similar recital outfit as Kestrel, allowing Starling to be dressed in purple sequins.

Ellis stared at Starling's eyeliner and eyelashes. "You do amazing things with makeup," complimented Ellis.

"I have two older sisters," answered Starling matter of factly. "Here," she said, handing Ellis the last piece to her costume.

Ellis placed the headband fitted with two long aluminum foil antennae on top her head, and nestled it into her unfamiliar looking hair. She then applied matching green lipstick and took another look at herself in the mirror.

Starling did the same, and deemed themselves perfect Martians. "From another world," Starling smiled. Ellis looked again in the mirror and returned the smile, the whites of her teeth bright against her green skin.

"You ready?" asked Ellis.

"Are you?" Starling replied back mischievously.

Ellis touched the hemline of her skirt, double checking the alignment of the pocket she had sewn onto the underside a few days ago. She mentally went over what she was about to do and she willed herself to remember every detail of the plan. "Let's go," she said.

They walked down the stairs, anticipating the first test.

"Hen," Ellis called out from the stairs before revealing herself.

Movement was heard from the kitchen table as Hen pushed the chair away and stood up. "Are you girls ready?"

Silently, Ellis and Starling ascended the remaining steps and walked into the kitchen.

Hen let out a short, excited scream. "Who is who?"

"It's me," said Ellis after several seconds, waiting first to see if Hen would be able to guess. *The first test was a success*, she thought.

Hen continued to look from one girl to another. "You are both so unrecognizable. I would never know. . . ."

Hen's confusion was a boost of confidence for Ellis.

"I can see why you two needed so long to get ready, but

you should get moving. The A Priori Open House has already started," said Hen.

Ellis and Starling went out the front door and down the walkway. It was a clear starry night. The nearly full moon seemed to be looking down on them and lighting their way as they walked.

The streets were busy with trick-or-treaters, silencing Ellis and Starling from discussing the plan. The sequined skirt provided no cloth for Ellis to wipe her cold and clammy hands. Starling was unusually quiet, making Ellis wonder if she too was nervous. Starling had been supportive from the moment Ellis asked for her help, but she also voiced her concern about Ellis needing to do something in such a secretive way.

Bourner Street was open to foot traffic only. A hundred luminaries lined the curb from one end to the other. A thin fog hovered a few inches from the cobblestone. The ornate A Priori and Apothecary signs were strewn with cobweb and inhabited by large black spiders. Doorways displayed meticulously carved jack-o'-lanterns.

Ellis was so entranced that it was Starling who reminded her it was time to do what they came for. "Oh, yeah," said Ellis, shaking her head as if to find her focus.

According to plan, Starling walked ahead of Ellis who lingered near the end of the street until Starling stood at the A Priori entrance. When Starling stepped inside A Priori, Ellis positioned herself in front of one of its windows.

Ellis took a deep breath and tried to keep calm as she gazed into the bookstore. She saw Starling inside, walking toward a large gathering. Ellis scrutinized the crowd further until she spotted Tori, who wore a red hooded cape and a German folk dress to take on the role of little red riding hood. Starling weaved in and out of the crowd, sometimes obscured, but Ellis was still able to track her moves by the bopping antennae, as

Starling had predicted.

Ellis needed to locate one more person before going in. She focused on finding Mr. Neumann, and it wasn't difficult to pick him out as the tall, gray-green skinned man with exaggerated facial stitches and the squarish head of Frankenstein. He had his arm extended offering treats from a large bucket.

After locating Starling again, who was glancing at the door not wanting to miss her cue, Ellis mustered as much confidence as she could and then walked inside. The store was elaborately decorated, helping Ellis feel a bit less conspicuous. Crepe paper in orange and black was twisted and hanging from tables and shelves. Cottony cobwebs stretched between cases from the highest shelves. Larger-than-life cardboard figures from literature were arranged to keep visitors in the front of the store — everything from Hester Prynne to Willy Wonka — and a huge raven floated from the ceiling.

After a momentary eye contact with Starling, Ellis headed toward the long wooden counter, trying to look as if that was where she was supposed to be going. She made sure to stay within the crowd as much as possible, while avoiding Mr. Neumann and Tori, who hopefully would not recognize her even if they noticed the green Martian.

Ellis approached the cardboard figures blocking off the counter and the back of the store. She maneuvered her way past an Oompa Loompa and then stood behind Sherlock Holmes before getting around Count Dracula. She slid behind The Cheshire Cat — which partially blocked the opening to the back of the counter — and then dropped to her hands and knees and crawled to the area where Tori kept the device.

A banging noise sent Ellis's heart racing even faster. She scooted on all fours as fast as she could to Daisy's bed and used her hand to stop the wagging tail from thumping the counter behind her. Daisy rolled onto her back and tilted her chin up in the air. Ellis obligingly rubbed the soft part of her neck and patted her belly. Within seconds Daisy was softly snoring.

Ellis carefully lifted her hand from Daisy and began searching the shelves and cubbies, pushing papers around and feeling into the nooks and crannies. She didn't see the small drawer from when she was last behind the counter.

Ellis thought she might throw up. She took a deep breath, stopped what she was doing, and looked with her mind's eye. The printer was in the same place, and she saw the shelves she remembered. But she also remembered there were more. She touched the area where she remembered seeing the drawer. The wooden panel gave way slightly. Ellis pushed on it and felt it move. She pushed the panel harder and it slid to reveal a set of small drawers.

With shaky hands and ice cold fingers, Ellis opened one drawer at a time. From the third one, she gingerly lifted out the device. It felt strange to be holding it in her hands without Hen and Tori at her side. She rubbed the smooth glass, thinking of the way Tori had rubbed the glass the first time Ellis saw it, reminding her of a genie and three wishes. She turned it over and saw the coordinates of the last thread. Ellis enclosed the device tightly in her hand and then closed the drawers, replaced the panel, and began crawling back from behind the counter. When she got to The Cheshire Cat, Ellis lifted herself to standing, crossing her fingers that only Starling would notice the antennae appearing from nowhere.

Chapter 39 ~ The Last Thread

A Priori was now packed. As nonchalantly as she could manage, Ellis moved along the perimeter of the crowd to get to the rear of the store. In some ways Ellis felt greater comfort in having more people to hide among, but the crowd was mostly Ida May kids and Ellis felt awkward playing the anonymous Martian, not saying hi to anyone. She kept her expression neutral and her eyes looking ahead as she walked by kids she knew. She garnered quizzical looks from Bea and Keri who were obviously trying to place her, but weren't sure enough to approach her. She kept moving, not wanting anyone to call her by name, which could alert Tori to her presence, and Ellis wasn't ready for that.

In front of the furthest aisle, The Three Musketeers were on guard, their two-dimensional cardboard swords drawn. Ellis walked with purpose, despite her legs feeling like rubber and her heart about to pound through her sequined top. She slipped behind The Three Musketeers and then stealthily peered past the cutout of their 17th century garb to check if anyone had seen her sneak away from the crowd.

Before she could lose her courage, or stupidity, as she was beginning to think, Ellis turned and jogged to the very back of the store. It was much quieter. It felt eerie and made her shiver. She immediately wanted to turn and go back and be part of the fun, receiving treats, and admiring the costumes of her new friends in her new life. But her perspective had changed. She had to trust her undeniable instinct to return to the last thread.

The tall ladder was still in the corner of the store, hooked to the top shelf of the floor to ceiling shelves along the back wall. Ellis reached out and grabbed a rung and pulled, testing the ladder's stability. It gave slightly, but Ellis could feel the sturdiness of the solid ladder. She pushed the ladder to position it. It moved stiffly on its wheeled base.

Ellis cautiously climbed the ladder, still clutching the device in her right hand, using her left to grab the rungs. She took her antennae off and held them in her hand as she continued to climb. Balancing the antennae and the device, Ellis climbed a few steps higher, stopping before her head would be seen above the slightly shorter shelves behind her.

Now high enough on the ladder to be less than an arm's length from the shelves in front of her, Ellis reached through the rungs and pushed books around to make a space where she gently laid the device. She tightly gripped her left hand to the ladder rung in front of her and then used the flexible antennae to bind her hand to the rung. The binding would never keep her from falling to the ground should she step off the ladder, but she hoped it would work as a reminder that she was on a tall ladder.

Ellis pulled a heavy hardbound book from the shelf and held it close for a few seconds while she mentally reviewed what she was about to do. It was now or never, she decided, and with all the force she could deliver, Ellis threw the book at the light just inches above her. As soon as she released the book, Ellis grabbed the device and pressed the button, returning to the last thread she visited.

Ellis couldn't remember what she was just thinking about. Why was she back up at the front of the bookstore? Why did everything look pink? Her mind was foggy in a way that made her feel as if she had been unconscious, yet she was standing.

And then she saw that her arms were no longer green . . . and she felt something heavy in her hand. Her heart raced with the realization that she was on a thread. She remembered that she needed to get back quickly, and then, more calmly, she reminded herself that the time on a thread amounts to just seconds on her main thread.

Ellis looked down at her costume. She was wearing a wildly bright flower print short dress with wide arms and white knee high boots. She touched her face and felt the wire frames of round rose colored glasses. Dangling from her arm was a bag printed with peace signs and partly filled with candy. Ellis slipped the device into the bottom of the bag, covering it with the candy.

"Why aren't you coming with us?" asked Harley, having doubled back from wherever she was. Her hair was braided beneath a cowboy hat and she wore a fringed shirt and skirt with cowboy boots.

Ellis tried to keep the surprise off her face. It was so odd to have Harley talk to her like a friend. Ellis wondered if she went through this same initial reaction on every thread where she and Harley are friends.

"Sorry. My glasses were bothering me," said Ellis, pushing the frames into place.

"Jules is waiting," Harley nodded toward a pirate.

Ellis followed Harley as they walked to join Jules at a table of refreshments. Ellis looked around, wondering what it was that made her want to come back to this thread. She saw Tori, dressed as a flapper with a long beaded necklace and a feather boa, handing out treat bags. Another woman, about the same age as Tori and also dressed as a flapper, was helping her. She wore a brightly beaded flapper headdress that completely enclosed her hair. She looked familiar.

Jules offered Ellis a cup of something green. The bowl of

punch sitting nearby was covered in a light green froth and appeared to have eye balls floating in it. Ellis took a sip. It was sweet and carbonated with a fruity taste. She hoped it would help settle her stomach.

Ellis, Jules, and Harley walked around the room, admiring costumes and talking with friends. Ellis was struck by the irony of this thread. Here she was enjoying the A Priori Halloween open house on a thread that she won't remember, when she could have just stayed on her main thread and enjoyed the open house with Starling and remembered it.

"You seem really quiet," Harley said to Ellis.

"Oh, I'm not feeling so great," Ellis only partly lied, her stomach still flip-flopping.

"Do you want something else to drink?" offered Jules.

"No, thanks," said Ellis, and then expressing regret for ruining her friends night out, she asked them to walk her home.

When they neared the familiar house on Elm Street, Ellis begged Jules and Harley to go back to A Priori and have fun. She would be fine, she promised.

Ellis stood on the sidewalk for a moment, deciding whether to go in the front door or the kitchen door on the side of the house. The lights were on, which meant that somebody was home. Ellis followed her instincts to go in through the front. Her stomach was really churning at this point. She wiped her hands on her synthetic flower dress, and opened the front door.

Ellis knew now why she had returned.

"Hello?" A man's voice called.

"It's me," replied Ellis casually, surprising herself at her natural sounding tone.

"Your mother and I are in the library. Come tell us about A Priori," Aiden called out.

"Be there in a minute," answered Ellis.

Ellis couldn't take her eyes off the framed picture hanging on the wall. She knew in her heart this is what she saw before, but imagined she didn't take a photo of it because the secret compartment in the pendulum clock seemed far more urgent. She rummaged through her peace bag until she felt the solid smoothness of what she was looking for.

"There you are."

Ellis let out a short scream.

"Are you okay?" her father asked.

Ellis released the device back into the bag and pulled her hand out holding a candy from The Apothecary instead.

"You scared me," Ellis forced a laugh.

"Boo!" her dad joked.

Ellis smiled. *He is so friendly and sweet*, she thought.

"You're home early," commented Aiden.

"Yeah, I was ready to come home."

"Come into the library," said Aiden. He was taller than Ellis expected. His thick dark hair was tinged with gray at the temples. He wore a simple button down shirt and tan khakis and peered at Ellis from the top of a pair of reading glasses that added to his distinguished but still young look.

Ellis nodded and followed her father into the next room. She felt light headed and reminded herself to breathe deeply, or to actually just breathe.

Maeve looked up from the chair she was sitting in — the same one Ellis sat in the day she and Hen unpacked the books and talked about her parents. She had her legs tucked up into the chair, looking relaxed.

"Hi," said Maeve. "How was A Priori?"

"Fun," said Ellis truthfully.

"Have a seat and tell us about the costumes," said Aiden, pointing to a footstool.

Ellis looked around the room. It was only slightly different from the way she and Hen arranged things. Her eyes rested on the small rectangular stool. She walked over and sat down, working to contain her emotions. She swallowed hard. Her eyes felt hot, warning her that she might cry at any moment. She was confused, and sad, and happy all at once.

"Well . . ." coaxed her dad.

Oh, yeah, thought Ellis, *the costumes*. They talked for a long time. At some point, Ellis forgot her apprehensions, forgot where she was and who she was, and was just there in the moment, not on a timeline, but just living a moment of her life. Ellis felt as if she were receiving an incredible gift. She may not remember the conversation, she thought, but somehow, she knew, she would carry the moment in her heart forever. This time with her parents was now a part of her and nothing could take away what she had lived.

Ellis stood to go to her room. She gave each of her parents a brief hug. They looked at her surprisingly. She smiled and left the room. She heard her father turn on some soft music. It will be enough noise, she thought, as she stopped by the front entry and pulled out the device and took a photo before heading up to her room where she returned from the thread.

"Tori!" yelled Starling, rushing through the startled crowd. "Tori! Wait!"

Tori looked at the purple Martian in front of her, but her eyes were unrecognizing and wild and unfocused. She tried to push her way past Starling.

"Tori, it's me, Starling."

Tori stopped and looked again.

"Ellis asked me to tell you to keep everyone up front. Give her a few seconds. She said to let you know the light broke and that it may spark and arc brightly," Starling recited the carefully practiced phrase.

Tori's face revealed both fury and fear, and it made Starling afraid.

"Tori, what's going on?" asked Mr. Neumann, his Frankenstein forehead wrinkled, making the drawn-on stitches look even more bizarre.

"It's okay, Dad," said Tori. "A light blew out. Please keep everyone up front."

Mr. Neumann began rounding up students and assuring them all was okay.

Tori headed to the back where the flash came from, while Starling nervously followed. Tori pushed The Three Musketeers aside and ran down the aisle. Starling stayed several paces behind, keeping a distance between her and Tori's reaction.

Ellis was coming out of a dream. Or was she? She felt a peacefulness and then confusion. She saw her hand, bound to a rung, and then she remembered. She was grasping the rung tightly, but when she looked through the ladder rungs to the floor twelve feet below, her heart rate spiked. She heard yelling behind her. Before she turned around, she slipped the device into the hidden pocket in her skirt.

"Ellis!" yelled Tori.

Ellis unwrapped the antennae and began descending the ladder. She went slowly. She was shaky.

"What are you doing?" said Tori in a brutal whisper.

Starling came up behind.

"I'm sorry. I wanted a book and I accidentally broke the light." Ellis lied easily, but felt guilty none the less.

Tori glanced over her shoulder, taking in Starling's presence, before looking straight into Ellis's eyes. "Please come up to the front now. We'll talk about this tomorrow with

Hen." It sounded like a threat. And then Tori turned and walked away.

Ellis had never seen Tori angry, and she felt unnerved by the experience, but somewhere deep inside there was a peacefulness that told her she did the right thing.

Starling stood patiently waiting. Ellis smiled at her. Starling smiled back. They walked down the aisle and past The Three Musketeers.

"Everything go okay?" Starling finally asked.

"Yes, thanks so much," said Ellis.

"You want to go home now?"

Ellis thought briefly, and not really understanding why, she said, "No, let's stay and have fun. I'm sorry I kept you from the open house."

"What are you talking about!" said Starling, "I've had a great time."

"I'm thirsty? Is there some punch around?" asked Ellis.

Chapter 40 ~ Henrietta

"Where is it?" asked Hen as soon as Ellis opened the door. The rumble of the jeep could still be heard as Kes drove away with Starling, Jules, and Myna. Ellis regarded the night as probably the most fun she had ever had in her life. After the incident, Tori didn't make contact in any way, and with that Ellis stopped worrying about the consequences. But she hadn't really considered Hen's reaction, or even that Tori might talk to Hen before tomorrow.

It was hard to tell how long Hen had been sitting at the kitchen table, a finished cup of tea in front of her. Hen rarely got angry with Ellis, and never at this level. With only a few words, Ellis knew Hen was in a state that she had never before witnessed.

Ellis found her resolve. With a stern look, she said, "I'll give it back tomorrow with the agreement that I can see the picture."

"You sound like you already know what the picture shows," said Hen, her voice wavering.

"I don't, but I know it's something important."

"How do you know that?"

"The first time I came back from that thread, I had a strong feeling I needed to go back again. Even without a memory of what happened on the thread, I knew something about it, and I knew there was something else to learn from it."

Hen had an unreadable expression. "It sounds like you're visiting threads too much," she said.

"I don't want to visit threads anymore. I don't know what happened tonight, but when I returned from the thread, I felt — well, I felt like it was okay to stop," said Ellis. "The lab books and notebook are on this thread — my main thread — and this is where I want to look for them from now on."

Hen was clearly upset, and she seemed to be at a loss for words.

"I'm sorry, Hen," said Ellis, a knot suddenly tightening in her chest, the heavy choking feeling of guilt. She never wanted to hurt her grandmother's feelings.

"I'm sorry too," said Hen. "You're right though," she added, a little more brightly, "There's no need to visit threads to find the notebook." She rubbed her eyes. Ellis thought she may have seen her rub away tears.

"Good night," said Ellis, and without waiting for a response she went up to her room and hid the device in the bottom of her backpack. She took a long shower, rinsing until no more green water swirled around her feet.

A towel still tightly wrapped around her head, Ellis sat down at her desk and pulled out the lab book. She reported what she knew, but without the printed photo, the experiment was incomplete. The rest would have to wait until tomorrow. She dried her hair and climbed into bed.

Ellis awoke early. The weight of what she had done seemed to make its presence fully known. She felt awkward going down to breakfast, and kept finding one thing after another to do in her room before she finally had to go downstairs or risk being late for school.

Hen was standing by the O'Keefe & Merritt, sipping her tea, too upset to sit down, Ellis guessed. A box of cereal had been placed in the middle of the table, but no bowl, spoon, or milk.

"Good morning," said Ellis without making eye contact.

"Good morning," answered Hen politely, her voice edgy.

"I'm going to leave now and stop at Madder's for a latte and kiffle."

"Are you tired?" asked Hen.

"A little," admitted Ellis.

"What you did was dangerous," said Hen.

Oh, no, thought Ellis, wanting to avoid this conversation for as long as possible. "I have to leave." Ellis put her jacket on and swung her backpack onto her shoulder.

"There's a lot you don't understand. What you did put yourself at risk, as well as me and Tori. You need to consider that."

"Well, maybe later you can explain to me what I don't understand," said Ellis tartly. "But right now I have to leave for school." She closed the kitchen door behind her and took a deep breathe, shoving her shaky hands into her pockets.

Ellis could eat only half the kiffle and the latte was not sitting well on her stomach. She tossed both before she entered Ida May. Starling was waiting for her at their lockers.

"Everything okay?" asked Starling, clearly reading Ellis's face.

"Hen is pretty upset with what happened."

"What did happen?" asked Starling. "You haven't explained to me why you broke the light."

Ellis had decided before she took the device that she would never visit a thread again after revisiting the last thread, and she didn't want to start breaking promises either, especially where Hen was involved. "I hope we're close enough friends that you will trust me on this. I can't tell you exactly what I did because I would be breaking a promise to Hen and Tori. But you helped me with something really important." Ellis left off, not knowing what else to say.

"Not breaking your promise to Hen and Tori is a good way to be," said Starling. "I won't tell anyone about what went on, but remember my parents are research scientists and so were yours. I have a pretty wild imagination when it comes to strange phenomena, like that crazy light arc."

Ellis smiled.

Hen was standing in the kitchen, ready to leave, as soon as Ellis walked in the door from school. "Get the device and let's go," she said.

Ellis wanted to run upstairs and lock herself in her room. She felt like Hen wasn't her grandmother anymore. She wanted to say something in her own defense, but her reasons all seemed very weak at this point and she found herself speechless. Instead, she trudged upstairs and dropped her backpack on the floor by her bed. She walked into her closet and went to a cardigan pressed between several sweaters and then reached into its pocket and pulled the device from its hiding place.

She held the device in her hand and looked closely. She had never taken the time to inspect it thoroughly. It was a really beautiful piece of glass, the center as dark as deep space fading to forget-me-not blue and then to a milky-white fog with a bluish cast at the perimeter. Ellis held the device by its edges and tilted it back and forth. The foggy edges looked like a swirling vapor and reminded Ellis of the mist that surrounded her thinking when she returned from a thread.

She slipped the device into her front jeans pocket. This is what she had been waiting for, but now she felt nervous about what she might see in the photo.

Hen led the way with Ellis trying to keep up to her pace.

She finally slowed down about a block from A Priori, but it was only to chastise Ellis even further. "Many of the kids at Ida May are the children of scientists. They know what it means for a light to arc, and what they saw was more than that. Tori has been putting out fires all day trying to explain what happened last night. What you did was beyond thoughtless."

"I'm sorry. I really am. I just had to get back to the last thread," said Ellis.

Hen turned to Ellis and delivered a wounding blow.

"I thought you trusted me, Ellis. I thought we had something special. I told you about your parents and then you turn around and do something thoughtless and careless, risking everything."

Ellis nearly crumbled. For a fleeting moment, she considered running back to the house and hiding the device. It was the only thing she could think of that might hurt Hen as much as she was hurting her. And then Ellis remembered how much she wanted to see the photo from the device.

Ellis ignored what was said and walked to A Priori without saying another word. Hen followed.

Tori was waiting for them at the door. She displayed the Closed sign and pulled the shade. From Tori's manner, Ellis decided there would be no support coming from her.

Tori immediately held out her hand. Ellis looked from Tori to Hen. "I want to be behind the counter while you're printing it."

"Why the distrust, Ellis?" Tori shot back. "We have been here for you and now you act like we're the enemy."

The words stung. "Somewhere in my memory, but not at a conscious level, I know there is something important that I learned on the last thread. I don't want you and Hen to try and hide anything anymore."

Hen gave Tori a wary look. Ellis detected guilt.

"Let's have a look," said Hen, and the three of them went behind the counter.

Tori placed the device on a small platform connected to the printer and then pressed a button on the platform. Printing started immediately. As the image appeared, Ellis began to recognize a photo of a framed picture.

She looked at Hen who was pressing her hand against her forehead and seemed to be holding her breath. Ellis turned to Tori and saw her expression was completely blank. Ellis thought she looked like she had resigned herself to some truth that could no longer be withheld.

The image continued printing, but Ellis was seeing enough to understand why she took the photo. "What's going on here? Who is that?" said Ellis.

Hen and Tori ignored her. There was silence until the printout was complete. Tori took the paper from the printer and walked toward the sitting area. They approached the same couch that Ellis sat on while awaiting the very first printout after her thread visit to Old Town Alexandria.

Tori waited for Ellis to sit and then she directed Hen to sit down as well before she handed Ellis the printout.

Ellis looked at it and felt overwhelmed with emotion, but wasn't sure why. She didn't understand what the picture meant, so she couldn't be upset about that yet, she reasoned. Somewhere deep inside though, she knew the last thread visit was special and the picture drew upon those emotions.

"I know these are my parents. And here I am at about eight or ten," Ellis was using her finger to touch each individual on the printout.

"But who is this?" Ellis touched the picture where an older teenager stood, a girl about eighteen.

Ellis wiped the wetness from her eyes before she looked over at Hen who was staring at the photo, tears flowing down her cheeks. Silent tears that streamed down her face and onto her chest and lap.

"It's me," choked Hen. She put a fist to her mouth and tried to stanch the raw emotion, her chest rising and falling in quick, jerky movements.

Ellis looked at Tori, who nodded her head and wiped away her own slow moving tears. "It's true," she said.

"But how? Who is Hen to me," said Ellis, confused and overwhelmed by a truth that she was not privy to.

Tori rubbed Hen's shoulder briefly, and then sat down in the high back chair to face them.

"Hen is your sister. When your parents disappeared, Hen was with them. It was the first time she visited a thread. Your parents had told Hen that when she was fourteen they would do something special with her. They took her with them to visit a thread, but we think something happened when they tried to return.

"One theory is that the device was dropped after your mother or father pressed the button to return. In the process the only one who returned was Hen. We think she aged because the device wasn't being held steady and therefore could not transport her properly from one thread to another.

"Your parents never returned at all. It may be that the device shattered during the fall. We don't know," said Tori.

Ellis was in shock and disbelief. "You're my sister?"

Hen nodded.

"How old are you?" asked Ellis, trying to piece together the information.

"I'm twenty-four," said Hen. She sat silently as if waiting for Ellis to pass judgment.

Tori continued, "Henrietta was my best friend from the time we were very young. We went all through grade school together. We had just started Ida May together when the accident happened." After a pause, Tori added, while looking only at Hen, "Henrietta is still my best friend."

"Henrietta?" asked Ellis.

Hen finally spoke without prompting, her tears subsiding slightly. "My name is Henrietta, and that's what I like to be called. But after the accident I didn't feel like myself anymore, so I chose the shorter name, and besides I needed you to think of me as your grandmother and forget your sister."

"Why don't I remember any of this?" asked Ellis, feeling absolutely dismayed.

"You were four. . . ." said Hen, "We think you were in shock. The Neumanns helped me out a lot for about two years. After that I knew my aging was permanent. We couldn't find our mother's notebook or lab books, and I was sixteen and felt trapped. I took you and we started moving around. We moved to places where I could do research. Big cities with research facilities and libraries. I spent as much time as I could learning about time theories, parallel universes, glass, whatever I thought might be related to their research and their discoveries about the device."

Ellis felt a strange sort of excitement. "I have a sister?"

Hen nodded.

"Maybe I'm in shock right now, but I have to say I'm excited to have a sister," said Ellis, surprising even herself with the revelation. She couldn't keep from staring at Hen. The thin, gray haired woman in front of her no longer bore a matronly appearance. Ellis recognized, seemingly for the first time, Hen's straight posture absent of stooped shoulders, her bright, albeit watery eyes that never needed reading glasses, and the always present sense of adventure. Why had the wrinkles and gray hair tricked her for so long? None the less, it was difficult to accept that Hen was her twenty-four year old sister.

Hen laughed for a few seconds, and then went back to a

serious expression. "I'm sorry," she said. "I put you in danger in hopes of finding our parents and finding a way to reverse my aging."

"Why didn't you visit threads?" asked Ellis, a million questions bombarding her thoughts.

"Tori and I and her parents talked about all the possibilities of what might happen if I visit a thread. Over and over we kept coming up with the same scenario: I show up on a thread as an old woman in place of a young girl and chaos breaks out."

"We need to find the notebook and lab books," said Ellis. "I will visit more threads if you think it will help. I can handle the déjà vu."

"No, Ellis," both Hen and Tori responded together in unison.

"Then what can we do? This isn't right," Ellis felt the anger welling up inside of her.

"Don't waste time being angry, Ellis. I'm not," said Hen, apparently sensing Ellis's frustration.

The three of them continued to sit together in the book store, talking and brainstorming on how to find the notebook. Ellis recognized Hen as completely relaxed for the first time ever. She noticed simple mannerisms — the way she kicked her foot when her legs were crossed, talking with her hands more, and the sparkle in her eyes. Hen and Tori acted so similar in age that Ellis couldn't understand how she had been fooled into thinking Hen was a grandmother.

"Did you have to learn how to act old?" asked Ellis, realizing that Hen acted differently around Ellis and in public.

"Yes, Mrs. Neumann helped me a lot with acting like an older woman," said Hen. "I was a quick study. I didn't want to risk being separated from you."

"Is that why we moved every year?"

"Partly . . . I was really afraid of being detected. I didn't want school officials or anyone else looking too deeply into why you were with your grandmother. We never stayed anywhere long enough to give someone a chance to learn about our past," said Hen.

Ellis felt a tingle of fear climb up her spine. "Can someone separate us?"

Hen smiled. "Not now. We're much safer being back in Harper. However, there are people here that remember you have an older sister. They think I went away to school and now, ten years later, they probably figure I am off living my own life.

"Ellis, today — right now — is the first time in ten years that I've been able to act like myself in front of someone besides Tori. I've only ever wanted to be your sister. I hope you're okay with knowing about me," said Hen, before she got quiet, waiting silently for a response.

Ellis smiled. "I'm so happy to know, but I'm afraid someone will find out. I want you to change back — to look like you do in the picture," admitted Ellis, holding up the printout and looking at it.

Ellis knew what she said was childish and selfish and even hurtful considering Hen knew of no way to change back. But she had lost a grandmother and gained a sister who she would never be able to speak to on that level in public.

Hen's expression fell. "Ellis, I'm not sure that will ever be possible. Please accept me for the way I am. Now that you know, things will be different between us, but you must never do anything to reveal my situation."

When they left the bookstore, Ellis noticed Hen went back to acting grandmotherly. She slightly hunched her shoulders and she lost her animated way of talking.

Ellis was determined to find her mother's notes.

Chapter 41 ~ The Notebook

"Something smells good," said Ellis, stepping into the kitchen. She had come down the front stairs, past the empty hooks on the wall, and envisioned the many pictures of her and Hen at different ages that probably used to hang there, and the family picture that most likely hung in the entrance. She understood now that the framed photos would never go back up unless Hen found a way to reverse her aging. Such photos would be too painful for Hen to see and raise too many questions among visitors that might see them.

"I made French toast," said Hen, standing at the O'Keefe & Merritt griddle, moving golden brown slices to a serving plate. "Sit down. I'll bring you a plate."

Ellis sat down at the table where a cup of tea was already at her place. In the center of the table, a small pitcher of warmed maple syrup gave off an aroma that reminded Ellis of The Apothecary. She felt awkward having her sister serve her, but the thought of changing their relationship felt even more awkward.

Hen brought over the plate of French toast and then sat down herself to eat breakfast. Ellis spread fresh butter and then poured on the warm syrup. Hen was the first to speak.

"I know it's a weird situation to be in," stated Hen, looking at her plate instead of Ellis.

"Weird?" said Ellis. "Does that really begin to describe it?" she added, trying to keep the sarcasm out of her voice.

"No . . . but it's what we have," said Hen.

Ellis took another bite of the crispy on the outside, soft on the inside sweet bread blending the tastes of rich vanilla, fresh maple syrup, and sweet cream butter.

"Do you want to stay home from school today?" asked Hen. "You've been through a lot."

Ellis watched Hen and reminded herself that this is her sister talking, not her grandmother. *She has the same eyes as* me, thought Ellis.

"No," answered Ellis, "actually I want to go to school and then stay downtown after because Madder's is having a hot cocoa cart at The Trivium, and Starling and I want to hang out there for a while."

Hen nodded. "Sure. Sounds like fun."

She's not talking like Hen anymore, at least not to me, thought Ellis.

"Do you want to invite Starling to sleep over?" asked Hen.

She's trying too hard, thought Ellis.

"Not tonight," said Ellis.

Tonight, thought Ellis, *I am looking for the notebook.* She had a nagging feeling that her house had secret hiding places. It may just be her strong desire to find the notebook, or déjà vu, or a combination of experiences, thread visits, and wishful thinking.

"What are you doing today?" asked Ellis. She had never before considered what Hen did all day.

Hen was visibly touched. "I like to read and do research. I also take courses online — I've never told you that because I didn't want you to suspect anything."

Ellis nodded because she was afraid to speak for fear her voice would crack or that the tears she was keeping at bay would start streaming down her face.

"I'm okay," assured Hen. "Tori and I are great friends. I have you. I'm really happy."

"Okay," said Ellis, her voice sounding hoarse, but she was feeling better inside.

Ellis took her dishes to the sink and grabbed her backpack before heading out the door to school.

Ellis wasn't even a block away when she heard a voice call from behind her say, "Hey". She turned around to see Harley closing in on her. Her first thought was to turn back around and keep walking to school, but an opposing emotion held her in place.

"Yeah," said Ellis.

"You know we used to be friends," said Harley.

Ellis raised her eyebrows, "Yeah, I heard."

They started walking together at a slow pace.

"I don't know what happened at A Priori the other night, but I think it's cool," said Harley.

Ellis laughed. A nervous laugh. And then a happy laugh.

"It's not that funny," barked Harley.

"I know." Ellis composed herself.

They walked a few more steps. Ellis thought her grandmother/sister reveal was weird enough. Now Harley — how much more could there be? she asked herself.

"I'm really not that good of friends with Vi," admitted Harley.

Ellis wasn't sure how to respond to the confession.

"She's really mean to Peyton," Harley went on.

"Why?" asked Ellis.

"I think it's just because she can be. Peyton is shy, but she's stuck with Vi as a friend," said Harley. "You know the whole glass kid thing — well, maybe you don't know. . . ."

Ellis hoped she wouldn't get tackled for saying, "Sounds like you and Peyton are friends. Why not do stuff with just her and forget about Vi?"

Harley gave her an exasperated look. "I've thought of that, obviously. It's just not that easy."

At that very second, Ellis stopped being angry and confused about all the moving around. She felt the heat rise to her cheeks, not from embarrassment, but because her heart was swelling with pride. "I've moved around a lot," started Ellis, "and I've learned that you can't control what others think or even how they act, so it's better to stay away from the ones that drag you down and find someone who will be there for you. Even if that means being your own best friend."

Harley gave her a bored look.

"What I mean is," smiled Ellis, "ignore Vi and be friends with Peyton."

Ellis and Harley walked on, not talking, but not separating either.

"You live in an old historic house, too, right?" asked Ellis.

Harley nodded.

"Do you think there are secret hiding places in the houses?" asked Ellis, following up on a feeling she had.

"There are a few in our house. You know, the walls, the fireplace mantel, and the wide window sills," Harley seemed to be looking with her mind's eye.

"I thought so . . ." Said Ellis, feeling the familiar tingle of déjà vu.

Ida May was within sight. "Do you still want to walk with me?" questioned Ellis.

Harley hunched her shoulders, signing indifference and said, "Sure."

They walked up the stone steps and then climbed the staircase to the second floor before going their separate ways.

Starling greeted Ellis with a smirk. "What was that?"

"We ran into each other walking to school," said Ellis, opening her locker and switching out books.

"Really?"

"She actually seems pretty nice." Ellis gave Starling a pleading look.

"Okay, okay . . ." conceded Starling before changing the subject. "Are we still going to The Trivium after school?"

"Yes, and I have to talk to you about something," hinted Ellis.

"Oooh," said Starling, waving to Jules as they entered Mrs. Dockleaf's class.

Ellis gave Jules a wave before sitting down. She pulled out her notebook and began copying the notes from the board, although she had no idea what she was writing because her thoughts kept going back to her sister.

It was cool and clear outside, leaves drifting from the tall oaks in front of Ida May. Ellis, Starling, and Jules joined countless other chatting groups of students heading east on East North Street toward The Trivium. As they approached the park, Ellis got her first real look of the area now clear of tents and festival crowds.

The Trivium was a backward L shape, with East North Street terminating at Locust Street to create the inside of the backwards L on the west side of the park. The outside of the backwards L, on the east side of the park, was formed by Leo Street. There wasn't exactly a juncture, like in the definition of trivium, but three roads formed the park.

Although Main Street wasn't accessible from this end of East North Street, the back of the courthouse and the clock tower were visible. The parking lot at the south end of the park was situated behind Hubbel's. Oaks, elms, sassafras, and maples randomly occupied the park, with benches scattered throughout, many positioned under the larger trees.

The three friends spotted the Madder Drinks cart, but without a second thought, Jules begged off to go sit on an unoccupied bench to make sketches.

"So what is it?" said Starling excitedly as soon as Jules was out of ear shot.

Ellis giggled at her friend's anticipation. And then she paused. Thinking about how what she wanted help with was serious. "My mom left behind research notes," she said seriously.

"Say no more. Let's get our drinks first," said Starling.

They headed straight for the hot cocoa cart, steam rising and a line of kids waiting. Starling was nonchalant and patient. Ellis wiped her hands on her jeans several times, but managed to be patient.

They each had a hot cocoa with fresh whipped cream and chocolate shavings. The cups were warm against their hands and the sweet steam slipping from beneath the cool whipped cream warmed their faces. They sat down on a bench near where they sat during the Harper Fall Festival.

Starling had a serious look. "What are you talking about?"

"My mom left behind some lab books and a notebook. I need to find them."

"The lab books are supposed to be kept at Connor Glass. . . ."

"I know — but they weren't. Will you help me find them?"

"Of course," said Starling.

They slurped on the hot cocoa and worked away at the whipped cream and chocolate shavings.

"I think they're in my house," said Ellis, licking at her whipped cream mustache.

"Why do you think that?"

"I just have a strong feeling," said Ellis, not wanting to discuss déjà vu.

Starling looked thoughtful.

"What about the creaky board by your bedroom door?"

"What?" Her response was rhetorical. *It was so obvious*, thought Ellis.

"You know the one that makes that squeaky noise."

Ellis nearly dropped her cup of cocoa. "Starling you're right. I — I have to go home. I'm sorry — I have to go." Ellis was looking around wildly, not wanting to leave her friend alone.

Starling stood up. "Are you okay? Kes is over there," she said, pointing near the Madder's cart. "Do you want me to ask her for a ride?"

Ellis knew Kes wasn't ready to leave yet and she didn't want to make her suspicious of anything.

"No, but you'll keep my secret, right?"

Starling gave her a look of indignation.

"Okay, I know you will," said Ellis. "Wish me luck!"

Ellis hurried out of the park, dropping the hot cocoa in the nearest trash bin.

"Hen? Hen!" Ellis threw her backpack into the corner of the kitchen. "Where are you?" She wiped her hands on her jeans.

Hen appeared from the library. "What's wrong?" she asked, her voice heavy with concern.

"I know where the lab books are. . . . I know where the notebook is." Ellis was breathless from running the whole way home, but her eyes were shining with excitement.

Hen looked at her with alarm. "Ellis, are you feeling okay?"

"Hen, where's the Squeaky book?"

Hen reached out to calm Ellis. "What are you talking about?"

"Where is it Hen!"

Hen walked into the library and Ellis followed. Hen reached up to the top shelf and pulled down "Squeaky".

Ellis grabbed it from Hen's hands and flipped it open to the inscription from her mother and read it aloud: "To Ellis, There are hidden treasures for you to find, Love Mom and Dad."

Ellis looked into Hen's eyes. "The books are here — in the house."

And then she flipped through the book until she came to the illustration of the young mouse's home under the floorboards.

"Hen, look," said Ellis, turning the book so Hen could see the illustration.

Hen glanced from the illustration to Ellis.

"Hen, I think our mother hid things under the floorboard. . . . The one by my bedroom door. The one that is *squeaky.*"

Hen shook her head. "I've tried to pry open those boards, but they don't budge. They are secure. . . ."

"Hen, there is a secret latch — one that works like the bookshelf entrance between A Priori and The Apothecary," said Ellis.

Hen looked thoughtful. "Your Squeaky book was always kept on the upstairs bookshelves. . . ."

They walked up the front staircase, each step more suspenseful than the last. At the top they stood still, looking at the bookshelf in the alcove of the hallway.

"Hen?" prompted Ellis.

Hen sighed. "I remember that we kept the children's books up here," she said, looking at the built-in bookshelf, which currently held several unpacked boxes.

Hen walked over and started moving the boxes off the shelves and stacking them on the opposite side of the wide hallway. Ellis helped.

"What is that?" asked Ellis in a quiet voice. Too afraid to

touch anything on the shelves, she stared at the bookend that appeared to be attached to the shelf. It was wrought iron and reminded her of the A Priori and Apothecary signs the way the metal twisted and turned in a filigree pattern.

"It's always been there," explained Hen. "I never thought anything of it before, but now that I think about it, mom always placed your Squeaky book against it."

Hen reached out and lightly traced its pattern with her fingertip. She applied more force to test if it would move. Ellis looked at the floor in front of her bedroom door and then shook her head at Hen when nothing happened.

Hen started feeling all around the bookend and then the bookshelf itself. She didn't look at the shelf directly. Her expression implied that she was concentrating on her sense of touch.

Ellis reached under the shelf and began tenderly dragging her finger pads along the smooth underside. She felt a seam in the wood — just barely. She wasn't even sure that what she felt was real.

"Hen, I think I feel something," said Ellis excitedly.

They both looked under the shelf. A square seam in the wood was barely visible through the paint.

Ellis positioned her thumb on the area that looked as if a wooden plug replaced an existing spot. She pushed up hard. But nothing happened.

Hen looked thoughtful. "Press again while I try to move the bookend."

Ellis pressed up again on the wooden plug while at the same time Hen wiggled the bookend and pushed down. Suddenly the bookend went straight down, gliding easily into a recess, disappearing below the shelf. When it was completely out of sight, they heard a click. And Ellis and Hen turned their heads.

The squeaky board popped up — just a couple inches.

Ellis looked wide-eyed in disbelief. Hen covered her mouth with one hand.

Ellis held tightly to Hen's arm as they walked down the hall toward Ellis's bedroom. In unison, they got down on their knees. Hen reached out and felt the raised edge of the board.

"This is it," she said.

Ellis crawled around and peered into the small opening. "I see something."

Hen pulled up on the board, but it wouldn't lift any further. "I can't get it to open."

Ellis squeezed her hand into the opening. "I can't reach inside all the way," she said. She pulled her hand out and then looked into the opening again.

"Wait. I think I see a button or something. . . ."

Ellis reached her hand in again, but this time she reached down, rather than back. On the joist, she felt the object she saw sticking out. She tried to press it, but it wasn't a button. Unable to look inside the opening while her hand filled the space, Ellis felt around the object. She realized it was a lever when she felt a cut in the wood support above it.

Ellis placed her finger below the lever and with a lot of effort it finally gave and moved up — the release causing Ellis to lose her balance and fall backwards from her squatting position.

Hen scrambled over to right Ellis and when they turned back to the board, a door in the floor had opened. Five boards across and nearly as tall as Ellis, the door had ragged edges that matched the layout of the floorboards. The compartment inside was only a few inches deep, but Ellis now understood what treasure Maeve was speaking of in the inscription.

"I'm afraid to even touch it," said Hen, moving closer. "This is it — this is mom and dad's work."

Ellis swallowed hard. "Let's see if we can change you back Hen."

Hen nodded. "Carefully hand me the books. Keep them in order — it may be important. Wait — let me get a piece of paper to write down how they are ordered in the floor."

Ellis nodded and waited, but wanted nothing more than to jump in and start looking through everything.

Within seconds, Hen was back with paper and pencil. She made a sketch of what the floorboard safe held.

"Okay," she said, nodding slightly.

Ellis stepped down into the cavity. Only the center was filled with books, leaving nearly half the space free. The area reeked of a slightly dusty and damp aroma.

She handed Hen the first pile, which contained a spiral notebook with a blue cover and two lab books. Hen remained focused and seemed to show no interest in what the books might contain. Ellis thought if it were her she might be flipping through the books as soon as she held them.

Next, Ellis handed up a second pile of three lab books. A third pile had two more lab books. Hen easily held them in her arms, placing one pile below the next for a total of one spiral and seven lab books.

Ellis double-checked the cavity for anything she may have missed. Satisfied, she stepped out and then closed the floorboard door, hearing it click in place. She glanced over at the bookshelf to see the bookend rise into place. She stepped on the board closest to her door and heard the familiar squeak.

Chapter 42 ~ Good-Bye

Before the whistle blow could gain full momentum Ellis turned off the gas burner of the O'Keefe & Merritt and picked up the kettle. She poured the steaming water into mugs holding tea bags ready for steeping. She customized each brew with the appropriate sugar and milk and then carried them to the table just to have Hen shoo her away.

"We can't have liquids near the books," warned Hen. "Leave the cups by the stove and we'll drink the tea when we take a break."

Ellis looked at the books spread out on the table, a numbered sticky note attached to each to indicate their order of recovery. Except for the notebook with its blue cover, which they both knew was on top and closest to the front. Ellis reached to open the notebook when Hen placed her hand on the cover.

She asked Ellis to please wait. She had called Tori to come over and wanted her to be here when they start reading. Ellis had her mouth open to protest when a knock at the front door interrupted her. Seconds later the door opened and they heard Tori say, "It's me."

She came into the kitchen with bags in her hands. "I picked up some soup for dinner." Without waiting for assistance, she put the cardboard containers in the refrigerator.

"Can it really be?" asked Tori.

Hen only nodded.

Tori looked at Hen more closely. "You haven't read

anything yet?" she questioned.

Hen shook her head.

"You have to be the one," said Tori pulling out a chair for Hen and then sitting down herself.

Ellis sat on the other side of Hen and waited.

Hen picked up the blue notebook and laid it open in front of her. Ellis could see the first page was filled with writing.

"It's notes about visiting threads," said Hen, her voice unsteady. She read silently for a few seconds and then started flipping through the pages.

"It's a logbook. Each entry notes if the device is set to visit a new thread or one already visited. And then there is an entry filled out after they return that lists the coordinates of the thread visited. Most of the entries also make a note that information was added to a lab book.

"The first log is dated when you were about two, Ellis. The same year as the inscription in the Squeaky book."

"What about the last entry, Hen?" asked Ellis.

Hen smiled, understanding Ellis's desire to find their parents. She flipped through the notebook until she came to the last page with writing on it.

She swallowed hard. "It lists a new thread — there are no coordinates listed — and the rest of the log is blank."

Ellis expected as much, but the confirmation made the reality even more bitter.

"They had to choose to visit a random thread when taking me for the first time because they had no way of knowing which threads I existed on," reasoned Hen.

Ellis nodded, but had no verbal response.

Hen flipped back to the first page. Her eyes scanned the page. "The ink is in different colors on this page. It makes me think that they kept adding on to their theories about threads. . . ."

After a few seconds she focused on a particular spot and began reading:

"We say the device appears to change perspective because it gives us the ability to view life from a different set of circumstances, i.e. changing our perspective. . . . We eventually accepted the feelings of déjà vu (for lack of a more scientific term) as confirmation that we visit parallel lives when removed from our current life by the device. . . ."

Ellis found herself tuning out. Hen's voice was droning on, but she just couldn't comprehend. Her thoughts drifted to the many lab books in front of her that had remained unopened.

"Hen," interrupted Ellis.

Hen stopped speaking and looked up from what she was reading.

"I want to go through the lab books."

Hen sighed. "You're right," she laughed. "This is taking forever. . . . Just keep the sticky notes in place."

Ellis picked up the lab book closest to her. It had a #1 sticky. The cover was very stiff and when Ellis opened it she saw a disc attached to the inside.

"Look, Hen."

"I guessed there would be electronic data. The disc is a glass data storage system invented at Connor."

The first page listed her mother's name and her father's name. As Ellis turned through several more pages, she saw notes, diagrams, drawing, and references to file names. Without understanding most of what she saw, Ellis read the word solar enough to realize this was probably the first lab book of findings related to the glass that was later used to make the device.

She set the book back in the pile and grabbed #4. Tori was intently reading a lab book herself and Hen was still studying the notebook.

Lab book #4 had no disc but every page was filled with details about experiments using the device itself. Ellis read that her parents began experimenting from the back of A Priori and allowing Catherine Neumann to observe. They hadn't known until then that they actually disappeared for a second or two. And because they had no memory of the thread, they hadn't realized that their groggy state was related to returning from a thread. Catherine was the one that suggested they should check for a photo. Perhaps they had taken one and not remembered, she told them. After that, visiting threads became routine with the goal of documenting as much glass research as possible to further the developments at Connor Glass on their main thread.

Ellis was preparing to inspect another lab book when Tori demanded they take a dinner break and discuss each other's findings. It actually felt good to get up and stretch.

Hen and Tori poured the chicken noodle soup into a pot and began heating it. Ellis grabbed bowls and set them near the stove before clearing the table, taking care to keep the books exactly as she found them.

It felt odd but nice to have Tori eating dinner with them. Never before could Ellis remember having someone else at their dinner table. The soup was amazing, and most likely tasted even better because they were several hours past their normal dinner time. Ellis hadn't realized until the first spoonful of wide noodles and broth just how hungry she was.

Tori reported that only the first three lab books — the oldest books — had a data disc. From what she could tell, those books were from Connor Glass. Without seeing the remaining lab books, Tori guessed they were all filled with information gathered from threads.

Ellis reported what she read in book #4. Her face felt a bit heated while she talked and she had to wipe her hands on her jeans a couple times. When Hen smiled back at her, she saw her sister in the aged face and was excited about exploring this mystery with her.

"Hen, what have you found out?" asked Tori.

"I'm not sure what to make of it . . ." Hen cleared her throat, "but the notebook had a few thoughts on visiting back and forth on threads and what might happen if there — if there are *changes*."

Ellis put down her spoon down. She noticed Tori had done the same.

"What do you mean, Hen?" stammered Ellis. "What kind of changes?"

Tori looked resolutely at Hen, waiting for her response.

"Well, it mentioned that when you visit a thread, you arrive as you should look in that thread. . . . When you return from the visit, you return as you were, for the most part. . . ."

"Go on," said Ellis.

"There is a note that if something happens on a thread, that it is possible to visit another thread and then return again to reverse the changes." Hen looked back and forth between Ellis and Tori.

Tori jumped out of her chair and shouted, "Yes!"

Ellis sensed apprehension and waited for Hen to finish.

"But I didn't change *on* a thread — I changed as I *returned* from a thread."

"I think you should try, Hen," said Tori excitedly.

Ellis felt Hen's eyes on her and she forced herself to look up, her chest tightening and her stomach lurching.

Ellis hesitated and then said, "Hen, I want you to go back to being yourself, but I am afraid of what might happen if a thread visit doesn't work."

After a few silent seconds that felt like minutes, Hen said, "I need to think about it some more."

"What about our parents, Hen?" asked Ellis, unable to avoid the topic any longer. "I've seen our mother on at least one thread. If she is alive on another thread, then why hasn't she and our father been able to come back to their main thread?"

Hen's eyes became teary even before she spoke. "They noted that if you stay on a thread beyond forty-eight hours that you may not be able to return. . . ."

"Did you read anything else?" asked Ellis, images of her lost parents anguished over being trapped in another life.

"Our main thread is a combination of all the threads we have together. . . . I'm not sure what is meant by that exactly, but it seems that our main thread is the way our life is meant to be, but influences from other threads can change the path of our main thread."

"So, we have a threaded destiny," commented Ellis.

"Yeah," Hen agreed.

Tori began clearing the table.

Hen had a faraway look and continued to look through her mind's eye as she spoke. What she was seeing Ellis couldn't be sure, but her voice was serene as she said, "I don't think our parents are sad or suffering. From reading their notes, I get the feeling they were at peace with any possible consequences. . . . They also seemed to believe that after forty-eight hours, you start to forget your main thread and your memories merge into the thread you're on and it sort of becomes your new life."

Ellis was reminded of the peacefulness she felt after her last thread visit. She believed Hen may be right about their parents.

The tears that streamed down Hen's face were tears of relief and forgiveness. She released herself of the guilt of leaving her parents, of not knowing how to bring them back, of raising a child when she was but a child. Ellis watched Hen say good-bye to their parents in a way that she never needed to. Having long ago accepted her parents as dead, the past couple months brought Ellis only surprises, a sense of self, happiness, and thankfulness for being able to visit her parents.

Ellis stayed home from school the next day. She wanted to be with Hen. They had stayed up reading the books until past midnight. Tori had left shortly after dinner with the promise that Hen would see her soon.

The sun was streaming through the kitchen windows while Ellis and Hen silently sipped their tea. Slivers of sunlight landed on the two piles of books on the other side of the table. The notebook and books #1 through #4 were in one pile — they were the books that made reference to the device and threads. Books #5 through #7 were filled front to back with notes on ways to use glass. Inventions that could change society and provide countless patents to Connor Glass. They were her parent's legacy and Ellis felt proud.

Ellis and Hen finished breakfast. The baked oatmeal, Hen said, was a recipe from their father's mother, also named Henrietta, but she had liked to be called Etta.

Hen picked up the first pile — those bearing evidence of the device and threads — and carried it upstairs. As agreed, Ellis pushed the bookend down to open the floorboard and then unlatched the floor door.

Hen bent down and arranged the books between the joists and then made to close the floor door.

"Wait," said Ellis. She ran into her bedroom, opened her desk drawer, and pulled out her own lab book. Ellis walked back out to the hallway and placed it with the others before Hen closed the door.

Tori was expecting them. She opened the A Priori door before they had a chance to touch the handle. She was clearly distraught. Ellis had the feeling the Closed sign had never been turned to read Open yet that day. Daisy, apparently sensing Tori's worry, stayed by her side.

"Are you sure?" asked Tori.

Hen nodded. "Ellis has convinced me to try."

Ellis felt a pang of guilt when Tori looked her way.

"You know what to do, right? You know — in case we don't return," questioned Hen.

"Don't even say it . . ." begged Tori. "What made you decide today? It feels so rushed. . . ."

Hen laughed. "Tori, you're my best friend, but I'm tired of being an old lady. It's been ten years. . . . I've waited long enough.

"Ellis and I talked last night. The more we read, the more it seemed that visiting a thread was worth a try," Hen looked at Ellis. "And Ellis is coming with me."

"What? Are you sure?" Tori addressed Ellis.

"I told Hen it was the only way I would let her visit a thread. I want to be there to bring us back if I need to."

Tori's gray eyes sparkled. "I'll meet you in the back." She turned and walked toward the counter, her bun bobbing, bits of hair sticking out.

Ellis and Hen walked to the back of the store. The tall ladder still in the position Ellis had moved it to on Halloween.

Ellis got wide eyed. "What if I don't recognize you on the thread? What if I'm confused or something?" said Ellis.

Hen smiled. "I'll recognize you. And besides you saw my picture of when I was eighteen."

"Oh, right," said Ellis, wiping her hands on her jeans.

Tori had a camera in one hand and the device in the other when she got to the back of the store.

"What's that for?" asked Hen, eying the camera.

"I want a picture of you and Ellis together," she said.

Hen angled her head and sort of smirked.

"Please," said Tori, her request sounding more like a command than a nicety.

Hen put her arm around Ellis and they smiled for the camera. Ellis couldn't remember ever having her picture taken with Hen before.

"Here." Tori put the device into Hen's hand.

Hen instinctively rubbed the smooth glass and then gave Tori a hug. "Thank you," she said.

Tori hugged Ellis next and then stepped back. "I'm waiting.
. . ."

Hen blanked the destination on the device and then linked arms with Ellis before extending her other arm. When the flash went off, Tori crumpled into the soft fur of Daisy, but before she could cry, Hen and Ellis were standing in front of her again.

Tori leapt to her feet and hugged Hen with such strength that she caused Hen to gasp.

Tori held her friend at a distance, both hands on her shoulders. She screamed and then pulled her in for another hug. She released her and said, "Look at yourself!"

Hen held up her shaking, unrecognizable hands and stared at them before putting both hands up to her face, feeling the smoothness. She ran her fingers through her hair and then pulled a handful of it away from her head so she could see the color. Just as her eyes matched Ellis's, so did her hair.

"Ellis?" asked Tori.

Out of habit, Ellis lifted her hand and gave Tori the device.

The action got Hen's attention. "Oh, Ellis. I'm sorry, I haven't asked about you." She hugged her. "Ellis? Are you okay?"

"I can't believe you're my sister. Even though I knew it was true, it never seemed real until now — now that I see you so young."

"What else is bothering you?"

Ellis knew her eyes were brimming with tears, but she refused to allow herself to cry at such a happy moment. "Will we have to move again? How do we explain this to people?"

"Oh, Ellis. No worries. Not today," consoled Hen, as she gave Ellis another hug. "We won't be moving, but your *grandmother* might be going back to her home now that your sister has come to live with you."

Ellis smiled. She put an arm around her sister's shoulders and said, "So tell me about this town, Henrietta."

Epilogue

Much of their walk was punctuated by the sound of leaves crunching beneath their feet. It seemed that overnight the time had come to switch from fall to winter, as marked by the surrender of leaves mulching the tree roots and flitting across the sidewalks and filling the gutters along the tree lined streets. The late afternoon sun was waning, the air chilling even as they walked. But the three friends strolled comfortably, laughing and talking.

"Your sister is awesome," said Starling. "My parents say she is great to work with."

Ellis smiled. Her cheeks were rosy from the brisk air.

"How's your grandmother?" asked Jules, sketch pad tucked under his arm.

"She loves Florida," answered Ellis.

The three of them had their Apothecary treats tucked in their coat pockets for the movie later that night. The route they took from Bourner Street had them walking down Harley's street. As they approached the big Victorian house they saw Harley and Peyton sitting outside on the wrap around porch. The three of them waved and said hi. Harley and Peyton waved back. "See you at the Pizza Den," Harley called out.

The elms in Ellis's yard were nearly bare. The Black Eyed Susans were now only fragments of what spring will bring, unlike the timeless glass models that Jules received a prestigious art award for.

They entered the house through the front door and took off their jackets, piling them on the bench in the entry. Hanging above the bench was a Bell family portrait picturing a smiling Ellis, Henrietta, Maeve, and Aiden. A new hook was added to the adjoining wall. There hung a framed picture of Ellis and her grandmother standing in front of the A Priori bookshelves.

Jules took a seat downstairs in the library, his sketch pad already open before Ellis and Starling left to change their clothes and get ready for the night out.

Upstairs, Ellis and Henrietta had worked hard to finish the unpacking. Chairs and benches were arranged at each bedroom door, and the small alcove with its stocked bookshelves had a comfortable sitting chair and foot stool. The creak at Ellis's threshold wasn't heard by the giggling girls stepping into her room.

On the desk was a framed picture of Ellis and Starling smiling bright like best friends do. Ellis was looking through her sweaters and Starling was in the bathroom when Ellis heard footsteps coming up the stairs.

"Hi, Henrietta. How was your day?" asked Ellis, peering out from her bedroom door.

"It was great," answered Henrietta, walking into her bedroom to drop her bags.

Ellis followed her into her room and sat on the bed.

"Starling's here. We're getting ready for the movie."

"I saw Jules downstairs." Henrietta took off her shoes and found her slippers.

"Everything is still going okay?" asked Ellis.

"Great," assured Henrietta. "Dr. Connor said we will be able to get several projects to patent stage within a few months." Henrietta was glowing.

"So, Starling's parents are staying?"

"Yes, and I'm their assistant along with Mrs. Slade. It's more than I ever dreamed of."

Henrietta sat down on the bed beside Ellis. "I think our parents would be proud."

Ellis smiled and said, "Me too."

Acknowledgements

Many thanks to the family and friends who helped make this book possible. First, my husband, Chris, for his endless patience while I spent hours, weeks, months, and years learning the craft of writing a novel on top of the actual writing of the novel itself. Thanks to my children, Tristan and Sage, who are my inspiration and ever present reminder of all that is good in the world. Love ya, love ya. My sisters, Debi Oliverio and Jodi McMasters for their editing, ideas, and support. My mother, Connie Bowser, whose stories of her youth brought fun to *Threaded Destiny*, including walking downtown for lunch in high school. A big thank you to my best friend Paula Lutz. Our many adventures together in junior high and beyond produced Connor Glass, the mysterious laboratory in the woods. Thanks to my good friend and former coworker Heidi Crane for her publishing expertise and support.

    Threaded Destiny is a work of fiction, composed entirely of fictional characters and situations. Some references, including redd up, egads, kiffles, shoo fly pie, and baked oatmeal are from the Pennsylvania Dutch and the culture of Western Pennsylvania. The Glass Flowers exhibit at Harvard University is breathtaking. The mystery behind the creation of the Glass Flowers as discussed in *Threaded Destiny* is real. I am grateful to my brother-in-law Keith Forest Brown for arranging the special tour several years ago that allowed my family to experience such wonderment. A road trip that led to a cupcake bakeries tour provided my family the culinary delights of Alexandria

Cupcake. I can still smell the delicious aroma of walking through the front door. From this same road trip, a visit to the Smithsonian where Julia Child's kitchen is displayed inspired the Bell's kitchen. I am grateful to my nephews Craig Warheit and Dana Warheit and their wives Maria Alii and Jennifer Koegler for the DC area adventure. While downtown Butler, Pennsylvania has been inspirational in the creation of Ida May and several Harper restaurants, the town of Harper and its buildings and residents are entirely imaginary.

Glass, its fascinating properties and its countless applications in our daily lives in everything from fiber optic cable for transmitting data to solar panels for generating electricity to our many electronic devices for making our lives more connected have deemed it an interesting topic for exploration in *Threaded Destiny*. The *Liquid or Solid?* journal article that Ellis reads in connection to the research at Connor Glass was inspired by a statement, which in part reads ". . . The transformation [of glass to a solid from a liquid] is apparent only when the system is viewed in both time and space." For their real-life glass research that led to this statement, credit is given to Juan Garrahan, School of Physics and Astronomy, University of Nottingham, David Chandler, Department of Chemistry, University of California, Berkeley, and Robert Jack, Department of Physics, University of Bath.

And finally, thank you to all the readers of fiction.

About the Author

Beth Brown has an engineering degree in computer science. She has written more than thirty-five computer science and computer applications textbooks. *Threaded Destiny* is her first novel. Beth lives in South Florida with her husband, her two teenage children, and two dogs.